SEED OF WAR

A SECONDARY WORLD FANTASY

UNEXPECTED HEROES
BOOK 2

MARTY C. LEE

Bookaholics Press

Book design and publication by Bookaholics Press LLC, Provo, Utah
Edited by Anna King
Front cover design by Brenda Camp Walter
Back cover and chapter heading illustrations by Naomi Rasmussen
Map by Michelle Allan and Naomi Rasmussen
Author photograph by Melissa C. Baxter

ISBN-13: 978-1-950230-04-4 (epub)
978-1-950230-05-1 (mobi)
978-1-950230-06-8 (paperback)
978-1-950230-07-5 (large print)
978-1-950230-27-3 (hardback)
978-1-950230-61-7 (audio)

Published by Bookaholics Press LLC
Provo, Utah bookaholicspress@gmail.com

Contact the author at MCLeeBooks.com

For Virginia, who liked all my writing,
and for Naomi, in hopes I atoned.

CONTENTS

Map of Darrendra

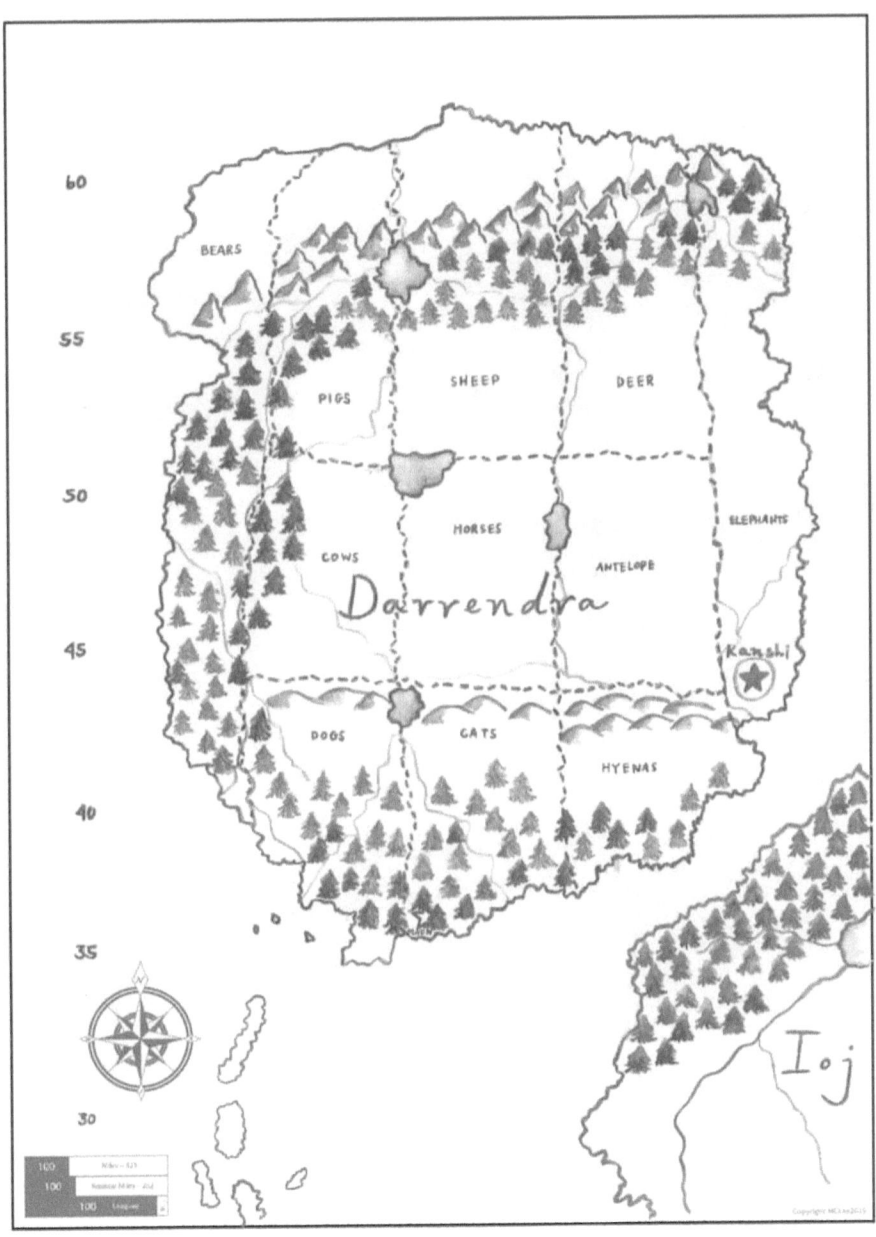

1. HUNT

(MAON, FELID TERRITORY, DARRENDRA)

A Darrendrakar bride and groom hunt for a sacrifice for their wedding ceremony. The catch is considered an omen for the success of their marriage.
Darrendran Religious Ceremonies

Life was nearly perfect. Ludik hummed happily as he laid out his wedding accessories. By the end of the day, he'd be married to Nemerra, and his only problem would be how much his cheeks hurt from smiling.

He looked out his window at the widely scattered village houses, glad to be home again after his last disastrous adventure. The little homes of the shapeshifting kindreds were cozier than any fancy building in Kanshi or Vasi, and more comfortable than Iskrin tents.

The scent of ripe apples and last night's rain filled the air. The gardens and orchards between the homes were in the final delicious stages of harvest. Papa and the other farmers would work right up until the last guests arrived, then pick up again as soon as the ceremony ended.

Despite his neighbors questioning the wisdom of inviting outkindred to his wedding, Ludik had insisted. How could he celebrate the best day of his life without his friends? There were ways to allow visitors from other countries into Darrendra, and wading through the bureaucracy was worth it. For the safe-conduct pendants left at the coast for them, he had even persuaded the village elders to use yellow rosebuds instead of a more neutral flower.

But the autumn sun had already passed mid-morning in the apricot sky, and his friends still weren't here. He'd expected them a day or two earlier, though travel across the ocean was difficult to predict. At least whichever ship had the honor of escorting them could pick up all three in a short arc between the other three countries.

The wedding hunt was ready, but if his friends didn't arrive soon, would he and Nemerra have to delay their wedding again? It was already two months late, and the wait had been torture.

He had been content to take his time finding a mate, but somehow, not long after adulthood, he found himself blissfully walking Nemerra around the fire in front of the village. The only flaw in their happiness was waiting the traditional year of betrothal.

Then everything had gone wrong. On his wedding day, he'd been in another land, tending a profoundly wounded friend while the fate of the world hung in suspense.

Ludik opened a drawer to look at Nemerra's stack of love notes. When he had arrived home, the mantel was buried beneath weeks of daily letters. It took him a day to read them all the first time, and he reread at least one daily. She had forgiven him, but he would spend a lifetime making it up to her.

He closed the drawer and looked out the window again. Still not here. Once they arrived, the hunt wouldn't take long, and then it would be time for the wedding itself.

His door burst open. Haider and Gurryon cursed as they wrestled each other through the doorway. Ever since Haider's broken leg had healed, Ludik's littermates had turned ruffian. Their desperate parents banned their antics from the family house.

"Hurry, Nemerra is waiting for you." Gurryon's silver eyes crinkled with amusement in his brown face. He'd grown his gold hair longer since last spring, now that he and Ludik weren't trying to fool the elders into thinking they were each other.

"The whole village is waiting." Haider looked more like Papa, with his long, tawny hair, gray eyes, and slightly less imposing height.

"Your friends are here." Gurryon dodged Haider's attempted trip, wrapping an arm around his neck and pulling him over sideways.

Haider let himself fall on top of Gurryon and then bounced free.

"They're here?" Ludik wiped his sweaty palms down his tunic. "Do I greet them or change first? Oh, Nemerra is waiting." He dashed for the bedroom, but his brothers caught him before he took three steps.

Haider pushed Ludik toward the door. "We welcomed them until Nemerra arrived, then we came for you. Go join her, then you can change. If you invite outkindred to your wedding, you should be polite to them."

Gurryon shoved Haider. "You don't want to annoy the most powerful priest in the world, do you? He might cancel the wedding."

"He wouldn't do that." Ludik stopped walking. "Is Ahjin that worried about the ceremony? Is he not feeling well again? Why didn't you tell me? Does Nemerra know?" He rubbed his hands over his freshly cropped hair.

Haider swore at Gurryon. "Now look what you did." He pushed Ludik toward the door again. "Ahjin is fine, and he's whispering the ceremony whenever anyone isn't talking to him. Everyone is waiting for you. All you have to do is go. Out. The. Door." He shoved Ludik over the threshold.

Ludik stumbled out and blinked in the bright sun. Wisps of clouds hovered on the horizon. Autumn's unpredictable weather was fortunately dry and still warm enough for an outdoor ceremony. The multi-colored mosaic of fallen leaves made a beautiful background for the wedding.

His littermates dragged him through the horde of villagers as neighbors called congratulations. His older brother whistled and beckoned toward the council fire next to the tiny guest houses.

Ludik couldn't see Nemerra yet, but his friends' paler faces stood out among the Darrendrakar browns. She had to be close to his friends.

"Well met," Niamolenulanami chirped. The pretty Nokai ran on bare feet and threw her arms around him for a brief hug. Lavender braids circled her head, then fell past the gills on her neck and down her back. Her golden skin glowed above the colorful ocean suit that hugged her curves with images of pink seaweed instead of Darrendran geometric designs. "Well met, brothers," she added with a cheerful wave at Gurryon and Haider.

"Good to see you, Nia," they chorused.

Their silly grins cleared Ludik's head. "Why don't you two bring your sweethearts to meet everyone?"

Haider darted for the pretty woman he had chosen from multiple admirers on the last day before the council would choose for him. Gurryon had let the council arrange his betrothal and now meandered toward his assigned lady.

Ludik's older siblings, whom Nia called twins, stood with their spouses, all of them with arms full of children. Hiranya, their long-awaited last sibling, bounced between them, grabbing at the babies.

And his sweetheart stood next to Mama, smiling and laughing. His heart exploded into a thousand butterflies. The sunlight streaked copper in her russet hair, and her honey-brown eyes shone as she talked to his other friends.

"I turned seventeen first," Nemerra was saying. "I had three months to plan how to get him to notice me. Of all the boys in the village, he is the kindest, most steadfast, and as wonderful as I knew he would be."

Ludik left Nia without a second thought and headed straight for Nemerra. "Are you ready?" He leaned for a kiss and bumped into her raised hand instead of her lips.

"You know it's bad luck to kiss before the ceremony." She gave him a hug instead. "I'm so glad your friends made it."

Ludik turned to face his friends, bowing to Zefra first. With the fifteen-year-old Iskrin's red hair covered by her usual dun scarf, her turquoise-and-yellow embroidered belt provided the only color to her tan desert robe and stark white skin.

At Ludik's side, Papa and Ahjin fumbled their greeting. Papa held out his left arm and Ahjin his right. Both apologized and switched arms. Behind Ludik, Nia giggled.

Zefra glanced sideways at Ahjin. The corner of her mouth twitched, and her tilted brown eyes crinkled under black eyebrows. Ludik tried to hide his own smile, not sure if it was funnier that Ahjin was muddling the etiquette or that he had tried in the first place.

Ahjin and Papa finally managed a proper arm clasp, and Papa switched places with Ludik to bow awkwardly to Zefra. Ludik held out his left arm with a grin, and Ahjin seized it with his own left, harder than customary.

"Are you all left-handed?" Ahjin asked. "You could have told me, you barbarian."

"Most of the men in our kindred are, yes. Are you ready?"

Ahjin had his usual narrow pack slung between his white wings and a fancy satchel at his feet. The new bag had five emblems burned into the leather. Four were those of the previously known gods; the star must indicate Kassian, the newly returned fifth.

Ahjin followed his gaze to the satchel and rolled his purple eyes. "That's my new uniform. The gods had a long argument about what it should look like and which part should represent whom. The result is garish, but Darravani said it should distract people from the rest of my appearance."

The sixteen-year-old Iojif did look scruffy with his wing feathers barely grown back. Otherwise, he seemed better than the last time Ludik had seen him. He wore a plain shirt and trousers so new they smelled of dye, and his white curls were neatly tied in a short tail at the back of his neck. Like Nia and Zefra, he wore a resin-preserved yellow rosebud around his neck. The lightning burns on his hands and face had faded to pink lines on his paler skin, and his wings finally hung properly.

Ludik sent more healing through their clasped hands, as the Iskrin healers had taught him.

Ahjin shook him off. "I'm fine, you sourpuss. Save it for someone who needs it. Speaking of healing, are you taking that apprenticeship in Iskra? Shri Okechuku is the best healer in the four lands."

Ludik ran his fingers over his hair. Stubborn cur. "No. I'm still arguing with the shaman and headman about being the village healer. I would rather remain a hunter."

"Will you go on the wedding hunt?" Nemerra asked. "You can't keep up in the chase, but you can walk with us until then."

Ludik was pleased she already felt comfortable enough with his friends to use contractions, though they wouldn't realize the importance.

"We'll come," Ahjin said.

Zefra smiled, and Nia cheered.

"And it is time," Mama said. "Go change. We will meet on the western edge of the village in five minutes." She clapped her hands, and everyone wisely scattered.

Ludik squeezed Nemerra's hand, then ran to his house while she headed for her parents' home. This was almost the last time he'd have to watch her leave. After tonight, she'd come with him, and then it would feel like home.

His small house was ready, with the gathering room and tiny bath on the ground floor next to the bedroom he would share with Nemerra, and an attic loft for their future children. Ludik had distracted himself the past three weeks by making repairs and painting or carving the surfaces. This week, he scrubbed and polished every inch of the house. The fragrance of beeswax-and-oil polish and the cedar mantel covered the last whiffs of soap and paint. It looked good to him, but what if Nemerra didn't like it? She was so sweet, she might never tell him if she was unhappy.

He threw his tunic into the corner before his bones shifted in seconds and his claws extended. Then he changed back from black jaguar long enough to fold his clothes and lay them next to his wedding gear. Nemerra must not think he was slovenly.

When he nosed open the door, their family members and friends were waiting. The clearing full of large cats was not a surprise, but the two-leggers... Ludik's mouth fell open, and Papa huffed in laughter. It seemed they had found a faster way for Ludik's friends to get to the hunt.

Ahjin sat stiffly on Papa's lion-back with his fingers wrapped gingerly in the long mane. Mama bore both Nia and Zefra on her long tiger's body. Nia had looped one of her many hair ribbons around Mama's neck for a handhold, while Zefra gripped Nia.

Nemerra stood next to Ludik's older sister. His sweetheart's sleek leopard form was dwarfed by Kalliona's pale golden tigress, but she filled Ludik's vision. She was so beautiful and kind and wonderful. If only the hunt were finished and they were on their way to their wedding cere-mony. How could he wait the long hours until tonight?

Nemerra caught him staring. She closed her eyes halfway and blinked her long lashes slowly three times in her usual quiet message.

Ludik blinked back. I. Love. You.

Papa would normally guide the hunt, but since he had a passenger, he jerked his head at Narrasiman. Ludik's older brother headed into the trees, his orange-and-black stripes disappearing into the shadows as the rest of the Cats bounded after him.

Nia cheerfully babbled about everything she saw.

This close to the village, the trees stood in orderly rows of orchard fruits and nuts. Beyond them, the wild forest spread to the horizon, an endless series of evergreens sprinkled with oak, yew, chestnut, and many others, including the occasional golden suvarna with its tri-colored leaves.

Small clearings let light into the woods, but, until the recent earthquakes had felled trees, this territory had few large open spaces besides the villages. In the thickest parts of the forest, the Felids could bound along the tree branches without ever touching a paw on the ground.

Ludik had heard the central territories had room to run for leagues. He imagined they might look like the Iskrin desert, only greener and cooler and with more to eat.

"Do you want to be in on the kill or dropped off before then?" Ludik asked, then realized some of his friends would only hear mewing.

Nia translated into trade tongue.

Ludik twitched his whiskers. A friend who spoke all languages was convenient.

"You can leave me somewhere," Ahjin answered in proficient Felid instead of the trade tongue he'd used before.

Ludik blinked. He'd been there when Ahjin received the same language gift as Nia, but he'd forgotten about it until now.

"I'll practice your ceremony while I wait," Ahjin continued.

Nia grinned. "I'll pick flowers instead. You can tell me what inappropriate messages I accidentally create."

All Darrendrakar learned the coded meanings of plants. In Nia's hands, they might be amusing.

"With no interpreter," Zefra said, "I will be in the way. I can wait."

Ludik turned to Nemerra. "Agu volunteered to leave early and track game for us. It's his wedding gift. We're to meet at the big pine for his report."

"That's thoughtful," Nemerra said. "I'll go meet him, dear. You can be the slow one today." She winked and bounded off while Ludik led his parents and their passengers down the faint forest trail.

"Darravani didn't have time to teach me much besides the ceremony," Ahjin said. "May I ask questions about the wedding customs? For instance, is the bride price like our dower, where the groom gives assets to the bride for her support in case of his death?"

"No," Ludik said. "I pay the bride's parents for her loss in their household and to acknowledge my debt to them for raising a wonderful daughter. I'm sure she'll control all my assets, anyway." He winked at Mama, who solemnly winked back.

"We use a dowry," Zefra said. "The bride's family gives it to the groom for her use and protection. She keeps all of it in divorce or widowhood. My parents have the first gold bracelet for my dowry."

"We cancel the dower in a divorce," Ahjin said.

"If I were ever stupid enough to divorce Nemerra," Ludik said, "I'd get back the bride price. Even if *she* left *me*, I'd get a refund, but I'll make sure she never wants to leave me."

"We don't have any of that," Nia said.

"No financial legalities in marriage?" Ahjin asked. "That's unusual."

"No, and no divorce, either," Nia said. "That's why most of us don't marry. There's no way out if we don't like it."

"Oh," Ludik said. "Well, I'll like it. Did you have more questions, Ahjin?"

"Yes," Ahjin said.

A sudden scream cut him off. It was followed by a cacophony of snarls, hisses, and screeches.

"Pardon." Papa tipped Ahjin from his back and ran through the trees with Ludik.

Mama caught up a moment later with Nia's ribbon still wrapped around her neck. "Your friends will follow."

A couple of very long minutes passed before Ludik and his parents worked through the yowling crowd to the source of the chaos. Bushes and plants lay crushed in all directions. Blood soaked the ground, tainting the air with a metallic reek.

An obviously dead fox lay next to an equally dead leopard.

Ludik's heart stopped.

"Is that Nemerra?"

2. BODY

(NEAR MAON)

Pink rose: grace and admiration. Red rose: love and respect. Red and white rose: unity. Heliotrope: devotion and faithfulness. Lily of the valley: sweetness. Gardenia: I am too happy. Orange blossom: eternal love.

Flowers and Their Meanings: A Guide for All Darrendrakar

Ludik's heart thumped with relief when he saw the body didn't have Nemerra's odd spot above her eyebrow.

"Where's Nemerra?"

Blood overwhelmed all other scents. Ludik whirled to search the frantic crowd. He couldn't see her. He whipped back to the dead bodies and double-checked.

Oh. Cold filled his belly. The dead leopard was Agu, the hunter scouting game as a wedding present. Ludik fought to swallow the lump in his throat. Agu didn't have a shift today, so if he hadn't been helping Ludik, he would have been safe at home.

Both Agu and the fox were covered in bites and claw marks. Leaves and broken branches littered the blood-soaked ground. It must have been a ferocious battle.

Behind Ludik, the villagers wailed in a furry mass of chaos.

Ludik jumped as someone touched his shoulder. He whirled, fangs bared, and Nemerra ducked aside. Nemerra. His whiskers sagged with relief.

Nemerra pressed against his side and shivered. "What do you think happened?"

"I don't know." He looked at both dead bodies again. "What is a Fox doing here, anyway?" The kindreds didn't cross borders except along trade routes. Though the Canids were their closest neighbors, Ludik had only seen them up close in a trade caravan.

"Agu was still alive when I got here," Narrasiman said. Ludik's older brother wiped one bloody foot on the ground, over and over. "I asked him what happened, and he said, 'The Fox,' and then 'See...' something. He was hard to understand, and then he died. I kept everyone back as much as I could, but I didn't know what else to do."

The headman, Asad, nodded. "You did well. Clear the area, please. Ludik, stay here."

Narrasiman bobbed his striped head and backed up, looking anywhere but at the bodies as he herded the gossiping villagers toward home.

Ludik watched everyone go. Home sounded like a wonderful place to be right now.

Most of Ludik's family left. Gurryon, although still an apprentice, stayed to help Shaman Akamu. The two lions huddled together, speaking quietly.

"We can walk back with Nemerra, if you'd like," Nia whispered.

Ludik hadn't noticed his friends had caught up.

Nia intently watched the trees away from the bodies, while Ahjin stared at his own feet. Zefra stood with one hand on Nemerra's back and squinted at the bodies.

"If you do not mind, Your Holiness," Asad said, "I would like you to stay, too."

Despite the situation, Ludik hid a smile. Ahjin's holiness was dubious. It was strange to think of him as the new "Mouth of All the Gods," especially for friends that knew his idiosyncrasies. Then again, his quirks had earned him the job.

"I know nothing about this kind of thing," Ahjin said. "I'd be in your way."

"With a casualty from another kindred," Asad said, "I prefer to have a neutral witness."

Ahjin sat on a tree stump. "As you wish," he said, but his wings drooped.

"Ludik, you worked with Agu," Asad said. "If Agu caught the Fox trespassing, he wouldn't have fought him, would he?"

"No," Ludik said, "he would have arrested him and brought him to you and the elders. It looks like he surprised the Fox, provoking an attack. Unless the Fox attacked him on purpose."

Both of them frowned.

In the background, Nia murmured a translation for Zefra.

"Why didn't they just stop fighting?" Ahjin asked from his stump.

"I wish I knew," Asad said. "Was Agu easily antagonized?"

Ludik shook his head. "Not really. Agu didn't like Dogs much, understandably, but he was level-headed. He would have fought hard against an intruder, but he wouldn't start trouble."

"He was running," Zefra said in trade tongue.

"What?"

Everyone turned to look at her.

"The Fox was running." Zefra pointed to broken shrubbery marking the Fox's path toward the village. Though not a hunter by trade, she had told them stories of how hunger and desperation on her rite of passage made her learn her hunting and tracking lessons well.

Ludik should have noticed the damage himself. The shock had distracted him. His heart still pounded from mistaking Agu for Nemerra. He glanced to make sure she was well.

"Asad, Ludik," Akamu said, "follow the Fox's path. We'll investigate here." The shaman and Gurryon turned back to the bodies.

Zefra followed Ludik and Asad, who sniffed all the twists and turns while she collected the sparse evidence caught on bushes and prickly weeds. They followed it for half a league before they lost the trail and turned back.

They had almost reached the others again when a different scent hit Ludik's nose.

"Do you smell... Bear?" he asked. "How many intruders are here today?" If he didn't know better, he'd think it was time for a trade festival.

"That is no Bear I know," Asad said, "but it isn't leopard or fox, either. Maybe it's one of the big Dogs? Did the Fox have a companion? Whoever he was, he was also injured. We should find him and ask him what happened."

They swept their heads from side to side, following the scent of the blood drops to a single heel print in the mud. The print was from someone bipedal but was too incomplete and smeared to tell anything more. They followed the scent trail a little farther until a skunk's den threw them off-track.

Ludik sat to think. "If that was one of the big Dogs, he must have been with the Fox. I don't know why they trespassed, but something obviously went wrong. The Fox probably ran into Agu, who defended himself, and the battle escalated from there. Agu and the Fox killed each other. The Dog caught up, saw what had happened, and ran back toward home, probably afraid of what would happen if more Cats arrived. Does that sound right?"

"I agree," Asad said. "He or she is likely traumatized. If we run after him, we'll only scare him more. If we leave him alone, he'll calm by the time he gets home. He must understand that since they're trespassers, this accident wasn't Agu's fault. Besides, the trail is gone now."

Ludik wasn't sure a stupid Dog would be so understanding, but ending this quickly was good. If something went wrong, the headman could deal with it. Ludik pulled himself to his feet and turned toward Maon.

When they returned to the accident scene, Ludik sat by Ahjin's stump. Nemerra curled up by Ludik, her presence comforting.

"What did you find?" Shaman Akamu asked.

"A few fox hairs caught on thorns and twigs." Ludik gestured to Zefra, who laid the small tufts of red fur in a line. "We also found this plant, and evidence of a witness."

Zefra laid the tiny scrap next to the fur.

Ludik explained about the scent and heel print. "And then a skunk scrambled the trail entirely," he finished.

Akamu frowned. "Unfortunately, it makes too much sense to have a third person involved."

"Why?" Asad asked. "Are these two not enough of a disaster?"

"Now that we've examined the bodies," the shaman said, "this is more complicated than we thought. The Fox died from Agu's claws and teeth, but Agu died from something much longer and broader, like a tree branch or spear. If we were much farther east, I would guess an elephant tusk."

Ludik laughed. "An elephant? Don't be ridiculous."

"We're in a forest; my first guess is a branch," Akamu repeated, pointing his chin at a fallen tree limb. "Since the Fox didn't have hands at the time, I assume it was the Fox's companion who grabbed whatever was available."

"That doesn't sound good," Ahjin said.

"It gets worse," Akamu warned.

Ludik flattened his ears. "How could it get worse?"

"Look at this." Gurryon rolled the dead fox with his foot to expose the stump of a tail.

"So? Agu is missing an ear," Asad said. "It looks like a fierce battle." He pointed to several of the leopard's wounds.

"The ear is right here," Akamu said. "We found it a few paces away. The tail is nowhere we can find."

Nia wrinkled her nose. "Why would someone cut off his tail?"

"Gurryon, where is the plant we found?" Akamu asked.

Gurryon produced a mangled stem with a few half-dried leaves.

Ludik took the shriveled plant and held it where Asad could also see. "I can't tell what it is."

"We found it on top of the Fox," Akamu said. "It's birdsfoot trefoil. I, too, thought it was random, until I heard of your witness."

"Birdsfoot trefoil." Ludik searched his memory. "I don't remember that one." He knew many ways to tell Nemerra he loved her, but he hadn't memorized the meanings of every single flower.

"It means 'revenge,'" Gurryon said.

Ludik's heart sank. "You think he took the tail for proof a Cat murdered his friend. Asad, we made a terrible mistake."

Asad shook his head and closed his eyes.

"What do you mean?" Ahjin asked. "I thought this was an accident, not murder."

"Agu didn't murder anyone," Ludik said. "But the Fox's companion must have arrived too late to understand the truth. All he saw was his friend dying, so he stabbed Agu with a fallen branch to end the fight.

Unfortunately, it was too late, and the Fox died anyway. We should have tracked down the Dog. We need to explain what really happened."

"Where is the branch now?" Zefra asked.

"He must have taken it with him in shock," Nia suggested, "then discarded it somewhere along his way."

Nemerra lowered her head to her paws and squeezed her eyes shut.

Ludik huffed. "This is why we guard the borders and the kindreds keep to themselves. Why can't Dogs behave?"

"The important question is if we can go back and catch him?" Asad asked.

"Even if we could before, he has too much of a lead now," Ludik said.

Nia walked around Ahjin's stump and stared at the bits Zefra had collected. "Would it help if we had an idea where he might be going?"

"How do you know?" Ahjin asked. "Can you scry in the water to see who he was?"

Nia shook her head and held up the shredded plant bit. "You know I can't see the past. But this is seaweed. Either the Fox or the other Dog must have recently been at the shore."

"That is too small to identify," Gurryon complained. "You cannot know that."

Nia narrowed her emerald green eyes and spread her webbed hands. "I live underwater, dimwit." She turned back to Ahjin. "I wouldn't tell you it's seaweed if I weren't sure. I can even tell you where this one grows."

Ahjin put a hand on her shoulder. "We believe you, Nia."

Asad sat heavily. "The Dogs do have a long coastline, and we are almost to the ocean ourselves. Ludik, you must follow the blood trail to the Canid border."

Ludik jumped to his paws. "Plague fleas, no! No, no, no. Not again," he snarled. He shouldered Nemerra toward the village. "Someone else can go this time. I'm getting married."

"I would go, but I'm old and must prepare the village in case you don't succeed." Asad tightened his shoulders. "Who else is familiar with the scent and the accident scene? Akamu and Gurryon are unfamiliar with tracking or hunting. We don't have time to wait for one of the border patrol."

"The Dog only defended his friend," Ahjin said. "Would you really charge him with murder?"

"That isn't my intent," Akamu said. "You don't understand how our kindreds think. He'll use the tail as proof Agu killed the Fox and rally his village against ours. We'll be stuck in a battle of revenge over a misunderstanding."

"You must convince him it was an accident," Asad said. "We will forgive Agu's death if they forgive the Fox's. The Dog only defended his friend against an apparent enemy. We would rather have peace than revenge for self-defense. You must go, Ludik."

Ludik snarled in his headman's face.

"Ludik," Nemerra gasped. "Behave. I think you should help. I waited for you before, and I'll wait again."

When Asad didn't respond, Ludik lowered his head and forced his mouth closed over his fangs. "If you can't find anyone else, I'll leave right after our wedding." He turned toward home again.

"I'm sorry, Ludik. We have no time." Asad gazed steadily at Ludik, but his tail twitched. "We can't wait for your wedding while the trail grows cold."

"It's an important task," Nemerra said, "and you're the best one to do it. The border isn't that far. It won't take long. You'll be back before I even have time to miss you." Her smile wobbled.

Just because lying Dogs couldn't be trusted to keep the peace didn't mean Ludik ought to be the one to make them see the truth. How could the headman ask him to miss his wedding again? It wasn't fair. He and Nemerra deserved their happiness at last.

It was Asad's fault Ludik missed his first wedding day, too. Last spring, when Ahjin and Nia came seeking help to rescue the gods, the village headman had sent Ludik along. His excuse was that pretending to be Gurryon during some of his healing lessons had made Ludik a half-trained healer.

Perhaps Ludik should blame Darravani instead. The goddess had told Asad to send Ahjin away, and the whole world nearly paid the price for her narrow viewpoint. Darravani had done her best to fix her mistakes, though.

Ludik could blame Kassian and Irajahan. The gods' stupid squabble had caused the entire disaster. But Kassian had been deceived by Irajahan's lies.

Yes, it was Irajahan's fault Ludik had missed his wedding.

He shouldn't have to pay for Irajahan's crimes.

Ludik opened his mouth to tell Asad to declaw himself and then stopped at the sight of the headman's regretfully twitching tail. He looked around.

Shaman Akamu and Gurryon covered the dead bodies in flowers, one stalk at a time. Nia and Zefra mourned a Darrendrakar they didn't even know. And Ahjin, whose life had changed more than anyone else's last summer, still waited to help. In a way, Ahjin would pay for Irajahan's crimes for the rest of his life, losing his dreams and almost his family, his wings, and his life.

Then Ludik looked at Nemerra. Her head hung low, but she stood by his side, twining her tail with his while he decided what to do. She had waited for him, though his tardiness gave her the right to annul their betrothal. Upon his return, she never spoke a word of blame.

Nemerra would stand by any decision he made, but she had said he should go. He wanted to be as good as she thought he was.

Ludik sighed and flattened his ears. Truthfully, missing their wedding was his own fault. He had stayed when he could have gone home, partly to help his new friends and partly to be the man Nemerra deserved.

It had been his choice in the end. No, he couldn't blame anyone else for last summer.

He dropped his head to his paws. It would be his fault now if the Dogs swarmed Maon. How would he feel if more bloodshed came to his village, his family, his sweetheart?

How could he marry when he couldn't be sure his sweetheart would live?

"I'll go," he croaked, as his heart shattered.

3. DEPARTURE
(MAON, FELID TERRITORY)

I make this record for my infant daughter, in case I don't get home. There is barely room in the healer's tent to add a pallet on the floor for me. Others have so many worse injuries that I have yet to be treated.
Torao, after The Battle of Sad Laughter

Ahjin rode astride Asad's back as they ran to the village, while Gurr-yon and Nemerra carried Nia and Zefra. Akamu and Ludik loped on either side of the group. They had left the bodies covered with flowers until the funerals could be held.

Ahjin had already seen enough death for a lifetime. This trip was supposed to be a vacation from his new job, though he was still on duty. Of course, he was *always* on duty now, and there was always something to learn or do. If he had been a skydancer like he wanted, everything would have been wonderful. His life had taken a flight for the worse this year.

His wings hurt from furling them too tightly, and he shook them loose. It didn't matter now what could have been. Somehow, he had to improve the way things were now. He needed to get his life under control.

While he was at it, he needed to help Ludik, who was obviously distraught. Every few minutes, Ludik brushed by Nemerra or entwined his tail with hers. She watched him constantly, smiling when he looked at her, worried whenever he glanced away.

"If it's so urgent to catch this Dog," Ahjin asked the others as they hurried back to the village, "why return to the village instead of chasing him now?" He spoke in trade tongue, for Zefra's sake.

"Yes," Ludik complained. "Why am I not already gone?"

"He has a head start," Shaman Akamu said, "and you need food, at least, and a blanket, in case you don't catch him today. It will only take a few minutes to gather supplies."

His mane shone lighter and redder than the chieftain's gray-sprinkled dark, while Gurryon's was long and golden. The two older lions ran as easily as the younger cats and wore gold hoops in their left ears. Ahjin swallowed at the reminder of a task yet to come and pondered instead how odd it was that Gurryon and Ludik looked so similar as men yet so different as cats.

Nia interrupted his thoughts. "What will you do if Ludik can't catch the Dog before he gets home?"

"Hmm, well," Asad cleared his throat. "I hope Ahjin will go with Ludik. It's hard to pass up the opportunity for an esteemed mediator with such impeccable authority. And so close at paw."

Ahjin grimaced. He already had plenty to do. Darravani had other priests who could help. Ahjin could ask one of them to go instead.

But it was Ahjin's fault Ludik had missed his wedding the first time. He owed him compensation for that, as well as gratitude for his life. "I don't know your land, and I have little experience, but I'll do what I can."

Nia chuckled. "Who needs experience when you have the gods on your side?"

On his side. Ahjin snorted. He faced a lifetime with people and gods demanding he fix everything, and on their terms. And Irajahan was still a difficult god. Nia knew all this, of course, she just thought it was funny.

He glared at her, and she stuck out her tongue.

Zefra sighed. "Enough. You need Ludik's skills. Ahjin will go as mediator. The question now is who else will go?"

Ludik twitched his whiskers. "I can run, and Ahjin can fly, but if we take others, can we move quickly enough to catch the Dog?"

Ahjin flexed his wings. Though healed, they were stiff from disuse.

His feathers had barely grown back after the lightning, and he hadn't gotten enough flying practice on the ship.

"I still can't fly for long," Ahjin admitted. "Wings won't help the situation much."

"Speed doesn't matter as much as you think," Akamu said. "Even if you arrive soon after he does, you can pacify his kin before they have time to leave."

"Ludik can't chase him as a jaguar, anyway," Asad said. "That might frighten him into running faster. And if you have to cross the border, you can't go on four legs and antagonize the same Canids you need to appease."

Gurryon surged forward to pace the shaman. "I will go with you. I could use the experience, Akamu. And I could reassure the Fox's family that he was buried properly."

Ahjin tightened his grip on Asad's mane. "It's fine with me." Even as an apprentice with authority limited to his own people and goddess, Gurryon had more experience as a priest than Ahjin did, and this was his country.

Perhaps Ahjin could get help with the Darrendran part of his vast, impending religious education. Gurryon might even help him recruit a few Darrendrakar workers for Arupa. With a little help, Ahjin could get his chaotic island under control. After Ludik's wedding and this new crisis, of course.

"Hmm, maybe, Gurryon." Akamu shook his mane. "But what will Il-ani think of your absence?"

"My betrothed will be glad to have me out of her mane," Gurryon drawled. "Maybe she'll miss me if I'm gone long enough."

When Akamu didn't reply, Gurryon fidgeted, bouncing Nia on his back. "Come on, let me go. Ludik had all the fun last time." His deep voice edged higher into a whine.

Nia gasped and clutched Gurryon's mane when he bounced again. "It doesn't sound like any more fun than last time. I don't want to go. I've had quite enough of death, thank you."

"We all have, so we must stop this before it turns into a battle," Asad rumbled.

Ahjin felt shivers run through the mighty lion, despite his calm voice.

Nia sniffed. "I don't see how I can help."

Ahjin tightened his shaking hands in Asad's mane. "Stay here and be safe."

Finding Nia's body last time had broken his heart. To distract himself from the bad memories, he translated the last bits of the conversation for Zefra.

"I will go with you," Zefra said. "I am the only one whose power is an offensive weapon."

She had almost died last time, too. Saving them with her magic left her gray and fading away.

"No," Ahjin protested. "You should stay safely with Nia." If he couldn't keep Ludik safe, he could at least protect the others.

"I do not need 'safe' in my job description," Zefra said. "I can follow and make maps, and I'm trained with sword, staff, bow, and knife. You might need my skills."

"We're trying to convince the Dog *not* to fight," Ludik said.

Zefra nodded. "Yes, but who can predict what will happen? It is better to prepare. He will expect you to be dangerous, but will he think it of me?" She waved her hand toward her skinny body.

Asad shook his mane. "There is no need to send children. Ahjin and the littermates will be sufficient, unless you want additional adults."

"Fine," Nia said. "Nemerra and I will stay in the village. I'll scry you, and we'll have everything ready for the wedding by the time you return."

"I am not a child," Zefra insisted. "Taking a woman will make you seem less threatening to your quarry."

"I ordered a breastplate like yours, Ludik," Gurryon blurted, "after you left on your adventure. I can bring it."

"We are trying to avoid a fight," Ludik repeated. "Civil war is too costly. The last war with the Hyenas wiped out a quarter of our kindred and half of theirs."

"Then why did you fight them?" Ahjin asked.

Asad turned his head to look at Ahjin on his back. "The Hyenas attacked us instead of taking the border dispute to the council. We had to defend ourselves until a council priest arrived from the temple. In that two months, the Hyenas carved a line through our territory."

"This time," Ahjin said, "we can settle this peacefully. And if the Dog does fight, he won't be as bad as squabbling gods. At least he's limited to mortal weapons and stray tree branches. We can handle it ourselves,

Asad. Zefra is right about the benefit of looking harmless, and we have more experience than you think."

W hen they reached the village, the Cats dropped them in front of the guest houses next to oak trees that meant hospitality.

Ahjin's little house had no loft, and the higher ceiling made it look bigger than the one the girls shared. An elaborately carved screen guarded the corner where two narrow cots were shoved together to accommodate his wings. At least the villagers had kept to an unusually minimal color scheme of pale greens with orange accents.

Unlike the girls' single pot of flowers, Ahjin had plants everywhere, sitting on every horizontal surface and hanging from the ceiling. He had researched some of them in Darravani's garden book. The yellow roses spoke of friendship and joy, the tiny white buckbean flowers on his pillow were for calm repose, and the sunflowers meant gratitude. The air smelled of herbs, including bay laurel for glory and sage for esteem, long life, and health.

He stopped reading the floral meanings when he discovered the oft-repeated grouping of yellow lilies, fritillaria, and wild geranium meant walking on air, power, and steadfast piety. Apparently, they were now his signature flowers. Despite the obvious respect, he preferred the yellow roses.

They'd left for the hunt so quickly Ahjin had merely dumped his things on the cots, so it took only moments to gather his pack and jacket. He left his fancy uniform and most of his religious texts, but after changing his mind three times, packed his newly repaired armor. Maka-navailea had suggested he bring it to Darrendra, though she hadn't mentioned any danger. Perhaps her advice was leftover distrust between the gods, or perhaps the Dog would react badly before Ahjin could mediate. He rubbed his back where scorpion claws had lacerated his flesh. If the Omniscient wished to advise her new Mouth, it was wise to listen to the goddess.

He arrived first in the public clearing, but Nia and Zefra arrived a few minutes later.

Zefra's short, curved sword hung at her side, mostly hidden in the folds of her tan robe. Her embroidered sash covered her sword belt. She carried her iron-bound staff openly as a walking stick, but Ahjin knew it was also a weapon.

"I like Ludik's family," Nia said. "His mama is packing food for you. Want to help me get it, Zefra? Ahjin can stay here and look official." She dragged Zefra toward Ludik's tall, sturdy mother.

Ahjin tried not to flinch at the gathering crowd. Everyone wore clothing as colorful as the Nokai's, although in different patterns. In a horde, they were eye-watering. Even their shoes were dyed and decorated, though a glimpse of plain brown drew his gaze downward.

That was strange. Ludik's tunic was as gaudy as everyone else's, but his travel-stained boots were undecorated. Until now, Ahjin hadn't realized they were unusual, except for their hidden steel greaves. The Iojif wore plain boots, as did the Iskrins. The Nokai rarely wore shoes at all. Nia's sandals had been made by Zefra after borrowed desert boots had blistered her feet bloody.

"He won't let me finish them," Nemerra said.

Ahjin turned to find her watching Ludik talk to his parents. "Finish what?"

"His boots. You were wondering why he wears such dull boots. I ran out of time to decorate them before he left with you last time. I offered to fix them, but he won't even let me sand down the gouges. He said he earned every one." She tilted her head in question.

"Probably from the giant scorpions." Ahjin rubbed the scars on his lower back. "Or the knee-high spiders."

Nemerra gasped. "*Giant* scorpions and spiders? He didn't mention their size. We teased him for having nightmares about little bugs. I didn't know—" She pressed her hand to her mouth. "Would you excuse me, please?"

She dashed to Nia and whispered frantically, then ran into the village.

Nia shoved her armload of plates at Gurryon and ran in a different direction, spewing curses.

Ahjin fidgeted. Poor Nemerra. Ludik had censored his adventures to spare her distress, but it was sure to come out sooner or later. He wouldn't tell Ludik he had ruined the secret.

Zefra returned with the food and the tall brothers, who wore white-flower pendants. Ahjin gobbled his hot lunch, stowed his share of the travel rations, and buckled his pack between his wings.

He was ready. This wouldn't be so hard. All they had to do was catch the Dog and convince him he made a mistake. Ahjin had done that sort of thing before, under harder circumstances. They could do it again, before Ludik's wedding was ruined.

Gurryon leaned toward the forest, and Ludik scowled at his little house. Their family and friends gathered in an erratic line to offer good wishes and embraces for the strangers as well as for Ludik and Gurryon. One after another, members of the family wept over their young men.

Ahjin twitched with every tear. "Do they think you're never coming back?" he muttered sideways. "Don't they trust you?"

"After I was late last time? No, I don't think so," Ludik murmured after he kissed his mother. "Besides, we're chasing a Dog. Who knows what he'll do?"

The next person was an old man who used a three-fingered hand to give Ahjin a small, handmade book with a worn cover. "I want you to take this with you. Read it as soon as you can."

Ludik frowned. "Grandpapa, your journal?"

"I want him to understand the seriousness of this. I want him to protect all my grandchildren." The old man turned to Ahjin again. "The Dogs cannot be trusted. Bring back my grandsons quickly. Keep them from war. Keep it from all of us." He clasped Ahjin's left arm and pressed their cheeks together. Then he embraced Gurryon and Ludik and left with tears running down his face.

Ahjin frowned. That seemed an over-reaction to a simple mistake they could explain to the Dog as soon as they caught him.

Nemerra and Nia were last in line, sliding breathlessly into place.

Ludik's lip quivered as he took his sweetheart's hand. "Keep well, Nemerra. I won't be long. We'll marry as soon as I return."

"Yes, soon," she said, "but I'm not waiting here for you."

"Don't give up on me," Ludik begged with heartbreak in his silver eyes.

She turned to show a small pack on her back. "I'm coming."

Ludik shook his head. "Oh, no."

Nemerra pressed her lips together and blinked. "My heart can't bear another day away from you. Ahjin will talk with that Dog, and that will be that. I'm coming, dear."

"No, you aren't. I won't allow it." He folded his arms across his chest and pulled himself taller.

As if he weren't already an intimidating height. Ahjin stretched his back and still only reached Ludik's shoulder.

"You can't stop me, darling." Nemerra kissed Ludik's cheek. "Are you ready to go?"

Ludik sputtered his way through a string of arguments. Nemerra ignored him while she helped Nia wrap the rest of her hair around her head and tie it with her rainbow of ribbons. The two commiserated about difficult men who didn't listen.

Ahjin hid a grin. Nemerra would keep Ludik's life interesting.

"Is this an important conversation, or should I ignore it?" Zefra whispered to Ahjin.

Nia froze. "Oops," she said in trade tongue. "Nemerra, we've been rude. I'm sorry, Zefra. I'll make sure you can understand from now on."

"You can't," Ahjin said. "You aren't coming." He suddenly empathized with Ludik.

"Blistering seas, I'm not staying here by myself." Nia turned to show her own pack and wave a shortened spear. "I'll go crazy waiting to find out if someone killed you for one of your pranks. Someone has to keep you out of trouble."

When Ahjin tried to argue, she put her hands over her ears and hummed loudly.

At least he could keep an eye on her if she came. "Fine, but wear your sandals for protection." He glared at her until she unpacked them.

After Nia tied her sandals with a flourish, she stomped her webbed feet and scowled. "Are we ready now?"

"You'll let Nemerra come?" Ludik protested.

"If you can't stop her, what chance do I have?" Ahjin raised an eyebrow. "You said this will be an easy mission. We explain the truth and come home again. She'll be fine."

Nemerra hooked her arm around Ludik's elbow and smiled at both of them.

"You could officially tell her to stay home," Ludik said.

"Could, but won't," Ahjin said. "If she's going to marry you, she has the right to come."

Ludik growled a rolling snarl, picked up his ax, and stalked out of the village. Nemerra trailed after him, shaking her head.

Nia went next, smacking innocent bushes with her spear and mouthing things best left unidentified. Everyone else followed quietly.

When they reached the accident scene, they waited while Ludik showed Gurryon the blood trail, which faded in less than a mile.

"I hope you are right about the seaweed, Nia," Gurryon said.

Ludik shifted his pack higher and kissed Nemerra's hand. "A straight line will end in Canid territory near the shore. Let's go calm down that Dog. I have other things to do."

Now the real work began. Ahjin rolled his shoulders and twitched his wings. If the flowers in his guest room were an accurate indication, perhaps the Dog would be impressed with Ahjin's new authority and listen. If they were lucky, they'd return for the wedding in no time.

Something good should come from his overwhelming new job.

4. FOREST

(SOUTHWEST FELID TERRITORY)

Any of the big Cats in the Felid kindred are called panthers when their fur is all black, regardless of their actual type.
A Brief Sketch of Mysterious Darrendra

Z efra frowned. They had walked for hours with no sign of the Dog, and the others did not seem to be hurrying enough.

"Shall we run?" she asked. "Do we not need to catch the Canid?"

"We might miss his tracks if we run," Ludik said. "As our shaman said, we can still prevent trouble if we catch him before he rouses an army."

Ludik and Nemerra walked hand in hand, whispering to each other as he scanned the ground. Zefra squinted under a prickly bush Ludik had missed. Her nose was nearly useless compared to the Felids, but her eyes and ears worked well. She was practical and skilled in the desert, but here, so many leaves continued to fall, it was difficult to see tracks before they were covered.

Gurryon poked at bushes with his staff and whistled softly. Nia stomped behind them with a ferocious scowl on her face. Ahjin walked with them, and that was a change. Before his injuries, he had flown most of the time.

Zefra glanced covertly at his wings. They looked recovered, but he folded them close to his body as if they still hurt. He maneuvered around grasping twigs, and the sudden mental picture of his wings tangled in branches explained everything. She glanced up but could not see more than glimpses of the sky through the leaves. That would make it hard for him to follow them from above the trees. And he was reading while he walked, which she had never seen him do while flying.

He squinted as he tilted the pages of the journal Torao had given him. "This handwriting is terrible," Ahjin complained, almost tripping on a root.

Nia frowned and crossed her arms. "Then give up."

Ludik brushed at leaves on the path with a disappointed frown, then stared at her before responding to Ahjin. "You saw Grandpapa. His injury happened in the war. He didn't have practice writing with his right hand yet."

Ahjin lowered the book. "I didn't realize." He rubbed one of the many lightning scars on his face and returned to reading.

It had only been two months since he was injured. Zefra prayed to Resef for his continued healing before scanning the forest again.

Zefra loved the scrubby green of oases and had always wanted to visit the Iskrin territories that grew most of Iskra's food. The Darrendran forest was greener than a thousand oases, greener than the largest garden. And the smell! The air was heavy with the spicy scents of growing things.

She split her attention between the layers of living green and watching for signs of their quarry. The sooner they found the Canid, the better. Despite the lovely forest, this was not a pleasure trip.

She would not miss Ludik's wedding, but after that, she must explore for Kassian. This detour disrupted her plans. If this hunt took too long, the winter storms would strand her on this continent until spring, delaying her first paid job. Unless the god decided to hire someone else because she was late.

Zefra walked faster until she had to work to breathe smoothly. The others sped up without comment, though Nia made a face.

Zefra still found no tracks. There was not even a real trail, just endless trees and layers of fallen leaves to cover any footsteps. Splitting up would cover more ground but defeat their reasons for traveling together. They needed a strategy.

"Which way is the Canid likely to have gone?" she asked. "Would he retrace his steps or take a different path? What is our best plan?"

"Slimy seaweed," Nia grumbled. "What difference does it make? We don't know his original path, anyway. How can we plan for wandering blindly through the woods?"

"We can make a strategic guess," Zefra said. "Plans can be adjusted with new information."

"If we'll have to change them," Nia snapped, "why bother in the first place?"

"Because plans help us succeed." Zefra shook her head. An intelligent woman like Nia should know that already.

"Why are we even chasing a murderer?" Nia complained.

"Oh, no," Nemerra said. "He's not a murderer. He was protecting the Fox. It's sad, of course, that Agu didn't speak their language so he could calm them, but it was still a misunderstanding. If the Dog had known Agu was only defending himself, things would have been different."

"Agu wasn't fighting the *Dog*," Nia said. "That makes it murder."

"It is still different," Nemerra insisted.

"It had better be different," Ludik muttered. He tucked Nemerra's hand in the crook of his elbow.

Zefra shook her head. "Murder is a matter of intent and law. The headman told me it counted as defense under their law. If they had entered Felid territory with the intent to kill Agu, then it would have been murder. But they did not even know Agu was there."

Nia stomped her feet. "I don't want to talk about this anymore." She turned away and yanked on her braids.

Zefra shuttered her inner eyelids and returned to watching for signs. She would make her own plans if no one would help. What was the most reasonable thing for a scared fugitive to do? Return home as quickly as possible. Therefore, they should continue in the straightest line possible toward the Canid's presumed home.

And she would watch. Nobody could avoid leaving some trace. Sooner or later, she would find something to tell her they were going the right way.

Nemerra stepped beside Zefra and gestured at the trees. "The tall ones make good masts and roof timbers, and smell them." She broke several of the needles and handed them to her.

"Oh, that is what I smelled." Zefra inhaled again before returning them.

"You may keep them," Nemerra said with a gentle smile. The tall woman waved her hand at the forest, easily matching Zefra's pace with her longer legs. "We have more than enough."

Her dress was as colorful as the brothers' tunics, although longer and fuller. Compared to them and Nia, Ahjin's simple colors were plain and Zefra's robe was dull. Although the Darrendran clothing was not camouflage, Zefra's tan stood out as much against the green and floral background as the Darrendrakar would have in her desert home.

"Thank you for the gift." Zefra carefully tucked the fragrant needles into her pouch and pointed to a shorter tree. "What are the ones with gray leaves and golden wood?"

"Those are suvarna. Earlier in the year, the leaves are rose and violet and silver. They are beautiful, though not as common as the evergreens."

Zefra stared around her. "'Tis all beautiful."

"They aren't that great," Nia muttered.

Zefra ignored her unusual rudeness. "Do you know any of the other plants?"

"I'm Darrendrakar. Of course I know the other plants." Nemerra chuckled and named flowers and bushes, mostly in Darrendran, but occasionally in trade tongue.

Nia grinned. "Do you make perfume from any of them?"

Zefra smiled. Ever since her brother, Izo, had given Nia some perfume as a flirtation gift, the girl was obsessed with fragrances. Izo was still disappointed she would not do more than flutter her eyelashes at him, though Zefra had told him Nia was still a child in her own culture.

Nemerra smiled ruefully. "I'm sure someone does, but I'm afraid I don't know which plants."

"That's sad," Nia said. "It would make this trip more fun. I don't have anything to do but translate for Zefra."

Zefra sniffed. She was fluent in trade tongue and could take care of herself.

Nemerra wrinkled her forehead. "But we might need you to translate when we catch the Dog, too. Every Darrendran territory has its own language. Languages, actually, since we use a different dialect when we're in our other forms."

"They are all different?" Zefra's eyes widened. "How many people will know trade tongue?"

"Many of the border guard, probably," Gurryon said. "The traders. Some of the shamans."

"Then it's a good thing I came," Nia snapped. "I can translate for our group, and Ahjin can translate for the people we meet."

That was enough. "Why are you so cranky, Nia?" Zefra asked. "Are your feet okay? Did something bite you? Are we walking too fast for your short legs?"

Nia wiggled her toes in her sandals and glared at Zefra. "My feet are fine, and my legs are long enough to reach the ground. I came here for a party, and now everything is ruined. I hoped we'd enjoy ourselves this time." She scowled and crossed her arms.

Zefra held her breath. She thought Nia liked surprises, oddly enough. Well, perhaps only good surprises, and so far, they had gotten the bad sort.

"We will catch the Canid before he tells everyone Agu is a vicious killer," Zefra said, "and we will have the wedding. I'm sure you will find some way to have fun. You always do."

She kept herself from rolling her eyes. Nia was almost as bad as Ahjin at making her own entertainment. It was wise to stay away from both of them when they got inspired.

"I'll let you know when I have fun," Nia said. "And now that you mention it, my feet *are* getting tired."

Ludik stopped scanning the ground to glance at the setting sun. The orange sky was already streaked with blue and purple. "We can't reach the border tonight. We should make camp."

"But the Dog will escape," Nia complained. "Why walk so fast if we won't even catch him?"

"He'll stop for the night, too." Ahjin patted her on the shoulder. "We'll find him tomorrow."

"If we keep going in the dark, we could walk right by his sleeping body," Zefra said. "There is a clearing ahead. Who has the tents?"

Gurryon laughed. "Who needs tents? There will be no rain tonight."

"I thought you would prepare." Zefra paused. "Is it likely to rain?"

"If it rains," Gurryon said, "and it will someday, we will cut branches to make shelters."

Zefra choked. "You will cut..." She could not bear to finish the sentence. "And what will you do with the branches in the morning? Will they not be heavier to carry than tents?"

Gurryon shrugged. "Leave them. We can cut more the next day, if we need to."

Zefra pressed a hand to her chest and took a deep breath. She tried to speak but failed. They could not mean they would discard the precious wood. When she inhaled again, Nia and Nemerra exchanged looks.

Nia took Zefra's arm. "Look at the thousands of trees."

Nemerra pointed. "So many saplings grow, we have to thin them regularly before they take over the forest. We get a lot of rain that makes everything grow quickly."

Nia elbowed Ahjin until he lowered his book.

His eyes flickered between the women and Gurryon. "Oh." He cleared his throat. "Don't worry, Zefra." He raised the journal again. "It won't hurt the forest or their economy."

"If it will make you feel better, Zefra," Gurryon said, "we will not cut any unnecessary wood." He bumped Ludik and whispered, "I didn't think it was such a problem."

Ludik did not bother to whisper. "You just didn't think."

Gurryon calmly tripped him.

The scuffle gave the others time to choose a camping spot and pull out a cold dinner. Zefra was doubly glad to avoid raw food and burning wood. Gurryon grumbled like a spoiled child who had never faced true hunger.

Nemerra sat on a fallen log at Ludik's right side and held his hand while they each ate with their other hand.

"These are the most portable of our wedding leftovers. Aren't they delicious?" She turned a wobbly smile on Ludik and blinked three times. He wrapped his arm around her without a return smile.

After washing the dishes, the men settled on one side of the little clearing and the women on the other. Zefra wrapped her scarf warmly around her head and rolled up in her blanket between Nemerra and Nia. She was almost asleep when a whimper echoed in her ear.

"Sorry," Nemerra whispered. Her blanket rustled, and the cloth muffled her sobs.

"We will catch him tomorrow," Zefra whispered. "Your wedding is only a couple of days away."

"I'm sorry," Nia murmured from on watch.

"Go to sleep," Gurryon grumbled. "It will seem better in the morning."

"Enough," Ludik growled. "Nemerra, come here." He towed her and both their blankets past the others to the closest tree. After wrapping one blanket around Nemerra, he sat with his back against the trunk and tugged her onto his lap. He tucked the other blanket around them both and pressed her head against his shoulder. "Everyone, go to sleep."

"Ludik," Zefra started, leaning on one elbow to remind them about the proprieties.

"I realize it isn't my wedding night anymore," Ludik snapped. "I still intend to comfort my beloved. Go to sleep."

Nemerra hiccupped. Ludik stroked her hair with one hand while his other arm held her tight. He murmured something Zefra could not hear, and Nemerra closed her eyes.

Zefra watched until Ludik leaned his head against Nemerra's and squeezed his eyes shut. A movement caught her gaze, and she looked over to see Ahjin watching the couple. His eyes shone with tears in the moonlight.

When he saw Zefra watching him, he rolled over and pulled his blanket over his head.

Zefra lay down and tucked her blanket under her chin. Ludik and Nemerra had already missed their wedding once. Missing it twice was ridiculous, and Nemerra had a reason to cry. She did not know why Ahjin wept. It was not his wedding or his fault. Tears were a waste of energy when he could plan how to help instead.

She fell asleep mentally reviewing her tracking lessons.

Ahjin woke Zefra before the sun had quite risen. "I loaded our little stove with deadfall twigs. Light it for breakfast, please. We need to leave as soon as we can see."

Zefra nodded stiffly, and he helped her stagger to her feet. Nia never woke early or quickly, but everyone else was already awake and folding blankets.

Ahjin frowned at Zefra. "Are you getting enough sunlight among the trees?"

She tried to reassure him, but her voice only croaked, and her hands shook on his supporting arm.

"Perhaps you shouldn't wear your scarf so you get the maximum light," he said. "I don't want a repeat of your problem in Ioj, and you need to keep up with the chase. If I didn't think he'd burn my ears for it, I'd tell Resef he made his people in a faulty design."

She tried to glare at him, then nodded. If she did not have enough energy for a decent glare this morning, he was right. If she was not careful, she might fall into hibernation from not enough sunlight to even stay awake.

Ahjin walked her to the cooking area, then started the long process of waking Nia.

"Does this look like enough cereal for all of us?" Gurryon tilted the pan.

Zefra shook her head, then leaned to light the fire with her finger. Nothing happened.

"I have a firestarter." Gurryon reached into his pack with a smirk. "Do you want it?"

"That is not necessary." Zefra sat, removed her scarf, rolled up her sleeves, and tugged her legs crossed. She rested her hands on her knees and tilted her face to the pale light.

Ah, that was better. She missed the bright sun of the desert and the heat that soaked through her bones by mid-morning. The cool shade of this scented forest made her listless.

When her energy climbed to the crown of her head a few minutes later, she opened her eyes. Gurryon's flint sat in front of her knees. She ignored it and snapped her fingers under his nose. When he yelped and jumped back from the flame that appeared, she lowered her hand and set the wood on fire.

"You're welcome," she said. "You can do it the hard way when 'tis your turn."

Nia woke in time to eat the last of breakfast. "You have pretty hair," she yawned, leaning against Zefra's shoulder. "You shouldn't cover it all the time." Her own braids fell in frizzy disarray until she plaited them all together and tied the braid-of-braids with one of her many ribbons.

Zefra tried not to blush. She poked her stray red waves of hair more or less into place in her braided crown and tucked her scarf into the back of the belt her little sisters had embroidered for her. Proper Iskrin maidens usually kept their hair covered in public for propriety as well as water conservation under the hot desert sun. Ahjin was right about her need for sunlight, though, and one advantage to outdweller friends was that nobody here knew she was being a little brazen.

"Will we run today?" Zefra asked.

Ludik frowned. "What if the Dog turns aside?"

"But we can go faster." Ahjin put his unopened scroll back in his pack and stretched. "Ready?"

All morning, the group walked so fast they had little breath for speech, but still did not catch the Canid.

Zefra kept careful watch as rear guard. The dappled sun bathed her skin until she felt normal again. She soothed her nerves by estimating how far away he could be if he ran all day, though even Darrendrakar could not do that.

"Look, more fox fur." Ludik interrupted her calculations, picking the red strands from a thorn bush. He sniffed them and gave them to her to stash in her pouch. "Same Fox. We're still on the right track. When will he calm enough for us to catch up?" He kicked the fallen leaves.

Zefra understood his frustration. Most surprises in life were unpleasant. Careful plans were the best way to reach satisfactory goals. She did not see any reason to change a winning motto.

"How do we know it's from the Dog carrying the tail?" Nia asked. "Maybe it's from the Fox's journey in."

"The Canid will retrace his steps to home," Zefra said. "Either way, it is likely the same path."

"Why don't we run?" Gurryon whined. "I don't know how we're too slow, but we haven't caught the half-witted Dog yet, and we're almost to the border."

Ludik stalked past Gurryon. "If I'd been running, I wouldn't have seen the fox fur. I hate this as much as you do."

"How close to the border are we?" Zefra asked.

"Only a couple of leagues," Gurryon said. "If he crosses the border before us, everything becomes more complicated."

"Mongrel curs," Ludik swore. "Is it better for us to cross the border, or to hope the Dog comes to his senses by himself? Which is less likely to cause trouble?"

Nemerra slid past everyone with an apologetic smile and wrapped her hand through Ludik's elbow. They set off at a trot, and the others followed.

Speed or care? It was a terrible choice. Ludik's pace was a risky compromise. Zefra watched for tracks or signs Ludik might have missed. It was harder to notice small signs in a crowded forest than an empty desert. Better to have extra eyes on the trail.

Where was that Canid?

It was early afternoon when Ludik raised his hand to stop the group again. "I smell the border. Do you see anyone around? Our quarry or any other Dogs?"

Nia put down her spear and shaded her eyes, looking into the distance.

"Nothing." Ahjin tucked the book into his pack. "Do we cross or wait?"

"I suppose we cross." Gurryon took a step across the border before anyone could stop him.

Zefra shook her head. Everyone knew a scout should go first, to make sure the route was correct and safe. This was foolish audacity in an unfriendly territory.

Gurryon took a second step and turned to see if the others followed.

A large wolf stepped from the forest and blocked their path, teeth bared. "You cannot cross."

Nemerra screamed, and Zefra reached for her sword.

5. BORDER
(FELID-CANID BORDER)

The Canid kindred are of two types: the Wolves, Dogs, and Jackals in the Canini, and the Vulpini Foxes.
A Brief Sketch of Mysterious Darrendra

Nia gasped. The wolf blocking the path was large enough to bite her in half. Where was her spear? She was right; this quest was no fun.

Ludik stepped in front of his sweetheart and raised his ax. Ahjin vanished into thin air. Everyone else grabbed their weapons.

Nia still couldn't find her spear. Did wolves normally grow that big around here? Didn't they have enough problems already? Why couldn't Dogs and Cats keep from fighting when they accidentally bumped into each other?

"Stop," Gurryon shouted. He raised his staff toward the massive wolf. "We have to cross in the name of peace."

Ludik crossed the invisible border to stand beside his brother. Nemerra took another step backward, fumbling for her knife and muttering a prayer.

Nia glared at the wolf. She had hoped Darrendra wouldn't be dangerous. It wasn't fair for such a pretty forest to be scary. Treacherous places should announce themselves with darkness and fog and ominous voices, so visitors could go somewhere else before it was too late. They shouldn't smell nice and be covered in flowers and majestic trees and then betray themselves with nastiness. That was bad manners.

At least Kassian's meadow had revealed its menace. By the depths of the ocean, Nia didn't want to think about that, and she couldn't take her attention from the wolf. His white teeth looked impressively sharp in his long muzzle. If he didn't let them cross the border, their quest would fail, and the Dogs would take their revenge on Maon. Would the Wolf allow them to chase one of his own kind?

The wolf sat on his haunches and held up his forepaws. He considered each person in their group before speaking in badly accented Felid. "Stop? What if I just... paws?" He howled with laughter.

He didn't sound menacing. Nia giggled and translated for Zefra. Now, this was finally fun.

Alas, the joke did not translate well. Zefra wrinkled her black eyebrows. "Is pause not the same as stop?"

Nia didn't have time to explain before Gurryon ruined everything.

"What are you, a Hyena?" Gurryon sneered, letting his staff dip.

The wolf dropped his feet on top of a dainty blue flower and narrowed his eyes. "I am not—" he pounced so quickly no one could stop him. "A Hyena," he growled, pinning Gurryon to the ground weaponless and with sharp teeth mere inches from his face.

Ludik lifted his ax, and Zefra raised her sword. Nia put her hand on Zefra's arm. The boys were making enough of a mess already. Nemerra's knife disappeared as Ahjin's invisible hand took it from her. A moment later, it reappeared in her sheath.

"Put down your weapons." The wolf leaned closer to Gurryon's face. "I can remove his nose before you can remove my head. I hate to do that to someone of such obviously... bad taste." He winked at Nia.

Nia smiled and then tried to look innocent when Gurryon glared at her.

"You think this is funny?" Gurryon stretched toward his staff. "Could you help instead of laughing?"

"Just apologize." Nia grabbed his staff, holding it out of reach. "You're the one with the bad taste to insult your neighbor."

"Oh, is that what he meant?" Gurryon muttered.

"I meant it both ways," the wolf said. "Shall I test the other before we discuss your invasion of my territory?" He licked his teeth and leaned toward Gurryon's nose.

"Ludik," Nemerra whispered urgently, peering over Zefra's head.

"Nia, I don't think you understand the seriousness of Darrendrakar interkindred relationships," Ludik said. "I don't think an apology will be enough." The ax in his hand twitched.

"I think it sounds like a good idea," the wolf said. "Unless you like my solution better." He grinned a toothy grin.

"Ludik," Nia said.

"That is not necessary. We ask your pardon for the insult." Ludik laid his ax on the ground and kicked Gurryon's foot.

Gurryon stopped reaching for his weapon and pushed the wolf. "Get off me."

The wolf growled and leaned closer.

Ludik kicked his brother harder.

"Fine." Gurryon kicked awkwardly at Ludik. "I am sorry, Wolf. I did not mean to insult you."

The wolf yawned in Gurryon's face, baring all his teeth again.

"You have to tell the truth in an apology," Ludik said.

Nia saw the corner of his mouth twitch and covered her own smile. The longer this encounter continued, the more her bad mood evaporated.

Gurryon sighed. "I was rude to insult you, and you are nothing like a Hyena."

The wolf tilted his head and stared at Gurryon for a minute. "Apology accepted." He licked Gurryon from chin to hair before jumping away. "Yep, bad taste."

Gurryon swore, then wiped his face and rolled to his feet.

Nia smothered a chuckle.

Ludik chuckled. "It serves you right. Now you know how gross it is when you do it to me."

Gurryon snatched his staff from Nia and shook it at his brother.

"We don't mean any harm," Ahjin said in Canid, popping back into view behind the wolf. He subtly resheathed the long dagger Izo had given him and walked around the wolf to rejoin the others.

The wolf twitched. "How did you get there?"

"We are sorry for crossing the border without warning," Ludik said.

"Normally, we would be happy to avoid it, but we are on an urgent errand and did not see you to ask permission. We are tracking a Dog who saw his friend killed in an accident with a Cat. We must keep him from leading his kin in mistaken revenge for mere self-defense. He moved too quickly for us to catch him before he reached the border. Have you seen him or his trail? May we continue tracking him?"

The wolf shook his head. "You want me, a border guard, to let you wander through my territory? I do not think so. It is my job to keep peace on this side of the border and trouble on the other. And you all seem like a lot of trouble. I have never met such a strange group." He smiled fiercely as he blocked their way, keeping one eye on Ahjin at all times.

He really was huge. His back came nearly to Nia's shoulders. She was the smallest of their group, but not that small. A delicate silver chain gleamed around his neck, mostly hidden in his thick, black-and-gray fur.

"But this is important," Ludik protested. "We need to protect our village."

Nemerra reached toward Ludik, then straightened her shoulders. She tucked her hands behind her back and raised her chin.

Nia frowned at the wolf. "I'm becoming disappointed in you. And we started so well."

Would it help their appeal if she rehearsed the debate about self-defense versus murder? Would the desire to stop the Dogs from fighting the Cats be enough to convince the Wolf, or was he more likely to let them cross if she said they wanted to stop a murderer from wandering through Canid territory? Would the Wolf care about a Dog who killed Cats, or would he cheer for him? The Dog hadn't killed any other Canids, so she couldn't use that as a reason for the Wolf to stop him.

While Ludik and Gurryon argued with the wolf, Nia quickly updated Zefra on the conversation.

Nia was still pondering her tactics for convincing the border guard when Zefra took one step forward.

"Excuse me, please," Zefra said in trade tongue, lowering her curved sword but not sheathing it. "Do you understand this language?"

The wolf nodded.

"How much do you know about recent world events? I know your country is more secluded, but perhaps you have heard the cause of the difficulties in the last few months?"

"You mean the natural disasters?"

Zefra looked at Nia, who translated the wolf's reply. He couldn't pronounce trade tongue with a wolf's muzzle. She wasn't sure if his poor Felid-accent was from the same cause or merely lack of practice.

"Yes, when the gods vanished," Zefra said. "Never mind the disasters for now. Did you hear what happened to the gods afterward?"

Ahjin groaned quietly but ducked under a low-hanging branch to stand near the wolf.

Nia knew Ahjin didn't like what had happened in the summer, but they needed to convince the wolf to let them pass, and Zefra's idea was a good one. If it worked, they wouldn't have to find out if the Wolf would cheer or jeer the idea of a Dog murdering Cats. Zefra's picky points of law didn't matter, either, as long as they caught the Dog.

The wolf looked from Zefra to Ahjin and back again. He narrowed his eyes. "The shamans told us the gods escaped, defeated their enemy, and restored the world. Then they appointed a mighty priest to serve them all and encourage intercultural cooperation and worship."

Ahjin slapped his forehead and groaned again.

Nia tried not to smile as she translated for Zefra. This would be fun, even if it bothered Ahjin. Especially if it bothered Ahjin. He needed to be harried more often, poor man, or he'd forget how to laugh. Wasn't that why he kept her around? She knew how to have fun. Real fun, not his unfunny pranks. Ludik liked insulting Ahjin and hanging Nia upside down, which shouldn't count as a sense of humor. Zefra understood irony but wouldn't recognize a real joke if it bit her.

"Oh. Well, that is... mostly true." Zefra smoothed her crown of flaming red braids. "The gods were actually rescued rather than escaped, and the enemy made peace with the help of the... mighty priest they appointed to serve them."

Nia laughed despite herself. Everything Zefra said was true, except maybe 'mighty.' If she said 'mighty stubborn,' that would be closer. Who else could out-stubborn a god?

"Are you saying our shamans lied?" the wolf snarled. "How dare you slur them and our goddess, outkindred? Of course they told us the truth. These Cats have lied to you, and I will find out why."

"Settle down." Gurryon tapped the tree badge on his shoulder. "I am the apprentice to our village's shaman. I serve Darravani even before my own kindred. Will you accept my word they are telling the truth?"

The wolf glowered at him. "I will think about it after you tell me why you believe them."

"I believe them because they are the ones who rescued the gods." Gurryon tapped his badge again.

Nia tried to look serious and responsible as the wolf examined each of them again, paying special attention to their safe-conduct pendants. Just this once, she envied Zefra's natural solemnity. The only way Nia could stay serious was to think about their horrible quest, and that was no fun at all.

"Not I," Gurryon said when the wolf looked back at him. "And not Nemerra. Just those four and two friends that are not here."

"These... children... rescued the gods? That is a fabulous joke." The wolf's smile bared his sharp teeth. "I thank you for the entertainment, but you still may not pass."

"Oh, sorry, I'm the only child," Nia waved cheerfully, "and I'm older than Zefra. It's a cultural thing." She shrugged. It was more fun to be a child than a responsible adult, and she intended to make the most of it until spring.

"You all look very young, but it is irrelevant. You are still liars." The wolf growled in a steady rumble, menacing enough to sober Nia. Where had his sense of humor gone?

Ludik elbowed Ahjin. "This is a good time for some proof, Oh-Mighty-One."

Ahjin slapped him away. "Give me a moment, please." He pulled a sheet of paper and a charcoal stick from his pocket. "Is there anything in particular you want to ask, or will any answer do?" he asked the wolf.

"Ask whom?" The wolf twitched his ears and stopped growling.

"Darravani, with Kassian's help. I don't have time to design a bouquet right now." Ahjin held the charcoal over the paper.

"Kassian? Is he one of your other friends? How will you send a message before I send you home?" The wolf took a step toward them.

"Very well, random message it is." Ahjin scribbled on the paper and threw it in the air, where it vanished. "Your shamans left out a lot. Kassian the Omnipresent is the elder brother of the other four gods."

"What a ridiculous story," the wolf said.

A paper fluttered into Ahjin's outstretched hand. He turned it right-side up and read, "Lyell Ulriksin, congratulations on the births of your pups. Your wife is well." He flipped over the paper. "Nope, that's it. That's a nice message. When were they born, Lyell?"

The wolf growled. "Who told you my name? How did you know my wife is expecting any day now?" He stalked toward Ahjin. "Are you spies? I will rip the truth from you."

Ahjin laid the paper at the wolf's feet. "See for yourself."

"Lyell... pups... fine," Lyell muttered. "I missed their births. Or you are lying to me." He turned over the paper to read Ahjin's original message. "Kassian, please ask Darravani to prove our identities to a stubborn Wolf." He sniffed. "How insulting." He wrinkled his nose and leaned closer to the paper, sniffing again. "I smell... I smell..." His voice drifted off. "I smell Darravani's flowers," he finished in a dreamy voice.

"Are you persuaded?" Nia winked at the wolf, good mood returning now that he seemed unlikely to rip out their throats.

Lyell shook his heavy fur and stared at Ahjin. "Who are you?"

"My name is Ahjin Machol. These are my friends: Nia, Ludik, and Zefra; Ludik's bride-to-be, Nemerra; and his brother, Gurryon."

Ludik's grin was irreverent. "Ahjin is the mighty priest the shamans told you about."

Nia pressed her lips together to contain a giggle.

The wolf walked around Ahjin and examined him from head to toe.

Nia made her own inspection of her best friend. Same long white curls, better combed than they used to be. Same plum eyes, more serious than last spring. Brand-new clothes in the same boring colors. Same stubborn expression. New scars, healing nicely as far as she could see. Same wings, with new white feathers instead of scorched black. She wrinkled her nose at the remembered nasty scent of burned feathers.

"Meet His Holiness, the Mouth of All the Gods." Nia said it with as much pomp as the title deserved, but a giggle ruined the fanfare. This wasn't the first time she'd gotten to announce him this way, but she still hadn't tired of the amusement. Poor Ahjin hated the reminder of his new life and didn't find any of it funny.

The wolf inhaled, then turned his head and walked around Ahjin to the side opposite Nia. He poked his nose between Ahjin's scruffy wings and sniffed again.

The mighty Mouth-of-the-Gods flinched.

"He's your best chance at getting the Cats out of your territory quickly," Zefra said.

The wolf smelled the paper again. "I still cannot have you wandering unsupervised. I suppose I will have to escort you, at least for a while. And you have a lot to tell me." He stepped sideways and let the girls cross the border.

Zefra sheathed her sword. Nemerra slipped her hand into Ludik's and leaned against him.

Nia finally found her short spear leaning against a tree. Now that the Wolf had let them into his territory, their worries were over. They would catch the Dog quickly and get back to Maon in no time. Ludik and Nemerra would have the best wedding of the year, and Nia would party with all the cute boys.

Gurryon pulled on Nia's elbow until she stepped aside. "I wish we could leave Lyell behind," he whispered. "How did you know he would not kill me?"

"Didn't you see the twinkle in his eyes?" Nia said. A companion with a proper sense of humor was a delightful addition.

"No," Gurryon drawled. "I was looking at his teeth."

"They are as sharp as his wit," Nia agreed, then ducked under his arm and darted out of reach under a prickly branch too low for the tall Darrendrakar to dodge. Gurryon, it seemed, was like his brother in several ways, and she didn't need an upside-down view of the forest.

6. CROSSING
(CANID TERRITORY)

And thus was changed the policy of the gods from autonomy to cooperation, with the help of His Holiness.
A Comprehensive History of the Gods, vol. 7

Ahjin watched the Wolf cautiously. "Are we ready to go?" He wasn't dancing with impatience like Ludik, but they did need to catch the running Dog before he spread his nasty gossip.

"Wait while I get my gear." The wolf pointed with his paw and growled, "Right here," before stalking behind a tall pine.

A series of howls echoed between the tree and the far distance. Ahjin was surprised to discover he understood them as well as he could the two-legged Darrendran languages. Makana's gift was broader than he had thought.

A man emerged shortly after, tugging his tunic smooth across his broad shoulders. He was half a foot taller than Ahjin, with brown skin a few shades lighter than the brothers and a little darker than Nemerra.

"I sent for a replacement guard for my route," Lyell said in trade tongue, repeating what Ahjin had heard in the howls. "He will arrive soon. It is good you did not move." He narrowed his light brown eyes and glared at everyone.

Ahjin raised his hands. "We want to prevent a problem, not start another. As long as you let us keep looking for our confused quarry, we'll obey."

Lyell sniffed. His nose was as long as Zefra's, but wider and crooked. "So you say. Tell me about this prey you are chasing." He buckled his belt around his waist and shifted two long knives, then threw a small pack over his shoulder. "Which way are we going?" He ran his hands through his black-and-gray hair until it stood on end and joined Ludik at the front of the group.

Ahjin dropped to the back with Gurryon to watch the guard as they walked.

Nia showed Lyell the scrap of seaweed Zefra dug from her pouch. "We think our quarry came from somewhere near the ocean. We know we were on the right trail this morning because he snagged the fox's tail in a thorn bush."

"That looks like seaweed," Lyell agreed. "You are tracking a sneaky Fox? It might be a trick."

"No, he is not a Fox," Gurryon said. "Well, he might be."

"You do not know what you track?" Lyell's mouth twitched at the corners when he looked behind him. "How will you know when you find him? Who else has a fox tail?" His grin widened.

Ahjin took a deep breath. "Perhaps we should start at the beginning."

"With your fantastic lie about the gods?"

Ahjin shook his head. "With Ludik and Nemerra's wedding hunt." He began the story, and everyone took turns explaining as they wound through the trees.

"So," Ludik concluded, "Agu did kill the Fox, but only in self-defense. Now we must catch the Dog before he claims murder and leads them in revenge against our village. We are not sure why the Dogs were in our territory, but if it was some minor trespass, we will forgive it. We will even forgive the Dog's killing of Agu, since he thought he was defending his friend."

"Even if I believed that is what *you* are doing," Lyell indicated the three Darrendrakar, "why are the rest of you here?"

"We're here for the wedding." Nia clapped her hands and skipped over a fallen branch.

Nemerra smiled at Ludik, blinking three times. He blinked back, obviously besotted.

Ahjin smiled to himself and recited the wedding ceremony. *We beg the gods to protect the ones we love. We...* Wait, he'd forgotten the last part, despite practicing every day for the last two weeks. How could he remember everything when the gods kept adding more to his duties?

The ceremony could wait, for duty currently required he pay attention to their new guide.

Lyell shook his head at Nia and touched a knife hilt. "Why have the Cats been foolish enough to let outkindred in their territory?"

"The way we met goes back to the fantastic truth about the gods," Nia said.

Ahjin hunched his wings and looked away. He hated the reminder of how his life was ruined.

Nia continued in an inappropriately cheerful voice. "Kassian, who delivered the message for you, is the older brother of the known gods. He left long ago because of certain lies, then returned this spring for revenge. He kidnapped Irajahan to stop all communication between the gods, but Irajahan could still talk to Ahjin because of a fluke."

Lyell squinted at Ahjin. "Hmph."

Ahjin managed not to wince. His life would be easier now if Kassian had more thoroughly blocked Irajahan's telepathy. Then again, the world might have been destroyed.

Zefra used her staff to vault a fat, fallen tree, and all the tall Darrendrakar stepped over it like a small branch. As if being tall were as good as flying. Ahjin stretched his legs over the trunk and helped Nia climb up.

"While Ahjin and I were looking for Irajahan," Nia said, sliding down the other side of the tree, "Kassian captured the rest of the gods. Their absence caused the earthquakes and other natural disasters."

"He made a mistake, though," Ahjin said. "Kassian didn't catch Resef until after he'd left a message for Zefra. We found her and the message during our search for the gods."

"Did you ever ask why he involved me?" Zefra interrupted.

"I did," Ahjin said. "You were praying. It was a mix of opportunity and confidence in you."

Zefra wrinkled her forehead. "I'm not sure if I should be flattered or worried."

"Resef's message helped us free all the gods," Nia continued, "though it nearly killed us." She blinked rapidly and took Ahjin's hand, running her thumb across one of his lightning scars.

Nemerra choked. When Ahjin glanced at her, she leaned into Ludik's shoulder.

Lyell frowned skeptically. "That cannot be right. Our shaman said the gods freed themselves."

"I'm sure some people prefer that story," Nia said.

"You must be wrong," Lyell insisted. "Why would our shamans change the story?"

Nia shrugged. "Maybe someone wanted to make Darravani look better or doesn't trust the part we outsiders played. Anyway, Darravani asked Ahjin to mediate their disagreement. Kassian declined until he learned he sought revenge for something that never happened. Then he wanted help, and Ahjin cleverly convinced everyone to behave."

Ahjin snorted. If the gods actually behaved, he wouldn't be stuck supervising them. Irajahan, at least, seemed incapable of being good.

"Hush, that's my story," Nia said. "If you don't like it, tell it yourself."

Ahjin shoved his hands in his pockets.

"And Ahjin agreed to continue arbitrating," Nia said.

Ahjin groaned. "Forever."

"The gods made him his own independent island, and now he speaks with — and for — all of them." Nia patted Ahjin on the elbow. "It's a hard job, but he's good at it."

Ludik and Zefra nodded. Nemerra smiled encouragingly, and even Gurryon didn't protest.

Ahjin snorted again. His main qualification was an immunity to Irajahan's charm.

"How should I believe all that?" Lyell asked. "You still look like children."

Ahjin shrugged. "I left all my regalia in Maon. Next time, I'll keep something with me."

Lyell shook his head. "Darravani did not tell that part of your story."

"Or maybe your shaman did not relay it." Gurryon pointed to the shaman's badge on his shoulder. "You can ask Darravani when you get to a shrine."

"Oh, I will," Lyell promised. "And if you have lied, you will not return across the border. Did the gods choose Ahjin because he can become invisible?"

"The invisibility's from Irajahan," Ahjin said. "As for being chosen, I was just in the wrong place at the wrong time."

Nia giggled. "No, it's because he doesn't give up or give in."

Lyell squinted at Ahjin. "That does not sound like much of a qualification."

Ahjin ruffled his wings. It wasn't.

Zefra pointed at something in the forest, and Lyell ran to investigate, followed by the others.

A tiny clearing was filled by a large mound of leaves with a circular depression in the middle.

"It's a campsite," Nia said. "The leaves would have been a comfy bed." She rubbed one hip.

"We can do the same tonight," Nemerra said.

"Do Dogs often camp here?" Ahjin asked, "or are we getting closer to our quarry?"

Gurryon sniffed the air. "It doesn't smell like Dog."

Lyell bent over the mound. "It does not smell like anything but pine needles, moldy leaves, and rodents. Any other scent was washed out by the rain two days ago." He stretched his arms to measure the rain-matted indentation in the middle.

Zefra poked the leaves with her staff. "If the scent is at least two days old, this must be where our quarry camped on his way to Maon. He likely took the same path back as he took out, but slept in a different spot."

Ahjin sighed with relief. "I worried we had missed the trail somehow."

"That hollow is too big for a Dog." Lyell squinted at the Darrendrakar. "It might be the right size for a lion or tiger, though."

"Why are you looking at us?" Ludik protested. "We just got here."

Lyell bared his teeth. "All that proves is that you did not camp here recently."

Gurryon tightened his grip on his staff. "Are you accusing us of something?"

"I have a theory," Lyell said. "This story of a Dog killing a Cat is nothing but a pack of lies, an excuse to get you across the border when I caught you spying. I think this is not your first trip here."

He kicked the pile of leaves and glared at Ahjin. "You have spied on the Dogs before, with someone keeping you unseen. And now you have returned to spy again but brashly neglected to hide. Maybe you think our border patrol incompetent and your magic unnecessary."

"Oh, no," Nemerra gasped.

"That is not logical," Zefra said. "Ahjin can only hide himself."

"Very well," Lyell said, "his magic is inadequate to the size of your current party."

"That is not what I meant," Zefra said.

Nia tugged on Zefra's elbow. "Hush, you're not helping."

Ahjin shook his head. "Lyell, we're strangers but not enemies. Why should we want to attack you?"

Lyell narrowed his eyes. "Who knows what lies the Cats have told you."

Ahjin struggled to keep his exasperation from his face. "No lies."

"We have always been uneasy neighbors," Ludik admitted, "but we are not your enemies."

Despite his peaceful words, he sneered, and Ahjin put a hand on his shoulder.

"We might be your enemy," Gurryon threatened, "if you do not want peace." He twisted his staff on the ground until pine needles crunched and released their spicy scent.

That was enough. Had all the Darrendrakar gone crazy? Ahjin raised his hands and stepped forward. "Calm down. Lyell, you're flying the wrong wind. None of us have ever been here before, and we'll happily leave as soon as we talk that Dog out of attacking the Cats."

"Attacking the Cats," Lyell growled. "Ha! You mean as soon as you help the Cats plan an attack on the Dogs. First you scout our land, looking for weaknesses left from the recent devastations. Next will come your army to take our land." He drew his long knives. "If you do not report back, the Cats might give up their plans."

Ludik fumbled for his ax, and Gurryon raised his staff.

"Stop right now." Ahjin stepped between the snarling men and turned his back on the brothers to face Lyell. "Nemerra, make Ludik behave. Nia and Zefra, hold Gurryon."

He kept his gaze on Lyell while the growls stopped behind him. "Lyell, put down the knives and listen. I know you don't believe us, but I promise, we told you only the truth. If we were lying, would we let you travel with us? If we were the forefront of an army, you would be nothing but a lump under a thin covering of earth. Go ahead, ask us anything you want. See if you can trip us in our story. In exchange, let's walk while you question us, so we don't lose more time."

Lyell bared his teeth in a grin. "If you do not answer sufficiently, it will not be me who sleeps under a dirt blanket."

He turned on one heel and strode forward, ignoring the Cats as if they didn't exist, but the hair on his neck stood up. "Tell me what you have done as Mouth of the Gods."

"I don't know what that has to do with anything," Ahjin protested. He followed Lyell with the girls and left Ludik and Gurryon to grouch in the rear.

"You said I could ask anything," Lyell said. "Humor me. I have a great sense of humor."

Nia spun around a sapling. She ducked under a low branch and bounced over pinecones.

At least someone was enjoying this journey. Ahjin scuffed his feet harder than necessary and sent a burst of fallen leaves into the air.

"It's only been five weeks," he said, "and half that was on the ship. Before I left, I started learning godly expectations and rites, including five different marriage ceremonies."

Behind him, Nemerra whispered something, and Ludik murmured in reply.

Theirs was the only marriage Ahjin ever wanted to perform.

"I weed the biggest garden I've ever seen while Darravani quizzes me on the plants. I really need to hire gardeners and guards." Ahjin rubbed his back. The journey here had taken long enough that he no longer ached from the work, but the memory was vivid.

He needed other staff, too. Cook, temple cleaner, who knew what else. Nia helped him, but sooner or later, she'd go home, and he'd be alone during his parents' frequent tours. He ran his fingers across the embroidered scarf he now used as a belt. His mother's handiwork had survived their last adventure in battered condition, but it still reminded him of his family.

"I will have to read every religious text in existence." Ahjin swallowed a sigh. "I try to make cranky, demanding gods be reasonable. Then I talk to cranky people that think they'll get a better answer through me instead of their old methods of prayer." His days of having time to himself were as dead as Nia's kraken.

Nia giggled again.

"And do they get better answers?" Lyell asked. "How does that work, exactly?" For the first time, his voice held more curiosity than hostility. He patted his pocket, rustling the note.

"It's easiest for me to speak to Irajahan telepathically," Ahjin reluctantly admitted, "but only his priests can hear his responses. He's difficult to deal with, anyway."

Irajahan was bad enough at the best of times, and he was still angry at Ahjin. He retaliated whenever he thought he could get away with it, so Ahjin avoided him as much as possible.

"Nobody else can see Makanavailea's messages in water." Ahjin grunted, brushed Nia's elbow from his ribs, and glared at her. "Except perhaps Nia. Darravani's messages can be read by anyone who knows how, but they are slower and sometimes ambiguous. Resef's runes are faster but nearly as obscure. When I need an answer for someone else, I prefer Kassian. He can reply quickly in any language."

He shrugged. "But no, people don't get a more favorable answer, although it might be faster and more clear. I'm most useful to contact someone who isn't your own god."

"He fends off toadies and predatory girls." Nia's giggles exploded out of control.

Ahjin glared at her. At least she had helped him chase off the troublemakers.

"Do you not like women?" Gurryon sounded shocked.

"Of course I do, but not when they fly overhead without proper leggings under their skirts."

Gurryon laughed, and Ahjin's face grew hot.

There was a slap behind him, and Gurryon said, "Ow."

Ahjin ducked around a tree large enough to give him a second to compose himself. Even if Ahjin wanted a wife right now — and he didn't — he'd want someone with more modesty and judgment.

"When I get back to Arupa," he continued, "I'll host dignitaries, mediate disputes, and write decrees under the tutelage of various leaders. I'm told this is only the first of my foreign visits."

He had always wanted to see the world, but as a skydancer in his parents' troupe, not a pretentious dignitary with a clashing wardrobe and no privacy. And Darrendra's resemblance to north-western Ioj put him a little on edge. He rubbed his back again, and not from the weeding, glad his wings hid the movement from his friends. At least the red and yellow autumn leaves broke the visual expanse of evergreens enough that he only sometimes remembered the spiders' forest.

Ahjin's new job stunk like a vulture, but his feathers had grown back, and he could already make short flights without his old aerobatics. On the ship, he had improved from across-the-deck hops to shadowing the ship for half an hour.

Lyell walked sideways to look at each person in the group, stopping back at Ahjin. "And are you the leader here, with your supposed divine authority?"

"That's what I'm told," Ahjin said.

Lyell frowned and tapped one of his knives. "They let an outkindred child lead?"

"I've been an adult for half a year," Ahjin objected.

Nia cleared her throat. "Under the circumstances, one of the Darren-drakar might be better."

Ahjin raised an eyebrow. "Didn't Akamu make me come for my supposed authority?"

"He did," Gurryon said.

Nia tilted her head toward Lyell. "I mean, for interkindred harmony."

Ahjin looked at the frowning Wolf, who didn't look convinced of Ahjin's credentials. Pressing the point would only antagonize Lyell. If the time came when his friends couldn't succeed without him, that would be soon enough. "Do you think Gurryon, as shaman, will be better?"

Zefra raised her hand. "I vote for Ludik. He has good reason to get this done quickly and right."

Everyone but Gurryon raised their hands.

Ludik looked at his brother. Nemerra cleared her throat.

"Oh, fine." Gurryon raised his hand. "But only until we get home, little brother."

He turned and stomped along the path. Lyell immediately followed him.

Ahjin looked from one identical tall brother to the other. Perhaps he was lucky he only had a much younger sister, too little to tease him. Then he looked at Nia, who slew crunchy leaves with her spear as she walked. His friends teased him enough.

His new job brought him no respect. If he couldn't convince Lyell he spoke for the gods, how would he ever convince the Dog they chased?

Ahjin forced his feet to move again, ignoring Nia's chatter and Gurr-yon's mutters. It was his fault Ludik missed his wedding the first time. What if this wasn't as easy to solve as Ludik thought? What if war did start? It was Ahjin's job to help the gods keep peace in the world.

What if Ahjin failed as Mouth of the Gods and his friends paid the price?

7. MURDER
(CANID TERRITORY)

Once my hand was stitched and bandaged, the healers put me to work hauling corpses. All day, I buried the victims of the filthy Hyenas in mass graves.
Torao, after The Battle of Sad Laughter

With Lyell to provide guidance through the territory, Ludik hoped to catch their quarry today. It was worth putting up with the Wolf to finish this quickly.

The Dogs' forest seemed brighter now. If Ludik admitted the truth to himself, it didn't look much different than the forest around his home village. It was just his mood that had made it seem gloomier. Ludik smiled at Nemerra and took her hand as they set out through the trees again. She smiled back, and he lost track of time.

Gurryon slugged his shoulder. "Hey, exalted leader, pay attention. We're trying to decide if we should follow in a straight line or try to cut off our quarry."

While they were still discussing, a big dog ran through the trees a short distance away. He stopped and watched them until Lyell waved, then continued toward the border.

"It seems even with an escort, the Dogs won't trust us," Ahjin said.

Lyell shrugged with a half-grin.

Ludik couldn't blame his suspicious neighbors. If he had seen Dogs in Felid territory, he would have watched them just as carefully. Canid territory made the hair on the back of his neck tingle.

"Perhaps that is another good reason not to take shortcuts," Zefra said. "If we follow the trail, we will show our trustworthiness and find any traces of our quarry."

Ludik sighed. "She's right." He liked the idea of the shortcut better. Sooner done, sooner home.

"Good," Zefra said. "Then we have a plan."

"That's a plan?" Nia complained.

"Yes," Zefra said. "We follow the trail and do not cause more problems."

Nia made a face at Ahjin behind Zefra's back. Ahjin patted her on her shoulder.

Nemerra squeezed Ludik's hand, and he pulled her closer as they wound around a giant cedar.

At their next rest, the group separated for brief privacy. The men went behind the thick bushes in one direction, while the women chose a line of trees with overlapping branches to block the view.

The women were still close enough for Ludik to eavesdrop. If he couldn't spend every minute with Nemerra, it was nice to hear her voice, even talking to someone else.

"So, Nemerra," Nia said, "what kind of party will we have when you marry your dashing beloved? Will boys attend?"

Zefra snorted.

Nemerra chuckled. "Yes, they will. They'll like you, I'm sure. If you wait a minute, I'll tell you about the men in the village who aren't betrothed."

Ludik grinned at the thought of the village men's reactions. Nia would turn them on their heads.

He was still imagining the romantic chaos when Nemerra gasped.

"Th... th... there is—" Nemerra screamed.

Ludik drew his knife and charged toward the women, cursing the stupid trees that kept him from seeing the danger. The other men pounded after him, skidding around the barrier and sliding to a halt by Nia, the only woman in sight.

Ludik lowered his knife in confusion. "Where is Nemerra?"

"Shark teeth," Nia squawked, staring behind a bush, her hands over her mouth.

Zefra pulled Nemerra from behind the bush. Nemerra still held a trowel in shaking hands. She turned green, and Zefra barely got her hair out of the way before she vomited.

Ludik lunged to help her, knife raised against danger. "Are you hurt?"

"We're fine," Nia blurted, holding out her hands to calm him. "She's fine."

Ludik handed his knife to Gurryon and wrapped his arms around his shaking sweetheart. "What happened?"

Nemerra buried her head in his shoulder. "There is a dead body back there."

Lyell put his hand on his knife and scowled. "Where? Who?"

"It's been dead for a while," Nia said. "Come give your expert opinions." She pried at Ludik's arms until he let go of Nemerra. "Come here, Nemerra, and don't think about it."

"We should distract her," Zefra muttered.

Nia nodded and led Nemerra toward their packs with a flow of gentle babbling.

Ludik watched them go until he was sure Nemerra was well, then sheathed his knife and stepped around the shrubbery. A dead yellow dog lay half under the bush. Flies and beetles crawled into its mouth, sunken eyes, and the hole in its chest. Dried blood matted its fur and darkened the earth around it.

Behind Ludik, Ahjin gulped.

Ludik exchanged glances with Gurryon. "Lyell, I am a hunter, and both Gurryon and I have some healer training. Long story. We will help you examine the body. Ahjin, you stand guard."

Ahjin nodded and turned his back, but as they discussed details of the wounds, he wheezed.

After a few minutes, Ludik turned to Ahjin. "Why don't you move farther away? If you get sick here, you might ruin information."

Ahjin walked several paces toward the women, and as the Darren-drakar lowered their voices, his wings relaxed.

Ludik and Gurryon used their training to find the time of death, explaining their old look-alike prank to Lyell as they worked. Lyell was more useful for the corpse's identity.

By the time they collected Ahjin and rejoined the women, Zefra had a fire started, and Nemerra stirred a quick soup.

"If we'll be here for a bit," Nia said, "we should eat. We walk enough to need the extra food."

Ahjin gagged quietly but collected the bowls. Ludik didn't have a medicinal tea for revulsion. Besides, Ahjin always refused non-vital treatments.

Ludik snaked an arm around Nemerra's waist, and she pressed his hand while she stirred.

"What did you discover?" Zefra asked.

Lyell ate his soup with a ferocious scowl on his face. "The Dog looks like a golden jackal, or maybe a dingo."

Ludik snagged flatbread and a bowl and sat with Nemerra. "He has the same deep wound as Agu."

Ahjin stirred his soup into a tiny whirlpool. "Agu was killed with a random tree branch. Who would do that here?"

Zefra sat on the ground by Nia and blew steam from her soup. "Could this be a coincidence?"

"The wound is an unusual shape," Ludik said. "And he was missing a paw, just like the Fox's tail."

"Beached whale," Nia swore. "The same dismemberment doesn't sound coincidental." She bit a spoonful of soup as if it were an escaping rabbit.

"That can't be right," Nemerra protested. "Our running Dog took the tail to prove Agu killed the Fox. Agu didn't kill this Dog. He wasn't even *here*."

"Then who could have killed him?" Ahjin asked. "And why?"

Lyell narrowed his eyes. "I am looking at a lot of suspects right now."

Ludik snarled at him. "We already told you—"

Ahjin leaned over and smacked the back of Ludik's head. "Lyell, the Darrendrakar don't welcome outsiders. Someone would have noticed us wandering around. We didn't do this."

Lyell frowned. "Are you suggesting someone took the branch used to kill your Cat and then came here to murder this Dog?"

"Even if he had a reason to kill this Dog," Gurryon asked, "why would he drag the branch all this way?"

"That is not important," Ludik said. "This killer cannot be our quarry. The yellow dog died a day or so *before* Agu and the fox."

"What if we have this backwards?" Nia said. "What if our killer chased the fox onto Felid land, killing this Dog on the way? Agu might have stumbled into the fox or the fight with his pursuer and been killed to cover the murderer's tracks. Maybe our quarry isn't afraid of us, but is going home."

"That is a terrible theory," Nemerra whispered.

"That might explain the body parts, too," Gurryon said. "I mean, if he was hunting the fox, maybe he needed proof of the kill. It doesn't explain why he would leave the trefoil to declare revenge on us, though."

"Perhaps he left it to indicate the kill was for his own revenge," Zefra said.

"But why?" Nia asked. "Are the Dogs involved in a civil war?"

"It is confusing." Lyell narrowed his eyes. "I have heard no such rumors. All I know is that trouble started when you showed up."

"We did not do anything," Ludik protested. "We are trying to fix things. If this was not all some sort of accident, then this Dog has already killed three people, so you ought to be grateful for our help." Lyell's suspicion was more evidence Dogs were dangerously paranoid and unstable.

Nemerra's lip quivered. "Asad didn't say we'd be chasing a murderer who chops off body parts."

Ludik took her spoon and dropped it in her bowl, then turned her around to fit her in his arms.

Everyone stopped eating to look at him and Ahjin.

Furballs. Ludik should have pushed Ahjin to be the leader instead of letting Nia dump it on him. "If someone is deliberately targeting Darrendrakar, is there anything we can do?"

"You had better do something," Lyell said, "or I will report your suspicious behavior before you even cross the border to home."

Ludik hid his silent snarl in Nemerra's hair.

"You could hunt the killer," Gurryon said. "Is it not your kind of job?"

Lyell laughed grimly. "Maybe I should arrest the suspicious characters I found wandering in my territory."

"That won't be necessary," Ahjin said. "We'll see our pursuit through, but we need your cooperation more than ever."

"I will listen to your theories," Lyell said, "but I will make my own conclusions."

"That's fair enough," Ahjin said. "Let's get back on the hunt."

Zefra held one hand over the fire, lowering her hand as the fire died. When the flames were gone, she stuck her hand in the coals for a minute. "'Tis safe to leave the fire pit now."

Lyell had watched her wide-eyed and now crouched by the fire to test the heat for himself, tossing tossed a cold, burned stick from hand to hand. "How did you do that?"

"We told you Resef needed me to do something for him," Zefra said. "He gave me a gift so I could help."

Lyell grunted and tested the ashes again.

While Nemerra washed the dishes, everyone else returned to the body to make sure they hadn't missed anything. Ludik searched the area until he found footprints on the other side of the bush. The prints, which Lyell identified as fox, traveled briefly down the path before disappearing.

"We haven't seen anyone else out here," Ahjin said. "I think it's highly likely the maker of these tracks is the murderer."

"And not us," Ludik grumbled.

"But there must be some kind of mistake," Lyell said. "I suppose a Fox could have killed another Dog, but why? Was he rabid?"

Gurryon leaned toward Lyell's face. "Why would he kill a leopard, hmm?"

Ludik put a warning hand on Gurryon's shoulder. He understood the impulse to attack the Wolf, but his brother's mouth was too smart for his own good.

"Stop it," Ahjin said.

"Because he was annoying, maybe." Lyell put one hand on each of his knives. "How about a lion, hmm? Or a li-ar."

Nia giggled despite the gravity of the situation.

Ahjin's voice thundered. "Stop it right now!"

Everyone jumped. Lyell and Gurryon leaned away from each other and eyed Ahjin.

"That's a great trick," Nia said. "Did you learn it from Irajahan?"

"How did you guess?" Ahjin smiled at her but kept a stern eye on the Darrendrakar.

Lyell and Gurryon glared at each other.

"I will bury the body," Lyell said.

"Do you want help?" Gurryon raised his hands. "No tricks. I am a shaman's apprentice, remember? I know the funeral rites. We do not have all the supplies for a full service, but I can do the vital basics. You could tell his family he was properly buried." He held out a trowel.

Lyell peered at him for a minute before taking the tool. "I will watch you."

The others repacked while they waited. Ludik made sure to complete his tasks by Nemerra in case she needed him again. Her smile was strained, but she chatted without other signs of distress. Even if she were merely hiding her fears, he was proud of her.

Zefra approached Ludik with a serious expression. "I need you to cut me a branch, at least a hand across, please."

Ludik bent his head closer to her. "I'm sorry, I must have misheard you. I thought you asked me to cut you a branch. From a living tree."

Zefra nodded solemnly.

He raised his eyebrows and chopped off the closest branch, as close to the narrow end as would fit her requirement.

She flinched with every stroke of his ax, and he nearly apologized. When it was down, she made him trim the leaves and twigs and split it in half vertically to make a rounded plank.

Zefra sat and traced her finger repeatedly over the wood. When Lyell and Gurryon returned, she handed them the crude board with a stylized flame burned on it. "To mark his grave," she said.

Lyell dropped a fine metal chain in his pocket. "I took his necklace to identify him to his wife and kin. Now I can tell them how to find him. I thank you."

Zefra bowed formally. "If someone is deliberately murdering people, perhaps bringing my armor was a good idea?"

She shrugged on her high-collared kazagand vest and fastened the lacquered leather from neck to waist. Her curved saif reached from her belt to the knee-length hem.

"I brought my shiny kikko armor," Nia crooned. "Oh, my pretty, I've missed you." She pulled the padded silk tunic down to her thighs and knocked on the overlapping scales of polished horn. "See, it works. I somehow forgot my helmet, though." Her eyes widened innocently.

"I'm sure you 'forgot' it," Ahjin said. "You're wonderful at forgetting what you don't want to remember."

He already wore his leather arm bracers but added a knee-length, leather forge apron, fringed for easy movement, and wrapped his weighted surujin around his waist.

Nia laughed and twirled her shortened spear. "I don't know what you mean."

Lyell straightened his shirt with a flourish. "I am ready."

Ludik looked at his armored friends. "I thought we decided we didn't need armor."

Gurryon cleared his throat and glanced at Lyell. "I brought mine. Just in case."

"So did I," Ludik admitted. "We must be a skeptical group."

Ludik and Gurryon had breastplates of segmented bands with buckles that came undone at a touch for rapid shapeshifting. Their boots hid steel greaves, though Gurryon's lacked a hidden knife sheath. Ludik's composite bow was stronger than Ahjin's simple recurve, and his wood ax had a metal-reinforced handle. Gurryon's staff was half-again as long as Zefra's.

"Nemerra, you don't have any armor?" Ludik mentally cursed.

Nemerra shook her head. "You said we didn't need it. I did get a longer knife." She patted her sheath with a pleased smile.

Ludik held his breastplate next to Nemerra, but it was obviously too big for her. Nothing fit Nemerra, except maybe Ahjin's apron. She might be wiser shifting to leopard for claws and more weight. Ludik frowned at Lyell. The sharp noses of the Dogs would detect her Cat scent even faster if she shifted. It wasn't worth it except in an emergency. He sighed and donned his own armor. It would protect Nemerra as long as his body was between her and danger.

Ludik hugged her. "You stay in the center of the group. You're too precious to risk." He blinked at her three times.

"Oh, how sweet." Nia flicked Ludik's elbow and picked up her spear. "This isn't the right time for you to drool over your pretty bride."

Ludik disagreed. It was always the time to admire Nemerra. And when she was finally his bride, the time would be even better.

Ahjin shoved Nia down the path. "Are we ready now?"

Nia waved at him and winked. When Ahjin rolled his eyes, she laughed.

Lyell stomped to the front of the group. Zefra slid between him and Gurryon and took a better grip on her staff, twitching a faint grin at Nia and Nemerra, who smiled back.

As they continued west, Ludik tried to understand the women, but it was a lost cause.

Lyell made a brief detour to stop at the grave one last time. The fire-marked board was barely visible from the path where Ludik and the others waited. Yellow zinnias covered the slight mound.

Nia sighed. "They're pretty flowers, but they're for another dead person. This adventure hasn't improved."

Lyell rejoined them. "This grave reminds me of when our neighbor's husband died. She was inconsolable. Everyone tried to help her, but she kept mourning. Then her garden bloomed in the spring. Somehow, her husband's name was spelled in scarlet geraniums on a background of yellow zinnias. When I asked my wife when our neighbor planted the flowers, she laughed." He smiled. "I later found the seed packets in a drawer."

"What do those flowers mean?" Zefra asked.

"The geraniums are for comfort, and the yellow zinnia are daily remembrance."

"That's sweet," Nia said. "I'd like to meet your wife sometime, if I get the chance."

"I am sure she would like that," Lyell said.

"Who will comfort the yellow dog's wife?" Nemerra whispered.

Ludik put his arm around Nemerra. She fretted only for the dead and for the bereaved family. He thought of a murderer wandering through the forest, possibly looking for a new victim.

He couldn't let Nemerra be the next prey.

8. STREAM

(CANID TERRITORY)

Bears are the second-largest Darrendrakar, after the Elephants, and have the best sense of smell, even better than the Dogs.
A Brief Sketch of Mysterious Darrendra

They walked quickly, and the murdered Dog's grave was soon lost from sight among the dense trees. Ludik held Nemerra's hand even after she started smiling again. She had a nice hand, slender, and soft between the leather-working calluses. Her fingers curled around his in the perfect fit. He would hold her hand all day if he could. In that way, this trip was better than being at home, where both of them were too busy to hold hands for long.

When he spotted a pretty flower nearly hidden in a pile of fallen leaves, he tucked it behind Nemerra's ear without a word. She smiled at him and blinked three times to say "I love you" before turning to talk to the other women. They seemed to be fond of each other already, and Ludik let their pleasant chatter wash over him while he watched for tracks or clues.

The smell of pine and cedar and dying leaves overwhelmed any faint scent trail the Dog might have left, and Ludik couldn't see any more footprints or snagged hairs. With no way of knowing they were on the right path, all they could do was keep going, watch carefully, and hope.

They soon found a stream burbling musically beside the path, with dappled sunlight dancing across the rippling current. He hated to let go of Nemerra's hand, but water was a vital necessity to live a long time with her.

"Give me your water jugs, Nemerra," he offered. "The ground is muddy."

"I made my boots as good as yours," his sweetheart said mildly as she shrugged out of her pack and unloaded her water jug. "I can get my own water. You spoil me."

"I feel spoiled with running water constantly available." Zefra pulled out her multiple water bags.

They still hadn't convinced her that streams would cross their path often enough for her to keep refilling only one or two.

"It isn't constantly available," Ludik quibbled, "just very common." In her desert, water was scarce, but she should believe him that they had plenty of water here.

"Very common, then," Zefra said. "Do you not prefer drinking real water to chewing cactus?"

The water jug in Nemerra's hand trembled. This was exactly why he had left out details when he told her and his family about his trip with Ahjin. She still didn't know everything, and he intended to keep it that way as long as possible.

"Don't worry," he said, leaning in for a hug. "That trouble is over now. I'm home."

Nia pointed at the stream. "What's that?"

Ludik reluctantly left Nemerra to look. A long drag mark stretched from the stream to the trees. Footprints in the slippery bank had distorted to crescents on either side of the line. He had never seen tracks quite like them.

"Nobody go near those," Lyell said. "There is an odd scent here, and I do not want you to mix it up."

He disappeared into the forest and came back a few minutes later as the huge wolf. He carefully sniffed the path, the footprints, the drag line, and the stream banks. Then he sniffed everyone in the search party.

Ludik curled his lip as the wolf nosed his hand. Suspicious Dog.

When the wolf reached Nia, she patted him on the nose and got her fingers licked in exchange. She wiped her wet fingers on the wolf's long fur as he turned to Ahjin.

Lyell reached Gurryon last and hung his tongue down to his chin.

"Do not dare," Gurryon said. "I had enough Dog slobber for a lifetime."

Lyell's snicker was clear, even in wolf form. "Back to work," he said, with Nia interpreting for Zefra. "This is getting odder. The tracks by the bush where the Dog was killed were clearly Canid. They looked and smelled like Fox. These tracks are different. They do not really smell like Dog. Maybe Bear, though not really." He paused to ponder, then shook his pelt. "Never mind. Luckily for you, they do not smell like any of you."

Ludik glanced at his brother and shook his head. Of course the tracks smelled like someone else. If the Wolf had any sense, he would have known that without sniffing. When would he trust them?

Ahjin looked in all directions with a hand on his unstrung bow. "Do Bear come through here?"

"No, they do not, and that worries me." Lyell shook himself again until his fur stood on end.

"There was an almost-Bear smell back by our village, too," Gurryon said.

"You did not tell me that," Lyell said. "You should smell this, too. Go put on your kitty suit and get your better nose over here."

"My kitty suit?" Gurryon lowered his staff to thump Lyell and hit Zefra's raised staff instead.

Zefra craned her neck to look up at Gurryon. "Just do it. You can be insulted later," she said with iron practicality.

Gurryon's curses as he stepped away made it clear he could shift and be insulted at the same time. When he came back as a lion, he confirmed it was the same scent as in Maon.

Ludik could have done the same thing, of course, but he'd rather stay with Nemerra. Gurryon had volunteered for this trip and should take some responsibility.

"Maybe we're looking for a Bear and not a Dog," Nemerra said. "I would love to meet one under better circumstances."

Ludik's hair stood on end. As bad as it would be fighting with the Dogs, the Bears would be worse. They were bigger and usually meaner and had a much larger territory with more resources. Fighting the Dogs and Bears at the same time would be an epic disaster. How much farther would the madness spread?

Chills raced up his neck. He checked behind them to see if anyone was following, but the trail was empty except for the occasional small bird.

"What motives might a Bear have?" Lyell asked.

"We have not even decided what motives a Dog might have," Zefra pointed out.

"We'll worry about that later," Ahjin said. "In the meantime, what would make that drag mark?"

Lyell bared his teeth. "I do not know, but when we find it, I will have something *pointed* to say."

"Can we get water?" Zefra asked. "Or do we need to wait?"

"Go ahead," Lyell said. "Gurryon and I will get dressed."

Ludik stepped carefully around the tracks on his way to the stream. The others watched his route and followed in his footsteps.

Lyell and Gurryon returned, dressed, before the others filled all the canteens.

Zefra drained her cup seven times before she returned it to her pack. "I drink when water is available," she explained to Nemerra, who had watched in amazement.

Ludik took an extra drink himself. Maybe he had picked up a few Iskrin habits. The good ones, not the scorpion-eating and cactus-chewing ones.

Everyone dragged on their packs and resumed walking west.

"Let's go over this again." Ahjin pulled on a strand of his loosened curls, then removed his hair tie and forced his hair back into submission, retying it with a jerk. "Because of our discovery of an earlier death, we no longer believe our quarry killed Agu merely to protect the Fox. Now he seems to be a deliberate murderer who followed the yellow Dog and the Fox, killed the Dog and took his paw, and continued past the border after the Fox. When Agu stumbled across them, he and the Fox fought each other. Maybe the Fox died from the wounds Agu gave him, and maybe not, but Agu was murdered with a long, round weapon like a tree branch. The Fox's tail was taken by the killer, who smelled a little like Dog and a little like Bear." He half-flared his wings for balance as he stepped over a newly fallen tree.

"Do not forget the trefoil to mark his revenge," Zefra said, "and the missing body parts to prove he caught his prey, which means he has to report to someone."

"Yuck." Nia shuddered. "What an awful thing to carry around with you."

Nemerra shivered and took a drink of water. Ludik silently growled. His friends should watch their mouths and not distress his sweetheart.

"We found fox tracks by this body," Lyell reminded them. "And drag marks by the stream along with the funny boot marks."

"You know," Nia said, "if the Dog hadn't been stabbed, I'd have been sure he drowned and was dragged from the stream and hidden under the bush. It would make perfect sense of the marks."

Ludik thought back to the track again. She was right. That was exactly what it had looked like.

"That would make sense," Gurryon said, "except he was stabbed."

"I know. That's what I said." Nia flipped her short spear and thumped Gurryon on the head with the dull end, then jumped a rotting tree stump to evade his reflexive grab.

Gurryon glared at her and stomped his feet for a few steps before Zefra shushed him.

Ludik grinned again. With both Nia and Zefra working on him, Gurryon didn't stand a chance.

"My point," Ahjin stubbornly continued, "is that we're looking for someone who smells Bearish but leaves Fox footprints when he isn't wearing pointed boots, uses a tree branch as a weapon, drags something through the forest, and has body parts in his pockets."

Everyone pondered his summary in silence. Their footsteps, quiet though they were, seemed to echo on the path. Ludik peered through the trees and touched his knife every time a bird chirped.

"You know, Ahjin," Nia finally said, sticking her fists on her hips, "that sounds ridiculous. If I weren't here with you, I'd think you invented the whole thing. Nobody will believe us."

"I did not believe you, either," Lyell said. "If I had not seen the body, I still would not."

"It doesn't matter if anyone believes us," Nemerra said. "Truth is truth. When it's over, we can laugh about the ridiculousness of it all."

Ludik squeezed Nemerra's hand and held aside a tree limb crossing the path.

Their original quest took time and energy he'd rather direct into his marriage, but a fast pursuit, a faster explanation about the self-defense, and they could have prevented battle in time for a quick wedding. Hunting a murderer was trickier and more dangerous. If he had known, he never would have brought Nemerra along, no matter what she said.

As if the increased danger weren't enough to complicate their mission, now all the evidence was pointing to a ridiculous set of characteristics.

He scanned the forest. He, Lyell, and Gurryon were big enough to deal with most Dogs. His friends were experienced enough with their weapons to help. Even Lyell, reluctant to admit one of his people could do something like this, would not want a traitorous killer running free through his territory.

But why would a Dog smell like a Bear? He subtly sniffed Lyell, then looked away when the Wolf turned his head. No, definitely Dog. Not a bit of Bear.

If they were looking for a Bear, how did it get through *two* foreign territories undetected?

At this point, it didn't matter how he had gotten here, only how they would deal with him. Bears tended to be large, and it would take everyone in their group working together, with a lot of luck, to take down a Bear. Otherwise the Bear would mow through them like a harvest sickle.

For either a Dog or a Bear, why would the murderer hunt Dogs? Had the Dogs done something horrible, or was the killer rabid, insane, or merely sadistic?

Nemerra's hand slipped from his. He pressed his elbow against his knife sheath and turned to check on her. She had dropped back to talk to Nia, her face lit up with a silent laugh.

Ludik scanned the surrounding forest again. All was quiet and still, except birds and rodents and the occasional falling leaf. Layers of red and yellow carpeted the forest floor, and the sky shone apricot through the sparser leaves on high branches. He relaxed his arm.

Gurryon led the way along the path, swinging his staff against defenseless bushes. Lyell strolled not-quite-casually at the back of the group behind the women.

Ahjin ducked away from the women, laughing, and worked his way forward to walk beside Ludik. "I think it's less dangerous up here."

Ludik grunted. After a minute, his worries overflowed. "If the Dogs committed some crime against the killer, he should have gone to the shamans for justice. Darravani doesn't approve of private feuds, since they can spread. Her children would have to be desperate to ignore her opinions. On the other paw, if that was what happened, calling in the shamans to deal with it should be enough. Can you judge a crime or stop a feud?"

Ahjin shrugged. "We don't yet know if that's the problem. But Gurr-yon is a shaman, and so am I. When we find our quarry, I'll talk to him. If he'll accept me, I can deal with it."

Ludik scanned the forest again. "A rabid Dog would explain the illogical attacks and can be dealt with in a final, merciful way. Insane or sadistic is less explainable, more dangerous, and the solution is not so obvious. And what do the missing body parts have to do with anything?" He threw up his hands in frustration. "Rabid seems the best option, but the trophies make that less likely. Everyone knows the other kindreds are crazy and hateful."

Ahjin narrowed his eyes. "Why do you say that?"

"The Hyenas attacked us without mercy. They took half of Grandpapa's hand and most of his family. They ruined his life, and all for no good reason."

"Nemerra doesn't feel like that about other kindreds." Ahjin spoke mildly, but he scowled.

"Her grandparents moved to the village *after* the battle," Ludik complained. "She doesn't know what it was like. Grandpapa was lucky to even survive. Women and children died, too, in villages overrun by the stinking Hyenas. And now some Dog has gone as crazy. Why would he do that?"

Ahjin shrugged again. "Perhaps your Grandpapa was right about us needing to prevent war. I don't think we'll know the answers to any of your questions until we find the killer and ask him. But if you rip off his head immediately, we'll never know."

Ludik bumped his elbow against his knife again. Could he convince

Nemerra to walk as a leopard for safety? He turned his head to check on her again. She still laughed with Nia, and Zefra had joined them, her face intent. Nemerra answered a question for Zefra, gesturing.

No, he would never convince her to shift and lose communication with Zefra. Why did she have to be so nice to everyone?

Ludik snorted. "How will we even find a Dog-Bear who wears pointed boots, drags something through the forest, and stabs people with branches? This is turning into a ridiculous chase for an unimaginable person. I would laugh at the absurdity if Nemerra weren't trapped in this impossible mess. She should go home."

Ahjin looked back at the others and grimaced. "You can't send her home with a killer wandering through the forest."

Ludik growled. "If there is a rabid Bear, I can't spare anyone to take her home, either."

9. RUKA
(CANID TERRITORY)

There are eleven Darrendrakar kindreds. Bear territory stretches along the west and Elephant along the east. Pig, Sheep, and Deer divide the north, with Cow, Horse, and Antelope in the interior. Dog, Cat, and Hyena cover the southern coast as a protective barrier from the rest of the world.
A Brief Sketch of Mysterious Darrendra

As they walked down the path, Zefra ducked under a low branch and frowned. She did not understand the squeamish reactions of the others to the dead body, especially since it was now buried. Death was a part of life.

If she had known Ahjin would react so badly, she would have let him help Nemerra while she inspected the body with the other men. Ludik's explanation of how he guessed the time of death by the age of the flies around the body was fascinating. Explorers needed a wide variety of skills, and she wanted to learn everything.

It was troubling the deaths were murders rather than an accidental skirmish, but it did no good to fuss about what could not be changed. All they could do was adjust their plans to better deal with the new information, starting with defending themselves if necessary.

Almost everyone in their group had decent weapons and armor.

Zefra did not know what fighting experience the other Darrendrakar had, but her three friends fought competently enough. She had done well enough in her clan's weapons classes and could take care of herself and help defend the others, too. They were as prepared as possible, considering how the situation had changed since they left Ludik's home.

As soon as they captured this killer, they could hotfoot it back to Maon for the wedding.

She scanned the path ahead for footprints or other marks. Still no more sign of their quarry.

Zefra took a step sideways into the sunshine filtering through the branches so her energy would be sufficient for whatever might happen. She tucked a stray lock into her braided crown, feeling exposed without her scarf.

Ahead of her, Ludik waved his hands as he explained again about the flies. Gurryon and Lyell dropped the occasional comment or question as they watched the trail. Nemerra cringed at every sentence, and Ahjin's wings twitched. Nia frowned at a smudge on her armor and polished it to a higher gleam. She did not seem to listen, but Zefra did not underestimate the intelligence hidden under Nia's frivolity.

"Have we talked about flies enough yet?" Nemerra turned to Lyell. "What is your wife's name? What is she like?"

"Her name is Ruka Sassabadin."

Ahjin interrupted. "Shouldn't she be Ulriksin now?" He stood straighter and relaxed his wings.

"She is not my brother." Lyell rolled his almond-shaped eyes, naturally lined with as much black as a woman dressed up on her wedding day.

"The Canids use patronymic surnames that designate both their papa's name and their own gender," Gurryon said. "They do not change them at marriage."

"Oh." Ahjin looked at Ludik and Nemerra. "Darravani didn't mention names when she taught me your wedding ceremony. What do you do?"

"What is there to do?" Ludik said. "We already have the same last name."

Ahjin stared until Nemerra blushed. "Are you related?" he asked. "I don't think I can marry—"

"Our surnames designate our home village," Nemerra explained. "Everyone has the same one."

Zefra let herself be distracted from their quarry for a minute. "That is interesting. None of the Iskrin clans have that particular tradition."

Ahjin gaped at Nemerra. "Everyone?"

Ludik glared at Ahjin. "Everyone in the village."

"How do you tell yourselves apart?" Ahjin asked.

"We know who we are," Ludik said.

Gurryon grinned openly as Ahjin turned red.

Zefra bowed. "Forgive my curiosity, but how do the other kindreds name themselves?"

The Iskrins placed great importance in the meanings of names. Her own name had gained "Kezhekori" this year to indicate she was flame-touched. It both warned of her "burning fire" and honored Resef.

Ahjin worked his hands behind his leather apron and crammed them in his pockets. He dropped back to rear-guard with Zefra, mouth pressed closed.

Gurryon stepped around Nemerra to walk at the front of the group. "I'll tell you all the different naming conventions later," he promised Zefra.

She made a mental note to remind him. It would make a good distraction the next time he caused trouble. And that was enough distraction for now.

"You were explaining about the flies, Ludik," she said.

"No," Nia said firmly. "Lyell was telling us about his wife." She gave her armor one last polish and skipped over a tree root.

Lyell grinned. "What do you want to know? We have been married eight years. This is our first litter, though." When Gurryon looked pointedly at his gray-streaked head, Lyell added, "My hair has always been this color." He tilted his head toward Ahjin's white curls.

Ahjin raised an eyebrow in return.

Before Zefra left home, she had never seen such variety in hair color and assumed any color was normal for other races. Except for the rare flame-touched like her, all Iskrins had dark hair, like her still-black eyebrows. Gray was closer to black than Nia's lavender or Ludik and Gurryon's gold.

"I miss Ruka," Lyell admitted. "I have been on patrol for a couple of weeks. It is bad luck my turn on the border came when she expected our pups." He turned to Ahjin. "Do you know how many babies? Or what day they were born?"

Ahjin spread his hands. "I don't know anything that wasn't in the note."

"As long as they are well." Lyell stuck his hand in his pocket, and Darravani's note rustled.

"You will be a great dad." Nia sighed. "Your children are so lucky. I wish I had a dad like you."

Lyell grinned at her. "Ruka is a historical cartographer, most often called to trace exact borders for court cases or inheritance disputes. Her pregnancy has kept her home since the earthquakes, but now that the pups are here, she will need to map the new coastline." He cast a suspicious glance at Ludik. "But the borders with our neighbors are not open to change."

Ludik glared at him. "How many times do I have to tell you we do not want your land?"

Perhaps the time for distraction had not yet passed. Zefra cleared her throat. "Our coastline changed, too, but that was not the worst catastrophe. The hail ripped through the spice farms, and hurricanes destroyed most of the gardens. Then the sun baked the surviving vegetables right in the earth and burned the grain."

She shrugged. The Iskrins were used to drought and short rations. A bountiful harvest was celebrated, not expected. Since the gods were back, Iskra would survive.

"It must have been terrifying on the islands." Nia put a hand to her gills. "Waves shook the shallows, so my clan tied the babies to their backs with fishing nets and hid in the deep ocean. With the gardens washed bare, they'll eat a lot of fish until the next harvest."

"Ioj shut the flying lanes and beached the boats." Ahjin spoke flatly, but his wings crimped so tightly his feathers curved. "The library survived, but the books all flew off the shelves. The printing press was just as bad. I hear they're still pulling type from the mouseholes. Half of Vasi collapsed from either the earthquakes or the tornadoes."

Nemerra took Ludik's hand. "Our trees fell over, and houses collapsed or lost roofs. They fixed our roof last, because you weren't back yet."

"It doesn't matter." Ludik raised her hand to his cheek. "It's ready for our home now."

"I didn't care about the house, either." Nemerra pulled him to a stop and leaned toward him. "I only worried about you. Every time the earth shook, I prayed you were somewhere safe. I prayed Darravani would hear me and protect you. But she couldn't hear me, and you weren't safe."

She sniffled. "Every day I learn more of your experiences, and every night I have worse dreams. Now I pray Darravani will help me protect you until we get married. Then everything will be well again." She dashed the tears from her face.

"I wasn't in danger the whole time," Ludik protested, taking her in his arms. "And the trouble is over now. I'm back, and nothing will stand in the way of our wedding."

Zefra chose not to contradict his assessment of how safe they had been while they searched for the gods or whether the trouble was over. They had no proof yet that the disasters would not send trouble into the future in ways they could not predict.

While she waited for them to pay attention to anything but each other, she examined the ground. Still no signs, and if they did not keep moving, they would get farther behind the killer.

Nemerra smiled at Ludik. "Everything will be perfect."

"And now back to your wife, Lyell." Nia poked Ludik until he and Nemerra walked again.

Zefra fell into step with the others, nodding her thanks to Nia.

"Ruka has beautiful brown hair and eyes as dark as this pup's." Lyell pointed to Zefra.

Zefra shrugged again. All Iskrins had brown eyes; it was nothing special.

Lyell smiled as devotedly as Ludik. "She is medium height and was slender before her pregnancy made her as round as a walrus. She is intelligent and kind and laughs at my jokes. Ruka is the light of my life and the heart of our home.

"We met when she was mapping roads between villages," Lyell continued. "I was on guard duty that day. I heard a noise in the trees and went to investigate. She fell off a branch, right at my feet. I almost cut her throat before I realized she had not ambushed me. I said, 'Isn't it usually leaves that fall in autumn?' She laughed and offered to 'leaf' if she was in my way, and I lost my heart." He smiled. "She snuck into my life and never left."

Zefra struggled to smile. This was amusing, but it had nothing to do with their quest. Nia and Nemerra had done too well at distracting the others.

"Love snuck up on you, but Nemerra stalked me," Ludik teased.

Nemerra smiled at him again. "I wanted to beat the competition."

Gurryon laughed. "What competition? Nobody else wanted him."

"They just couldn't tell the two of you apart," Nemerra said. "Who wants a husband you can't identify? But I can tell, and I chose the best in the village."

Ludik leaned toward Nemerra, then stopped and pulled himself up again, groaning. "Since it isn't our wedding day anymore, is it still bad luck to kiss you?"

"How much more bad luck can we have?" Nemerra said. "And the tradition only forbids it on the actual day." She looked at Ludik from under her eyelashes and ran her hand up his arm. "Are we getting married today?" She blinked three times.

Ludik grinned and drew her into his arms.

Zefra sighed. Another delay. She politely looked away from the sweethearts.

"Aww," Nia said.

Gurryon made an exaggerated gagging noise.

Ludik spun toward his brother and shook a fist. "One of these days." His frown softened as he pulled Nemerra behind a large tree. "Go on without us."

Gurryon stomped past the tree, cursing under his breath. Nia giggled and skipped after him, dragging Ahjin with her. Lyell whistled as he followed. He ran his fingers along the silver chain around his neck and reread the note from Darravani, ducking under branches without looking at them. Zefra guarded the rear and kept a watch behind them, in case something threatened the distracted suitors.

When Ludik and Nemerra caught up to them a minute later, Nemerra's hair was mussed, and Ludik grinned from ear to ear. Now that she no longer had to guard two groups, Zefra returned to the prior conversation.

"My people make maps, too," she told Lyell. "My mother taught me the basics. I would love to see your wife's work sometime."

"Ruka would like that. She loves showing her collection and telling stories about it. She can talk for days about why this map is more accurate than that one, and how politics or myth distorted the accuracy of others."

"Our maps are so accurate, the best mapmakers in our clan are famous," Zefra said.

Nia made a rude noise. "Your maps might be accurate, Zefra, but not everyone is as good, and you know myths generally warp the truth. We've listened to myths from all over, Lyell, and all were wrong. Irajahan claimed he created every bit of the world, for instance. That's one of the things that caused the recent crisis. Some of the other gods objected to his lies."

"I would object, too," Lyell said. "Irajahan's tale is crazy. Ruka would like it, though. She collects odd stories. I remember she told me one that claimed a Darrendrakar kindred was lost millennia ago. She has not found a single bit of corroborating evidence, of course."

"Isn't it possible?" Nia asked.

"Of course not," Gurryon said. "What kindred is missing?"

"Ooh!" Nia bounced on her toes. "They could be dragons!"

All the Darrendrakar stared at her in complete silence, then burst out laughing.

Zefra imagined a fierce, fire-breathing dragon belonging to Darravani and smiled. Dragons did not exist, but if they did, Resef was more likely to have one. Or perhaps Kassian, who already claimed several kinds of monsters.

Nemerra was the first to stop laughing. "Sorry, Nia, but that is unbelievable."

When Gurryon could breathe again, he said, "Seriously, where would another kindred even live?"

Lyell shook his head. "The boundaries between kindreds have been fixed for thousands of years. Darravani disapproves of anything but the tiniest of shifts back and forth across the current border. There is no room for another territory."

"During the war with the Hyenas in our Grandpapa's time," Ludik said, "the temple priest judged our side correct after hearing only fifteen minutes of testimony. The Elephants chased the Hyenas back to their territory after that. No one sane stands against the Elephants, not even the scruffy Hyenas."

The conversation died, and they walked in silence. While Nia picked flowers and threaded them through her braids, Zefra scrutinized the ground for prints. What bad luck kept them from finding a trace?

As twilight fell, she raised her voice just enough to carry to the front of the line. "Gurryon, can you smell anything pertinent? Are we still on the right track?"

Gurryon rolled his shoulders in an exaggerated shrug. "Nothing, but there has been nothing leading away, either. Have you seen anything?"

Zefra bent low, squinting in the fading light. "There are so many fallen leaves covering the ground, and new ones all the time. Even our prints do not show for long. Ludik, you see better in the dark. Will you take over now?"

Ahjin glanced at the purple-dark sky. "It's getting too dark for anyone to see details. We should eat and camp and start again in the morning."

Zefra sighed. Another day without success.

She quickly found a suitable clearing with overhanging branches. "We will be fairly hidden, and safe enough for a small fire," she explained.

Ahjin asked, "Will you join us, Lyell, or keep yourself in impartial separation?"

Lyell grinned sarcastically. "I would rather keep a close eye on you, if you do not mind."

Gurryon shoved a pan at Lyell. "Then it is your turn to cook."

After a tasty dinner had been devoured and the pan scraped clean, the men did the dishes in the flickering light of the tiny fire while the women made the beds. Nia decided on a new layout and convinced Nemerra to go along with it, outvoting Zefra.

"The beds are ready, boys." Nia grinned. "You'll find them more comfortable than a tree tonight, Ludik."

Ludik went to see her arrangements. Instead of blankets on opposite sides of the fire like the night before, Nia had put them nearly in a circle. Ludik's blanket lay at the center of the arc, next to Nemerra's.

"Nia, we should separate the genders," Zefra protested for the third time.

"Ahjin needs more space for his wings, and we have to make room for

Lyell, too, so I scooted everyone else closer together," Nia said. "I'm afraid that means Ludik will have to sleep next to the girls." She shook her head with mock regret and then laughed.

Gurryon winked at Nia. "If you don't want to, I will."

"That would make me break your arm, bro, and I don't feel like fixing it today. You can sleep on my other side." Ludik leaned over and kissed Nia's forehead, then went to talk to Nemerra.

Nia chuckled and sat on her own blankets, facing the darkness for the first watch.

Zefra cooled the fire and lay down, prepared to listen for misbehavior and throw a pebble at Ludik's head if he did not mind his manners during the night. Any noise would wake her, as would the smallest alarm from the person on watch. If only that were the biggest problem on the journey.

Ahjin yawned and pulled his blanket over his head. Gurryon was already snoring. Zefra did not understand why everyone ignored the continued danger of chasing a murderer. At least Nia would watch now and wake the next person, and so forth through the night. The killer could not sneak up unnoticed in the middle of the night.

Just before Zefra fell asleep, she remembered the murderer could creep in disguised as an animal. And dogs could see better in the dark than she could.

10.GODS
(CANID TERRITORY)

His Holiness, Ahjin the Great, was dignified and wise in all his doings.
A Comprehensive History of the Gods, vol. 7

Ahjin woke before the sun rose and crept through the woods alone. He undressed and slid into the cold stream, stretching his twenty-two-foot wingspan above the waist-high water.

His uneasy dreams had been full of the murderer they chased. It wasn't just that the killer might circle around if he knew he was pursued, although now Ahjin had thought of that, it did worry him. He was more concerned about the number of deaths and lack of surviving witnesses.

It was ridiculous to fret so much. For all they knew, many people had seen their quarry and lived. Just because they had found no survivors didn't mean they didn't exist.

Ahjin grabbed his soap. He'd looked for help in some of his religious texts but had found nothing useful.

Now that they knew they chased a deliberate killer, he doubted he *could* help. A mediator advised quarreling parties or smoothed misunderstandings, but what could he negotiate between a murderer and his potential victims? It seemed like a job for soldiers and courts.

He tossed the soap onto the bank and rinsed. Even being the Mouth of the Gods didn't seem helpful, unless the killer was pious enough to stop on religious grounds. But if he was, he probably wouldn't have killed three people.

Ahjin finished bathing and donned his pants. Since he was awake and alone, it was time for his daily religious observances. Resef first, with blue dawn shimmering on the water. Ahjin sat cross-legged on the bank and started his prayers. After only a few words, he stopped.

As the Mouth of the Gods, why hadn't he asked the gods for help? They must want to prevent war between their peoples as well as among themselves.

He had left his religious supplies in his pack, but Resef could adapt. Ahjin laid out twigs in the rune for "message" and the upright triangle for "fire." He restarted his prayers and explained the situation to Resef. Then he waited. After a minute, the twigs rearranged to form three new runes.

One rune, meaning confinement or limitation, took the position that meant Resef or the gods in general. The two representing the petitioner were runes for endurance and caution.

Ahjin pondered for a moment. He was already being careful, and if Resef was limited, what good would enduring do?

What a waste of time. This was Darravani's land; he should have asked her first. Perhaps he could fly two winds at the same time. He plucked a yellow leaf for parchment and a handful of red berries for ink. Ahjin printed as small as possible with a twig and summarized the problem, but he still filled both sides of the leaf.

"Kassian," he prayed, "would you and Darravani please see if either of you can answer this?"

The leaf vanished.

While he waited, he performed his morning routines for the two gods. When he finished, a yellow carnation and a meadowsweet bloomed in front of him.

"No and uselessness," Ahjin interpreted. He reached to snap off the flower heads, then flicked the petals instead. "That's not helpful," he muttered.

Pine needles rained over him, and a white oak leaf fluttered into his lap. Pine was hope in adversity. White oak meant independence, and a single word was etched on the leaf. "Sorry."

Ahjin held his breath. He was on his own.

This was ridiculous. He needed to actually talk to someone. It was easy — too easy, sometimes — to talk to Irajahan with his inherent telepathy. It took a little more effort and Makana's good will to connect to her, but her way was less intrusive than Irajahan's and less complicated than the other gods' methods.

There was plenty of water here to contact Makana. He reached for his shirt, then changed his mind. Makanavailea liked men shirtless. He normally ignored that preference, but he seemed to need every advantage with the gods today.

Ahjin scooted to the edge of the bank to clearly see the burbling stream. He rolled his pants to his knees and dangled his feet in the water. After a deep breath to cool his already-burning cheeks, he called Makana. There was no answer.

Ahjin leaned above the water and called again. This time, Makana's image appeared in the stream. She was laughing, and music pounded in the background.

"Well met." She took a closer look and grinned. "Why, Ahjin, I'm flattered. What can I do for you?"

He launched into her favorite compliments, starting with her beautiful rainbow hair. When she waved off more of them, he explained the quest for a murderer. "Can you help us find him?" he finished.

"I'd love to, cutie," Makana said, "but although Darravani and I are talking now, I don't think she'd appreciate me scouring her land for information. Who knows what else I might see? I'll try to keep an eye out, but that's the best I can do. Pleasant journey, and keep in touch." She smiled as she eyed him again, then winked and disappeared.

Ahjin groaned. As much as he hated the idea, Irajahan was the only one left.

"Oh, Irajahan." He winced as his heartfelt lack of enthusiasm crept into his voice. "Great God of Air, I humbly beg for a minute of your time." His groveling might not matter. Irajahan was difficult.

"What do *you* want?" Irajahan snarled in the back of Ahjin's head.

Ahjin ran through the story again.

Irajahan laughed. "You mean you're in danger, chasing through a foreign land after a murderer you won't recognize if you find him? The other gods won't help, and you're asking me?" He laughed harder. "No." He disappeared from Ahjin's mind.

That was about as useless as Ahjin had expected.

He didn't know how to tell Ludik he'd be no help. Perhaps he shouldn't mention his failed attempts.

Ahjin was stretching his wings when the other three men ran through the woods, laughing and whooping. He whipped his wings shut across his back, a moment too late. The gasps and curses made it clear Lyell and Gurryon had seen his ugly scars as they jumped into the stream.

Ahjin knew the gashes from the giant scorpion's claw crisscrossed in vivid red through the skin and muscle of his waist. Lightning scars crawled across his entire body in branching ferns of purple, pink, and white. The combination looked horrific.

Ludik was silent. As Ahjin's healer, he knew how the scars looked. He was a very talented healer and should take the Iskrin apprenticeship. Ludik and Darravani had improved the appearance of Ahjin's face and hands, as well as the proper function of his body, which was more important. They hadn't worried about what didn't show.

Ahjin was used to the way he looked now, not that it should matter. Now that he could fly basic maneuvers again, the only things that still bothered him were the memories and the appalled expressions of strangers. He was learning to deal with the memories and tried to believe it didn't matter what people thought. His folded wings still made a welcome shield to cover his back.

Behind Ahjin, Lyell had gone silent, but Gurryon's exclamations continued. A splash and a gurgle made Ahjin turn.

Ludik smiled brightly at him. Gurryon had disappeared, and it took Ahjin a moment to find him underwater. Ludik sat on his brother's back and held down his arms with his hands.

"Good to see you, Ahjin," Ludik said. "The women thought we should hurry so they can take their time bathing after us. How is that fair?"

"Sometimes life isn't fair," Ahjin drawled as the bubbles rising to the surface slowed. "Are you studying how to heal drowning victims?" He pulled on his shirt, leaving the back panel unlaced.

"Oh, I suppose not." Ludik let go of his brother and stepped back.

Gurryon popped to the surface, spitting water and curses in nearly equal amounts. He lunged for Ludik, but fell short when Lyell yanked his leg. When Gurryon surfaced again, he sputtered, "Listen, Wolf."

"You listen," Lyell growled. "Better yet, think." He jerked his head toward Ahjin.

"What?" Gurryon turned to follow Lyell's gesture.

Ahjin met Gurryon's gaze, then sat to put on his boots. *It doesn't matter what other people think.* He repeated it to himself twice.

Gurryon growled and splashed Ludik. Ludik splashed back. In seconds, the stream turned into a three-way fountain.

Ahjin grabbed his towel and ran for dry safety. When he reached the edge of camp, he draped his towel over a branch and laced down the shirt panel between his wings. Nia wouldn't care if he were half-dressed, but the other girls would, and so would he. And if Nemerra saw the wreck of his back, she would worry about Ludik more and fret over Ahjin, too. He yanked the laces tight and knotted the ends, watching the girls clean up breakfast.

Nemerra and Nia chatted while they washed the dishes. Zefra dried them with a bored look on her face.

The other men returned from their baths more quickly than Ahjin expected. Ludik and Gurryon barreled up the path first, swatting each other with towels.

Ludik paused to let Gurryon pass, then smacked Ahjin on the shoulder. "Gurryon never learned manners."

Lyell strolled in drying his hair and nodded at Ahjin as he hung his towel on the branch.

Ahjin took a breath and followed Lyell into camp.

Nia threw the dish cloth at Ludik. "Is it our turn yet?"

"The water is cold," Ahjin warned.

Nia made a face.

"I can keep you from freezing," Zefra said.

"I knew bringing you was a good idea," Nia said. "Get your towels, ladies."

"Ahjin, what happened to your back?" Gurryon asked.

Ludik shoved his brother. "We'll finish the dishes, Nemerra. Hurry, we need to leave."

"Ahjin, did you hear me?" Gurryon said. "What did you tangle with to do that much ugly damage to you?"

"What?" Nemerra slowed on her way out and looked at Ahjin.

Nia hurried her down the path. "Oh, Nemerra, you don't want to know." She looked over her shoulder and mouthed "sorry" at Ahjin.

"But I do," Gurryon persisted.

"You don't need to know," Ahjin said.

Ludik wrapped an arm around Gurryon's neck. "Leave him alone. Come help me finish the dishes."

Gurryon needed to not ask rude questions. Ahjin had an idea how to teach him. He volunteered to fold the blankets while the brothers finished the dishes and Lyell cleaned the rest of camp.

The Darrendrakar hadn't worn their boots to the stream. Ahjin wandered to his pack, put away his blanket, and retrieved one of his hidden surprises. He meandered past Gurryon's boots and dropped the present inside, then placed everyone else's blankets on their packs.

Though he avoided watching, he knew when Gurryon put on his boots right after the girls returned to camp. Gurryon's cursing was louder than Ludik's shrieks of laughter.

Nemerra rushed to help. "Ludik, fetch your healing kit and stop laughing. Gurryon, sit. Sit! Put your foot in the air and hold still. Whatever did you do?"

Ahjin watched from the corner of his eye as Gurryon dumped his boot upside down.

"What is that?" Nemerra asked.

Gurryon howled again. "I don't know."

Ahjin indulged in a smile.

Ludik reached for his brother's foot. "Nia, would you investigate, please?"

Nia walked straight to Ahjin. "How did you get a sea urchin out here?"

"It's dried. I saved it for a special occasion."

"Did you at least choose one of the nontoxic ones?" Nia asked.

"Of course." Ahjin sniffed, insulted. "I even chose the one with the shortest spines. They're barely prickles."

Nia walked back to Ludik. "It's not venomous. Pick out the spines and use your magic goop."

Ahjin grinned all through Gurryon's treatment.

After Ludik bandaged him, Gurryon carefully pulled on his boots and hobbled to Ahjin. "Why not just swear at me? If I knew you were so upset, I would have apologized."

"Swearing isn't my style," Ahjin said. "It shows a deplorable lack of imagination. Besides, some things you say are offensive to the gods."

"They do not care," Gurryon said. "It is not as if they are listening to me."

Ahjin raised an eyebrow.

Gurryon looked over his shoulder. "Are they listening?"

Ahjin shrugged. "You can hope they aren't listening to you. I certainly won't risk it."

"I see your point," Gurryon said. "And I do apologize. I should not have asked about your scars. If you ever want to tell me what happened, I am interested, but I will not ask again."

Zefra swung her pack on her back and picked up her staff. "Are we ready, then?"

Ludik took Nemerra's hand and walked after Zefra. "We could have been gone if Gurryon hadn't created a healing emergency this morning."

Gurryon limped after them. "It wasn't my fault."

"Oh, I think it was," Nia said.

She and Lyell fell in line behind Gurryon. Every time he tried to talk to Ahjin, they blocked him.

"Pay attention to the track, Gurryon." "Be quiet, Gurryon." "Don't alert the killer, Gurryon."

Ahjin smiled and took rear guard.

After an hour, Ludik took point, and Ahjin tucked his wings so Lyell could trade positions with him.

"Is it awkward squeezing your wings through the trees?" Lyell asked. "Why are we plodding on foot when you could fly overhead and track our quarry from the air?"

"I can fly," Ahjin said, "but I can't see through the tree branches."

"Oh." Lyell grunted. "It would have been convenient."

Ahjin preferred to fly, but besides lacking visibility, he didn't have enough stamina for a long flight yet. If he flew above the trees, he couldn't talk to the others, and below the branches, he had no room. Breaking his wings twice already was two times too many.

"Speaking of convenient, have you tried scrying yet, Nia?" Ahjin asked. If Makana feared trespassing, perhaps Nia's attempts would be less intrusive.

"No," Nia said. "Silly me. The first day, it seemed like we'd catch the Dog quickly. Then all that nastiness happened yesterday, and I didn't think of it."

"Should you try now?" Ludik spoke through gritted teeth from the front of the group.

Nia shot him a disgusted look and stopped walking. "I had decided that, yes."

"Wait." Lyell stopped right before he ran into Ahjin's wings. "What scrying? Are you talking about a spyglass or some magical gibberish?"

"Oh, definitely the magical gibberish." Nia rolled her eyes and rummaged through her pack. "I'll tell Makana how you described her gift."

"Never mind," Lyell said. "I do not want to put you to any trouble. Will you explain it to me, though?"

"Better yet, I'll show you." Nia poured half her bottle of water into a bowl. "If I stare into the water with the right mental twist, I can see... nothing right now." She drank the water. "Sorry, Ludik, it didn't work."

"Why not?" Zefra stretched her back and legs and shook out her arms.

"I don't know," Nia said. "Sometimes it doesn't. We might be too far away, or maybe nothing is happening. Or I don't know where to look. I can't see everything, you know, and if I don't know what I'm looking for..."

"Don't worry, Nia," Ahjin said. "You can try later. By the way, I had a chat with Makana about you last month."

"About what?" Nia narrowed her eyes at him.

"I asked when your birthday is."

"You know my six-thousandth day is in spring. I'll invite you to my party so you can celebrate me becoming an adult. Why ask Makana about that?"

"I know that part," Ahjin said. "I wanted to know when you were *born* so I could give you a birthday present." He reached in his pocket and pulled out the package he had bought in Ioj. "Happy sixteenth birthday."

Nia's mouth dropped open. "What, today? Are you sure?"

"Makana said so." Ahjin held the package closer to her, but she didn't take it.

"She doesn't know when she was born?" Nemerra asked.

"They count differently," Zefra murmured. "Listen."

"But we don't celebrate our birthdays," Nia protested.

"Does that mean you don't want your present?" Ahjin waved it in front of her.

Nia snatched the small parcel. "Don't be silly."

She untied the ribbon around it and stuffed it into her shirt, then yanked off the wrapping to reveal a miniature, obsidian dolphin. She held it to the leaf-filtered light, admiring the different angles and the silvery chain to hook to her belt. "It looks like Ya'eel."

"I thought so, too," Ahjin said.

"Thank you." Nia flung her arms around his neck and squeezed him, then went back to examining her gift. Nemerra took her elbow to guide her as the group walked again.

Ahjin smiled. That worked well. Since he was no longer rear guard, he wiggled Torao's journal from his bag and read while he walked. There was never enough time to study on this journey. By the time he returned to Arupa, he'd be hopelessly behind in the gods' assignments. He made a face.

"What's wrong?" Lyell asked.

"With five gods to please, my reading list is endless," Ahjin said. "Now I have this journal on top of everything else. After an hour or two, my head aches. I'd rather fly."

"You don't have to read Grandpapa's journal," Ludik turned sideways to talk. "It talks about the rotten Hyenas, not the Dogs."

"He seemed to think it was important. It might have something useful for our situation."

"The only thing that would be useful is if we caught the stinking Dog and got out of this lousy territory," Ludik muttered almost too quietly to be heard.

Lyell glared at him but spoke to Ahjin. "My wife is not a teacher, but in her free time, Ruka helps at the village school. She showed up daily until the teacher assigned her children to help. She tutored those children for a year. When the oldest one finished school, he brought flowers for both his mama and Ruka. He said he could not have made it without either of them."

"That's kind of her," Ahjin said, "but what does that have to do with us?"

"Oh, I thought we could take turns reading out loud."

Ahjin handed the journal to Lyell, then stuck his hands in his pockets while he listened. When his head pounded again, he pulled out one hand to rub it.

"I can give you some medicine for your headache," Ludik said.

Ahjin cringed and shook his head. Ludik's medicines were nasty.

"You should know he's too stubborn." Nia untied Ahjin's embroidered scarf-belt. She folded it in a long strip and poured water in the middle, right where she had mended the tears from the scorpion attack. Before he could protest the abuse of his scarf, she reached up and tied the cold, wet patch on his forehead.

"The medicine would work better," she said, taking the journal from Lyell. "Don't argue; just keep listening."

Ahjin listened to Nia read another of Torao's rants and thought about Ludik. *Rotten Hyenas*, Ludik had said again. And he obviously didn't trust the Dogs, either, not even Lyell. It seemed he hated the other kindreds as badly as his grandfather did. What would he do when they encountered other Dogs in their search for the murderer?

Would Ludik change his heart before his animosity triggered the war they were sent to prevent?

11. TRACKING

(CANID TERRITORY)

Every day, the casualty lists rotate through the healers' tents. We read who died in other tents and add the names of those the Hyenas stole from us.

Torao, after The Battle of Sad Laughter

Nia was miserable. Though it was almost midday, the air was still cold, and her feet were tired. She wasn't sure if either problem was worse than the boredom of endless plodding. This wasn't her idea of a fun adventure. There should be delicious food, beautiful music, and good company.

Here, there wasn't even comfort for her feet. She would never admit it to Ahjin, but she was glad he'd made her wear sandals. The Darrendran forest was beautiful, but her beach sand was softer than layers of twigs and dry evergreen needles. Even Ahjin's island had a combination of grass, smooth paving stones, and well-turned garden dirt.

Enough complaining. It didn't solve anything, and she could at least reduce the boredom. She beckoned Nemerra.

"Give me Torao's journal. I'll take another turn." The journal was depressing, but reading it aloud made the time pass faster and helped Ahjin. It also reminded Nia why they were on this dismal journey.

"The Hyenas outnumbered us," she read aloud as she walked, turning the thick pages of handmade paper, "and they pounced from branches and behind trees. Anyone lagging behind the group was sure to be killed."

When she stumbled, Ahjin put a hand under her elbow. How *did* he manage to read while he walked?

Unfortunately, the journal continued with depressing casualty statistics, including a shocking number of Ludik and Gurryon's relatives, which didn't distract her from her worries. Nia had thought Torao was overreacting when he asked Ahjin to prevent war. Nobody would be stupid enough to start a war once Ludik and Ahjin explained Agu had only defended himself against the panicking Fox. But they'd been wrong, and now their quest was so much ickier. Torao might be right about the danger of war.

Nia shuddered. She had fought monsters in their last misadventure, but it had been self-defense, and none of them were people. How could someone kill another person on purpose? He was like a piranha or a crazed dolphin. Nobody wanted to get any closer to someone like that, but they couldn't let him roam around killing people.

"Annoying anemones," she said, interrupting her own reading. "What will we do with the killer when we catch him? Drag him all the way back to Maon?"

Ahjin glanced at Nemerra. "We might not have enough people for that."

"Leave him with the Dogs?" Nia suggested.

Ludik and Gurryon looked at each other, then narrowed their silver eyes at Lyell.

"The Cats would prefer to be sure of his fate," Ludik said.

Lyell bared his teeth and bumped his knives with his elbows. "*We* are trustworthy. We also want to be sure of this murderer's future."

"Execution is foolproof," Zefra said.

Nemerra gulped.

Nia huffed. No, this adventure was no fun at all. The last thing she needed was to watch an execution. What could be worse? She thumbed the pages as she read the journal to Ahjin again, wondering if the entire book was full of war and death.

Instead of coming on this stupid trip, she should have stayed in Maon to play with Ludik's younger sister and his siblings' children and sleep in a real, warm bed, which was almost as good as a hammock. She would have missed her friends, but when they came back, they would have the wedding and party.

Nia loved parties. Could they throw one when they caught the murderer? It would make her perfectly happy to celebrate his capture. She thought of Zefra's comment and shuddered. Celebrating an execution was in horribly poor style.

Nia shivered. The last two days had been warmer, and even anticipating a party couldn't take her mind off the weather's betrayal. Nokailana's winter was cool and wet, but it never got cold.

She pulled her borrowed Darrendran cloak tighter around her. It didn't help much. Her nose was cold, and her ears were cold, and her fingers froze around the edge of the cloak.

The Darrendrakar looked perfectly comfortable.

Nia paused her reading again to ask Nemerra, "How do you deal with this cold?"

"Cold?" Nemerra said. "It's a little chilly today, but it's only autumn. It won't get frosty for at least a couple of weeks. Smell the fallen leaves and the cool snap of the pines. I'll always associate these scents with my wedding."

She smiled at Ludik, and he smiled back. They interlaced their fingers and drifted off in one of their frequent mutual admiration episodes.

Nia usually found their habit sweet and entertaining, but not when freezing in obviously winter weather. This was their home, so it made sense they were used to the cold. She wiped her nose on her shoulder. They didn't have to enjoy it so much. Didn't they care that she was miserable?

Pleasant thoughts, Nia. She stomped her feet to a mental tune as she walked, but the fallen leaves smothered the rhythm.

She glanced around the group. Only Ludik and Nemerra smiled, and only at each other. This was such a grumpy bunch. Nobody had a sense of humor except for Lyell.

Ooh, they did have a perfect excuse for a different party. She gave up on reading and slid the book into Ahjin's pack.

"Oh, Lyell," Nia said, "what are the Canid party traditions for new babies?"

"We usually do not have one," Lyell said. "They are babies. How much partying can they do?"

"They can't, but we can. You're such a great dad, you certainly want to celebrate your children. If you don't have any traditions, then we can do whatever we like."

"I suppose." Lyell sounded dubious. "Ruka visited new mamas when their babies were born. She did not party, but she loved to rock the little ones to sleep so their mamas could rest. Now she finally has babies of her own. She might like a celebration. I can ask her when I get home."

"Well, let's do a little planning before we get there," Nia said. "If we don't make it that far, you'll have all the ideas you need. If we do go to your home, we can be the life of your village." She ignored Ludik's groan and listed food and games and decorations as fast as she thought of them.

Lyell finally laughed. "That's more than enough suggestions. We cannot do a fraction of them."

"I haven't gotten to the songs yet," Nia protested. "Here's one of my favorites." She burst into a lively song but didn't get past the second line before Gurryon hushed her.

"Nia, you're too loud." The tall sourpuss glared at her from the front of the group. "If we're closer to the killer than we think, you might alert him."

"That's not fair," Nia said. "We've been reading out loud."

"Yes, but quietly." Ahjin touched her shoulder. "You have a lovely but powerful singing voice. Don't give me that look. You know you do."

"But, Ahjin, I'm bored." Nia wrapped her arms around herself and shivered.

"I know. Do you want to scry again? It's about time for a rest break, and if we can get a better idea where we need to go, we might shave off some distance."

"Fine." While everyone stopped for a drink, Nia pulled out her bowl and repeated her scrying attempt. The water shimmered, and then lavender waves lapped against the inside of the bowl.

"I see the ocean," Nia murmured. "Look at the warm water." She shivered as the cold wind blew in her ear.

"We already knew the Dog came from the shore," Ludik complained. "This doesn't help us."

"It's confirmation," Nemerra said.

"Unless her vision is affected by her homesickness," Zefra said.

"Who says I'm homesick?" Nia denied.

Zefra blinked. "You obviously miss the ocean."

Nia sniffed. "That doesn't make a difference to the scrying."

Lyell shrugged. "Then it tells us nothing we did not already know."

The sun went behind a cloud, and the temperature dropped more. Without walking to warm her, cold crept through Nia's webbed feet. She shivered again. Boots might have been better than sandals; they would have kept her webbing from turning to shards of ice.

Ahjin must have felt the cold, too, since he pulled on his jacket.

Nia smoothed the middle back between his wings. "You take the right ribbons," she stuttered through chattering teeth.

She laced the satin ribbons down the left side of his jacket below his wings. The blue fabric was decorated with beautiful embroidery in more shades of blue. Waves bounced around the hem, while birds, dolphins, and fish danced across his torso. It made her even more homesick.

"Did you already have that," Nemerra asked, "or is it something they gave you as a priest? It's beautiful."

"I brought it from home, but Nia's mother mended it with the embroidery." Ahjin fastened his jacket to his chin, wrapped his scarf around his neck, and pulled on gloves. After that, he seemed unaffected by the cold.

He had told Nia that flying in higher altitudes could be cold. That was why his mom made his scarf for him. So, of course, his jacket was also made for those conditions. Not fair.

She should have accepted her mom's offer of a coat for the trip, but no, she would be back before winter, and it wouldn't be that bad, and she could go inside or sit by a fire if she got cold. If she told Mom she'd been right, Mom would just smile. Ugh!

"Are we ready to go?" Gurryon asked.

Zefra drained a water pouch and nodded. The others put on their packs while Nia drank the water she had used for scrying. As Nia put away her bowl, she saw the perfume given to her by Zefra's brother, darling Izo.

"Ooh, the perfect thing to brighten my day." She grabbed the small, cut-glass bottle and worked out the stopper. Before she could splash it on herself, Ahjin snatched it.

Nia grabbed for it, but Ahjin held the bottle over his head, out of her reach even on tiptoe. "You give that back, you thieving magpie," she insisted in her loudest whisper.

He unfolded a wing to keep her away. "I will, as soon as you agree not to wear it."

Nia dodged his white wall of feathers and swiped at the perfume again. "I don't care if you hate it. It's mine, and I like it."

"Nia, you can't. Think about it. Why do you wear perfume?"

"Because it smells pretty. You're so dumb sometimes."

Ahjin ignored the insult. "And where are we now?"

Nia put her hands on her hips. "In the middle of a forest. Will the squirrels object?"

Lyell ran his hand through his hair until it stood on end. "We are in a Canid forest. If you put on your perfume, every Dog for leagues around can track you. The killer will smell us before he can hear or see us."

"It's not that strong," Nia protested.

"How do you think I found you at the border?" Lyell asked. "I knew you were strangers by your speech, but I first detected you from the scent of roses."

Nia glanced nervously around the forest, then pouted and held out her hand. When Ahjin gave her the perfume, she crammed in the cork and scowled at him. "Don't think I'll forget this."

"Of course not." Ahjin smiled. "Fortunately, I can turn invisible and fly away."

Nia glared. "Irajahan didn't give you invisibility for your silly pranks, and I can make sure you can be tracked by scent."

She threatened him with the bottle of perfume before repacking it and shrugging her pack onto her frozen shoulders.

As she followed Zefra between the trees again, she scuffed the pine needles into broken bits and inhaled. It was apparently the only fragrance she could enjoy on this trip.

"Will we see anything but trees and dead bodies on this trip? Please tell me we'll at least meet people, see the towns, taste the local cooking?"

"I don't know," Ludik said. "This isn't an entertainment tour. If the track doesn't go through a town, neither do we."

"She has a good idea," Ahjin said. "We could ask for help. Even if we don't find any, I'd still like to try hiring workers for Arupa."

"That would be nice," Nia said. "I'm tired of weeding half your giant garden every week. I'd rather welcome visitors and give tours of the island. And you have more important demands for your time."

She hated watching his shoulders slump every morning when another shipload of visitors landed wanting to talk to His Holiness, the majestic priest that must be hidden somewhere behind the scrubby young Iojif with the molting feathers.

"More important," Ahjin muttered.

Nia patted his elbow. "If you can't remember what you've done, you should ask Kassian."

"I mean since then," Ahjin argued.

Nia wrapped her arm around his waist. "You're important to me."

Ahjin gave her a quick hug, then looked at Lyell.

"I am not sure your chances are high," Lyell said. "Most Darrendrakar are unwilling to live outside their own territory."

"If you give word enough time to spread," Ludik said, "you might find a few adventurers willing to go. But they won't get a ship across during winter, so you have a limited amount of time to gather people this year."

"I'll do that, too, but spring is so far away," Ahjin said. "What we're doing is important, but if we get even close to any towns, I can fly ahead and then catch up to you without you losing any time."

"There is nothing for at least a day," Lyell said. "And that depends on the route."

Ahjin made a face and pulled out a scroll to read. Nia offered to read again until she discovered it was one of Irajahan's old scrolls, instructing his priests how to worship his majesty. She wouldn't suffer through that egomaniacal rubbish, not even for Ahjin.

Next to Nia, Zefra shivered, too. She struggled to wrap her cloak around her, but it was trapped under the straps of her pack. She couldn't lift and pull at the same time, especially while shaking.

At least Nia wasn't the only tropical flower around here. She grabbed one of the straps and lifted enough for Zefra to wiggle her cloak around her arms.

"That is better," Zefra said. "I need to trap the warm air, or it will dissipate before it heats me."

"What warm air?" Nia asked.

Zefra blew on her hands for a minute. "Warm bath, warm air. I would thank Resef for his flame-calling if I were not afraid of what else he might give me." She tucked herself into her cloak and sighed happily.

"You can warm yourself as well as start a fire?" Nia pulled her cold fingers inside her cloak. Where was *her* warm air? The cloak slipped from her fingers and parted its full length to let in the cold breeze. She fumbled for the edges to pull it around her again.

This was a miserable adventure. Maybe they wouldn't have to worry about finding the killer or what to do with him, because they'd freeze first.

12. RAIN
(CANID TERRITORY)

Southern Darrendra is pleasant in the summer, but cold in the winter. Northern Darrendra sinks under feet of ice and snow for many months.

A Brief Sketch of Mysterious Darrendra

Ludik agreed with Nemerra about the cool air and scents of autumn. It would be his favorite season now, always reminding him of their wedding. He smiled at her again, admiring the way her russet hair mimicked the red and orange leaves against the background of the fir trees. At least their walk through the forest gave him plenty of time to look at her.

When Ahjin jiggled his elbow, Ludik barely avoided swatting him for interrupting his pleasant thoughts. "What?" he growled.

"It will rain tonight," Ahjin said. "We should plan on an early stop so we can build shelters. Sorry, Zefra, but we'll need to cut some branches."

Lyell looked at the clear sky. "Why do you say it will rain?"

"The air pressure is changing."

Lyell raised his eyebrows. "Is it?"

When everyone else stopped and either strapped their packs tightly closed or covered them, Lyell's eyebrows climbed even higher.

"Birds know weather," Nia whispered to Lyell. She winked as she passed him and linked arms with Zefra.

Ludik chuckled and turned to walk again. After a minute, he frowned. "If it rains, we might lose the scent trail, at least until our quarry moves after the rain."

Nia shrugged. "You haven't found much scent, anyway. He's stayed on a straight path so far. We'll try to pick it up again after the rain, unless we catch him first. More importantly, if it will be colder and wet tonight, I think we should have a warm stew for supper. It will be filling even if we can't cook flatbread to go with it. How does that sound?"

"Stew takes too long," Gurryon complained.

Nia waved off his objection. "I have an idea I want to try, if you'll catch a fat rabbit or something."

She and Zefra talked in low voices for a few minutes, then Nia pulled a ball of twine from her borrowed cloak, and they started what looked like a giant game of cat's-cradle.

While Ludik and Lyell gathered other stray vegetables beyond the path, Nemerra showed Ahjin how to recognize wild onions. By the time Gurryon caught a rabbit, they had enough ingredients for a large potful.

At the next rest break, Gurryon cleaned the rabbit while Nia bossed everyone else into chopping the vegetables. She added spices and water, then tied the lid to the pot. She slid the pot into the cat's-cradle and slipped a folded pad of fabric on one side.

"Okay, Zefra, it's ready," Nia said.

Zefra donned her pack again, and then Nia helped her slide the netted pot over her shoulders. It rested in front of her with the pad between the pot and her chest. Zefra placed both hands on the sides of the pot.

"We're ready to go," Nia said.

Ahjin laughed. "Same brilliant Nia."

Ludik stared at Zefra and then chuckled as he figured out her plan. They would have the evening meal ready before they set up camp.

"You'll like this trick, Nemerra." He slapped Nia's upraised hand as Gurryon took the lead for a while.

"It will not cook by itself, you know," Lyell drawled.

Zefra opened her mouth, and Nia clapped her hand over it.

"But, Nia," Zefra mumbled.

"Oh, don't spoil the surprise." Nia giggled. "He has a good sense of humor, remember?"

Zefra nodded, and Nia removed her hand.

Nemerra stepped beside them. "Will you tell me your plan while we walk?"

She laughed at their enthusiastic nods and bent her head to hear their whispers as they followed Gurryon.

Ludik grinned as Lyell watched them march down the path, his arms crossed and eyebrows still raised.

After a few hours, a faint but delicious scent of roasting meat and vegetables hovered around Zefra. When she put down the netted pot during a rest break, Lyell reached for the lid.

"No!" Zefra slapped his hand away. "Are you crazy? You will be burned."

"You cannot possibly put out enough heat to cook the stew," Lyell scoffed. "Resef's gift might allow you to extinguish a small fire, but it cannot turn you into one."

Zefra opened her mouth, then shut it again when Nia cleared her throat. She shrugged and picked up the pot again. "Whatever you say."

As they fought through a section of underbrush, the clouds rolled in. By late afternoon, a gentle sprinkle turned into a downpour that ran inside their collars and dripped into their boots.

Ludik wrapped his cloak around himself and walked faster. "We're stopping at the next adequate place."

A few minutes later, they found a clearing even better than he'd hoped. The large trees around the edges crossed their branches almost to the center of the clearing, thinning the rain deluge. A heavy blanket of old pine needles and dead leaves softened the ground and kept the travelers out of the mud. The stream was close enough to make fetching water easier than waiting for rain to fill a bucket.

Zefra surrounded her pot with the packs to keep off some of the rain that sizzled as it bounced off the hot metal. Ludik chopped a few branches for their shelters, and everyone else gathered dead wood.

Nia directed the building efforts to make three triangular shelters assembled in a rough circle. The larger support branches were covered with smaller ones lined up closely and then topped with layers of leafy or needled boughs to make them nearly watertight.

"The larger one is for the girls," Nia said, and Zefra and Nemerra scrambled to pull their packs from the pile. She grabbed her own pack and dove in after them. "We'll be back in a minute for supper," she called over her shoulder.

Gurryon waved at the remaining two shelters. "Who is sharing with whom?"

"I am used to Ahjin's wings," Ludik volunteered quickly. He would rather have shared with Nemerra, but since that was impossible, at least he could avoid the Wolf. And Ahjin was more peaceful than Gurryon.

"Oh, no, you cannot do that to me," Lyell protested, glaring at Gurryon.

"You cannot do that to *me*," Gurryon objected.

Ahjin rolled his eyes. "I'm taking this one, and anyone is welcome to join me." He picked up his pack and crawled into the closer shelter.

Ludik and Gurryon glared at each other, then looked at Lyell. The brothers threw their packs in the other shelter at the same time.

Lyell shrugged and joined Ahjin, silently arranging his single blanket and his small pack.

Ludik shamelessly watched the Wolf. If Lyell tried anything against Ahjin, he wouldn't get away with it.

Lyell cleared his throat and rubbed his hands on his knees. "Shall we see how long we still need to cook the stew?"

Ahjin nodded toward the women and pulled his spoon and bowl from his pack. "They're serving it now."

Lyell gaped at the steaming pot, rapidly cooling as the rain bounced rings in the thick sauce.

Ahjin grinned. "You should hurry before your food gets cold." He scrambled into the rain and sat on a log next to Nia.

Ludik smothered his own grin and sat beside Ahjin, bowl balanced on his knees. He pulled Nemerra to his right side so they could hold hands while they ate. It was his favorite benefit from her being right-handed instead of left.

The stew was full of delicious spices and cooked perfectly, and Ludik devoured half of his in the seconds it took Lyell to join them and take his first bite.

"This is as good as Ruka's food," Lyell said, "and she is a good cook, although she always cooked more than we could eat." He smiled. "If there were not several guests at the table, then I knew I would make a delivery after we finished eating."

"My compliments to the cook." Ahjin nodded at Nia. "And the stove." He winked at Zefra, who bowed with a grin and then shivered.

"Is your rain always this cold?" Zefra asked. "I was not so cold before it rained."

"It's autumn now," Nemerra said. "It will keep getting colder, and wet clothes drain the heat." She drank the last of her stew and moved to Zefra's side to put an arm around her. "You should take the middle tonight. You'll be warmer with Nia and me on either side of you."

"I'm sorry, Zefra," Nia said. "I shouldn't have tried this when you were already trying to keep warm."

Zefra shivered again. "Is it time for bed?" She glanced at the not-quite-setting sun and drooped.

Nia slurped the last of her stew. "Yes. It's the boys' turn to do dishes."

When Gurryon protested, Ludik thumped him.

"Hush," Ludik murmured. "You do realize that without fuel, Zefra used her own energy to create heat, don't you? Between the cold, the rain, and cooking the stew, she's drained. We should have realized the forest shade and the cloudy sky would affect her too much."

Gurryon winced. "I'll get the water."

Ludik turned to Zefra. "I shouldn't have let you do it."

Zefra shivered harder, and her soup sloshed in her bowl. "I agreed to it. It was not your choice."

Nemerra held Zefra's bowl and helped her finish eating, then the women retired. Nia hung Zefra's wet cloak across their shelter's entrance.

Ludik finished his stew, then stood next to the women's shelter in case Zefra needed healing.

"Come on, you need to get dry," Nia's muffled voice crooned. "Take off your wet clothes, that's it. Give them to me. Good girl. Now the dry clothes. Lift your arms for Nemerra. No, don't worry about it; let Nemerra do the work, you just hold out your arms. Almost done. There you go, climb under your blankets. Okay, Nemerra, you next."

There was a murmur from Nemerra.

"Leave them in a pile in the corner," Nia said. "We'll dry them tomorrow. Scoot next to Zefra; it's my turn." There was a pause. "Oh, blessed dryness."

Nia stuck out her head from behind the cloak across the entrance and looked at Ludik. "I thought you'd be there. Don't worry, we got her settled. The four of you can share the watches tonight. We'll see you in the morning." She pulled her head back in, and a chorus of sighs faded into silence.

Zefra would be well. That was a relief. Ludik rejoined the men to wash dishes in cold water.

"Ahjin, go to bed," Ludik said. "Your feathers will already take too long to dry. You can take the last watch in the morning."

Ahjin dropped the clean spoons into the stack of clean bowls. "Yes, bossy. There's only the pot left, anyway. There's no point trying to dry the dishes tonight."

"Do you think it will rain tomorrow?" Ludik asked.

Ahjin stretched his wings and yawned. "It should stop by breakfast. We'll dry while we walk. Good night, everyone." He raised his voice. "Good night, ladies."

"Go to bed, Ahjin," Nia mumbled.

"I will take the first watch," Ludik volunteered.

"I will take the second," Lyell said, "and even finish washing the pot."

"Great, four hours of sleep before I have to get up," Gurryon said. "Sounds good to me." He crawled into bed almost as quickly as Ahjin.

Lyell finished the dishes and changed to wolf. He smelled like wet dog as he crawled into the shelter next to Ahjin, who was already asleep.

Ludik wrapped a blanket around himself and sat just inside his shelter for the best view, wrinkling his nose at the stench of wet fur and feathers.

What an awful day! He would be glad it was over, except they had failed again. At this rate, it would be winter before he got married, if war didn't prevent them entirely.

He looked across the clearing at the women's hut. Zefra's cloak still blocked his view to the interior. It was bad enough he couldn't sleep by Nemerra; he hated not being able to see her. He liked it better when they slept in the open.

Ludik leaned his head carefully against the shelter frame. This was the third day of their hunt, and there was still no end in sight. This should have been a simple chase, but self-defense had turned out to be murder. That wasn't progress.

Even if they caught him — or her — how would they stop someone who *wanted* to start trouble? War seemed more likely now. Grandpapa had been right.

Ludik banged his head against the branch in frustration. Water promptly dripped down his face.

Furballs. He wanted to go home and get married.

He could do that, if he convinced Nemerra to give up. They could turn over the chase to Gurryon and Ahjin. But then Ahjin couldn't marry them. And Ludik wasn't likely to convince Nemerra to abandon their responsibility now that it was more important than before.

Ludik frowned. It would sound like he didn't care if there were a war between the kindreds.

Even though no Cat in his right mind wanted to be in Dog territory, he had to go forward, had to catch the murderer. His village depended on him, and so did Nemerra.

He spent the rest of his watch planning different wedding bouquets.

In the shelter across from him, Lyell woke, shook himself with a yawn, and crawled to the entrance. He laid his muzzle on his paws and watched Ludik for a few minutes.

Ludik didn't say anything. Nothing would help at this point.

Lyell lifted his head and looked toward the women's shelter, then resettled himself.

"It's hard missing them, is it not?" Lyell said. "I'll take over now. You go dream of Nemerra."

He had used contractions. It was the first real sign of trust Ludik had heard from him. The thought of doing the same made Ludik's stomach bubble. How could he trust a Wolf?

But Lyell did give excellent advice. Ludik curled up in his blanket and took it.

In the morning, Nemerra woke Ludik with a soft kiss on the forehead. "The meal is almost ready," she whispered.

He sat up for a proper kiss.

Nemerra leaned out of reach and tapped his nose. "Go wash." She smiled and returned to the fire.

Ludik took another look. One shelter had already been turned into a fire to cook the cereal. Zefra obviously had enough energy this morning to make damp wood burn. The second shelter was collapsed into a tidy stack of firewood for the next travelers in the area.

Everyone but Gurryon was already awake. Ahjin dried his wings by the fire, and the women and Lyell basked under the strongest sunbeams.

Ludik choked back a laugh at Zefra's appearance. Her normal tan robe must still be wet, because she had borrowed a dress from Nemerra. The height difference between Zefra and his sweetheart was obvious, and he was sure the sedate Iskrin had never worn so many colors in her life, much less all at once. She usually had color only in her embroidered belt and her red hair.

He poked Gurryon. "Wake up. It's time to eat."

Gurryon finally stretched and opened his eyes. When he glanced out the shelter, he chuckled.

"Say nothing to Zefra," Ludik said, "or you might be the next stew."

Gurryon's shoulders shook as he folded his blanket and stuffed it into his pack. "I'll try."

Ludik packed his own belongings, and when both brothers left the shelter, he kicked it down before devouring his cereal.

"I had to put on new socks this morning," Zefra complained as she washed dishes. "The ones I wore yesterday were still cold and soggy. Does anything dry around here?"

"I don't have wet socks." Nia's round, green eyes grew even wider with fake innocence.

Zefra closed her eyes for a moment. With her long, black eyelashes shading the glint in her eyes, she said, "You do not wear socks, Nia."

"Well, barnacles, that does make it easier." Nia wiggled her bare, webbed toes in her sandals and chortled.

"I liked rain in the desert," Zefra continued. "I thought you were so lucky to have rain all the time. I did not know it got so cold and... wet." She held up her damp cloak and grimaced.

Lyell sat with a thump and hid his face in his arms, but his shoulders shook.

Gurryon dropped his spoon and howled with laughter.

Zefra shoved her dishes in her pack. "'Tis not funny. You can catch up when you have finished being rude."

She flung her cloak around her shoulders and stomped angrily from the clearing, holding up Nemerra's long dress to keep from tripping.

The sound of her squishy footsteps sent everyone into peals of laughter. Nemerra and Ahjin covered their mouths, and Lyell kept his head down. Nia and the brothers roared openly.

Nemerra was the first to stop laughing. "We'd better not let her get too far ahead," she said. "We don't want her to get lost or run into the killer by herself."

They quickly packed and followed Zefra. Gurryon's shoulders shook as they lengthened their stride between the dripping trees, no matter how many times Ludik shoved him.

It didn't take long to catch up to Zefra. She wasn't even walking anymore. She stood by the path and stared with her mouth clamped tight.

A line wavered along the muddy path, as if something heavy had been dragged. The prints of pointed boots marched along either side of it.

13.FOX

(CANID TERRITORY)

Two of my brothers were brought to this healing tent today. One of them had died on the way.

Torao, after The Battle of Sad Laughter

Zefra stood by the tracks in the muddy path, swallowing the last of the water in her second bag. She had already drained her first pouch while she waited for the others to stop laughing at her and catch up. Now that they were here, she smoothed the anger from her face. She should be too adult to stay angry at their childish mockery, especially considering more important matters.

Their detour was almost over. Four days back to Maon, a day for the wedding — she could be on a ship within a week and home before the first winter storms. If she gathered maps and supplies during the rains, she would be ready to work in spring. Anticipation rushed to her feet and made them twitch in her boots.

The only thing delaying her now was the immaturity of her traveling companions. Gurryon still smirked when he thought she was not looking, instead of focusing on the task at hand.

"What took you so long?" Zefra indicated the pointed boot prints. "Do you think those are the kind of boots that would smear to crescent marks in slippery mud? Could this be our killer?"

The prints were bigger than her own feet, but smaller than the men's, and the trail dragged in a fairly straight line into the woods. It was clear enough for her to follow in the early morning light, but waiting for the muscle of the group was more practical than tackling a killer by herself. Though she was competent, she was not invincible.

Zefra unbuckled her armor, used one of Nia's ribbons for a belt, and pulled a handspan of Nemerra's dress over the ribbon to shorten it for running. Then she refastened her armor and sword belt, ignoring Gurryon's snicker.

Lyell turned to follow the prints, loosening his knives in their sheaths. "I intend to find out if this is the right track. No killer gets to wander free in my woods."

"This could be the end of it, Nemerra," Ludik murmured. "If we can catch him, we can go home for our wedding. No more waiting!"

Nemerra smiled. "Oh, darling, isn't that wonderful?"

"But it's the wrong direction," Nia complained. "We need to head toward the ocean. There's no seaweed in the forest."

"There's no guarantee he kept going the same way," Ahjin pointed out. "That's why we've been following him rather than trying to cut off his path. It wouldn't do any good to reach the ocean and discover he went somewhere else."

"Perhaps you should leave the tracking to the experts," Zefra said.

She was surprised when Nia glared at her. Nia's talents lay in other areas, such as the ocean.

Nia turned up her nose and followed Lyell, spearing fallen leaves. The others formed a line, weapons ready, with Nemerra protected in the middle. Zefra sighed and took rear guard, trying to deduce how the truth was an insult. If this chase included sailing, Zefra would gladly yield to Nia's expertise.

They followed the trail for half a league. The prints appeared and disappeared depending on the thickness of the fallen leaves, but the drag mark cut through the layers, leaving a clear trail even for the novice trackers. Finally, the group reached a clearing where the tracks dead-ended at a strange cargo litter. No one was in sight.

Lyell pointed at the litter. "There is the cause of the drag mark."

The two poles that formed both the frame and the handles were separated on one end and tied together on the other, with leather stretched between them in a long triangle. The connected end of the poles sat in the drag track. The poles ran past the leather platform and ended as handles that rested on short, upright posts when not in use. A basket of sharp stakes and two large, wrapped bundles tied with twine sat on the litter.

"Stakes. That makes sense," Ludik said. "They could make a wound like the ones we've seen. And if the killer already carried them, he wouldn't need to cut a branch."

Zefra nodded. "'Tis more practical than our original speculation and explains why we never found a bloody branch discarded in the trees."

"He must have left his litter here while he chased the Fox across the border," Gurryon said. "That is why we didn't see the drag trail by Maon. It is easy enough to take a couple of stakes with him. Now he's come back to retrieve the litter. His prints say he's around here somewhere."

"We still don't know why he killed the Dogs," Ahjin reminded him. "Let's hear his side of the story before we do anything rash."

Lyell sniffed. "I smell raw meat. And Bear."

Zefra inhaled. Only a faint whiff reached her nose, not enough for identification. Having the Darrendrakar along was convenient.

"Do you think those packages are more bodies?" Nia asked.

"They had better not be," Lyell growled. He stalked toward the litter, knives drawn.

Nia shielded Ludik's sweetheart. "I've got Nemerra."

While Ludik, Gurryon, and Ahjin guarded the other directions, Zefra followed Lyell.

Lyell inspected the litter itself, then the stakes. "The litter smells like blood," he said, just loudly enough to reach their ears.

He frowned, resheathed one knife, and pulled a stake from the basket. The sharp end was discolored a dark red. He grabbed several more. Half of them had the same red stain. He dropped them back in the basket with a clatter, then poked at the other package, which squished under his finger.

"Ew," Nemerra said.

Zefra searched the rest of the litter for evidence. The worn handles were developing splinters, and something was snagged on one of them.

"Look." She wiggled free the chunk of red fur and handed it to Lyell.

"Fox fur," Lyell said. It sounded like a curse.

"This is your territory," Ahjin said. "How do you want to handle it?"

"I want to cut down the murderer where he stands, but I'll settle for dragging him back to justice," Lyell said. "With your permission, Ludik, since he killed one of yours, too."

"Go ahead," Ludik said. "You can give him what he deserves."

"I will give him..." Lyell's threat dissolved into muttered curses in his own language.

Instead of asking Nia for a translation, Zefra turned to look for other clues in the area.

"Now we have to actually find him," Ludik said. "Where do we look from here?"

"We should follow the footprints." Zefra pointed to prints that led away from the litter and into the forest. Ludik must be very upset to miss such an obvious trail.

"We can't all go," Ahjin said. "Someone has to stay here to protect Nemerra and the evidence."

"I am going," Lyell said.

"I am staying." Ludik's gaze was fixed on Nemerra.

"I will go," Zefra offered. She was probably the best visual tracker after Ludik, and her skills made a good complement to Lyell's nose. Though she could take care of herself, they ought to have one more person to help with the arrest. "Gurryon can come with us. Ahjin's wings are a liability in the trees."

Ahjin shrugged. "Fine with me."

"I'll go," Nia offered. "I can understand all of you and carry messages if you need something from the others."

Zefra nodded at the practical strategy.

As they turned to follow the footprints, someone came into view from the middle of the forest. Ludik shoved Nemerra behind a tree and guarded her with his body while the others also slid behind trees.

The short Canid had silver-streaked red hair and looked a bit older than Lyell. He hummed to himself as he walked between the trees, leaving pointy-toed footprints in the damp earth. A stake spun in endless circles, flipping from one hand to the other. As he did a little dance step, he threw the stake higher, spun around, and caught it behind his back with an extravagant flourish and a stomp of his pointed boots.

Zefra shook her head. Did murder bring such joy to his heart, or did he merely not care? And how could someone so inattentive be the fierce murderer they sought?

"Look at his hair," Lyell muttered from behind the tree next to Zefra. "He's a Fox. And those boots made the prints."

"Does his scent match?" Zefra whispered.

Lyell inhaled the wind blowing in their direction and winced. "His soap stinks too badly. I can't tell. But the litter smelled similar." He stepped from behind the tree.

Gurryon drew his knife and followed him. Zefra kept her saif sheathed and remained out of sight, hoping they could settle this without edged weapons. The idea was to capture the killer, discover his motives, take him back for trial, and prevent a war. If a dead suspect started yet another blood feud, the situation would not improve.

The man turned back around, caught sight of Lyell and Gurryon, and flipped the stake to an attack position.

Zefra would not be worried by such a pitiful weapon if she had not already seen two dead bodies killed by it. At least he had enough sense to be wary of weapons pointed at him.

Ahjin and Nia joined the two Darrendrakar in the open. Ludik left Nemerra behind the tree and stood with the others.

"Who are you?" The Fox looked between them, eyes widening at the sight of the outdwellers. "What are you? What are you doing here? You should not hunt here. This area is off-limits now." He stepped forward.

This was not going well. Zefra slid farther into the forest and circled around the clearing, keeping her staff close to her body so it did not tangle in the branches. If she snuck behind the Fox unnoticed, she could keep the suspect alive for questioning. She did not want to consider what Ludik might do if he thought Nemerra was in danger.

"Do not move," Lyell shouted. He threw one of his knives past the man's ear into a nearby tree.

The man ducked. "What are you doing?" he screamed. "Are you crazy? You cannot throw sharp things at people like that."

"I told you not to move," Lyell threatened.

"Movement is not cause for throwing knives," the man countered. "I did nothing to you." He took a step back from Lyell, shifting his grip on the stake again.

Zefra was close enough and out of time. She swung her staff. When it cracked against the man's head, he collapsed, dropping the stake.

Nemerra gasped and ran into the clearing, staring at the fallen Fox with hands over her mouth.

Zefra raised her staff and looked at Lyell. "Why argue with him when he has a weapon? Will someone throw me some rope?"

Gurryon handed Zefra rope from his pack.

"What will you do to him?" Nemerra asked.

"Now we turn him over to Lyell," Ludik gloated, "and hurry home." He wrapped his arm around Nemerra and leaned for a kiss.

"You could help me transport him to the nearest village," Lyell said. "Orrik is only a few hours away."

"I suppose we could," Ludik said. "We need to stop somewhere for the night, anyway, and it is easier to confine our prisoner in a building than the middle of the forest."

"We should at least make sure this is the right man," Nia said.

Zefra nodded at Nia. That was another sensible idea.

"He matches all our criteria," Lyell said. "Do you think more than one person fits such an odd description?"

"The litter smells Bearish," Ludik listed, "though he is a Fox. He wears pointed boots, carries branch-like stakes, and drags a litter loaded with meat through the forest. I do not know how you can get much closer to the clues."

"It does seem unlikely," Ahjin said, "but it's important to be sure."

Zefra tied the man's hands and feet and confiscated his knife. "I did not hit him hard enough to be asleep for long, so choose your questions quickly." They ought to be certain, so their case would be fireproof.

"I've already made up my mind," Lyell said. "We can take him to Orrik now."

"I am ready to go," Ludik said. "Should we wait for the Fox to wake up or drag him on his own litter?"

"Wait." Gurryon met Ludik's glare steadily. "I agree with Ahjin. We have to be sure."

"He'll lie about it," Ludik said. "Can't you be happy we caught him? Or if you insist, the Canids can question him when Lyell drags him back. Even Dogs can handle that."

Lyell bared his teeth in what was probably supposed to be a grin. Zefra had a smoking suspicion the Canids would question the Fox with more than mere words, despite the foolishness.

"Torture is unkind in general and unjust if the Fox is somehow innocent," she said. "And answers obtained under duress are more likely to be false than true. It is not practical to risk missing the truth because of violence and fear."

"I think I can help," Ahjin said. "Keep him from lying, or detect the truth, I mean. I do have a few resources at my disposal."

He removed his pack and rummaged through it, finally emerging with a green bag of seeds and a small green book.

"How many books do you have with you?" Nia asked.

"Not as many as you think," Ahjin said, "but it's a good thing now."

"If you think your plan will work, go ahead." Ludik pulled Nemerra back into his arms and scowled at the unconscious Fox.

Ahjin looked up at Lyell, who stared back, drawing himself to his full height.

Zefra rolled her eyes. What was it with men and posturing?

Ahjin's mouth twitched as he waved at the Felid brothers. "If I'm not intimidated by these two giants, then you won't scare me, either. Besides, I can fly away from you." He wiggled the tips of his wings.

Nia giggled.

Zefra frowned. That was not necessarily logical. Ludik and Gurryon were friendly, but Lyell was at best an uneasy ally. A little fear might be a reasonable precaution. How would Ahjin survive the politics of his new vocation if he did not learn to be wary?

Lyell barked a laugh. "If you think there is a feather of a chance" — he flicked Ahjin's wing — "of you determining the truth, I'll let you try before we take him to Orrik." He moved to stand near the prisoner, sharpening his knife.

"We caught him," Ludik murmured to Nemerra. "Another hour here, a brief stop in Orrik, and four days to home."

Zefra drew her saif and sat to wait for the Fox to regain consciousness.

14.FORESTER
(CANID TERRITORY)

Any Darrendrakar can petition their goddess. Darravani will bloom flowers in reply, which can be interpreted personally or with the help of the shamans.
Darrendran Religious Ceremonies

While the others guarded the Canid until he awoke, Ahjin sat on a stump and pored through a pocket version of Darravani's garden book until he found an appropriate plant for the experiment he wanted to try.

When the unconscious man stirred, Ahjin put down his book and picked up his bow. Everyone but Nemerra raised their weapons. As the man sat and held his bound hands to his head, Lyell loomed over him.

"We know about the Fox." He held up the tuft of fur Zefra had found in the litter poles. "And the others you murdered."

Ahjin frowned. It might be easier to get the truth if they didn't offend the man with their first statement.

"Murdered?" The red-headed man choked. "That is my fur," he said. "I caught my tail on the litter yesterday morning."

"Your tail?" Zefra asked.

"Yes, mine. Why does a scrap of fur make you think I murdered anyone?"

He jerked on the ropes around his wrists, then reached for his ankles. When Lyell raised his knife, the Fox stilled, though he kept talking. "What is going on here?"

"We found your tracks by a dead jackal two days ago." Ludik explained.

"I beg your pardon," the Fox-man gasped. "You did not!"

He sounded so appalled that Ahjin set his arrow across his knee and reached into his pack. Did he have the flower he needed in dried or seed form?

With his bow still in one hand, he rummaged through the packet of flower and herb bits Darravani had given him to use when he wanted to speak to her. It would be easier to involve Kassian, but that wouldn't be appropriate in this instance. Only Darravani's word would be trusted by the Fox, and probably by Lyell, too.

"Yes, we did." Lyell pointed back the way they had come. "The body was poorly hidden under a bush just past your footprints on the trail. We also found your prints leading to the stream where you washed off the blood so no one would see or smell it."

The Fox shook his head as if to clear it. "You are all crazy. You must be. I have not even seen a dead body recently, much less created one. What makes you think they were my footprints?"

"Fox paw prints by the trail, and pointy boot prints by the stream." Lyell pointed at the Fox's footwear. "And both of them had a drag line between them that smelled like Bear." He pointed at the cargo litter.

"All right, the fox prints might have been mine, I suppose, although I could confirm or deny it better if you told me exactly where you were. I walked a lot of trails this morning, and all this week, actually — without knowing there was a dead body, my goodness — but the boot prints are not mine. I always walk barefoot on stream banks. It is a good time to air out my feet, and it keeps my boots cleaner."

He lifted one foot. His highly polished boots showed a bit of trail dust, but there wasn't a speck of mud on them.

"What besides your litter makes a drag mark like that? And we have not met anyone else with those ridiculous boots. It has to be you." Ludik sounded desperate to settle the problem, and he clutched Nemerra's hand so tightly his knuckles paled.

Ahjin sympathized. If this Fox wasn't the killer, Ludik still couldn't go home and get married. The possibility must feel like torture.

The Fox threw his tied arms in the air. "I do not know who it is. I only know it is not me. And my litter smells like Bear because I bought it from the Ursids. A Bear made the thing. I spend a lot of time on the western border, and I deal with a lot of Bears. A Bear made my boots, too, so do not be surprised if they also smell like Bear. Now, will you at least stop pointing those arrows at me while we talk? You make me nervous, and I am answering your questions, am I not?"

Ahjin dropped the arrow back in his quiver. He wasn't ready to believe the Fox yet, but either he was outstandingly good at making up believable answers to odd questions at a moment's notice, or his guilt should be doubted.

Ludik let go of his bowstring but ran a finger over his arrowhead. Zefra sheathed her sword and took a two-handed grip on her staff instead, looking deceptively less deadly.

"Thank you," the Fox said. "I will sit here on this tree root with my hands in plain sight, and you all try not to get too excited. Now, please explain what started you on this absurd quest of yours. Murder, indeed! I have never been so much as accused of scaring people with a nasty look."

He scooted onto the root, leaning back against the tree trunk with a sigh.

"We have been chasing a murderer." Lyell did not sheathe his dagger or sit. "I intend to get him out of my district."

"We have come all the way from Maon in Felid territory," Ludik continued, "and have already found three bodies, two with wounds made with something like these stakes."

"Three bodies?" The Fox swallowed visibly. "Well, it was not me. I am a forester. I use these stakes in my work, but not for killing. I mark where to cut trees, or where other work needs to be done. There is no point dragging my big saw and other equipment all through the forest when I do not know where I need them. After I mark everything, I come back with help and get the real work done. And I do not even go hunting, if I can help it. I hate killing things. I prefer my meals to show up on my plate ready to eat."

Lyell dangled one stake in front of the man's face. "That does not explain the bloodstains on these."

The forester recoiled from the stake as if it were poison. "The red is clay, you dolt. I reuse my stakes as long as possible, and the last time I used these was farther north in an area with red clay. Not blood! Ew."

"That is a good lie, but I do not believe it," Lyell said.

Ahjin stacked the seed packet on top of the green book and waited. When the others calmed, he'd be ready.

The Fox dropped his head in his bound hands and muttered to himself for several seconds. He finally raised his head and glared at Lyell with a clenched jaw. "Why not?"

"I can smell the blood," Lyell said. "We have caught you at last."

Ahjin couldn't smell anything, but he wasn't Darrendrakar, either.

"You are Canid, are you not?" the Fox said. "Move *away* from the litter and stick the stake under your nose, you idiot."

Lyell sneered, took one step from the litter, and waved the stake dramatically under his nose. His face fell. He grabbed another stake and smelled it, and then another and another.

"Oh. Well, we still have more evidence you have not explained."

"Like what?" The Fox dropped his head against the tree and closed his eyes.

"Like these packages on your litter that smell like blood and raw meat. I am guessing they are either a new body or the trophy pieces you cut from your previous victims."

"That is the most disgusting thing I have heard all day," the forester said without opening his eyes. "And I have heard a lot of disgusting things in the last ten minutes. Go ahead and open the packages. Go on. I will wait here for you." He raised his bound hands with a faint grin.

Lyell strode to the litter, cut the twine, and ripped open both packages.

Ahjin winced in anticipation, but one bundle held only chopped logs and small branches. The squishy one held a large pile of dead rabbits.

"Why do you wrap your wood?" Nia asked.

Zefra stirred the wood with her staff. The branches rattled together as she rearranged all of them, revealing only more wood.

"It rained last night. I wanted to keep it dry to make a nice fire tonight." The Fox sighed heavily. "At this point, I would be happy to be alone for a quiet meal and some undisturbed sleep."

Nia made a sympathetic noise. Ahjin smiled to himself. The Fox already had another person on his side.

"And the rabbits?" Gurryon asked.

"I have been following a poacher and emptying his traps. It is part of my job. I did not even kill the poor things, much less a person or three."

"But it has to be you," Ludik whined.

"It is most definitely not me," the Fox insisted.

Lyell ran a finger along the edge of his knife. "How can we believe you?"

The Fox pressed himself against the tree, wide-eyed.

Ahjin cleared his throat and stood before it was too late. "There's a better way to settle this. Will you take Darravani's word for the truth?"

"Yes!" the Fox exclaimed. "Yes, let us ask her, please." He extended his tied hands toward Ahjin.

Lyell's "yes" came from between bared teeth.

Ahjin pulled a few more sheets of paper from his bag. He either needed to talk to the gods about getting a few more supplies, or he needed to stock his island market with actual merchants and useful goods.

"Lyell and Ludik, which of you wants to speak on the accuser's side?"

"It is your territory," Ludik said. "You choose."

Lyell held out a hand for a piece of paper. "I will do it."

Ahjin gave another piece to the Fox and returned the rest to his bag. He gave the charcoal to Lyell.

"You first. I want you both to write your version of the story on the paper. I'll ask Darravani to tell us which is right."

Lyell dragged the charcoal across the parchment with angry jerks.

The Fox narrowed his eyes. "Forgive me, but you are not Darrendrakar. What makes you think Darravani will listen to you?"

"She will listen," Gurryon said. "As Maon's apprentice shaman, I guarantee it. But if you do not want him, I can petition her, too."

"Oh, feel free to convince me this outkindred will be more fair and effective than a Cat." The Fox smiled crookedly at Ahjin.

Nia giggled. "Oh, let me tell him," she begged. Without waiting for permission, she continued. "This is His Holiness, Ahjin Machol, the new Mouth of the Gods. He could introduce you to the gods if you wanted." She winked. "I wouldn't ask, if I were you."

Ahjin shook his head. She was right, but not as funny as she thought.

Nemerra spoke over Nia's head. "If you are worried about Darravani taking his side, do not be. She is still our goddess and would never betray us."

Lyell finished writing and handed the charcoal to the Fox with a flourish.

"The mouth of gods?" the Fox asked Ahjin. "You seem a little... young. What makes you qualified for the job? And if you want me to write, untie my hands."

Ahjin shrugged, feeling his face flush. "I'm old enough for the gods to conscript, and it wasn't my idea."

He knelt and untied the prisoner's hands but left his feet bound. He didn't want to discuss his qualifications or lack of them.

"And what happened to your face?"

"That wasn't my idea, either," Ahjin said. "Are you doing this or not?"

"Hrmph." The Fox wrote one line with an eye on Lyell. He held the charcoal above the paper for a moment, then shrugged and handed both back to Ahjin. "I am ready."

"Is that all you want to write?" Ahjin asked. "We can wait for you to explain as much as you'd like." For everyone involved to accept the results, he must be as fair as possible.

"It says 'I did not kill anyone.' What else is needed? I am ready," the Fox repeated.

"If you'll both fold your papers in half." Ahjin waited for them to obey. "Lyell, put yours at the base of this tree, and Zefra, put the Fox's by that tree. Now, everyone back away, thank you."

Zefra stepped beside the Fox to guard him with her staff.

The Fox folded his arms, leaned back against the tree, and looked longingly at his tied ankles.

Ahjin reached into his pocket and removed the dried rhubarb leaf he'd dug out of his kit, placing it on the ground halfway between the two papers.

"Darravani," he said, as if she stood right in front of him, "we'd like some advice, please."

He stepped back with the others and stuck his thumbs in his belt, waiting for her to notice his appeal.

Nothing happened.

Lyell opened his mouth to protest, and Ahjin put his finger to his lips. Darravani appreciated respect and patience.

The rhubarb leaf and both pieces of paper suddenly sank into the ground and disappeared.

Lyell snapped his mouth shut, and the Fox gasped.

Everyone held their breath while they waited. A moment later, a white chrysanthemum sprouted in front of the tree that had been designated the Fox's.

Ahjin pulled out his book and showed everyone the pertinent page. "The Fox spoke truth."

"Truth," Gurryon confirmed.

"Truth?" Ludik complained. His shoulders slumped.

Nemerra wrapped her arms around him and whispered in his ear.

The Fox whooped for joy. "I told you so." He took his knife from Zefra's open hand, cut his ankles loose, and jumped to his feet. "Now that you know I am innocent," he continued, "do you mind leaving? I want to get back to work, and you make me nervous."

He picked up the stake he had dropped and tossed it into the basket. Zefra and Nia rewrapped and tied his packages for him.

Ahjin watched the Darrendrakar, but Lyell merely slammed his dagger back into its sheath while Ludik glared.

Nemerra handed the Fox one of the sweet biscuits left from breakfast. "We are sorry for disturbing you. You seem like a nice man, and I am glad you do not kill people."

"Apology accepted," the Fox said. "If there is a murderer roaming around, I understand why you are anxious to catch him. But next time, be a little more careful when you accuse people, hmm? Not everyone will take it as calmly as I did."

He ate the biscuit in two bites. "Delithuth, thankth," he mumbled with a full mouth. He grabbed the front poles of the litter and trundled into the forest.

Nia glared at Lyell. "I told you it was the wrong direction. Are you ready to head for the ocean?"

"Now what do we do?" Ludik asked.

Ahjin retied his escaped curls behind his neck. "We've been foolish. Not only is a fox not large enough to make the impression in the bed of leaves we found, the murderer is dragging around the dead fox's tail. If he's being careless with it, that could leave the hairs we've found. Now that we know the footprints belonged to our innocent forester, the killer could be anybody. Probably Dog or Bear, based on the scent."

"I haven't been to Orrik in a couple of years," Lyell said, "but they used to have a large guard company. They could help."

"More Dogs?" Ludik complained. "Why would they help us hunt down one of their own?"

Ahjin reached up to thump the back of his head. "Because," he said, "like our *host*, they will be interested in the truth and in the safety of their people."

Lyell glared at Ludik. "You can have them help search a greater area and find who really did it, Fox or not. You might even turn over the hunt to them and go home."

Ludik smiled at Nemerra. "A tempting idea. I will think about it."

"You?" Ahjin repeated. "Not we? You won't continue with us?"

That was good news, mostly. If they had convinced Lyell they were trustworthy, they had a chance at convincing the other Dogs. And with help from Orrik, they wouldn't need Lyell.

"I want to see my wife and new babies, if you don't mind," Lyell said. "And after that, I need to get back to my patrol."

"I thought you didn't trust us to roam around alone," Nia teased.

Lyell flicked Nia's braids. "You won't be alone. Any searchers that join you can keep an eye on you. Besides, I suppose you are acceptable. For a bunch of Cats and outkindred, that is."

He swiped a biscuit from Nemerra and crammed it in his mouth. "Thith rilly ith delithuth."

"Thank you," Nemerra said. "I'd love to trade recipes with Ruka."

Lyell nodded and licked his fingers.

Ludik squared his shoulders. "Are we ready to go, then?"

Nemerra snuck her arm around his waist.

Ahjin repacked his books and flowers and slid his pack between his wings. "We're ready."

"My village is a day to the west," Lyell said. "Orrik is closer to the southwest, and the local patrols might have seen something. I'll take you there before I go home."

"We should trade for more supplies, too," Zefra said. "We're getting short on food."

"That explains Nia," Lyell said, "but what about the two hulks there?" He motioned toward Ludik and Gurryon.

Ahjin grinned. He got teased for being short, though he was average for an Iojif, so the change of flight pattern was refreshing.

"I'm sorry," Zefra said. "I must have used the wrong word. I meant we're running out of food, not that we're shrinking."

Nia giggled, and Lyell howled with laughter.

"You said it right, Zefra," Gurryon assured her. "You have to keep in mind that having one greater sense, like smell, is often offset by another weaker one. Like a feeble sense of humor."

Lyell stopped laughing. Ahjin struggled to drop his grin.

Nia laughed harder. "Come walk with me, Zefra, and I'll explain a few things to you."

"Come walk with me, Gurryon, and I will explain a few things to you," Lyell growled. He beckoned to Gurryon with one hand and touched a knife with the other.

Gurryon grinned and adjusted his grip on his staff. "I already understand all I need to know."

"I doubt it." Lyell brushed past Gurryon with an offended sniff. "Everyone, turn right after that fallen tree."

Ahjin's smile faded as he followed. Lyell's continued escort was a good idea, since everyone thought Ahjin was too young to be who he claimed. Would he be an old man with a long beard before anyone trusted his competence or was willing to come work for him?

If Lyell could convince Orrik's patrol to help them hunt, Ahjin would worry about his own reputation later.

15. ORRIK

(CANID TERRITORY)

The Felid kindred are of three breeds: the smaller Felines, the large Panthera, and the long-toothed Makarodonts.
A Brief Sketch of Mysterious Darrendra

Though they were only temporarily diverting from the killer's trail, it still felt like a reprieve to Nia. Now she could enjoy the forest scenery on the way to Orrik and have pleasant conversations that did not include death or blood. As soon as they got to the village, the others could ask about killers and Bear scents and funny tracks, and she would find someone nice to chat with about the weather or food or local music. There was still a chance for this to be a fun adventure.

By the time they reached the gardens and orchards on the outskirts of Orrik in time for lunch, she was quite cheerful, despite their mission.

That changed when a large, brown-spotted hound darted from behind a tree and barked in her face, "Stop there!"

Nia skidded to a halt and held up her hands. "Hey, buddy, calm down. We won't hurt you. Sit, dog. Heel."

The dog barked even louder and herded her backward into the rest of the group. "Strangers, strangers!"

He was a young dog, brave, obviously headstrong, and maybe not too smart.

"Calm down," she tried again.

It was frequently hard to talk to animals, even in their own language. They didn't think the same way as people. This one was obsessed with alerting someone and stopping them.

Gurryon stepped in front of her and addressed the dog in trade tongue. "I am sure the rest of your patrol has heard you by now, so you can stop barking. We are not going anywhere. Look, we will sit and wait." He sat, pulling Nia with him.

While everyone else sat, Lyell questioned the dog about any strange visitors or scents, keeping his hands conspicuously away from his knives.

As the dog calmed and answered in complete, although uninformative, sentences, Nia blushed.

"Oh, he's not a *dog* dog." If he had spoken more intelligently earlier, she would have known.

"No, Nia, he's Canid," Nemerra whispered. "You speak animal languages? Didn't you hear the difference?"

"Not really," Nia muttered. "I understand every language so automatically that if I don't listen specifically for the differences, I don't hear them." She looked at the Dog, who still had his teeth bared. "I hope his entire village isn't this unfriendly."

"They could be," Ludik said pessimistically. "But some guards are touchy, and that one is young. Don't worry yet."

"And speaking of guards." Ahjin pointed at the dozen men and a few women now walking through the trees toward them, weapons in hand.

"Let me handle it." Lyell stepped toward the approaching group and explained their errand.

Nia remembered her job and whispered translations of their Canid speech to the others.

The soldiers wore identical insignia over a mismatched variety of colorful Darrendran tunics. They slouched, half-bored, and denied finding similar scent or tracks to the ones the Felids were following. When Lyell asked permission to search the grounds, they jerked to indignant attention.

"Absolutely not." Their stocky, dark-haired leader stalked forward until Lyell retreated almost to Gurryon's knees. "Go back the way you came. You are not welcome here."

"Yet more guards telling us we're unwanted," Gurryon muttered.

"It must be your fault," Lyell said. "I never have problems when I am alone."

Gurryon hissed until Nia kicked him.

"It seems we cannot leave the hunt to them," Ludik murmured. "They do not even want to listen."

"Can we recruit help from the village to search?" Ahjin asked. "We'd be happy to leave as soon as possible, so if you have anyone ready to come with us, we could go now."

The patrol leader shook his fist. "I already told you no one is interested in helping you. And do not speak to me, outkindred."

The other guards raised their weapons and yelled. The barking hound went crazy at their feet.

Nia stopped listening after the first handful of insults. They weren't imaginative, anyway. The Nokai sailors at the annual cursing competition were much better.

"If you would listen," Lyell started.

One of the guards stuck a dagger under Lyell's chin until the Wolf closed his mouth.

"It seems we cannot trust you warmongering foreigners to obey," the patrol leader said. "We will have to try something else. What do you say to a trial?"

The thunderous reply of howls made Nia cover her ears. She stared at Lyell in distress, but he merely scowled and watched the soldiers with narrowed eyes. So much for Ludik's suggestion not to worry yet. A little worry seemed appropriate.

The guards hauled everyone to their feet and escorted them toward the village. The stupid hound nipped at Nia's heels the whole way, and Ahjin wouldn't let her kick the mutt. He based his long, whispered argument on calming interkindred animosity, but she gave in because her sandals didn't protect against teeth. She really needed to talk to Nemerra about new boots.

The orchard thinned just before the first houses. Walking into the village with drawn bows at their backs ruined the excitement of visiting somewhere new. The village seemed nice enough, moderate-sized, with mostly wooden buildings. Many houses had flowers in window boxes or around the front steps. As the patrol escorted the visitors down the main street, the brightly colored doors and shutters made a pretty picture even after the villagers slammed them shut.

"Friendly bunch," Lyell said.

"We didn't do anything to them," Nia protested.

One of their guards poked the end of his bow into Lyell's back. "Shut up."

Lyell raised his hands higher and made a face. "Ow. Dogged, aren't they?" He winked at Nia.

Gurryon shook his head subtly.

Nia didn't laugh. This wasn't going well, and Lyell's jokes weren't helping this time.

"How are dogs and trees alike?" Lyell asked.

Nobody answered him. Nia shook her head emphatically, but he ignored the warning.

Lyell grinned. "They are both wooden under their bark."

One of the guards bashed Lyell's head. Lyell went down like a stunned fish, despite the twins' attempt to catch him.

Nia opened her mouth to yell at the Dogs but found her curses muffled by Zefra's hand.

Nemerra tugged on Nia's elbow and whispered desperately in Felid, "Be quiet."

Two guards threw Lyell's arms across their shoulders and dragged him to the base of the stairs of a stone building. Their comrades shoved Nia and the others to the same place.

Guard House and Jail, said the sign above the door. That was not a nice sign. It should say Inn and Bakery, in Nia's opinion. Was Ludik smart enough to worry *now*?

"Hey, Captain!" the patrol leader shouted.

A minute later, a burly man with heavy jowls stomped out the door at the top of the stairs. A fancy badge hung on his multi-colored shoulder in the same place Gurryon's did. Instead of Darravani's tree, it showed a crossed sword and knife.

"What do we have here?"

"We caught trespassing hooligans, Captain. They would not go away when we generously offered to let them go, so we brought them back for a trial. If they will not leave, they are obviously up to no good."

Nia crossed her arms. Someone was up to no good, but it wasn't her friends. When they had a chance, she'd ask Ludik if poisoned wells could cause insanity. Maybe that explained the crazy Dogs.

The guard captain thumped down the stairs, glanced at Lyell's dumped body, and eyed the rest of them.

"A trial sounds like a good idea, but you know the headman does not want to be disturbed today for piddling trespassers. I will question them myself, in case they are hiding greater crimes. Which of you miscreants is the leader of this group?"

"I am," Ludik said. "We did not mean to trespass, and we mean no harm. We are chasing a killer who murdered at least two Dogs and a Cat. If you would help us track him, it would be appreciated, but otherwise, let us go so we can find him. You do not want his sort running free around here, do you?"

"Watch your smart mouth. What do these outkindred have to do with anything?"

Ludik simplified the long story. "This is Ahjin, the Mouth of the Gods, and his friends."

Nia nodded. That was wise. The captain wouldn't care about Ludik's wedding, and Ahjin was the biggest authority they had. It would help if the captain were impressed by His Holiness.

"I call upon you," Ahjin said, "in the name of the gods, to help us in our search."

He held himself straight, but Nia saw his clenched fists. Considering how much he hated his job, he must detest trying to awe someone with his rank.

The captain howled with laughter until he had to lean against the railing to support himself. Other guards laughed almost as hard. The hound rolled hysterically in the dusty street until his spots turned gray.

"You do not speak for the gods," the captain gasped. "That is the most imaginative lie I have heard all week. Do you have any more?"

"I can prove it." A slow flush crept up Ahjin's face. His scars showed starkly against the added color.

The captain stopped laughing and sneered into Ahjin's face. "Now why would an ugly cur like you ever be chosen by the gods for anything but Bear bait?"

The hound continued to snicker until his tongue slobbered in the dirt.

Nia grabbed Ahjin's hand and squeezed. Lyell had already been inca-
pacitated. This boorish officer obviously had no sense of humor or
decency. Now would be a good time for Ahjin to practice the diplomacy
he'd learned while mediating for the gods, especially if the guards weren't
impressed by his prestige.

"I can get a message from Darravani for you." Ahjin reached for his
pack, but stopped when one of the guards pricked him with an arrow.
"I'm only looking for my seed bag. If you'd prefer, you can get it for me.
It's the green one on top, just under the flap."

"Planting a seed you choose proves nothing," the captain said. "It
seems you are determined to compound one lie upon another. I think we
do need a trial. Throw them in jail, boys, and let us find the headman!"

The guards howled again and swarmed Nia and her friends. They
dragged Lyell and jostled the others up the stairs, into the building, and
downstairs again to a small dungeon. Lyell's heels thumped on every step.
At least it wasn't his hard head banging on the floor.

The basement was nice enough for a dungeon. The cells had hard,
narrow cots, but the lanterns were lit, and more light came through the
barred window. No obvious instruments of torture decorated the room,
unless you counted the desk piled high with scrolls and accompanied by
a chair that looked as uncomfortable as the beds.

Their packs were thrown into a heap in the far corner. Nia chattered
as much as she dared while the guards confiscated the prisoners'
weapons. Her babble distracted them enough they overlooked the
hidden knife in Ludik's boot.

The girls were shoved together in the cell closest to the window. The
guards divided Ludik and Gurryon into different cells — to keep the
look-alikes from mischief, they said — and debated how to allocate Lyell
and Ahjin.

"Put the Wolf with me," Ludik said. "I am... a healer. Let me fix his
head. Please. You do not want him to die before the big trial, do you?"

The soldiers dithered until Ahjin cleared his throat and sidled into
Gurryon's cell, hands up. He smiled, lay on the nearest cot, and closed his
eyes.

Nia hid a grin. Whenever Ahjin looked so innocent, someone was in
for trouble. She didn't see how they would escape this situation, but with
Ahjin on her side, they'd manage somehow.

The soldiers shrugged and dropped Lyell into Ludik's cell.

"May I have my healing supplies, please?" Ludik asked. "They are right in the top of my pack."

"No." The guards locked the cell doors and left.

Ludik dragged Lyell to a cot and sat beside him. "Dogs are stupid," the healer muttered as he laid his hands on the Wolf's head.

Ahjin sat up. "What do we do next? Whatever the plan, I don't think it will include me hiring workers here. I've never seen such hostile people in my life. Why are they so paranoid?"

Nia clutched the bars. "I think it's bad water. We should wait to talk to the headman. Maybe he'll be more reasonable."

Her wild imagination suggested several unpleasant alternatives if their leader was also irrational.

"It probably isn't the water," Ludik said, "but if the headman isn't any wiser, we'll need Lyell in working condition. It will take me a while to heal his concussion, especially with none of my medicines, so we might as well wait." He cast a nasty glance at the stairs and turned back to Lyell.

"What if we just leave?" Zefra asked. "Can we escape?"

"Not right now," Nia said. "We don't know where we're going, we aren't familiar with the patrol schedule, we don't have our things, we're too tired, and Lyell is unconscious. I think that's a few too many obstacles, don't you? Why don't we wait until morning and see how our trial goes? They should let us go when we explain." She shoved her worries to the back of her mind and smiled cheerfully.

Ahjin lay back on the cot. "Then we wait. Wake me when someone comes."

Zefra removed her boots and spread her stockings across her cot. She ran her hands down one, over and over, then flipped it and repeated the process on the other side.

"What are you doing?" Nia asked.

"If we're stuck here for a while, I want dry stockings." Zefra switched to the other one. When her magically warm hands had dried both of them, she pulled them back onto her feet.

"I will take the floor," she offered. She pulled the extra length of Nemerra's dress out of her belt to cover her feet and rolled up in her cloak under the window.

Nemerra took the other cot, pulling the threadbare blanket as high as it would go.

Dead seaweed, this was boring. Nia wandered to the cell corner and stood on tiptoe, singing to herself as she peered out the window. More pretty houses. Flowers, trees. People walked past and stared. Some of them turned and walked the other way. Others pointed and made rude comments.

Nia grunted. They didn't know her, so maybe they could be excused for assuming she was a felon. Did she look like a dangerous criminal? She couldn't possibly look dangerous, on her tiptoes and still barely tall enough to see out the window.

Ooh, a curly-haired dog with a waving tail wandered down the street.

"Hi, there," Nia said in her friendliest voice.

He perked an ear at the sound of her voice and moved closer, finally sticking his head through the bars to look inside the jail.

Nia waved at him. He was the first person who had come close enough for a conversation. "How are you today? Isn't it a lovely day?"

The dog pulled back his head, raised a leg, and watered the flowers outside the window. When he finished, he sauntered down the road, jauntily wagging his tail.

Nia turned around and stared at Gurryon. "Please tell me that was a *dog* dog."

He turned away and lay down, pulling his knees to his chest to fit on the short cot.

"I do not like this village," Nia muttered. "Everyone is so rude."

It was obviously time to worry. Had all the Dogs gone crazy? Could she do anything to improve their chances of a fair trial?

16. TRIAL

(ORRIK, CANID TERRITORY)

Each village has its own headman (or woman) and local council, which serve under a kindred council. The temple priests oversee interkindred matters.

A Brief Sketch of Mysterious Darrendra

As he spent several hours trying to heal Lyell, Ludik's frustration grew. He'd never mended a concussion with his healing magic before and had to guess as he went along. If he had access to his pack, he would have mixed a medicine to help, as Akamu had taught him. The only blessing now was that a jail full of sleeping people was quiet enough for him to concentrate as he fumbled with his still unfamiliar magic.

In his brief experiences in Iskra, he had learned only the most basic magical skills. His first lesson had been limited to "think about him healing well." Since then, he'd learned to mentally feel damage as an incorrect texture in his patients' bodies. Touching the injured areas helped, when possible. Ludik ran his fingers over the goose-egg on Lyell's head and did his best to smooth the roughness inside the Wolf's mind with his magic.

Hunting was easier and more fun, both good reasons to keep his old job and resist the new position as the village healer.

While Ludik continued the healing, one of the guards returned. All the sleepers except Lyell woke to watch him. The soldier sat at the overflowing desk and worked his way through stacks of records. After a while, he cursed and shoved the scrolls on the floor.

Nia winked at Ahjin and leaned against her cell bars. "Oh, that must be so frustrating," she cooed to the guard in trade tongue. "Why do they have a nice, strong man like you shuffling records? You should protect the village."

The guard was a foot and a half taller than Nia, and his belly made him even bigger. He puffed out his chest and replied in the same language. "Yeah, I am the best. But someone has gotta do this, and Captain is busy. He relies on me to run the place because I always do what he says."

If he ran the place, then his impression of them could be important. If Nia made friends with the soldier, maybe he'd speak up for them when they talked to the headman. Ludik glanced at Ahjin, who raised an eyebrow, apparently of the same opinion.

Nia chatted a storm of flirtatious silliness through her jail bars while the fat guard worked. After an hour, they talked like old friends, and he laughed at all her jokes.

While Ludik concentrated on healing and the others watched Nia, Zefra sat on the cot closest to the window, sunlight pouring over her, and observed the soldiers patrolling around the jail.

When Ludik had done as much to help the Wolf as possible, he left Lyell in a healing sleep and dozed until the mongrel guards announced their return with raucous calls. Two of them clattered down the stairs, making enough noise to wake all the sleepers, even Lyell. Everyone sat up on their cots except Lyell, who put his hands to his head and watched.

The short guard carried a tray with seven small bowls and cups of water. The tall one had a long sword strapped at his waist and a dagger in his hands.

"You are in luck," the tall guard chortled. "The headman agreed to hear your case tomorrow."

The short guard slid the food and water under the bars. "We will return for the bowls in a few minutes, so eat quickly."

Both guards left, as did the soldier at the desk.

Lyell struggled upright, and Ludik handed one of their cell's bowls to the Wolf.

Nia jiggled the thick gray mush. "This is disgusting. And they didn't give us spoons."

Gurryon grimaced at his own bowl. "Spoons can be sharpened into a weapon. Of sorts."

"You will taste the food less if you swallow it fast." Zefra demonstrated, lowering an empty bowl a minute later. "'Tis not that bad, just very bland."

Nemerra cringed as she copied Zefra. Ludik tried to do the same, but it took him three attempts. He didn't want to know what Zefra had eaten in the past that made this palatable.

"I'm still hungry," Nia murmured.

Ludik ignored his own complaining stomach.

Zefra pulled on her boots and stood. "Your stomach will growl, but we will be gone from here tomorrow, and it takes days of scant meals to harm you."

Ludik hoped she wasn't still speaking from experience. He turned to his patient.

"Lyell, how do you feel?"

"Mmm," the Wolf said, unhelpfully. He gulped his terrible mush and made a face, then rubbed the back of his head.

Ludik helped Lyell work himself to his feet and stroll around the cell. He was still wavering when the guards returned and blew out all the lamps but the smallest one above the desk.

In the morning, two guards brought the morning meal, more of the gray glop from the night before. Ludik gulped it as fast as possible, saving his water to wash out his mouth.

After the meal, the guards took the dishes upstairs. When they returned, there were a dozen guards: one for each of the women, two for each of the men, and an extra to give orders. The men's hands were bound behind their backs. Ahjin winced as his wings were smashed against his back.

When the guards got to the women's cell, Ludik tensed. If they hurt

Nemerra, it wouldn't matter how much rope they had wrapped around him, he'd string them up by their mangy tails.

Fortunately for the guards' continued existence, they were kinder to the women. Ludik glared at the guard who held Nemerra's arm, trying to drill a warning through the back of the Dog's head.

Nemerra smiled at Ludik and patted the guard's hand. Her elegance made it look as if he escorted her to a festival rather than a trial.

"Where are we going?" Nia asked. "Is it far? Do we get to go outside for some fresh air? Is your judge in a good mood this morning?"

The guard shook her. "Shut your mouth, or I will shut it for you."

Ludik watched Lyell, prepared to protest if it looked like he wouldn't make the trip to the council house, but the guards only took them upstairs to a large room at the back of the building.

The room held a makeshift desk at one end and two rows of chairs in the middle. The patrol captain stood by the desk. Villagers peered through the windows on three walls, between the shoulders of the armed guards that ringed the room.

Ludik glanced at his friends. No, they still looked like themselves and not like ravening monsters. Had something terrified this village, or was it merely a sign of the unreasoning hatred he expected from paranoid Dogs?

Their escorts shoved the Darrendrakar into the front row of chairs and the outkindred behind them. Ludik leaned a little sideways until he felt the brush of Nemerra's shoulder against his arm.

Finally, an elderly man walked past them and sat at the desk. He had soft eyes and wavy white hair, and his tunic was rumpled. He looked kind and thoughtful and very unlike the boorish guards.

After the headman yawned, he looked at the captain. "Please explain about this invasion. I will be unhappy if I woke early for an imaginary threat."

The guard captain and patrol leader took turns reciting a fictional report full of supposed verbal threats and outkindred threatening guards with weapons.

Ludik and Gurryon tried to rise to their feet, but the guards held them down.

"That entire story is a lie," Ludik protested, swallowing the insults he wanted to hurl at the guards. "We never threatened anyone. We are not invaders. There *is* no invasion. We have been authorized to retrieve someone who killed a Cat and at least two Dogs. Once we find him, we will leave your territory immediately. We wanted help from you but will settle for a few answers."

The headman yawned again and propped his head on his fist. "We will return to your questions later. Please, convince me our guards overreacted. Your entrance into this territory was authorized by whom?"

Gurryon turned his shoulder to show his shaman-apprentice badge. "The shaman and headman of Maon sent us."

"Hush, Cat." The headman closed his eyes. "We do not recognize the authority of the Felids. They have always hated us. Does anyone else have an acceptable answer?"

"I am a border guard from Durriel." Lyell had a touch of a slur in his speech. "I told them they could cross the border to continue their search, and I escorted them to keep them out of trouble."

Ludik nodded, a little surprised the Wolf was defending them against his own people.

"It does not seem to have worked, has it? And Durriel has no authority over this village." The headman shook his head and straightened. "Three Felids and three outkindred, wandering unauthorized through Canid territory on a flimsy excuse. And all of them armed and armored. Innocent travelers do not need weapons. It looks like an invasion to me. We must take steps to protect our village from the bloodthirsty Cats."

The patrol leader and the guard captain smiled at each other and gripped their weapons. An excited murmur spread through the guards along the walls.

Lyell tried again, desperation creeping through the slur in his voice. "I was with them when they found one of the dead Dogs. His wedding chain is in my pack, or I can take you to his grave. I have seen most of the evidence and am convinced their story is true. Their weapons and armor are protection against the killer they seek. He already murdered three and would not balk at a few more deaths."

Ludik nodded again. Bringing Lyell with them had been a better idea than he would have believed at the border.

"Adding a renegade Wolf to the story does not make the Cats' lies more believable," the headman gently chided. "I tell you, bringing weapons into our lands is a declaration of war."

Ludik frowned. How could they disbelieve one of their own so easily? He looked hopefully at the fat guard Nia had befriended, but the soldier stared at the wall, steadfastly ignoring the prisoners.

Ahjin groaned behind Ludik. "Excuse me. Darravani knows we are here and approves of our errand. Is that enough authority for you?"

"And who are you to say Darravani approves of you, outkindred?" the headman asked. "You are not one of her people."

"I'm Ahjin Machol, the Mouth of All the Gods." In a nearly inaudible voice, Ahjin muttered, "If that helps anything."

The guards burst out laughing. The headman covered his face with his hands, shoulders trembling. After the room calmed, the headman lowered his hands.

"You are the Mouth of the Gods. All the gods. Including Darravani?" His mouth twitched. "You are obviously not Darrendrakar. Even if you did not have wings, I know you are a stranger by your fable about Darravani uniting with the other gods. Why should we believe that lie?"

Ahjin's feet shuffled behind Ludik. "Ask your shaman to confirm my identity. All of them should have gotten word from Darravani."

The headman covered his eyes sadly. "Our shaman and his apprentices died in the earthquakes two months ago. We have not replaced them yet."

"I have seen him communicate with the gods, including Darravani," Lyell said.

His slur was getting worse. Ludik squinted at him, checking the size of his pupils. They were growing uneven again. Ludik had apparently not healed his concussion. He wasn't a good enough healer for anyone to depend on him. Staying a hunter was definitely a better idea.

"I think it says more about your gullibility than his identity, Wolf," the headman continued. "You are too stupid to understand you were tricked. Even if Darravani would talk to an outkindred, and she would not, she certainly would not talk to an ugly pup. She would look for someone older and more dignified." He brushed his white hair back from his face and smiled.

Lyell snarled until a guard slapped him.

A single tear ran down Nemerra's face, and Ludik leaned harder against her shoulder. She was braver than he had known, but even her courage had limits.

He glared at the mangy Dogs. When one touched his knife and scowled back, Ludik jerked his gaze to his knees and held his breath. He couldn't afford to antagonize the guards when he couldn't defend himself or the others.

"I'll prove it to you," Ahjin offered. "It would be easier if you untied my hands, but even if you don't, it will just take a little longer. Oh, Iraja-han—"

Two thuds echoed behind Ludik, and Ahjin's voice stopped. Ludik concentrated on not shifting to jaguar and tearing out the guards' throats.

"You didn't need to hit him!" Nia protested. "Won't you at least pick him up off the floor?" She fell silent when a guard moved toward her.

This situation was rapidly going to the dogs. Ludik winced. The Felid saying had never been so accurate before. More importantly, how could they escape this mess?

The others were all wisely frozen in place.

He was supposed to be the leader. Ludik took a calming breath and tried again. "Please let us explain about the trail we followed. We need to know if you have noticed any of the tracks or scents. Surely you prefer the murderer is caught before he finds your village."

"I think that will not be necessary," the headman said. "I have heard enough. Since the Cats sent this invasion to our land, we have no choice but to execute their scouts and prepare for a return strike. We will chop off your heads to stop your lying tongues. Guards, throw these spies back in jail. Gather the army. Send word to the next towns. Tomorrow we will witness the deaths of the spies before we march. War is upon us."

The captain removed their safe-conduct pendants and shook them over his head. The guards and the villagers peering in the windows all howled before the villagers rushed toward their homes.

Ludik's stomach churned. Not only was the murderer still on the loose, but with Orrik out for blood, Maon could be hit with two armies. There had to be some way to stop the hateful Dogs from attacking.

His vision blurred until he took a deep breath. First the seedling, then the tree. They wouldn't be able to help his village if they couldn't escape their own execution.

Nemerra sat with her head bowed. When Ludik pressed harder against her shoulder, she straightened in her seat and twitched a smile.

The guards hauled Ludik's friends downstairs to the jail. They had to support Lyell and carry Ahjin's unconscious body entirely, and they were not careful. Ludik flinched every time they banged Ahjin's wings into another wall. How would he face Ahjin if he let his wings get broken again?

Ludik couldn't convince the guards to put Ahjin in the center cell with him, but being locked up again was almost a relief. At least there were bars between them and the ruthless Dogs.

The guards double-checked the cell doors. After a few choice insults, the troop sauntered up the stairs, laughing at their prisoners.

Zefra waited until the guards were out of earshot before speaking. "May we escape now? As soon as Lyell is functioning properly — sorry, Lyell — and Ahjin is conscious, I mean. Then all we have to worry about is a town full of bloodthirsty Dogs, the bars of our cages, an impending execution, and no weapons."

"Oh, is that all?" Lyell mumbled. "When you put it that way, it sounds too easy. Ludik, I need sleep. You take care of Ahjin now and heal me later."

He flopped onto his cot and closed his eyes. A few minutes later, horrific snoring filled the jail.

Nemerra reached her hands through the bars of the cell toward Ludik. "I have faith in you, darling. Heal Ahjin, and we'll deal with the rest later." She leaned her head against the bars until Ludik pressed a kiss to her soft lips.

Ludik rubbed his hands across his cropped hair and turned to the other cell. "Teeth and claws, this will be tricky. Gurryon, I need your help, please."

Gurryon carefully picked up Ahjin and smiled at Ludik. "Tell me what to do."

His brother's trust steadied Ludik. "I need Ahjin on the floor next to the bars so I can reach him. Make sure his wings aren't crimped under him. Yes, right there. Turn him a little so his head is closer to me. That is all you can do now. Go ahead and sleep."

"I'll wait." Gurryon walked to the edge of the cell and squinted at the prison in the dim light.

Ludik reached through the bars and brushed Ahjin's curls from his face. The guard's punch had left a bruise on the avian's jaw. If Ludik ran out of energy dealing with internal injuries, the bruise could stay.

He closed his eyes to concentrate and wormed his mind inside Ahjin's head. After a while, he knew they were lucky. Working on Lyell had given him practice, and Ahjin had less damage. He should be recovered by evening. In fact, he should wake soon.

Ludik stretched to heal Ahjin's bruise, and his friend twitched.

Ahjin feebly brushed Ludik's fingers off his chin. "Stop tickling me."

Ludik gave up on the bruise. "How do you feel?"

Ahjin raised an eyebrow, eyes still closed. "I'm fine. Is everyone else well?"

"We're all here."

But if they didn't escape tonight, they would all die tomorrow.

17. JAIL
(ORRIK, CANID TERRITORY)

**The Hyenas tried to take our land by force, proving the distrust
between the Hyenas and the Cats is justified.**
Torao, after The Battle of Sad Laughter

It was obviously still morning, since the jail window faced east and the
sun was stabbing through Ahjin's eyes and into his brain.

Everyone was here, miraculously in one piece if he didn't count his
splitting head. Zefra basked in the striped sunlight under the window,
talking to Nia. Ludik whispered to Lyell and Gurryon while he held
Nemerra's hand between the cell bars.

Ahjin rubbed his bruised jaw. It hurt almost as much as his head, but
he wouldn't mention either. Ludik needed to help Lyell, whose continued
slurring indicated his concussion was not fully healed. Ahjin's mere
headache was tolerable. As Nia had commented far too many times, he
was hard-headed.

A trumpet blared, jolting Ahjin's headache. All the guards pounded
from the building and assembled in the courtyard.

Ahjin stood on his cot and watched the rows of soldiers fill the
meadow outside the window. Dozens of guards marched over the grass,
well-armed, and judging by their polished drills, well-trained. They
weren't as intimidating as warring gods, but the sight wasn't encouraging,

either. Why did a small town have so many soldiers, and how could Ahjin and his friends escape them?

While Ludik healed Lyell again, the girls watched the soldiers and the limited view of the grounds. Nia and Zefra laughed and chatted as if idly gossiping, but if the guards outside had understood their Iskrit, they'd have objected to the volume of martial data in their conversation.

Ahjin flipped back his thin mattress and stared at the bed boards. "Ludik, may I borrow your boot knife?"

Ludik drew his knife from its hidden sheath and tapped it on his finger. "If you dull it, I'll sharpen it on your skull."

Ahjin ignored the threat, holding out his hand until the knife slipped between the bars. Based on the girls' reports, he scratched rough exterior maps and a guard census on the bed boards. When the girls switched to dissecting fighting styles, he gave the knife to Gurryon to map the interior of the jail on his bed.

The guards separated after an hour of drills, some heading to patrols, some presumably home, and some returning to the building. Two of them clattered down the stairs, giving enough warning for the prisoners to replace the thin mattresses over the maps.

The fat guard from the day before returned to his overflowing desk.

"I'd sit with a handsome man like you," Nia offered, "if I weren't locked in this nasty cell." She ran her hand up and down the bars and fluttered her eyelashes at him.

Gurryon pretended to gag.

"Shh," Ahjin breathed. They had to take risks to escape, but Nia's scheme could go horribly wrong, even without Gurryon making it worse.

"Oh, I would let you out, but I cannot." The guard brushed crumbs from his wrinkled uniform and beamed at Nia. "Keep the prisoners locked up where they cannot hurt anybody, Captain says."

"You're afraid of me hurting someone?" Nia laughed. "I'm a little girl. You must be two or three times my size, a big, strong man like you."

He frowned and squinted at her.

"Oh, please," Nia said. "What can I do while you hold my friends hostage?"

The guard rubbed his chin.

Ahjin held his breath. Perhaps the lummox just needed a little push to go along with her.

"Don't do it, Nia." Ahjin winked discreetly. "The bars protect you from him, too."

Nia smiled at the guard again. "He won't hurt me. I'm so bored in this cell. I'll stay out of the way. Please?" She bounced on her toes and pressed herself against the bars.

The guard squared his shoulders and eyed Nia's curvy body in her form-fitting ocean suit. He glanced at the barred window and up the stairs, where the faint sound of footsteps echoed. "If you promise to be good, I guess it would do no harm."

"I'll be so good, you won't believe it," Nia promised.

Ahjin raised an eyebrow at her. They needed a friend here before they could heal the interkindred relationships, but she'd better behave.

The guard pointed at Nemerra and Zefra. "You two, against the wall."

After the other girls retreated, Nia skipped from the cell. The fat soldier relocked the iron bars and returned the key to his pocket.

Ludik sat by his cell door with his hands dangling by his hidden boot knife. Ahjin shook his head subtly. Nia was safe for now. A hostage wouldn't help, and a dead guard would only make things worse.

Nia stood, hands behind her back, and waited prettily for the guard to pull a second chair next to the desk.

"I dunno, maybe this isn't a good idea." The guard spread his hands across the reports. "I don't think you should read these scrolls."

Nia widened her emerald eyes. "Do you have any written in Noki?"

"What? No. Ohhh." The guard laughed. "Silly me, of course you cannot read Darrendran." He gathered the scrolls he'd thrown on the floor and sorted them into piles. After he had them arranged, he read through each one, making notes on a separate sheet.

Eventually, Ludik relaxed his guard and slid back to hold Nemerra's hand through the bars.

Ahjin kept watching Nia.

By the time the trumpet sounded again an hour later, the guard had even let her refill his pitcher of water from the pipe in the corner.

"I'm sorry, miss, but I gotta put you back in the cell now," he said. "That is the call for drill, and I gotta go or I'll be in big trouble."

"Oh, no worries." Nia sighed dramatically. "I'll be fine while I wait for you to return."

"I've got other duties today. Maybe I can trade shifts to bring you your evening meal." He looked sad. "It will be a shame when they cut off your pretty head in the morning."

"It will be a shame, won't it?" Nia said with a straight face. Once in the cell, she fluttered her eyelashes at the Dog while he locked her door. "I look forward to seeing you again, one last time."

After he left, she sat on her cot and laughed.

"What was that about?" Lyell asked. "Are you trying to get him to take you home instead of execute you? You'd make a good pet, if you want." His voice was unfortunately no longer slurred.

Nia glared at him.

Before she started cursing, Ahjin interrupted. "Tell us what you learned, Nia."

"Most of the records were boring, but I found the number of guards. I know the times of the shift changes and the post locations."

"I understand you reading the numbers, I guess," Lyell said, "but how can you know what they mean?"

"I *can* read Darrendran." She sniffed. "What did you think I was doing? Flirting with the lout?"

Ahjin grinned. "If you flirt a little harder, perhaps he'll save your pretty head."

"Oh, no." Nia's voice dripped sarcasm. "Captain relies on him to keep the prisoners locked up safe."

Gurryon moved the mattress and took notes as she recited details.

"We have a good start," Ludik said. "What else do we need to plan?"

"I will watch outside," Zefra offered. "I might see something useful in their drills."

"We still need a way out of these cells," Lyell said. "I could help if I had my lock picks. Nia, can you get them from my pack the next time you're flirting with the guard?"

"I could try. I think he'd notice, though."

"What are lock picks?" Zefra asked.

Lyell looked a bit sheepish. "Thin metal or wire shapes that allow me to open a lock without a key. We're not supposed to have them, but I made some anyway."

"If you know how to make them, I have a better idea than flirting," Zefra said. "Nia, may I borrow one of your hair ribbons?"

Gurryon chuckled. "You can't pick a lock with hair ribbons."

Nia pulled one of the many rainbow ribbons from her hair. Zefra undid her fiery crown of braids. Her white skin flushed a pale pink as she made a pile of hairpins next to her, then rebraided her hair in a single plait and tied it with Nia's ribbon.

"Now we can have lock picks without making the guard suspicious," Zefra said.

She returned to her post at the window while Lyell twisted the hairpins into new shapes.

Ahjin flipped back the mattresses to study the maps again.

Zefra interrupted. "I think this is important. They hauled a big stump and are celebrating too much for it to be meaningless."

Nia and Nemerra joined her at the window, and the men stood on their cots to see.

The soldiers positioned the stump in clear view of the window, then took turns chopping it with an ax. Each time a soldier got a solid hit, the company howled. After every guard had a chance, they saluted the jail window, sheathed their weapons, and wandered in different directions with raucous laughter.

Nia dropped from her tiptoes and sank on a cot. "Our guard is the only one who thinks it's a shame, and even he won't stop it."

Nemerra sat next to Ludik's bars and reached for his hand again. Lyell growled wordlessly and threw himself on a cot. Ahjin exchanged grim looks with Gurryon. Escape was up to them, and they were outnumbered ten-to-one.

Zefra shrugged. "It does not matter; we will not be here tomorrow."

"And what if we don't get out?" Nia asked.

"Then we will be dead, and it still will not matter." Zefra spoke as calmly as if she discussed the weather.

"I don't like the way you think," Nia said. "Nemerra and I should learn how to pick locks. What if they hit Lyell again? Besides, it looks like fun."

Zefra shrugged again and returned to the window.

Ahjin studied the maps. "Gurryon, come tell me how long you can run with a burden when you're shifted."

They debated distances and speeds and abilities, twisting the information into a risky plan.

Nia and Nemerra conquered lock-picking fast enough that Lyell whistled. "Have you done this before?"

Ahjin didn't know Nemerra well enough to make judgements, but he'd learned to never underestimate Nia, particularly when having fun.

"No," Nia said. "Let's go now." She glanced out the window at the stump, then opened her cell door.

"Be reasonable," Ahjin said. "Let's finish a decent plan and leave after dark. We don't even know why they don't post guards down here. Are they so confident in their locks?"

"I'll look." Nia handed the picks to Nemerra and snuck halfway up the stairs before creeping down again, shoulders slumped. "They don't leave any guards here because the room upstairs is full of them."

"Let us take advantage of our temporary freedom," Nemerra said.

She and Nia rummaged through the luggage for anything useful and small enough to hide, including knives and Lyell's actual lockpicks. Ludik asked for his herb kit, and Zefra pulled out her damp robe. Ahjin requested several of his religious supplies and Torao's journal.

They hid everything under their mattresses and locked themselves in their cells before lunch. This time, it wasn't gray glop. It was brown glop, covered in salty brown gravy. If the soldiers got the same food, it was no surprise they were unpleasant.

Ahjin eyed the guards as they collected the bowls. More likely, they had been frightened by the recent catastrophes and the temporary disappearance of the gods. And with their shamans dead, they didn't have anyone to reassure them things were back to more-or-less normal. They were grasping at feathers in the wind to make sense of the world.

"Darravani is back now," he tried, clutching the cell bars. "You can speak to her at her shrines, or I'd be happy to relay messages until you get a replacement shaman."

A guard ran his sword across the bars toward Ahjin's fingers, making him jump back.

"No outkindred can talk to our goddess," the guard snarled. "We will get a shaman when we are ready, and until then she can keep her nose out of our affairs."

Yes, that definitely sounded like fear and abandonment speaking. Ahjin added it to his mental list of problems to discuss with Darravani, right below interkindred cooperation.

"You should hope she does not hear you say that," Gurryon commented mildly. He tapped the badge on his shoulder and pulled Ahjin to the wall, turning his back on the guard. "So, Ahjin, tell me how your family fares."

They chatted, pretending to ignore the guards until they finally left.

Zefra returned to her window observations, running her hot hands across her robe to dry it. Nia and Nemerra picked all the locks several times for practice, and Gurryon and Ludik searched the room for weaknesses. Lyell dug around two window bars to loosen them, repacking the scratches with the debris.

Ahjin sat with his books. The others would tell him if they needed him, and this was the first time they had stayed still for long. He needed to finish several religious books by the time he returned to the island, and he wasn't a particularly fast reader. And if he was lucky, Torao's journal might give a few insights into their current situation, since it chronicled the last interkindred war.

If he wasn't lucky, he'd be an even slower reader without his head.

Which should come first, religion or journal? He finally alternated chapters, starting with one of the brief scrolls Kassian had given him. Since little was known about the mysterious older brother of the gods, it was a good place to start.

This one was a report on the creation of the world. Ahjin couldn't help comparing it to the biased myths commonly known. Kassian scrupulously gave credit to each of his siblings for their parts of creation, all as precisely explained as his own. Ahjin tied the scroll with a red ribbon to remind him to educate the world on the actual dynamics of the gods. Religious politics would change radically in the next few years.

The journal was more depressing. The numbers of casualties were shocking enough, but Torao's description of the ferocity of the attackers was frightening. Hyenas had cut a swath of devastation straight into the side of Felid territory, with no regard for life or limb. It had been remarkably effective, despite the Hyenas' own losses. Torao's bitterness leaked from every page of the journal.

After one chapter, Ahjin couldn't take any more war stories. It struck too close to home. He laid the journal on the floor and curved his wings above his face. If the guards were careless tomorrow morning, he might be able to fly away, but his friends would all die.

Unacceptable. He'd thought himself the only survivor before, and death was easier than the guilt.

A shadow blocked the light and crouched over the journal. The pages rustled, slowly and then faster, until Lyell slammed the book shut.

"I thought you exaggerated about the war," Lyell said. "Surely people would be less cruel. But this is horrific. And now the Dogs are falling to the same madness? I thought we were more sensible."

Ludik muttered something that didn't sound complimentary.

Ahjin lowered his wings to shoot Ludik a warning glare. "This isn't your village, Lyell. It's not your fault. If you help us catch the killer, you'll have done enough."

"Still, I thought Canids were better than this." Lyell returned the journal to Ahjin and shuffled toward the stairs. "We've done everything we can for our escape. You should rest before the guards return for the evening meal. I'll keep watch."

Ahjin steeled himself and opened the journal to the next chapter. The Dogs weren't the only ones suffering from madness. Ludik hadn't acted like himself since they'd found Agu's body, and the delay in his wedding didn't explain it all. Even before they knew the deaths were murders, Ludik had held a grudge against the Canids.

Grandpapa Torao had asked Ahjin to keep his grandchildren from war. Ahjin still hoped to accomplish that, somehow, but how could he keep war from Ludik's heart? Torao had taught his grandsons the wrong lessons, and retraining them seemed almost as difficult as keeping peace between the gods. Ahjin left the journal open but watched his friends above the pages.

Ludik and Nemerra snuggled in a corner, murmuring with worried looks. Lyell read and reread Darravani's note about his family. Nia entertained herself by mocking the competence of the soldiers drilling outside, while Zefra drew the closest patrol routes on the map under the mattress.

Gurryon stole parchment from the desk and scribbled for a while, then brought it to Ahjin. "Will you review this and add anything needed?"

He had written a letter to the unknown replacement shaman, including the cause of the recent disasters, the truce among the gods, and the attitudes now rampant in Orrik. He finished by recommending the villagers immediately comply with Darravani's policies, including peace with other territories.

"I think you covered most of it," Ahjin said. At the bottom, he added an invitation for additional training on the new changes and offered employment for anyone interested. He signed his name and his full title, "His Holiness, the Mouth of the Gods."

It probably wouldn't work, but at least he'd tried.

Gurryon hid the scroll under his mattress, to be left on the desk as they left. "Why don't you ask the gods to rescue us?"

"We're developing a plan to handle it ourselves," Ahjin said. "The gods might advise, but they don't actively meddle in our affairs. It complicates matters too much. Also, I serve the gods, not the other way around." He shrugged. "I'll ask for help if we can't escape. That's the best I can do."

"You sound an awful lot like Akamu," Gurryon said. "Were you always so pious? Is that why they chose you?"

Ahjin laughed and laughed. He couldn't stop, even as he struggled to catch his breath.

When Gurryon repeated his questions after the others came to investigate the noise, Nia and Ludik laughed so hard they had to sit.

"No," Zefra said, "they chose him because he was too stubborn to give up."

Ahjin finally stopped laughing. "When I was called as one of Irajahan's priests, I was sure the god was only a convenient myth so the priests could maintain power. Now I serve all the gods faithfully, but I don't call myself devout."

Nonetheless, he spent the rest of the evening alternating between his religious books and their escape plans. It was true he needed the time to study, but the stump outside the window was a constant reminder of other stakes.

Not only were their own lives at risk, but if they couldn't escape, who would warn the Cats about the army coming for them?

18.ESCAPE
(ORRIK, CANID TERRITORY)

Today, my second brother died. I wrote both names on the casualty lists below Papa and all his brothers. I will never forgive the Hyenas for this.

Torao, after The Battle of Sad Laughter

Dinner was late, almost at twilight, and was more of the bland pulp. Zefra drank hers while the others played with theirs.

"Food is better than hunger," Zefra said. "We will need strength for our escape."

Nia stuck out her tongue, but everyone choked down the food.

The desk guard stayed after the meal and let out Nia to entertain him again. "If I gotta stay here while everyone else patrols, I might as well have pretty company," he said.

"How long will you be here?" Nia asked, with the brainless, wide-eyed look Zefra had never been able to copy.

"I'll be here for hours, trying to get these—" He glanced at Nia and blushed. "These scrolls sorted."

Zefra found his delicacy amusing, considering Nia would probably be cursing now if it fit with her current act as innocent lady.

The more important issue was what to do about the guard. Ludik's plan was risky. If it went wrong, they needed a way to eliminate the guard. Zefra eyed the scrolls. So much parchment would make excellent tinder.

Perhaps it would be better not to let Nia take the risk. Zefra could burn him fast enough to prevent screams. She looked at the others and rubbed her hands together, then nodded at the guard and raised her eyebrows in question.

Ahjin and Ludik both shook their heads.

Perhaps they did not understand. Zefra motioned again, less subtly. They shook their heads harder.

Ludik slid his hand under his mattress. After a moment, he walked to the front bars of his cell and complained, "I am thirsty, guard. May we have water?"

"I am busy," the guard said. "You had water with your meal. You can wait."

Nia nodded to Ludik. "Your pitcher is nearly empty," she told the guard. "Why don't you let me water the prisoners and refill your water, too. Your work is too important to interrupt. I'd love to help such a capable soldier." She smiled at the guard until he agreed.

Zefra watched carefully, but she still could not tell how Nia could attractively flutter her eyelashes instead of looking like she had a bee stuck in her eye. There must be a trick to it.

Nia held the pitcher against her chest and minced to the water pipe. She filled the pitcher and walked along the row of cells, filling the prisoners' cups. Zefra drank her first cup fast enough to get a second before Nia moved on.

When Nia got to Ludik, she held the water away. "Complainers go last, Ludik."

She ran out of water after giving it to everyone else and had to go back for more. Ludik grumbled the whole time, and the guard chortled.

Nia poured Ludik's cup half-full. "Short rations might teach you to hold your tongue."

"That is not enough," he complained, grabbing the top of the pitcher.

Nia let him pour another splash and then stepped out of reach. Even from the next cell, Zefra had barely seen the powder Ludik dropped into the water.

Nia swirled the pitcher temptingly in front of Ludik. "No more for you."

After the powder dissolved, she carried it back to the desk and refilled the guard's cup, then resumed her flirtations.

Zefra nodded at Nia. She had accomplished step one like a champion. Now they would see if it worked as planned or if the desk and the soldier needed to be flamed.

Everyone fidgeted in silence, covertly watching the guard. Most of them had a hand out of sight, and Zefra assumed they, like she, had some small weapon ready to use if things went wrong.

The guard chatted with Nia while he worked on his records. After a few drinks, he slowed, finally drooping onto the desk, fast asleep. His horrific snores did not pause when Nia pulled the key from his pocket and threw it to Ahjin.

Step two done. Zefra prayed to Resef that the entire plan would go as smoothly.

While the men turned their backs, Zefra changed into her now-dry robe. She gave Nemerra back her dress while the others grabbed their packs.

Nia poured out the water to hide the evidence. "How long will he sleep, Ludik?"

"An hour or two." Ludik dropped one herb pouch on his cot and stuffed the rest in his bag. "The long-lasting drugs are more noticeable in both taste and effect. We'll have to move quickly."

"I could have burned the guard too fast for him to stop me," Zefra said. "Then we would not have to worry about him waking."

"Sharp-tailed scorpions," Nia swore.

"Listen, you bloodthirsty barbarian," Gurryon said, "we don't kill anyone if we can help it."

Zefra stomped her feet into her boots instead of kicking the manner-less lout. "I'm not bloodthirsty, I'm practical. Do you really think we can escape without killing anyone? Which is better, him dead or all of us?"

Ahjin stuffed his last book into his pack. "Perhaps we can escape without any deaths, and perhaps not, but we'll look for alternatives. We can discuss relative moral philosophy after we escape."

"It's almost dark," Nemerra said. "Are we ready to go?"

Lyell, Gurryon, and Ludik wrenched the two loosened bars from the window.

Nia returned the guard's key to his pocket. "It was more fun to pick the locks."

"Be realistic," Lyell said. "We had no way of knowing the guard would have the key down here. Besides, this wouldn't have worked if Ludik didn't have his herbs."

"I'm keeping the lock picks," Nia insisted. "I'll buy you new hairpins, Zefra."

Zefra touched the braid falling down her back and sighed. Even with extra pins in her pack, she did not have time to put it up.

"Hush," Nemerra hissed, waving frantically.

She pressed herself against the wall next to the window and peered sideways into the darkness. Ludik squeezed himself into the corner next to her.

Gurryon and Zefra kicked the packs under their cots, then threw themselves on the most visible beds and pretended to sleep. Ahjin vanished, and everyone else ducked out of sight of the window.

Outside the jail, the crunch of boots drew near. Someone whistled off key.

Zefra forced herself to breathe evenly. *Please, Resef, let him move on.* She watched the window through the narrowest crack of her eyelids, but the night was too dark to see anything.

Nia remained flat on the floor against the wall, her ears tilted toward the window and fingers clenched white around her spear. Behind Zefra, Lyell's knives hissed free of their sheaths, and his boots tapped slowly toward the stairs.

No one said a word as the minutes stretched into eternity. This was the problem with a plan based on guesswork — so much relied on luck. Zefra preferred a plan based on facts.

Please, Resef, do not let the sentry notice the missing bars. As the steps faded, she realized she had been holding her breath.

Nemerra whispered shakily, "He turned the corner. Hurry."

They shoved four of the packs out the window, followed by most of the weapons.

"Be careful, girls," Ahjin said. "We'll watch for your signal."

"*You* be careful." Nia stuffed a handful of records from the desk into her shirt and went next, cursing Ludik for pushing too fast while she wriggled her curves between the remaining bars. She picked up her short spear and stood guard.

Now it was Zefra's turn. She grabbed the windowsill and pulled as Ludik lifted. Skinnier than Nia, she slid through easily, but tumbled in a heap when her foot caught in her robe. As soon as she could stand, she pulled the hem of her robe forward between her legs and tucked it into her belt. She couldn't afford to trip again, and it was too dark for anyone to see her bare legs.

She looked down and changed her mind. Even the moonlight was enough to make her white skin glow like a lantern. Zefra rubbed handfuls of dirt over her legs until the gleam dimmed. She buckled her sword belt around her waist and slid her pack on her back with Lyell's strapped to it.

Once Zefra was ready, Nia put on her own pack with Ahjin's on top and gathered the other weapons.

Zefra peeked inside the jail. All four Darrendrakar had shifted to their alternate shapes for speed and better night vision. Their natural weaponry was substantial, though close-range. They could even carry the others once they were reunited.

The three giant cats wore their own packs, which Nemerra had made to accommodate both shapes and would give their riders a makeshift harness to clutch.

The wolf and Ahjin, without packs, would be the first up the stairs. As the only one left with hands inside the jail, Ahjin had his bow and his weighted rope.

"Make the distraction big, Zefra," Ahjin whispered from the window.

He crossed to the bottom of the stairs, and the predators lined up with Nemerra in the middle.

"Here," Nia whispered in the dark, pulling the crumpled scrolls from her shirt. "I thought tinder might help." She snuck out a few paces and waved to Zefra.

Zefra crawled toward the execution stump. This was the trickiest part of the escape, as far as subtlety went. If they were caught now, they would all die tonight.

She glanced behind her. The dim light from the jail window outlined the edge of Nia's shadow, her head turning slowly as she scanned the meadow.

Zefra returned to her crawl. The grass was soft under her hands and knees and damp enough to moisten her robe as the long strands brushed against her shoulders. Damp was good; she did not need fire spreading to cut off the others' escape.

The triple-moonlight cast odd shadows in the meadow. Bushes looked like sentries with drawn bows, and trees looked like monsters. She could ignore the monsters, but what if she missed a real sentry?

Zefra crawled through the shadows, heart pounding. When the soldiers had first hauled the stump to the yard, she thought it was too close, too good a view of her friends' deaths. Now it seemed a league away, and danger haunted every pace.

She froze at a sudden noise.

No, just an owl, but Zefra's heart raced. She inched forward, and a tall bush turned its head and revealed himself a real sentry.

She pressed herself against the ground. When had he appeared? Had he seen her?

His footsteps drew closer, and still closer. She held her breath. If he sounded the alarm, she would burn the guard for the distraction, despite Gurryon's opinion. Her hands shook as she reached for the flame inside her, raising her head enough to see her target.

And then the sentry passed her and kept walking.

Zefra dropped her head to the ground and trembled with relief.

When the soldier was out of sight, she wriggled forward, cautious of dry twigs in the grass. Concentrating on the placement of each hand and knee helped drown the voice in her head that insisted she had bungled the patrol patterns. Had her incompetence missed something else? What hole in their plan would lead to their deaths?

Finally, here was the stump. She stuffed the scrolls into a crack in the side, then glanced back. When she was sure she had Nia's attention, she gave a tiny wave and crawled away.

At the limit of her throwing range, Zefra flattened herself in the tall grass and scanned the area.

Where was Nia?

A petite shadow flitted into the trees, waving right before she disappeared.

It was time. Zefra checked for soldiers, but only shadowy monsters faced her. Whether they were trees or not, she was out of time.

She called fire into her hand. When she had a solid flame, she stood and threw it hard at the dry stump. It was a perfect hit.

The scrolls caught, and Zefra ran for the trees. The stump whooshed into a pillar of fire. The scent of burning oak accentuated the crackle of the bonfire.

The area erupted with running soldiers from the village and the jail. Few were left to stop her friends from escaping up the stairs.

But if she did not hide, they might stop her. Zefra skidded into the cover of the forest and slid behind a fat tree, covering her mouth to quiet her panting.

The captain's brash voice bellowed over the commotion. "Get buckets! Form a line! Don't let it spread to the buildings!"

The soldiers ran for the nearest well.

Ahjin burst around the corner of the building with a wolf by his side and a panther, leopard, and lion behind him. For the first dozen paces, they were unnoticed. Then shouts arose, and guards wavered between them and the fire.

Zefra's friends made it halfway to the firelight before a soldier opposed them. Gurryon bounded to the front, bowling over the guard like tumbleweed beneath a horse's hooves.

Ahjin spread his wings and jumped into flight. As soon as he reached head-height above the ground, he disappeared between one wingbeat and the next.

The giant cats and the wolf had crossed half the yard and were now illuminated by the flaming stump. They kept going, just ahead of the guards streaming after them.

Zefra clenched her fists and prayed Resef lent them the speed of a forest fire.

Then the captain was suddenly in front of them, swinging his sword at Nemerra.

She squirmed sideways and rolled barely out of range, skidding to her feet and pelting for the trees. Her ears flattened to her head, and her fur stood on end.

The captain followed close on her tail, slashing with every step.

Zefra shot fire at the captain and missed. He continued after Nemerra, howling outrage. Zefra grappled for more fire, but she was too slow. The captain swung at Nemerra again.

His sword missed as he jerked backward, one of Ahjin's arrows in his shoulder. He did not have a chance to rise before Ludik slashed his throat.

Zefra snorted. So much for moral philosophy.

She jumped as a shadow rose in front of her. Just before she flamed it, she recognized Nia.

Zefra clenched her fist to smother the fire. "Ashes," she swore. "Warn me next time."

"Here." Nia shoved Ludik's bow into one hand and an arrow in the other.

As quickly as Zefra shot an arrow at the weapon-waving shadows, Nia handed her the next, but there were dozens of soldiers chasing her friends.

Zefra's arms shook from the effort of having called flame after sundown. Despite her shaky aim, the volley of arrows scattered the bellowing guards and bought the prisoners time. Perhaps her "warning shots" would make Gurryon happy; she would have preferred to reduce the number of armed pursuers.

The wolf and three cats scrambled into the forest and slid to a halt next to the women. Grass and leaves stuck to Nemerra's back. The bloodstains on Ludik's black fur showed only as glistening patches of more black.

Ahjin popped back into visibility and perched on a branch to continue shooting. Zefra and Nia climbed onto the backs of Nemerra and Lyell, leaving the biggest cats free to fight.

They were ready to go. Zefra whistled at Ahjin, and Nemerra launched herself immediately. Zefra's head snapped back, and she barely clutched the pack strap in time to stay on. Next time, she scolded herself, grab first, whistle second.

Nia whooped until Ahjin shushed her. Zefra shook her head. While she agreed with the sentiment, the noise was a foolish risk. She crouched lower over Nemerra's pack, lowering wind resistance and keeping her head from branches. It also made her less of a target.

The last step in their plan was to get far enough ahead to lose the Canids. Ludik had rubbed an herb on the Darrendrakar feet that he claimed would confuse their scent trail.

Lyell led the way, with Gurryon and Nemerra running at the wolf's top speed and Ludik guarding the rear. Zefra's skin crawled as howls rose behind her. Some of the guards must have shifted.

She tucked her face lower and shuttered her inner eyelids against the wind. They had only a small head start, and it was too early to know if Ludik's herb worked. Now, it was outrun or die.

Ahjin and his bow guarded their escape from above. Anytime Zefra heard a bark too close for comfort, the next sounds were the snap of a bowstring and a yelp. Soldiers crashed through the forest behind them for twenty minutes, lagging farther and farther behind. Dogs bayed in the distance for even longer.

Zefra counted the seconds between each howl. At each silence, she took a breath. Were they finally clear? More barking always charred her hopes.

After an hour of shaking the Canids only for them to catch up again, Zefra nearly gave up. Finally, the sound of baying drifted to silence. The party slowed to a lope.

Zefra shifted her seat on Nemerra to be a little more comfortable. They continued in near silence with Ahjin's wingbeats a comforting whisper above them, running in the featureless dark until the only measure of time was the dance of the three moons above them. The large, golden moon was a waning crescent, while its tiny, pale blue companion chased its lavender twin across the heavens. The tree branches overhead crossed the dim light and blocked most of it, flashing shadows across the ground in hypnotic patterns.

Some time later, Nemerra stopped with a jerk, waking Zefra from near-slumber. She blinked. According to the moons, it had been about three hours since they last heard the Canids.

Nia stood by Zefra, pulling her to the ground. "Ahjin needs a beacon to land," Nia whispered, shaking Zefra when she did not respond.

"A beacon." Zefra yawned.

She rubbed her cold hands together and looked for the fire inside her. She snapped her fingers. Nothing. She reached deeper and called a small flame into her hand, shaking with the effort. The light showed the others standing wearily at one side of a clearing.

Gurryon poked his head under bushes and behind trees. "All clear," he said.

Zefra held up the light. "Are we spending the night here?"

Ahjin swooped low, thumped to the ground, and fell to his knees. "Ow." He half-folded his wings, then stopped with a whimper. "I haven't flown so much in months."

Nia shook herself and left with the water bags. Ludik and Nemerra dragged the packs one at a time to the high branches of a tree and lodged them in forks. Lyell piled fallen sticks above a depression in the ground to make a large den.

"Can you make it up a tree?" Nia asked Ahjin when she returned with more water.

"Can I get a boost?"

Nemerra stayed in the tree, but Ludik climbed down and braced himself against the trunk.

"Zefra, you first," Nia said. "Climb on his back and then up the tree. Nemerra will help you reach a higher branch."

Zefra clambered up the tree, too fatigued to be embarrassed by her bare legs. Nemerra pushed her to another branch and helped her wedge herself next to her pack. By the time Zefra pillowed her head on her pack, Nia and Ahjin had settled nearby.

Ludik sprawled next to Nemerra, while Gurryon stretched himself on a lower branch. Lyell crawled into his makeshift den and pulled a branch across the entrance.

"Hey, Gurryon," Ahjin called softly. "Did you leave the letter for the shaman?"

A low growl drifted up the tree.

Ahjin yawned. "See you in the morning."

"This would have been easier if the gods helped," Zefra murmured as sleep dragged on her eyelids.

Nia yawned. "Ahjin told you they can't. We managed fine." Her words drifted softly through the branches, ending in a whisper and a sigh.

"The Canids might still follow us," Zefra said, but if anyone replied, she did not hear.

19. HOMEWARD

(BETWEEN ORRIK AND DURRIEL, CANID TERRITORY)

Just as Darravani speaks to her people in the language of flowers, they can give messages to each other the same way.
Flowers and Their Meanings: A Guide for All Darrendrakar, Introduction

Ludik woke with the sunrise and turned his head to check on Nemerra. She was so close to him in the tree, lying head-to-head along the branch, that his cheek brushed hers. Yes, that was the right distance. He closed his eyes again and inhaled her leopard scent. He had worried so much about her the last couple of days. Their arrest and imprisonment had been bad enough to turn his whiskers gray, but when that soldier almost cut her in half, his heart stopped. He didn't regret killing the guard. Better him than Nemerra.

Even hiding in a tree was a relief. He pushed away nagging thoughts of the tasks still looming. Nemerra was here, safe and wonderful. Life couldn't get any better until their wedding. The hunt for the killer could wait.

When Nia slid down from her higher branch and stepped on his tail, he forgot his wishful thinking and almost bit her.

"What are you doing up?" he growled softly. "You're never awake early."

"Sorry," she whispered. "Pinecones jabbed me all night long. Shouldn't we get up now, anyway?"

Nemerra chuckled near his ear. "She has a point, dear. We need to go." She yawned, stretched, and jumped to the ground.

Ludik cursed silently.

Nia also stepped on Gurryon on her way down. His startled yowl woke everyone.

"Sorry," Nia said. "I don't think I'm good at climbing trees." She slithered the rest of the way to the ground. "Will you lower my pack, please?"

Ludik moved just in time. Zefra stepped to his branch, took each pack from Ahjin perched above them, and lowered them to Nia.

Gurryon climbed down and stalked off, muttering something about checking their back trail.

Apparently, the time to sleep was over. Ludik dragged his pack behind a bush, shifted out of his fur, and put on his tunic and boots, grumbling about the lost chance to admire Nemerra.

When he emerged, Nemerra had also changed, Zefra was lighting a small fire, and Nia had refilled all the water jugs again.

"Where did Lyell and Ahjin go?" Ludik asked.

"Lyell smelled rabbits and thought fresh meat would taste good after the jail food." Nemerra kissed his cheek, then rummaged through her pack for spices and bread.

"I'm still up here," Ahjin moaned. "Save me some breakfast."

"Not a chance," Nia said. "Get down here or go without."

"Heartless girl."

After a few minutes, the branches shook as Ahjin crept down the tree. When he hit the ground, he fell to his knees and stayed there, face wrinkled in pain and wings half-extended.

Ludik fetched his healing kit. As long as Ahjin was holding still, it was a good time to check his wings. He had made a long flight last night, despite not having much practice since Darravani healed his wings.

The exam went quickly. "My friend, you're lucky," Ludik said. "They're only strained from overuse. You're supposed to get back in shape gradually." He ignored Ahjin's long-suffering sigh. "No more flying for a while."

"No worries." Ahjin gingerly folded his wings and climbed to his feet. "I like your plan. No flying."

Everyone divided the chores, and by the time the Wolf returned with a half-dozen rabbits dangling from his mouth, the bread was sliced, and the bowls were waiting. Zefra had the pan hot, ready to fry the rabbits as soon as they were skinned and gutted.

T he rabbits were indeed much better than the so-called food they had been served in jail. Ludik tried not to drool as he gobbled his share.

Gurryon returned at the end of the meal. After he changed, he shoveled food into his mouth while he reported.

"I didn't see, hear, or smell anybody from Orrik," he mumbled, "but I think I caught a whiff of that Dog-Bear scent. If I'm right, we're close to his trail again. I'll take Lyell to confirm it as soon as I finish eating."

"At the rate you're inhaling your food, that won't take long," Nia said.

Gurryon snarled at her and shoved the last two bites in at once. Lyell chuckled, but didn't say anything as he followed Gurryon into the forest.

Ludik, Ahjin, and the women cleaned the camp while the two were gone. Helping Nemerra was a handy excuse for Ludik to stay close enough to touch her at every other step.

They finished before the scouts returned, so Nemerra pulled her brush from her pack.

"Good idea," Nia said, and tied her frizzy braids around her head with her ribbons.

Zefra found more hairpins and restored her hair to its normal coronet.

"Ouch," Nemerra complained, yanking on knots. "Maybe I should have braided mine, too."

"Let me." Ludik took her brush and stood behind her to gently untangle one knot at a time. He ran his fingers through her silky hair as each lock came free, leaning forward to catch her scent. Then he kept brushing until the shimmering russet cascaded smoothly down her back.

When Nemerra reached for the brush, he held it out of reach while he kissed her on the cheek, then returned to brushing.

Lyell and Gurryon finally returned, to Nia's impatient sigh and Ludik's disappointed one.

"Are we still on the right trail?" Ludik asked.

To his further disappointment, Nemerra borrowed a ribbon and confined her beautiful hair to a thick braid.

"He's our fellow," Lyell said. "Our run last night made up for much of the time we lost in jail, so we're still less than a day behind. It looks like he'll pass within an hour or two of Durriel. When we get closer, I'll leave you to your chase and go home to my family."

"You trust us on our own now?" Ahjin asked.

Ludik had noted the contractions in Lyell's speech and already suspected the answer.

And to Ludik's surprise, the Wolf had proved at least one Dog was worth knowing.

Ludik cleared his throat. "We are — we're grateful you trust us."

Lyell shot him a startled glance and grinned. "Oh, I think you can behave yourselves. Or else." His grin widened to show most of his teeth. "I'll talk to our village shaman about sending one of his upper apprentices back to Orrik and a message to the temple in Kanshi. Come to Durriel after you catch the killer, and I'll help you decide what to do with him. Ahjin, you can even ask around and see if anyone there is crazy enough to work for you."

"How generous of you," Ahjin drawled. "I'll do it anyway, thanks."

"Don't worry, Ahjin," Nemerra said, "You'll convince them. All you need is enough time for them to learn what a wonderful person you are and how hard you work with the gods to make the world better."

Ludik didn't laugh. While her attitude was a little optimistic, he more or less agreed with her. He might have a stronger opinion of Ahjin's annoying qualities, but that wasn't relevant to his competence.

Lyell smiled at Nemerra. "You remind me of Ruka. You're as kind and thoughtful as she is. And you have her curiosity and bravery," he said to Zefra.

Nia winked at him. "What about me?"

"You have her zest for life and her sense of humor." He flicked her ear.

Gurryon scoffed. "Are you sure you are not imagining the perfect woman?"

Ludik smiled at Nemerra. *He* had the perfect woman.

Lyell pulled Darravani's note from his pocket. "See, it says right here, she exists." He smirked at Gurryon and tucked the note back into his pocket. "And now we have perfect little babies, too. As soon as I get rid of you, we'll have a perfect life."

"Then the bigger question is why she married you," Gurryon said.

"The obvious answer is that I'm the perfect husband." Lyell put a modest hand on his chest and smiled.

Gurryon's protests were drowned in a roar of laughter from everyone else.

"And since I'm also the perfect hunter," Lyell continued when the laughter died, "let us follow the trail."

Ludik held Nemerra's hand as they walked. She was in a cheerful mood this morning, chattering about the wedding feast they'd have to recook, and her dress that he wasn't allowed to see until the ceremony, and wondering how long it would take to get their house arranged.

"I'll fix it any way you want," Ludik said. "Your wish is my happiness."

"Stop before I gag," Gurryon said. "Why couldn't you go for an arranged marriage like me and not make everyone around you sick?"

"Gurryon, I know Ilani," Nemerra said, "and I'm sure you'll grow to love her before your betrothal year is done. She's a sweet girl and determined to make a good life with you. We've already talked about how she can support you as a shaman. She asked your mama how to cook your favorite dishes and your papa for stories about you as a child. If you aren't nice to her, I'll, I'll..."

Ludik winked at Ahjin. "I'll ask Ahjin to come back and prank you. He's a master."

Nia scowled.

Ahjin half-bowed without breaking step. "Should I say thank you or blush?"

Nemerra wrinkled her forehead and looked from one to the other. "What are you talking about?"

"For instance," Ludik said, "Ahjin once dyed the end of Nia's braid. She was—" He saw Nia's glare and settled for "displeased." It was an understatement. Her tantrum had been impressive.

Ahjin winked at Nemerra with a straight face.

"And what about the fishbone?" Nia retorted. "Or popping out of invisibility all those times?"

Ludik snarled. "That fishbone! Askari should have cut off Ahjin's head."

Ahjin laughed.

That started a round of whispered stories that lasted an hour. Ludik and his friends kept to the lighter parts of their first adventure as they followed the scent trail. Nemerra exclaimed in all the right places. Lyell laughed until he doubled over, despite Zefra's reminders to hush.

Gurryon asked Ahjin for paper and scribbled while they walked, between sly glances at Lyell and Ludik.

"You're taking notes?" Ludik said. "What have I done? Ahjin, keep him in check."

Ahjin laughed. "He's your brother. Do it yourself." He ignored Ludik's sigh and turned to Lyell. "How old is the scent now?"

Lyell sniffed deeply. "We seem closer than before. If all of you are recovered from yesterday, we can walk faster."

Ludik grinned at the Wolf. "We can walk as fast as you can."

"Ludik," Nemerra chided as she stretched her legs to match Ludik's longer step.

Ludik shrugged. Cats were faster than Dogs. Everyone knew that.

Zefra and Ahjin quickened their pace. Nia sighed and broke into a half-jog.

They alternated a half hour of the faster pace with fifteen minutes at a walk and kept it up until they stopped for the midday meal.

A fter they ate, they walked again, despite Nia's yawns. Nemerra let go of Ludik's hand to keep Nia from running into low-hanging branches.

Since Nemerra was busy, Ludik dropped back for a turn at rear guard.

In front of him, Ahjin pulled a parchment from his pocket, reading silently.

"Is that one of your religious texts?" Zefra asked.

"No, Kassian delivered a message from Darravani," Ahjin said. "She says the village of Kairri has gone silent, with no prayers in days. She'd like us to check on it and make sure everyone is fine."

"Where is Kairri, exactly?" Zefra asked.

"It's about a day past Durriel," Lyell said, "right on the coast."

"If we have time," Ludik called up to them, "after we finish our other mission." He still hoped for a fast return to Maon.

"Do you suppose we'll actually catch him?" Nemerra's voice was wistful. "How much longer will it take?" She looked over her shoulder at Ludik and blinked three times.

I, love, you, he blinked back.

"Don't worry," Lyell said. "If we maintain this pace, we should catch him by evening. The Orrik guards did us a favor, driving us faster after our escape."

Nia wrinkled her nose. "That was a favor? Remind me not to ask for any more."

"Speaking of favors, though," Nemerra said, "Darravani told us the forester wasn't the murderer. Couldn't she tell us who is? And where to find him?"

"It doesn't work that way," Ahjin explained. "In the case of the forester, Darravani read his heart and knew he told the truth about his innocence. Unless the murderer has talked to Darravani recently, she won't know who it is. She's not omniscient like Makanavailea, and even Makana has to look for the answer before she can find it. And no, Makana won't trespass in Darravani's territory."

Stupid gods, Ludik mouthed. He knew better than to say that out loud.

Gurryon scowled. "If we're looking for someone who hasn't talked to Darravani lately, maybe we need to go back to Orrik."

"If we go back there, we need a much larger group," Ludik said. "But we don't need to return, because there was no scent in the village. We're back on the trail, and it leads away from Orrik."

"Oh, Ahjin," Nemerra said, "will you read the note from Darravani again? Didn't she say the other village hasn't been talking to her, either?"

Ahjin examined the note again. "Kairri has gone silent, yes. As of several days ago." He stopped in the path until Nia tugged his elbow. "Now I want to know exactly how many days. Agu was killed almost a week ago. Could 'several days' mean a week?"

"They might be like Orrik," Nia said, "missing a shaman. Keep walking, Ahjin."

"Even without a shaman," Ahjin said, "I'm sure someone in Orrik still prays."

"Then why would all of Kairri go silent?" Zefra asked.

Nemerra gasped. "You don't suppose the killer murdered the whole village, do you?"

"One person?" Gurryon scoffed. "Don't be silly. Kairri has guards and hunters and lots of people living there. It does have lots of people, doesn't it, Lyell? It isn't a little twig with a couple dozen residents?" He exchanged glances with Ludik and increased the pace again.

If the killer were in Kairri, the sooner they got there, the better for everyone.

Lyell frowned. "They're almost as big as Durriel, about half the size of Orrik. Not too large, but able to defend themselves from anything short of an invasion force. Is it possible the killer is from Kairri and everyone is keeping his secret?"

"I'm sure their silence is a coincidence," Ahjin said. "It's harvest-time. They've probably been too busy to think about their religious duties. By the time we catch the murderer and get to Durriel to meet Ruka and the new babies, we'll have another message from Darravani, telling us everything is fine in Kairri and we only have to worry about taking the killer back for justice."

"I vote we throw him in the jail at Orrik," Ludik said. "We won't have to execute him. Eating that food every day will be worse than death."

"Ludik," Nemerra gasped. "That's not nice."

Ludik didn't feel nice. Their visit to Orrik had sunk his already low opinion of Dogs to an abysmal level. Only Lyell kept his assessment from hitting rock-bottom.

"It's a great idea, though," Nia said. "That food is a wonderful punishment."

Zefra shook her head. "I pity you all in a famine year. None of you would last a month."

"I'm not worried," Ludik said. "Nemerra is a good cook."

"I'd better not tell my wife about the jail food," Lyell said. "She'd trek there every week to bring better food and teach their cook how to do his job properly."

"Ruka is too good for you," Gurryon said.

"I object," Lyell said. "She's perfect for me. When we get to Durriel,

I'll introduce you, and when she whacks you with the teakettle for being rude, you'll see she has a weakness."

"I'm not sure whacking Gurryon is a weakness," Nia said. "I look forward to meeting Ruka." She sidestepped Gurryon and jogged to the other side of Lyell.

Ludik grinned at his brother's offended expression. Maybe he would add the legendary Ruka to his short list of likeable Dogs.

20.SMOKE

(NEAR DURRIEL, CANID TERRITORY)

All my friends went to war. Few returned home. I have one brother left of five.

Torao, after The Battle of Sad Laughter

This was ridiculous. After a couple of hours keeping up with everyone's longer legs and faster pace, Nia was exhausted. They chased and chased and never caught up to the murderer that had ruined what could have been a delightful trip to Darrendra. It was only the reassurance of Lyell's fabulous Wolf nose that kept her going. He said they got closer to their quarry every hour. Ludik said they had to keep moving. Nia thought they were both pains in the feet.

If Lyell hadn't promised they were almost to Durriel, she would have staged a revolt and insisted they stop for the night. But sleeping in a real bed sounded better than another night camping on the ground, and she counted on Ruka being as good of a cook as Lyell claimed.

If she was as wonderful in all the ways he said, Nia looked forward to a marvelous evening. She could show Ruka her new dolphin statuette, and hold the babies, and wrap herself in a warm blanket, and stay off her feet until morning. It sounded perfect.

Zefra lifted her nose to the sky and sniffed. "Do you smell smoke?"

"I'm almost home," Lyell said. "We're bound to smell someone's chimney from here. Don't worry your pretty head. You'll enjoy the warmth." He whistled a happy melody.

Nia's stomach growled. "I hope those chimneys send smoke from a perfectly cooked supper."

Zefra sniffed the air again. "I do not think 'tis dinner. What do you do around here if a lot of trees burn?"

Lyell's whistle faltered. "How many trees? When there is an actual forest fire, we evacuate the nearby villages and pray for rain. If the woods get an infection, the foresters sometimes clear a section with firebreaks. I haven't heard of any planned for this month, though."

Zefra set her pack on the ground and pulled out three water pouches. "Not all goes as planned."

"How many trees are burning?" Lyell asked. "How can you tell?"

Zefra shrugged. "It seems I can sense large bodies of heat. I had not realized before, but my abilities are still new. Are there any villages nearby besides yours? Do we need to warn anyone else?"

A distant howl echoed through the forest.

"Fire. Run," Nia translated. Her heart drowned. That was no chimney smoke and no well-cooked supper.

Lyell stared at the western sky, threw down his pack, and kicked off his boots. "There's no one else to warn," he whispered, "just my village."

He darted through the trees toward the smoke billowing into the clear sky, ripping off his belt and tunic as he ran. In seconds, the huge black-and-gray wolf sped through the forest.

"Ahjin, pray." Zefra hiked her robe to her knees and ran after Lyell with her water bags.

"His family," Nia gasped. Ruka and the babies were in the village. How would she get them out by herself?

Everyone gaped at the black fumes. Gurryon swore. Ludik rummaged through his pack for his healing kit while the others grabbed every water bag they had. Now Nia wished she carried as many as Zefra did.

When Ahjin started to do the same, Nia grabbed his pack from him. "Zefra was right. You need to pray. We need rain, and we need it now. You're the only one who can help."

"Darravani can't make rain," Ahjin protested, "and even if she gives permission for the other gods to help in her land, it would take too long to get them to cooperate. The village can't do anything but evacuate. We're wasting time here. We need to go help."

Nia glanced at the cloud of smoke piling higher, black against the bright apricot autumn sky. She shook Ahjin, hoping sense would bounce into his brain. "Dark, dank, and drippy, Ahjin." She emptied one of his water bags into the cooking pot and shoved it at him. "We'll do what we can until the gods help, but it won't be enough without rain. The gods wanted you to keep them working together. They made you Mouth so you could do it, so make the gods see sense. And do it quickly!"

He jerked back as if she had slapped him, but he took the pot.

Leaving him to deal with the gods, she wrapped Lyell's discarded clothes around the rest of the water jugs and slid everything into the net she'd made for Zefra's cooking experiment. She slung it onto her back and ran through the forest after the Darrendrakar. In front of her, she saw a flash of Nemerra's dress and barely a hint of color from the brothers' tunics and Zefra's tan robe. The wolf was much too fast to still be in sight. If the Darrendrakar didn't like bright colors as much as her own Nokai, Nia might be lost already.

If she didn't move faster, she would get lost anyway.

Wait, think. Ahjin would come behind her. Other than the general direction of the smoke, he would have no idea which way to go, and the smoke would spread a lot by the time he came. With an entire horizon to search, he'd be completely lost. How could she mark the trail for him? Could she leave rock piles or wooden pointers? No, it would take too long.

And what if he flew? He couldn't see any markers from above.

She looked up, stumbling over rocks and pinecones. No, he wouldn't fly. The smoke was thickening rapidly, and he couldn't breathe in it. And his wings surely still ached from his flight last night. So he would run. Ground level, two-legged speed.

Oh, it would be handy to be Darrendrakar right now, with the ability to change to four legs. But she wasn't, and neither was Ahjin, and most of the Darrendrakar hadn't given up the use of their hands for the sake of speed.

Never mind, it didn't matter. How could she mark the path for Ahjin? She paused for a breath and brushed her sweaty, frizzy hair out of her face. Her hair ribbons!

She ripped the first ribbon she found from the end of a braid without untying it. Ahjin was two hands taller than she, so if she tied it... here, on the end of a branch, he should see it even while running.

Nia ran again, clumsily, as she untied ribbons and stuffed them down the front of her shirt to be ready for use. She'd have to talk to Mom about adding pockets to her ocean suits, or get a pouch like Zefra's.

This was so awful. Why did the fire have to be around Durriel? Lyell was so happy to return home, but his homecoming was spoiled by this fire. If he had to help clean the forest, he wouldn't get to spend much time with Ruka and his new babies.

Maybe with Nia and the others here to help, Lyell could at least steal a few minutes to meet his children and kiss his wife. That sounded like a good idea. She'd have to tell the others. Even Gurryon would go along with it, if she twisted his arm.

And when Nia tired of cleaning, she could help Ruka with the children. That sounded like an even better idea.

She looked for Nemerra's dress in front of her. Still there, far ahead. Nia used her fastest knot to tie a ribbon around a handy branch for Ahjin. Time to run again. Faster, this time.

Nia sucked in a ragged breath. She couldn't go much faster.

The smoke grew thicker. A light sprang up in the distance. That must be the fire growing. Not good. It wouldn't spread to the village, would it? No, that was unlikely. Zefra said trees were burning, not buildings. Surely the village would fight it off. They must have plans for forest fires.

This was not the time to remember Zefra saying all doesn't go as planned. The villagers would be fine. They had to be.

Run, tie a ribbon. Run again. Could she still see the others? Just barely in the distance.

How much farther to the village? Lyell had said they were almost there, but almost-there on a long trek wasn't necessarily the same as almost-there at a headlong run. He must be so frantic now. The fire was spreading so fast, and his wife had who-knows-how-many new babies to take with her. But her neighbors would help.

What if the neighbors were busy with their own families?

Ruka was smart. She would find a way. And Lyell was a fast and loving Wolf; he'd whisk them from any danger before Ruka had to worry about it. His children were lucky to have such a great dad.

Tie another ribbon. Nia turned to check for Ahjin, sucking in great breaths of air while she had the chance. He wasn't behind her, so she took another breath. Time to run again. Her feet throbbed in protest.

Now she saw the flames themselves instead of just their light. The fire spread quickly, jumping from pine to cypress like lightning strikes, overtaking the forest in both width and depth. The pretty, tri-colored suvarna smoldered, but the evergreens burned like torches, popping and snapping and throwing sparks like Iskrin flares. Zefra would have a fit when she saw the damage to the forest. Even the underbrush smoked.

If Ahjin didn't hurry with the gods, this would be out of control in less time than it took a piranha to strip a dolphin to bones. *Please, gods, please listen to Ahjin. Makana, send us rain. Irajahan, blow the storm above the fire. Resef, steal the heat of the flames. Darravani, let them help. Please, Ahjin, make them send rain.*

She hoped the others prayed, too. Maybe more voices would help convince the gods to listen to Ahjin's petition in time to save the village.

Nia forced her legs to keep staggering. She could swim all day, but running was different. And if she had any brains at all, she'd run away from the fire instead of to it. Adventures should be fun. Danger always seemed like a betrayal.

Poor Lyell. This wasn't fun for him, either. *Run faster, Lyell. Get out of town, Ruka.*

Time for another ribbon, but no time for knots. She snagged it on prickly — and hot — twigs and hoped it wouldn't burn before Ahjin saw it. If he got lost in a forest fire — he just couldn't. She wouldn't allow it.

The air was hot. Even the ground was hot. She missed the cool ocean and the seaside breeze.

She accidentally kicked a smoldering pinecone and yelped. At least she wasn't running barefoot. If she thanked Ahjin for making her wear the sandals, would it make his head swell too much?

Where was the rain?

She had to keep running. How much farther did she have to go? How much farther *could* she go? But she couldn't stop. Running was her only choice. She could barely see Zefra's robe in the distance, tan against the orange flames.

"Ah!" She yanked to a halt as her unraveling braids caught on a grasping pine branch.

She fumbled with her braid but couldn't get free. The fire crept down the branch, devouring the oil-rich needles like children with a jar of festival sweets, reaching hungry tendrils toward her.

Nia pulled, stretching her hair its full length. It gained her an ell of cooler distance, but not for long. The fire crawled toward her, smoking and crackling.

She coughed and ducked toward the fire, trying to untangle her hair with shaking fingers. The fire was too close, too hot. She swiped at the sweat running into her eyes and retreated as far as possible, jerking her hair up, then sideways.

It was too snarled. The only way to get it free was to cut it.

She had left her knife in her pack. Kraken tentacles! She should have worn it on her belt today. But no, she thought all the big men around her would take care of any cutting. She yanked harder. Stupid, stupid. She would never again be without her knife at hand on an adventure.

The fire sparked onto the branch that held her trapped, then writhed toward her. Nia coughed again and turned away from the scorching heat.

Who was she fooling? She would never go on another adventure. She would find her fun in her home ocean.

Nia yanked again. If she didn't get free, she wouldn't go anywhere but a pile of ash.

Lyell's knives! She reached for the net on her back. If she could get it open...

The fire reached the end of the branch and lit her hair, racing up the strands. She screamed and pulled until the burning hair snapped.

She beat out the remaining flames and wrapped her hair around her neck to keep it from becoming a wick as she ran. The ends were hot and crispy, and some tresses were a hand or more shorter than the rest.

No time to worry about it now. Run! As the fire grew, time shrank.

Her tangled hair had delayed her too long. She could no longer see the others. They were too far ahead, and the smoke was too thick. Unless the village was close, she was in trouble. She ran as straight as the burning branches allowed, hoping she wouldn't end up surrounded by flaming trees. Hoping she still ran in the right direction.

If she couldn't find the way, she would be lost inside the fire. Running in a straight line might not work, but running in circles would certainly be fatal.

She was almost out of ribbons. Ahjin had better come soon, or he'd be lost in the inferno, too. *Please, Resef, don't let the ribbons burn until he gets through.*

The rain had better come even sooner than Ahjin. This fire was out of control. Soon, every tree would burn and there would be no escape. Where was the rain?

A burning branch cracked above her head. Nia lurched to one side as it crashed to the ground and set the grass on fire. She should have listened to Ahjin about the boots.

Nia held her hand to her aching side and forced her legs to stumble faster. She squinted through the smoke irritating her eyes.

The line of trees to her left burst into flame, and she dashed to the right.

Would she burn alive in the forest before she found her way out?

Was that a break in the trees? She saw buildings. It must be the village.

Please, let it be the village.

A light flickered behind the buildings. *Please let it be the village not-burning.*

Nia stuck another ribbon on another branch and staggered onward. Just a little farther. She could make it, if she could catch her breath. The smoke burned her lungs and made her cough.

It was too hard to breathe.

Where were the others? She still couldn't see them.

Nia lurched into the village and jerked to a halt, gasping for air. Thicker smoke filled her lungs, and she coughed.

Where was everyone?

Where was the rain?

Light glowed through the dark smoke in front of her.

This was bad. This was so bad.

21.FIRE

(DURRIEL, CANID TERRITORY)

Multiple births are common in many of the Darrendrakar kindreds.

A Brief Sketch of Mysterious Darrendra

Ahjin fell to his knees before the pot of water, fumbling for his runes and dried flowers. "Hail, gods. Hear my plea."

He glanced toward the billowing smoke. Though the gods usually told him they wouldn't help, there was no one else who could. If he couldn't convince them to make an exception, Lyell's village was doomed.

Ahjin had never wanted this job, this Mouth of the Stupid Gods, but now he was stuck with it. There was no rule book to tell him what to do, no predecessor to train him, no traditions to follow. His life was out of control, adrift in the winds of uncertainty. He had to chart a course by himself, and now was an excellent time to start.

Irajahan answered quickly, in his usual cranky mood. It took a couple of minutes longer for Makana's image to appear in the pot of water. She was smiling, and smothered laughter came from somewhere behind her, probably from one of her famous parties.

The smoke was blacker now and spreading fast.

As he explained the situation to Makana and Irajahan, Ahjin scribbled a brief note with the same information. While Irajahan argued, as usual, and Makana sent away her guests, Ahjin dropped a dried rosebay and the rune for fire on top of the note to alert Darravani and Resef to his message.

Darravani's permission for the other gods to work in her land bloomed as a fluffy yellow goldenrod. Not just agreement, but encouragement. Resef scorched only a single vertical line at the bottom of Ahjin's note, the rune for 'ice.' Two gods down, three to go.

Irajahan sent his numerous protests to both Ahjin and Makana. At the end, he smirked. "I don't see why I should help you. You're always reminding me to mind my own affairs."

"Oh, weeping whales," Makana said. "Enough! If you don't help, I'll come hit you again. Kassian will help me." She balled a fist. "I will make a nice soggy rain cloud, and you will blow it to the fire while Resef pulls away the heat. Ahjin, tell him!"

Ahjin threw his seeds, runes, and paper into his pack. "I've been telling him."

Smoke covered half the sky. There was no more time to debate. "Irajahan, I'm making it official. By the authority you all gave me, I require you to help Makana put out this fire."

Ahjin braced his head between his hands. It was a trick he'd learned the hard way, thanks to the god's frequent outbursts. This time, the hurricane Irajahan mentally blew into his brain only lasted a moment, and then the god was thankfully gone.

Ahjin didn't know if Kassian could help, but just in case, he transported the note to him, leaving help to his discretion.

By the time the first drops of rain fell, the sky was steaming hot and filled with smoke. Ahjin gave the other gods his heartfelt thanks as quickly as etiquette allowed. He shoved the pot under the bushes with all the abandoned packs.

Nia had already taken Ahjin's water jugs, so he grabbed Lyell's boots to protect his feet from embers and ash when he shifted back to his two-legged form.

The rain poured harder, flowing like a waterfall over the cliffs of Ioj. The last time he'd been in a storm this impressive, the weather had been berserk because the world was ending. Makana had apparently taken notes. While he appreciated the attempt to quench the fire quickly, he couldn't breathe water like Nia could. He threw his jacket over his head to block the water from his nose.

Now to get to the village as quickly as possible. When he tried to fly, he made it above the treetops but had to land within a minute. Not only did his strained wings protest, but the smoke was now so thick he couldn't breathe the billowing fumes, and the sheets of rain soaked his feathers to uselessness in seconds.

He would have to run. He had thanked Darravani for healing his shredded back, but perhaps he hadn't thanked her enough for the gift of movement. If he found some good gardeners, he would make her garden on Arupa as beautiful as the one in Kanshi.

But for now, it was time to run.

He wasn't sure which way the others had gone, besides west, but as he stumbled through the dripping, smoke-darkened forest, he found a blue ribbon hung at eye-level. He pulled it down and looked around. From there, he could just see a pink ribbon on a farther tree.

He followed the trail of ribbons for several minutes. Some trees had scorch marks, although the rain had doused the fire here. He let himself hope the gods had worked quickly enough.

The rain steamed in the overwhelming heat, adding fog to the smoke. Visibility shrank. Ahjin flapped his wings slowly, trying to stir the air enough for him to see which way to go.

The farther west he went, the more trees had burn scars. As he brushed against leaves, their crispy skeletons dissolved into ash. He leaned a hand on an unburned tree to rest for a minute and yanked away with a hiss. The trunk was too hot to touch. He kicked the fallen leaves on the forest floor and jumped back from the escaping steam. The deluge flattened the leaves back into the mud.

He spotted a yellow ribbon in the distance and pushed himself into a run. Flying would have been faster.

The air cooled to a hot summer's day. Resef was having an effect. Surely the village was safe now.

Ahjin's gasps pulled in as much smoke as air. Every breath turned into a cough. He stopped to tie his scarf across his nose and mouth, barely finishing before his sizzling boot-soles encouraged him to run again. His fragile hope dissolved in the smoky air. How could Durriel survive this fire?

A glimpse of lavender caught his eye. Another ribbon, seared onto a tree branch.

No, that was no ribbon; it was a lock of Nia's hair!

After a frantic search, he found no other trace of her and pushed himself into a faster run.

The temperature fell to late summer. The fog lightened.

When he reached an orange ribbon, he heard coughing shouts. A green ribbon beckoned him, but the direction he should go was clear now. He grabbed the ribbon and grudgingly slowed to a trot, struggling for breath. The torrent of rain had soaked through his clothes. His wet scarf clung to his face, and his hair dripped a waterfall inside his collar.

The trees were mere trunks now, and the bushes were stumps. Ahjin scuffed soggy ash with every step as he strained for a glimpse of the others.

A stone fence suddenly loomed through the smoke, steaming in the pouring rain. Beyond it was half a wall and a charred floor. A collapsed barn sagged against the stone wall on the other edge of the yard.

The air cooled to autumn again.

Ahjin leaned over and rested with his hands on his knees. Where were the people? The near part of the town was devastated, but the far end had less damage. Some of the farthest houses were merely scorched or smoke-blackened. There was a prominent well in the village square, so the residents could have fought the fire when it was small. If it hadn't grown so quickly.

The rain slowed to a steady trickle. The air continued to chill.

Ahjin gasped for breath through a racking cough. When he half-straightened, a brown hand held a dipper of water in front of him. He dragged himself upright and reached for the dipper.

"I already added a cough remedy, so don't spit it out." Ludik said.

Ahjin pulled down his scarf and emptied the dipper gratefully, despite the nasty taste. "Where is everyone else?" he croaked. "Are they okay?"

"We're searching the houses," Ludik said. "We found a few old folks that died, but it looks like almost everyone ran. Without the rain, though, the whole town would have burned, and the refugees would have fried as they ran through the woods."

"I'm glad it worked." Ahjin took another drink.

Ludik handed him the bucket. "Take it around to everyone else." He headed left into the village, and Ahjin went right.

Ahjin soon found Nia and Nemerra laying bodies in a large garden between two houses. They drank from the treated bucket between coughs. Ahjin covered the casualties with sheets and tablecloths the girls had collected from the less-damaged houses.

"Thank you," Nemerra whispered. She wiped her eyes and dragged her feet toward another house.

Nia hugged Ahjin. "Please give these to Lyell when you find him." She handed him Lyell's discarded tunic and knives before following Nemerra.

Nia's many braids had been fastened together into one tail with a single red ribbon and then looped up with the ends tied at the nape of her neck. Ahjin would return her ribbons later, when they were less busy.

Ahjin peeked in and around every house along the edge of the village before he found Gurryon. The tall Darrendrakar crouched by two bodies in the back path. One corpse held a knife clenched in his hand. The other hadn't even drawn his before he died. Darkness covered a patch of dirt around them.

The rain beat into the dark circle and flowed out in pink streams.

Ahjin swallowed hard. "Um, Gurryon," he started.

Gurryon jerked to his feet and drew his knife. He was halfway to Ahjin before he stopped. "Oh, Ahjin, it's you." He sheathed his knife and coughed. "Come look at these and tell me what you think."

Ahjin reluctantly approached. Hadn't he seen enough death yet?

Gurryon rolled the first body halfway to its side for a better view. "Look." He pointed to a long hole in the man's side. "I might be wrong, but this wound looks the same shape as the one that killed Agu and the other Dog." He let the body fall and turned over the second one. "As I feared. This one is the same."

"We should warn the girls to leave the bodies here," Ahjin said, "until we have a chance to investigate more. We don't want to ruin any evidence. Anything left by the rain, anyway."

Gurryon rubbed his hands on his tunic. "Why were these people killed? What do they have to do with anything? Are we chasing a madman who kills for no reason?"

"I don't know," Ahjin said. "We'll ask Lyell and Ludik what they think. Lyell knows the area and the people, and Ludik can give his healer's opinion."

Gurryon pushed his soggy hair out of his eyes. "Those were my healing lessons Ludik borrowed, you know."

"True," Ahjin said. "Are you as good as he is?"

"Not really." Gurryon stood and coughed. "We should ask him, too."

Ahjin handed Gurryon a dipper of medicated water and glared at him when he started to spit it out. "Swallow," Ahjin commanded. "You can complain to your brother about the taste. I still haven't given everyone their dose. Can you talk to Nia and Nemerra, that way," he pointed, "while I find the others?"

Gurryon swallowed with a grimace. "I'm supposed to help them anyway." He slapped Ahjin on the shoulder and headed back into town.

Ahjin wove through the houses until he found Zefra with an armful of wet linens. Her cloak was missing, and the downpour had pulled red tendrils from her braided crown until they trailed down her neck in a cold parody of fire. Her lips quivered.

"Hey, it's over now," Ahjin murmured. He took the linens in one arm and held out the bucket of water with the other. "Ludik made cough medicine." He waited until she put the dipper to her lips before he continued. "Most of the people escaped the fire. And the trees will grow back." When she took back the linens, he patted her on the back.

Tears joined the rain streaming down her face. "You do not understand," Zefra said. "The burned forest is terrible and will take years to regrow. The villagers are worse. But Lyell—" She choked to a halt.

"Lyell was with us when the fire started," Ahjin said. "Was he injured before I arrived? The gods argued forever. I'm sorry. I'll tell Ludik that Lyell needs help." He took only one step before Zefra grabbed his arm.

She took a breath to speak, then dissolved into a fit of coughing sobs. "I sent Ludik—"

She took another breath, then gave up and pointed toward the burned end of town, in the corner Ahjin hadn't yet visited. She pressed her lips together tightly and scurried toward the other girls.

Ahjin hurried in the direction Zefra had pointed. As he reached houses with extensive damage, he spotted Ludik and Lyell.

Ludik disappeared around the corner of a half-burned house. It was a pretty wooden house, with a gravel path to the front door. Half the roof had collapsed. The Canid sat against the blackened wall with his eyes closed, covered by Zefra's cloak.

Ahjin knelt by Lyell's side and gently shook his shoulder. "Are you all right? I have water for you, and your tunic and boots."

He looked at Lyell's hands, limp in the mud. Blisters covered his palms and fingers.

"I'll hold the ladle for you," Ahjin offered. "Then you can get dressed."

Lyell didn't move or open his eyes. He did have a pulse, though.

Ahjin shook him harder. "Hey, are you well?" he asked in a louder voice.

"Ahjin? Is that you?" Ludik's voice came around the corner. "Come help me, please? Bring the water with you."

Ahjin left Lyell and carried the bucket around to the front of the house.

Ludik crouched by the doorway, near a woman who lay halfway across the threshold.

Ahjin hurried closer. The woman wore a scorched blue dress. The fire that had burned her home had singed her brown hair unevenly short. Eyes as dark as Zefra's stared sightlessly at Ahjin. Her outstretched hand rested on the edge of a large basket still mostly hidden behind Ludik.

The healer searched the basket, not even looking at the woman. Ahjin didn't understand why until he peeked inside the house. A burned rafter had fallen across the woman, crushing her lower torso. She was beyond help.

"Hurry, Ahjin." Ludik touched one area of the basket for a few seconds before moving to the next. With every touch, he whispered a curse.

Ahjin finally got close enough to see what kept Ludik's attention. Inside the basket was a heap of four tiny babies, curled together in colorful blankets.

None of them moved, and he didn't see any breathing. Their skin was blue under the ash.

"Plague fleas." Ludik dropped to his knees. He rested his forehead on the basket.

Ahjin let the water bucket sag in his hands. He had been too slow for Lyell's family.

22.PUP

(DURRIEL, CANID TERRITORY)

Red carnation: my heart aches for you. Helenium: tears. Primrose: I can't live without you. Locust tree: affection beyond the grave. Rosemary: remembrance.
Flowers & Their Meanings: A Guide for All Darrendrakar

Ludik pushed the baby basket next to Ruka's dead body and took the bucket from Ahjin. He hated losing patients, even if it wasn't his fault, and children were worse than adults. What good was healing magic if it couldn't save everyone?

Being a hunter was much better than being a healer. If he came home without a deer, they could eat apples for a day. When he got home, he would tell Asad and Akamu they needed to find someone else to be the healer for Maon.

But until Durriel's healer came back, he couldn't avoid his current task. He was too late for Ruka and the babies, but he still had one patient to help. He walked around the house to where Lyell sat in the mud, barely covered by Zefra's cloak.

The Wolf still hadn't moved. His skin was coated in ash despite the rain, and his hands had second-level burns across his palms and fingers. He didn't open his eyes as Ludik approached.

"Lyell. Lyell, I know you are awake. It is time to move." Ludik tipped back Lyell's head and poured water in his mouth.

Lyell flinched and swallowed to keep from drowning.

"I'm very sorry, Lyell, but letting yourself die won't help." Ludik pulled out his healing kit and took one of Lyell's hands.

They would have to deal with his emotional wounds later. He didn't know how to do that, but there must be someone who did. Durriel's shaman, or maybe Gurryon.

Ludik finished washing one hand and reached for the other.

Lyell stiffened. "Did you hear that?" His voice was thick with unshed tears.

"No." Maybe grief, exhaustion, and his injuries were causing hallucinations. Ludik might need to put Lyell to sleep for a while, after bandaging his burns.

As he reached for the water again, he heard a whine from the fire-damaged beams. Lyell shot to his feet and dashed around the corner of the house, throwing Zefra's cloak around his neck to cover his naked body.

Ludik followed close behind. The Wolf was obviously grief-crazed and needed someone to keep him out of trouble.

Lyell stood in the front yard, looking from one side to the other and inhaling deeply.

Between the pounding rain, the smoke, and the aromas of scorched wood and flesh, Ludik smelled nothing useful. "Lyell, sit and let me wash your hand."

Ahjin looked up, letting the last corner of a burned curtain fall across the basket and Ruka's face. "What are you doing?"

"Nothing." Lyell rubbed his eyes. "I thought I heard—"

He broke off when a bush rustled. He stalked softly across the yard and crouched to look underneath the bush.

"Hey, there," he whispered. "Come here, I've got you." He squeaked gently and knelt, stretching an arm beneath the leaves. "Come a little closer, dear."

When he pulled back his hand, he cradled a black wolf pup not much bigger than a double handful, fur flattened in the rain. The pup tried to stand, but its spindly legs were too weak, and it toppled with a yelp.

Shivers racked it from nose to scrawny tail as it closed its dark blue eyes and licked Lyell's thumb.

Ludik reached for the pup, relief flooding him from toes to nose. Someone had survived.

Lyell ignored him and cradled the baby, tears running down his cheeks.

"You have a smart child," Ahjin said, joining them to gawk at the puppy, "to know crawling on four legs would let him escape."

Lyell clenched his mouth until his lips stopped quivering enough to talk. "Infants cannot change on purpose at such a young age. It was luck that saved her life."

He turned to Ludik. "She is too cold, though. She should not be out of the house or away from her ma—" He swallowed. "Mama yet. This rain will kill her. What can we do?"

And Lyell was back to using no contractions. Was it just the stress of the situation or a change of heart?

Ludik reached for the pup. "Let me check her for injuries. Go find Zefra. Bring her back here as quickly as you can."

"Zefra? Why?" Lyell half-turned to keep his daughter away from Ludik.

Ludik glared at him. "Give her to me and get Zefra before it is too late. Move!" He held out his hands until Lyell handed him the shaking ball of wet fur. "Ahjin, keep the rain off us for a few minutes."

Lyell shifted to wolf shape, dropped Zefra's cloak, and ran toward the center of town.

Ahjin unfolded a wing and bent it above Ludik and the pup. "Is this what you had in mind?"

"That is perfect, thanks. As long as you're standing there, you might as well pray for the rain to stop, too." He ignored Ahjin's glower and examined the sopping-wet baby.

Ahjin made another face, but he did mutter to the gods while Ludik worked.

The pup suffered from smoke inhalation and early hypothermia. None of that was a surprise. She did have a full belly, which improved her chances of survival. He would have to ask Lyell about milk nurses or typical milk substitutes.

Ahjin's feathers rustled. "Are you finished yet? The rain should stop soon. Ah, there it goes." He mopped his face and folded his wing as the rain finally died.

Ludik dipped a soft rag in the cough-medicated water and let the puppy suck on it. Her paws were miraculously unburned, though he had to pluck a thorn from one.

In only a few minutes, Lyell bounded back with Zefra running behind.

"Here I am." Zefra skidded to a stop as the wolf edged around Ludik to sniff his pup. "Nia told me to follow Lyell to you."

"I need you to warm this baby," Ludik said. "You can do that without fire, right?"

"I can. 'Tis like drying my socks." She rubbed her hands under her armpits, the driest part of her robe, and scooped the pup out from under Lyell's nose.

Ludik's patient kept her eyes closed, but her shivers gradually slowed. He had Zefra dry his handkerchief and showed her how to rub the pup gently to dry her fur and increase her circulation.

The wolf watched until the pup's body relaxed and her breath softened into sleep, then he grabbed his clothes from Ahjin and went into the house. When Lyell reemerged a few minutes later, he was two-legged, dressed, and carrying an assortment of smoke-blackened objects.

"I found a small carry basket, a bottle, and a few supplies. I have nothing to feed her yet, but I hope to find one of the village goats that escaped."

He stuffed everything but the basket and a blanket into a bag that had only a few burn holes. "Here. At least it is dry." He handed the blanket to Zefra and hung the basket's long strap over one shoulder and across his torso.

"I'm sorry," Ludik said, "but Zefra must carry your daughter. We have to keep her warm or she'll die."

They would have to keep giving her the cough medicine, too, when she woke. At least her mama saved her from the actual flames and gave her a chance to fight for her life.

"I can keep her warm enough," Lyell shouted, reaching for the pup. "You will burn her. Give me back my daughter!"

Ludik didn't blame him for the outburst. He wouldn't wish the last hours on his worst enemy, and Dog though he was, Lyell was no longer his enemy. Ludik would happily listen to his shouts if it meant the Wolf was ready to live again.

Zefra wrapped the pup in the blanket and tucked her into the crook of one elbow, then put her free hand on top of Lyell's.

After a few seconds, he sighed. "I see." He helped settle the carry basket on Zefra, then took his baby, kissed her fuzzy head, and slipped her into the basket. "Where do we go now?"

Zefra settled both warm hands over the ball of black fur.

Ahjin squeezed water from his curls. "There are two dead bodies on the other side of town you two should see," he said flatly. "They were killed with a weapon, not by the fire."

Ludik threw his hands in the air. "Don't we have enough trouble? If they're already dead, they won't get worse while I treat Lyell's hand. Ahjin, go help the others finish gathering the deceased, and we'll meet you — where?"

"I'll leave you a signal. Or Lyell can track me by scent, now the rain has stopped." Ahjin squished through the mud toward the center of the village.

Ludik pulled ointment and bandages from his healing kit and grabbed Lyell's hand. "Is there a flag or something we can use to signal your townspeople it's safe to come home, or do we have to wait for them to decide it's safe?"

"Or something, yes." Lyell threw back his head and howled, long and loud.

Return howls echoed from all directions.

"They are coming," Lyell said.

Lyell's hands now had bits of leaves, dirt, ash, and puppy fuzz embedded in the burns, as well as the soot and blood still on the untreated hand. Ludik mentally cursed difficult patients while he cleaned the wounds. He used an extra long bandage to wrap Lyell's hands, hoping the awkward bulk would keep him out of trouble for at least a few minutes.

"Let's go join the others," Ludik said.

"Yes." Zefra gently rocked the basket.

Lyell looked between his burned house and his sleeping daughter. "No."

Ludik growled at him. "We don't have time to dawdle. Two murdered men and an unknown number of dead villagers still wait for us."

"It will not take long," Lyell said. "I want to stop by the town registry and see if Ruka recorded the children's names. She wanted to surprise me with them."

Ludik winced, regretting his impatience. "We can do that. Is there anything else you want from your house right now?"

"Yes, if you will help me." Lyell hopped back through the window and tugged on the rafter on his wife's body. He strained, arms quivering, as his bandages turned gray with ash.

Ludik should have thought of that himself. He was an idiot.

He stepped carefully around Ruka to take the other end of the beam, and together they tossed it aside.

Lyell picked up Ruka's broken body and carried her through the half-burned house and into the bedroom. Zefra carried the basket of dead babies on the opposite hip from their littermate.

The blankets on the bed were thrown aside as if Ruka had suddenly awakened and jumped up. Tears stung Ludik's eyes. She hadn't left the house when it first started burning because she had been asleep. She hadn't woken until it was too late.

Lyell laid his wife on the bed. Zefra set the basket of dead babies next to her.

Lyell rubbed his hands over his face. He unfastened the silver chain from his neck and draped it next to the matching chain around Ruka's throat. Then he pulled the blankets over his family.

Zefra and Ludik went outside to give him privacy.

Lyell's singing voice carried softly through the doorway in a pleasant but unremarkable baritone.

"We will walk along with your hand in mine. You are mine lifelong; I am always thine.

"You are still my light and my everything. With you, life is bright, and my heart will sing.

"At the end of day, I will sit with you, share my heart's bouquet and my love renew.

"You are still my light and my everything. With you, life is bright, and my heart will sing.

"When you leave in death at the final end, you will take my breath, and I cannot mend.

"You have been my light and my everything. With you, life was bright, and my heart did sing."

Zefra sniffled and patted the fuzzy wolf pup.

Ludik cleared his throat several times and tried not to think how he'd feel when Nemerra died, even as an old grandmama decades from now.

When Lyell walked out, he carried an inkwell and a piece of parchment. He handed both to Ludik and motioned for Zefra to give him his daughter. He dripped ink on one baby paw and pressed it against the paper. After waving the parchment to dry it, he took the ink inside.

Ludik washed the pup's foot and resettled her in the carry basket.

Lyell returned, still waving the parchment. "Now I am ready. The town hall is that way." He pointed toward the center of the village.

It was a short walk to the only stone building. The windowsills and door had burned, but the walls and slate roof were intact. Instead of a gravel path to the front door, it had real paving stones.

Ludik waited in the street with Zefra, glaring at the stone hall. If the villagers had stone homes, more people might have survived. It would at least have reduced the burns, even if it didn't prevent smoke inhalation. Stone was more expensive and harder to work with, but were records more important than people?

But the house Ludik built for Nemerra was also wooden. It was traditional, easy to build and decorate, and convenient in the middle of a forest.

The thought of a fire running through Maon kept him silent while they waited, and Zefra was too busy petting the wolf pup to speak.

They had identified Ahjin's signal — a yellow curtain hanging in a tree — by the time Lyell emerged. Ludik caught a glimpse of several names written on the parchment before Lyell shoved it awkwardly into his pocket with a bandaged hand.

Lyell touched the baby's head. "This one is Tala. She was second-born. I am ready to go now."

They walked silently across town to Ahjin's yellow signal. The others already stood around the bodies and the blood-stained dirt.

Ludik crouched by the bodies and turned their heads so Lyell could see their faces. "Did you know them?"

"Yes, two of the village guards. They did not have border shifts, just local patrols."

Ludik rotated the bodies to examine their injuries. The wounds were the same as those on Agu and the yellow dog in the forest, deep and round and ending in a point. They were undoubtedly killed by the same weapon. The murderer had struck again.

If only they had caught him before now. They were too slow, always too slow. At least the fire was an accident.

Or was it? They had been getting closer to their quarry. He could have set the fire to scare them off the track. Or did the killer hope his trackers would be caught in the blaze?

If Orrik hadn't delayed them for a day, could they have caught him before he reached Durriel?

Mongrel curs. How many more would die before they caught this monster?

23. DURRIEL

(DURRIEL, CANID TERRITORY)

A proper Darrendran funeral includes planting flowers on the grave. In winter or times of hardship, scattering seeds is adequate.

Darrendran Religious Ceremonies

Nia leaned against the charred door jamb, unable to stop crying. She and Nemerra had been searching for dead villagers with Gurryon since they arrived, which was already a miserable task. Then Zefra had come to help, and she told them about Lyell's family. Nia and Nemerra had been crying steadily since then, even after Lyell ran up and dragged Zefra away.

"I don't think I can put Lyell's babies with the other dead," Nia bawled into the smoky wood. "They're just babies. How do I tell Lyell how sorry I am? I planned a party to celebrate their birth, with Ruka's permission, and now they're dead. And Ruka, too."

She mopped her face with her already soggy handkerchief. This was the last house, and there were no dead to mark for removal. In the whole village, there had only been a dozen or so deaths, mostly those too old to evacuate. Considering the amount of damage to the buildings, it could have been worse. But even one was too many, and including Lyell's family was a piranha-faced tragedy.

Ahjin strolled up, hands in his pockets and curls dripping over his soggy jacket. "Did Lyell tell you about his baby?" he asked.

Nemerra nodded, wiping her eyes. "Zefra told us. It's so sad."

"Oh, you didn't hear," Ahjin said. "One survived. Zefra didn't know earlier, and I guess Lyell was too busy to mention her."

"All he said was that Ludik needed Zefra." It was wonderful news, but Nia still couldn't stop crying.

Ahjin patted Nia on the shoulder. "The baby isn't in good shape, but Ludik thinks she'll make it. Zefra will care for her until she gets stronger."

Nia and Nemerra exchanged glances. Zefra was a wonderful girl, and very competent in some ways, but she wasn't so much the nurturing type.

They wiped their eyes and followed Ahjin and Gurryon to the murdered guards at the edge of town to wait for the others to come. Nia sat on a fallen log with Nemerra and refused to look for evidence around the body. Enough was enough, and this was more than enough.

A few minutes later, the others arrived. Ludik headed directly for the corpses and poked at their wounds with a ferocious scowl on his face.

How could he stand to do such disgusting things? Ick.

Lyell had his clothes back. His eyes were red, and his shoulders slumped. He hovered around Zefra like a shark around a shipwreck, clenching his fists and glaring at anyone who approached.

Zefra kept one hand in the basket hung around her torso and one under it.

Nia edged past Lyell. "Zefra, show us what you have in there." She tugged on the edge of the basket until Zefra let her look inside.

Curled in a small blanket was the cutest ball of black fluff ever created. Her pointed ears were half-flattened against her head, and one paw lay across her tiny nose.

"Oooh. I want to hold her," Nia demanded. Here was the perfect antidote to tears.

"No," Ludik said behind her.

She turned to glare at him. When the water ran pink as he washed his hands, she turned away.

"If anyone holds her, it will be me," Lyell grouched.

"She's not warm enough yet," Zefra said. "Later." She fluffed the pup's fur with her fingers. "After she's dry. Worry about the bodies and let me worry about the puppy."

"When will the killing stop?" Nemerra asked. "Why would someone do this?"

"This much death hints at a deadly enemy rather than a personal grudge." Ludik rubbed his hands over his face.

Nia gulped. He'd better have washed them well.

"If he is an enemy of the Cats, why is he killing Dogs?" Lyell growled.

"If he is an enemy of the Dogs, what was he doing in Felid territory?" Gurryon snarled.

Nia stomped her foot. "Why is he anyone's enemy at all? We don't know who he is or what he wants."

"When we catch him, those are excellent questions to ask," Ludik said. "And to catch him, we need more information. Lyell, you know the area better. While you search for evidence we might have missed, we'll take these guards to the other deceased."

Lyell reached for his daughter, then growled and stomped toward the forest without her.

While Nia gathered flowers with Nemerra and Zefra, the men dragged the bodies into town and laid them by the smoke casualties.

Nia cried steadily again as they sprinkled the flowers over the bodies.

Lyell returned and sat with his back to the dead. "I circled the town," he said. "The rain washed out the scents, but I found a few signs. It looks like one of the culprits hid in the forest. When the others arrived from the southwest, they met with him and snuck around to set fires on the other side of town. It was probably a distraction to allow our quarry to escape us, since they all went southwest again after that. I think the guards caught them on the way out."

Nia gasped. "They set fire to houses as a distraction?" She sat beside Lyell and put her head between her knees. Could this adventure go any more wrong?

Zefra asked, "Was it the man we have been following, or the one he met here?"

"I do not know the answer to either question," Lyell admitted. "It looks like the fire was set in that barn on the edge of town. It spread quickly, but I cannot tell if that was on purpose or not."

"How long ago did they leave?" Ludik asked. "Can we catch them?"

"It depends how quickly they are traveling," Lyell said. "The fire started shortly before we arrived. We have been cleaning for a while, though."

"We could shift to four feet," Gurryon suggested.

"Not all of us can do that," Zefra said. "Did you plan to leave us behind or let us ride you again? And what about the baby?"

Gurryon threw his arms in the air and muttered rude words. At least he said them in Felid instead of trade tongue. Nia didn't translate them for Zefra.

"I can scout ahead," Lyell said.

"Thank you for escorting us this far," Ahjin said, "but you don't have to continue."

"Tala should be well enough by morning for blankets to keep her warm," Ludik said.

Lyell ran a finger over Tala's ears and frowned. "We can discuss this after I find the shaman."

He walked away, and Zefra tucked the blanket close around his baby.

Nia frowned. When would it be her turn to hold the furry little puppy?

"All the villagers are coming back," Gurryon said. "Nia, come translate for me."

Despite her protests, he dragged her through the burned town and into the square, ruining her chance at fuzzy joy and dumping her back into the horror she wanted to forget. The wails of distress at the burned houses rang even louder when the villagers found the row of bodies.

Gurryon talked to everyone about what they might have seen, making Nia repeat questions two or three times when he got no response from the mourning villagers.

In the end, the information was scarce. Few people had seen anything. Some had fought the fire, but when it spread too quickly, they called for evacuation instead. Those who tried to escape to the west had been chased back by arrows. The two guards sent to deal with that problem hadn't been seen again until now. And that was all anyone in the village knew, no matter how many times Gurryon made Nia ask.

She finally folded her arms and refused to translate. Since the villagers didn't know anything, they should be left in peace to clean up and mourn their dead.

Lyell returned with the shaman, Tema, and Nia's group clustered around them.

"The town of Orrik lost their shamans in the recent earthquakes," Gurryon explained, "and with neither access to Darravani while she was captured nor a shaman to reassure them, they have lost their faith and trust. They need a new temporary shaman as quickly as possible while they wait for a permanent replacement. Since they know you and you have not been escorting Cats, they will trust you. You need to go there now."

Lyell frowned. "We need to hold the funerals tonight."

"Do not worry," Tema said. "I can leave first thing in the morning."

Nia stomped her foot. "But they're arming for war right now. There's no time to lose. We're already hours from those Dogs. If someone doesn't stop them, who knows how soon they might attack the Cats? They might have already left, unless we left them in enough disarray to delay them."

Tema looked at Lyell and shook his head. "I cannot leave my people without the comfort of proper funerals. My apprentice is not ready for the task. Tomorrow is the best I can do."

Nia shared a dismayed glance with Ahjin. Tomorrow would be too late to prevent Orrik from leaving for Maon, if it weren't already.

Gurryon pulled Ahjin closer. "What if we hold the funerals? I am only an apprentice, but I am well-trained and approaching full priest status. Ahjin is the Mouth of the Gods and has Darravani's authority to perform Darrendran rites."

Tema gasped. "His Holiness? I heard about you. I am honored to meet you." He clasped arms with Ahjin as the avian turned red. "Yes, I suppose you two will do well enough. I will pack a bag and be on my way."

"Wait," Ahjin said. "If we stay for the funerals, we won't make it out of here before morning."

"We still must retrieve our packs," Zefra said. "Dark will fall in just over an hour. Unless you want to follow our quarry after sunset, we cannot leave tonight."

"Chase a killer in an unfamiliar forest in the dark?" Nia shuddered. "Please, tell me you aren't that stupid."

"Fine, we aren't that stupid." Ahjin ruffled her hair until she ducked.

"If we can't leave tonight, then we should perform the funerals so Tema can go to Orrik. We'll leave at sunrise."

Ludik followed the shaman toward his house. "I will tell you about our experience in Orrik and make sure you have directions. Don't hold the funerals without me," he called over his shoulder.

He was back in the village square in a few minutes with a green bundle in his arms.

"All right, everyone," Gurryon called to the villagers, "please bring your dead to the cemetery. We will start in a few minutes."

He waited until the crowd dispersed. "Ludik, we have a problem. Neither Ahjin nor I have the correct clothing to officiate, and Ahjin left all his seeds in his pack."

"No worries." Ludik unfolded his package. "Tema thought of that. Here's his spare robe for you and his apprentice's for Ahjin. It's the only one that might fit, and I assured him you won't be insulted. He left the usual assortment of funeral seeds, too, and told the headman you're doing the funeral. Tema and his guards are traveling on four legs to get to Orrik by morning."

Ludik helped Gurryon dress, while Nia helped Ahjin adjust the robe as much as possible over his wings. The hem hiked up a foot in the back no matter how much she tugged on it.

"That is what you looked like the first time I met you," Zefra said to Ahjin. "I thought you were a hunchback. I was quite surprised when I saw you fly."

Ahjin wrinkled his nose at her. "A hunchback? Really?"

Nia giggled despite her unhappiness. He did look like a hunchback. She smoothed her face when he turned to look at her. "Don't mind her," she said. "I think you look fine. Green is a good color on you."

When he turned back, she smiled again. The next time he was annoying, she could call him a hunchback.

Her smile died when Lyell asked her and Nemerra to carry his children to the cemetery. He cradled his wife in his arms and led the way.

The slow procession was full of noisy weeping, Nia's included. The babies in her arms were adorable, but so cold and still. Her shoulders trembled so badly that, if the babies had been alive, they surely would have protested the motion. Nemerra walked steadily beside Nia, but silent tears ran down her cheeks and dripped onto the babies she held.

Those that did not carry the deceased hauled shovels and spare linens. The entire village helped dig the graves, side by side under scorched trees, then wrapped the dead and laid them to rest.

Lyell did not cry. His face was stiff as he lowered his wife into her grave, pressed a tender kiss to her forehead, and laid their babies in her arms.

While Gurryon and Ahjin conducted the brief funeral service, the sunset cast a blue glow across the silent bodies, making them look bruised from head to foot.

Nia shivered. The entire village might have died. And nobody knew how many more could die before they caught the murderer. Murderers, as if they needed more than one.

Nemerra fed Zefra a steady stream of fence slats that had been donated by the village headman, Mingan. He identified each dead villager for her in a choked voice, and she burned their names on the grave markers. Nia handed each one to the family members.

When Lyell stepped up for his wife's marker, Nia looked at Ruka's name with four smaller names under it. Fresh tears covered her cheeks, but Lyell was silent.

It wasn't until dirt was shoveled over the graves and Ahjin sprinkled seeds across them that a single tear slipped from Lyell's eye. He swiped it away and dropped a yellow zinnia across the seeds.

"My neighbor picked it from her husband's grave for me. It is from the flowers Ruka planted." Lyell rubbed baby Tala's head and left for the village.

Some of the mourners stayed at the gravesites, while others followed Lyell. Nia and her friends plodded behind them, watching Mingan encourage and comfort stragglers. Ludik frowned the entire time.

Once the villagers seemed well on their way, Mingan dropped back. "Thank you for helping. Since you cannot leave until morning, we found beds for you, and baths, and food, and a wet nurse for the baby."

Nia silently cheered. All those sounded wonderful. It had been hours since Ruka had died, and the puppy's whimpers must mean she was hungry. The rest of the offer was generous, considering the villagers who still had homes already sheltered those who had lost theirs. At least they didn't have to travel after dark again. It was bad enough running away from killers in the dark, without running toward them.

"Thank you," Ahjin said. "We'll collect our packs and be back soon."

"We can speed things a little," Nia said. "How do you men feel about fetching all the packs while we ladies feed Tala and bathe? If we hurry, we can finish by the time you get back, and then you can take your turn."

Since the boys bathed first last time, it was the girls' turn to go first, anyway. Nia rubbed her hands together. Warm water and a real bed. Maybe a real bed? A real roof, anyway. And the puppy would sleep with Zefra. Nia was happy to sleep on the other side of the fuzzball, to keep her from falling off the bed, of course. And if she petted the puppy in her sleep, who would know?

Ahjin nodded, and the men turned back toward the forest, stretching their legs in a near jog.

"Taking turns is a good idea," Mingan said. "It would take a long time to draw and heat enough water for all of you to bathe at once."

"If you fill one tub with cold water, I can heat it while you heat the water for the other tub," Zefra said.

"How will you do that?" Mingan asked.

Nia waved her hand wearily to indicate mysterious doings. "Magic, of course."

"Whatever you say," Mingan said. "Let us know if you need anything."

"Great. I get to hold the puppy while Zefra bathes." Nia skipped for a couple of steps before she remembered why Zefra had Tala in the first place.

Holding the pup would not make up for the rest of the disaster.

She would try again to see the murderer in her bath water. Maybe she'd be lucky this time.

24.PURSUIT

(DURRIEL, CANID TERRITORY)

Our defensive circle failed today. The despicable Hyenas slaughtered women and children before we pushed them back.
Torao, after The Battle of Sad Laughter

Ludik wasn't happy about fetching their abandoned packs while the women prepared the baths. He wanted to wash off the ash and smoke, but he didn't feel comfortable leaving Nemerra. Half the town had burned, and who knew if the culprits would return?

Mingan had lent them lanterns, but it was a more dangerous trip through the burned forest than Ludik expected. The ground and trees had cooled, but the lanterns did not cast enough light to tell which trees were safe to walk under. Weakened branches fell at random, snapping under their own weight, and broken stubs snagged feet and clothes.

Ludik's and Gurryon's better night vision gave them an advantage in the dark. After the second falling branch nearly broke a wing, Ahjin tucked his wings tightly and let the brothers drag him away from hazard after hazard.

Gurryon cursed his way through the forest, but Ludik kept his mouth shut and fumed. They wouldn't be in this danger if the Dogs kept their teeth to themselves.

By the time Ludik, Gurryon, and Ahjin got back to town with the packs, they were exhausted. They didn't get the chance to ask Mingan where to find their women before the villagers swarmed them, tear tracks outlining their angry mouths.

"This is war," one said. "They murdered our families. Tell us who did this, so we can kill them."

"Settle down," Ahjin said. "We'll find out who is responsible, and you won't kill anybody. We want to stop a war, not start another one."

Ludik didn't want a war, but he understood how the Durriel villagers felt. His Grandpapa had struggled with his mutilated hand for decades, and there was a row of family graves in the Maon forest that spoke of the greater damage left from the Hyenas. Where was justice for the victims?

"You do not understand," the villagers shouted from every side. "We want to punish them." "We want them to suffer the way we suffer." "They do not deserve to live." Their anger was nearly a visible force.

Ludik didn't know how to make the crowd see reason. Would they attack him and his friends in their desperation for revenge?

"You know Darravani forbids war," Gurryon said. "Would you risk her wrath? Do you want the temple shamans to trample you under their Elephant feet?"

"They will not do that," one man protested. "This war is not over territory or trivial concerns. This retribution is justice. Darravani will understand."

"I tell you, she will not." Gurryon set his shoulders and stood tall, speaking slowly. "She accepts no excuse for war among her children. We priests have strict instructions."

Ludik had never seen his brother take his role of shaman so seriously. Didn't he feel the anger that made Ludik's hair stand on end? He narrowed his eyes and examined his brother.

Though Gurryon faced the crowd earnestly, the corners of his mouth were tight and his hands were fisted behind his back. Yes, he felt it, too.

How could he ignore the urge for revenge? What would it take to break the control Shaman Akamu must have taught him?

The crowd pressed forward. "You are only an apprentice," someone shouted.

Gurryon tried to speak again.

They shouted over him. "If Tema were here, he would understand."

Ludik put a hand on his knife. He didn't want to aggravate the situation, but he would defend himself and the others if the Dogs attacked. He was almost ready to give up their hunt as useless and return home to guard the border. If they couldn't stop the war, maybe they could still win it.

A thump made everyone turn to look at Ahjin, who had dropped his pack on the ground and now rapidly hunted through it. He pulled out Torao's book and raised it high.

"Here's a journal from someone who fought in the last interkindred war. He tells of death and maiming and devastation. He lost half a hand, and he was lucky. Many of his friends died. His father and uncles died. Most of his brothers died. More than half the men in his village died, and a high percentage of the women and children, too. The Cats and the Hyenas took years to recover, if you can call it recovering with so many deaths."

The crowd stopped shouting and gaped at him.

Ludik stared at Ahjin. How would reminding them of that injustice help?

Ahjin shook the journal at them. "You are asking for this to happen again. Is war really what you want?"

"It will not come to that," someone said. "If we wipe out the murderers, it will end. Our kin will be paid for with blood and can rest in peace."

"I tell you, it won't work," Ahjin shouted. "War is evil, and it breeds evil. Anger feeds on anger, and hate grows hate. Even the gods would tell you grudges and revenge lead to devastation. That's what led to the near-destruction of the world this summer. Don't let your thirst for vengeance bring another massacre. Let us end this conflict. We will still bring justice to your families."

Gurryon knocked Ludik's hand from his hilt and gripped his shoulder. Ludik nodded once. He would wait to see if Ahjin could pacify the raging Dogs.

"What kind of justice?" someone yelled.

Gurryon raised his hands. "Darravani will bring you true peace."

"What if it doesn't work?" the man muttered.

"We can kill them later," someone else whispered. "Let them try for a few days."

Ahjin held the journal above his head. He stared at each person in the crowd until they looked away. One by one, the villagers scuttled to their homes.

Ahjin waited until they all left, then repacked the journal and shrugged his pack on his shoulder. "Are we ready for those baths, then?"

Ludik clapped Ahjin and Gurryon on the shoulders. "Well done."

Gurryon shook his head. "That was amazing, Ahjin."

"That was the unfortunate truth," Ahjin said. "Both of you should change your own attitudes. It's time to make peace with the other kindreds. If the gods can start cooperating, the Darrendrakar can let go of past wrongs and do the same."

"It's not that easy," Ludik protested. "Have you considered our current situation? We were sent to catch a harmless person from spreading a dangerous misunderstanding. Now we're chasing someone so ruthless they would burn a whole village."

His statement hung in the air all the way through town.

As Ludik emerged from his bath in clean clothes, the women had food ready next to a small fire in the village square. Everyone sat on the ground and tried not to look at the burned houses around them, eating as if they hadn't had food since yesterday.

Ludik crammed half a roll into his mouth. "At least this food is better than that slop in the jail."

He reached for another as Nemerra frowned at him. When he shrugged an apology for his bad manners, she laughed and handed him the roll. He ate it one polite bite at a time, watching her steadfastly until he finished.

Nemerra smiled under his scrutiny, but a tempting pink crept up her neck to her cheeks. As soon as she and Nia finished eating, they convinced Zefra the baby would be fine out of her basket for a few minutes. They passed her back and forth, wrapped in her blanket, until she whined and Zefra took her back.

"She just ate, so she's probably cold." Zefra tucked Tala into the basket and put a warm hand over her.

"It's late," Nemerra said. "Why don't you go to bed. Tala can snuggle next to you for warmth."

"I'm cold," Ludik murmured. "You can snuggle by me."

Nemerra swatted his shoulder without sparing him a glance from her beautiful eyes.

Nia yawned. "Bed is a great idea. I vote yes. Who will ask Mingan where we're sleeping?"

"I will," Ahjin said. "Since we aren't leaving tonight, I want to ask him if I can leave a note in the town hall about hiring workers for Arupa."

"I'll walk with you," Ludik said. "I want to make sure Lyell's bandages didn't get too dirty at the graves."

This pending war wasn't the Wolf's fault, and he was suffering as much as anyone. Dogs loved their families as much as Cats did.

Gurryon and the women stayed to clean up and smother the fire.

Ludik left Ahjin at Mingan's house, next to the town hall, and continued to Lyell's burned home. If he wasn't there, Ludik would check the cemetery.

His hunch was correct. A heap of debris was stacked outside the window, and Lyell was sweeping his home, one slow stroke after another, working by the light of a tiny lamp.

Ludik stood in the doorway, half in the dark. "Lyell, why are you doing that?"

The Wolf kept his gaze on the fire-blackened floor. "Ruka always kept our home tidy. She would never let it get so messy."

"It can wait until I check your bandages."

Lyell held his hands to the light. "They are fine. Anything else?" He turned back to his task without waiting for an answer.

Ludik looked at the broom strokes in the ash. There was a pale spot at his feet where Ruka had fallen, blocking the floor from more soot. For a moment, his imagination replaced the house in front of him with his own home. If war came to Maon, a pale patch on the floor might be his last memory of Nemerra.

He took a desperate breath and blinked, and Lyell's house was back in front of him.

"We're leaving at sunrise," Ludik finally said. "Will you be ready to take Tala?"

"Yes."

After a few minutes listening to the swish of the broom, Ludik left.

He'd always thought the other kindreds must somehow be different in order to be as cruel and deceitful as Grandpapa described them. Orrik had been no surprise. But Lyell, though fierce, was kind, honest, and heartbreakingly familiar in his love and grief.

Ludik walked back to the town hall and found Ahjin by the moonlight on his white wings.

"How did it go with Mingan?" Ludik asked as he fell into step toward the village square.

Ahjin shrugged, wings rustling. "I got directions for housing. Mingan hinted some villagers want to go with us tomorrow, but since they're out for blood, I declined the offer. Breakfast will be ready at sunrise. I've also been informed that no one here will ever be interested in working for outkindred, Mouth of the Gods or not, though I can post my note if I feel like wasting my time and ink. I did, and I'll check on it on our way back. How was Lyell?"

Ludik sighed. "He's sweeping his floor. He'll get Tala in the morning."

"Oh." Ahjin didn't say anything else until they reached the women and he had to give directions.

The men and women separated again. Ludik hugged Nemerra and went to bed, but it was a long time before he fell asleep in the smoke-scented house.

How could their quarry be ruthless enough to burn an entire village and risk the lives of all the people? But this was someone who had brutally killed three times before this. What if they meant to kill the villagers rather than merely create a distraction? If they were savage enough to do it on purpose, Ludik and his group might walk into the hands of people with no conscience at all.

He could expose Nemerra to the worst sort of danger.

Should he leave her behind? Durriel was nothing like Orrik. She could help the villagers clean up and rebuild, and enjoy their company. It might be a pleasant vacation for her, instead of a relentless chase through the forest.

The village hadn't saved Ruka.

No, he would keep Nemerra with him and protect her himself.

When he finally fell asleep, he slept poorly.

The nightmares woke him even before Ahjin's wings rustled.

"Are you awake?" Ahjin whispered in the dark.

"Yes," Ludik said.

"No," Gurryon grumbled.

"Let's go," Ahjin said.

They dressed and packed without a lamp and stumbled outside to wait for the women.

Nemerra and Zefra arrived almost immediately. Nia miraculously showed up soon after, though she glared continuously at Zefra and kept rubbing her arm. Lyell was the only one missing.

Ahjin's eyes were as red as Ludik's felt, and he winced in the first rays of the sun. They lined up to collect hot, delicious-smelling stuffed rolls from the basket a sleepy villager held.

"I guess Lyell changed his mind about meeting us," Ludik said. "Everyone, eat while you walk so we have time to take Tala home."

Lyell could find somewhere to stay that wasn't filled with the memory of Ruka's voice. Ludik kissed Nemerra's fingers.

Zefra rocked the pup and tucked her blanket in more securely. "I miss her already," she whispered. "She's such a sweet little baby, so quiet and soft."

"She's not yours," Nemerra reminded her softly. She patted Zefra's shoulder, then helped her slide her pack straps over the carrier harness. "I'm sure Lyell will let you visit her on our way back."

"'Tis not the same." Zefra stroked Tala's fur the whole way to Lyell's house.

They found Lyell with a large pack on his back, frantically throwing blankets and a wooden bucket into a basket. A bleating goat yanked on the leash tied to a tree outside the door.

"I am sorry I am late," he said. "I had to bargain with my neighbor for the goat." He handed the goat's lead rope to Gurryon and pulled a bottle from the basket. Someone had wrapped his hands with lighter bandages. "Can I hold Tala long enough to feed her?"

Zefra lifted the pup from her carry basket and handed her to Lyell. "She's better today, but she might not be hungry. The wet nurse fed her again this morning."

"We can at least discover if she likes goat's milk," Lyell said. "And look, she does. That is good."

He smiled at his daughter, who sucked on the nipple as she clutched her tiny paws around the bottle. "If someone will carry the basket for me, I will take it back as soon as Tala eats."

"Where are we escorting you?" Ludik asked.

Lyell scowled. "I am escorting you. You no longer have the safe-conduct pendants, and I would *love*" — he growled the word — "to meet the person who killed my family."

Ahjin tightened his shoulders. "That's not a good idea."

Ludik squeezed Nemerra's hand. "Yes, it is." Lyell deserved to see the capture of his wife's murderer. And maybe letting him come would restore his trust in the Felids.

Nia scowled at him. "I think the deaths were an accident. You said yourself they didn't light any of the houses."

Lyell's eyes glistened. "They set the fire on purpose. I do not care if they meant for people to die or not."

"What about Tala?" Ludik asked.

"I hoped Zefra would still help me with her."

"You should leave her with a neighbor," Nemerra said. "Zefra has warmed her enough. It's too dangerous to take her with us."

Lyell narrowed his eyes. "No more dangerous than being at home yesterday. I will never let her out of my sight again. I will find my wife's murderer, and then I will never come back."

"Oh, you don't mean that," Nemerra gasped. "You'll change your mind later."

Lyell reached for the chain he no longer wore, then looked away.

Ludik's eyes stung. It was from lack of sleep, he lied to himself.

Ahjin watched Lyell for a few minutes. "If you ride this current to the end," he said, "I can offer you a job. Come to Arupa when your daughter is strong enough for the trip, and we'll find something that works for us both."

"Thank you, but no," Lyell said. "I do not want to move to another country."

Ahjin shrugged. "The offer won't expire, but I understand if you aren't interested."

"You can't bring a goat," Gurryon said. "We're going to move faster now."

"I bought my neighbor's fastest goat," Lyell said. "She will be fine. If she isn't fast enough, we will follow behind, but I think she can outrun you."

Gurryon folded his arms. "I doubt it. But if you are coming with us, you can take care of your own goat."

Lyell nodded toward his armful of puppy and bottle. "I am afraid my hands are full right now. Will you hold on to her for me? Maybe she will drag you along fast enough to keep up."

"Ludik can do it."

Ludik smiled and picked up the large basket. "Sorry, my hands are full, too." This was too good an opportunity to tease his brother.

Nia giggled.

Gurryon groaned and snatched the goat's rope. "You owe me for this."

"We need to get moving," Ludik said. "Lyell, you said the tracks go southwest again. What is the next village in that direction?"

"Kairri is the next town over. We will be there by midday."

"That's handy, I suppose," Ahjin said. "At least I can make sure they are well and reassure Darravani. So far, I've failed at everything else."

"What?" Nia protested. "That's not true."

"I didn't convince the gods to douse the fire in time, and my failure will haunt me for the rest of my life." Ahjin's shoulders slumped under his pack. "I didn't convince Durriel to give up the idea of war, although perhaps they'll think about what I said. I haven't studied enough. I didn't convince Orrik that we were innocent or that I spoke for the gods. We haven't caught the murderer, much less prevented war. I haven't hired a single person. I haven't succeeded at the important things *or* the little ones."

Lyell bared his teeth. "I will remember your part in my wife's death."

Ahjin bowed his head. "I am so, so sorry, Lyell."

Ludik glared at the Wolf. That was unfair. He turned to Ahjin. "The success or failure of most of those have yet to be determined. Either way, you tried. Doesn't that count for anything?"

Ahjin shrugged and looked at his boots.

Ludik sputtered and tried to think how to convince him.

Nemerra put her hand on Ahjin's arm. "Ludik is right. It's too bad Ruka was sleeping, but look how many people you did save. Fewer than twenty died in the whole town. And you saved Tala before the fire caught her. She never would have crawled more than a few feet."

Lyell choked. His arms shook, and the puppy whined.

Zefra tsked at him. "Do not drop her." She took the baby and put her in the carry basket.

Lyell stood with his empty arms still extended, flexing his bandaged hands.

Ludik looked away. Should he tell Zefra to give back the baby? Should he say something to Lyell? What could he say that would help?

Nemerra patted Ahjin again and moved to Lyell. She put her arms around him and hugged him. He stood frozen, arms outstretched. After a minute, he began to sob. He lowered his head to Nemerra's shoulder to hide the tears flowing down his cheeks.

She waved her hand at Ludik until he caught on and ushered everyone else down the path. Nemerra would know what to say. She was always kind and wouldn't know an enemy if one bit her.

Why didn't their hostility with the Dogs bother her? How did she love so easily?

As they hurried through the forest, his conscience itched. Could he learn to be like Nemerra, if he tried?

25. MAPS
(KAIRRI, CANID TERRITORY)

While the gods contended, the world crumbled.
A Comprehensive History of the Gods, vol. 6

As they hurried past the last house and through the farms and orchards surrounding Durriel, Zefra held the bottle for the puppy. Tala soon lost interest and curled into a fluffy ball.

Gurryon confirmed the scent trail continued toward Kairri, and they soon entered the true forest again. This section had been on the leeward side of the fire, so there was little damage.

Zefra breathed freely for the first time in a day. She inhaled the scent of pine and reminded herself most of the other trees would recover. The forest would be as thick as ever in a few years.

She had wedged her staff under her pack to have two hands free for the puppy. If she was not careful how she moved, her staff banged her head, but mostly it worked well enough.

When Nemerra and Lyell caught up to them a while later, Lyell's eyes were red.

Zefra handed Tala back to Lyell, without the bottle and well-wrapped in her blanket. "I told you she is not hungry."

"I have a present for you, Zefra." Lyell shifted Tala to one arm and fumbled a leather parcel from his pack. "Maybe it will repay you in advance for your care of my daughter." He handed her the packet with a sharp inhale and lengthened his stride to walk in front of her.

Zefra untied the clasp and carefully withdrew a sheaf of old parchment. She slowed her steps as she leafed through the crackling, faded pages. "Maps! Where did you get so many wonderful old maps?" Heat rushed to her cheeks. That was undiplomatic. They must be his wife's. "Oh, I see. I'm honored, Lyell. Are you sure Ruka would want me to have these?"

"I am sure," Lyell said over his shoulder. "She would not want her work to die with her. I thought about giving them to her fellow cartographers, but they mostly have copies already. I want you to have hers."

"These really are wonderful." Zefra walked behind the others, but her attention was already on the maps. "Here is one of Iskra. Hmm, 'tis inaccurate, but I suppose few Darrendrakar have visited the interior. Oh, here is the original date. Unbelievable. 'Tis from more than five hundred years ago. Even this copy is a hundred years old. This is priceless. Lyell—"

"I am sure," Lyell interrupted hoarsely. "Please keep them." He turned away to babble at his daughter.

Zefra turned back to the maps, picking her way across the uneven ground by feel. "This one of Darrendra must be even older," she murmured, barely touching the fragile parchment.

Names of mapmakers who had copied it marched down the side of the map in tiny script. The first half of the list did not even have dates. "The oldest copy date here is a thousand years ago," she said, "and the original was even older than that."

"Really?" Gurryon looked over her shoulder. "Oh, no. That one is wrong. See, it continues too far south for Darrendra. And it has one large island instead of all the little Murron Isles."

"Oh. Well, 'tis still beautifully drawn," Zefra said. "Copying it will give me something to do at home between explorations, and then I can file it in our legends category."

"You have a category for maps of legends?" Nia peered over Zefra's other elbow. "That's amazing. How many maps do you have in that section?"

"Not me personally," Zefra explained. "But my clan's map library includes hundreds of myths and legends. We sort them by country of origin and chronology. We have cartographers who specialize in understanding the old stories and how they relate to historical events and cultural ideas. If you ever want to visit, you would enjoy hearing all the stories."

"That's a great idea," Nia said. "I love stories. Do any of them have songs, too?"

"A few do," Zefra said. "You could ask to hear them."

"If they don't," Nia said, "I can make up my own." She hummed a line of tune and then modified it.

Zefra smiled absently as she turned her attention back to the maps. The wind rustled the old parchment. It would be nice to stop walking and take a proper look at them.

"Here is a new one. It has dotted lines on the coast. What is this one, Lyell?" She turned it around for him to see.

"That is the one Ruka planned to work on after the babies were born," he said. "I told you, she wanted to mark the new coastline. The dotted lines mark the border visitors and traders told her about. She planned to double-check their reports and fill in the missing pieces." He sighed and turned back to Tala. "I arranged for some time away from patrol. We wanted to take the family and make a trip of it."

"I'm sorry," Nia whispered.

Zefra looked at the maps again, turning pages as she walked. These were an intellectual treasure. The mapmakers in her clan would be delighted to see them. Even the completely inaccurate one of Iskra would be evidence of the way the rest of the world had seen her country at that point in time. It would be a great addition to the history and cultural bias section.

Tala whined.

Zefra ignored the fuss and turned another page.

"Zefra."

This map was equally fascinating. It did not have any political borders, but seemed to show geological resources. Mother had been raised as a cartographer before she married Father, and she would love this.

Tala whimpered.

"Zefra..."

The map was of Darrendra, though. That made sense for Ruka.

Regardless, could her clan take advantage of the information? If not, could they make a similar map for Iskra? Imagine how useful it would be when her clan sold information on trade routes.

"Zefra!" Ludik shouted in her ear.

She slammed to a halt and almost dropped the fragile maps. "Be more careful, please. Why are you yelling at me?"

"Because you weren't listening," Ludik said.

Zefra sniffed. There was no need to interrupt her to say she was not listening. She unrolled the maps and took a step.

Nia pulled her to a stop. "Give me the maps."

"They're mine. Lyell gave them to me." Zefra rolled them and cradled them to her chest.

"I'll put them away while you take the puppy from Lyell," Nia said.

"He asked to hold her for a while, and I'm busy." Zefra held the maps above Nia's head.

"Zefra!" Nemerra said. "Tala's getting too cold. You need to take her back now."

Zefra looked over Nia's head. Lyell frowned, cuddling his daughter. Ludik scowled.

"Oh. All right, give her to me." Zefra let Nia take the maps and leather parcel. She put Tala in the basket while she made sure Nia carefully put away the maps.

The puppy really was chilled. Zefra put both hands around her and pulled heat to her fingers. Not too much, just enough to be like soaking in warm bath water or sitting by the fire. There, that should be enough. But with both hands around the puppy, there was no chance she could examine her maps for now.

Ahjin read while he walked again. That seemed particularly unfair when Zefra could not. This time, he was not reading Torao's journal, but some scroll written in terrible writing. He kept wrinkling his forehead and tilting the scroll to the light, but it did not seem to help.

"Would it help your studying if you read out loud?" Zefra offered.

Ahjin shook his head and squinted at the scroll again.

It was too bad he would not let her help. Holding the baby did not occupy her mind. Zefra looked at Lyell. He stared at the baby again, with a familiar troubled look on his face.

Zefra stroked Tala's fur. "Perhaps you should check the trail, Lyell. Make sure we are still going the right way."

Lyell shook himself and stalked off silently. He returned a short time later with a worried look on his face. After a chat with Gurryon, they handed the goat's leash to Nia and left together.

Ludik furrowed his brow but pulled Nemerra's hand through the crook of his arm and kept the group moving.

Nia poked Ahjin until he put away his book and paid attention to the forest. Zefra kept watch but saw nothing.

In less than an hour, they reached a small river. The water burbled south, and delicious-looking fish swam in the current. Zefra wished for a net. Not far away, a narrow bridge crossed the river, not much more than a flattened log with a rope railing above it.

Ludik waited at the end of the bridge until his brother and Lyell came back, one on each side of the river. Lyell scowled on the opposite bank while Gurryon spouted furious gibberish on the near side.

Zefra did not ask Nia to translate.

"Stop swearing, Gurryon," Ludik said, "and tell us what you found."

"We lost the scent," Gurryon stated bluntly. "They must have swum for a while. We each took a bank, but we can't find where they got out."

Ludik bit off whatever he started to say.

Zefra cleared her throat. "The best we can do is keep going toward the ocean. We will probably find the trail later."

"You're right," Nemerra said. "It will be fine. I have faith in our hunters." She smiled encouragingly and wrapped her fingers in Ludik's.

"You'll find the trail eventually," Nia said. "They have to get out of the river sometime."

"Onward, then," Ahjin said. He crossed the bridge with his wings half-extended for balance.

The Darrendrakar crossed with enviable grace, and Nia scampered across like a squirrel, even with the goat.

Zefra put one hand across the basket and gripped the rope with the other. One step at a time, in no hurry. She kept her gaze on her feet, even after another pair of boots appeared at the edge of her vision. Those colorful boots walked backward, matching her pace.

When she stepped off the log, she looked up and saw Lyell's bandaged hands drop to his sides as he turned away.

Nia sighed. "Back to the chase. Will we ever catch up?"

Ludik twitched. "Does everyone have their weapons ready?" He looked at Nemerra, who only had a long knife.

A chorus of "yes" answered him. Everyone but Nemerra wore armor and carried weapons. Even Lyell had added a leather jacket this morning.

"It will be fine, dear," Nemerra said. "We're ready."

Gurryon rattled a long sentence that was not in trade tongue and looked around frantically.

Nemerra blushed. Nia looked amused but did not translate for Zefra, and Zefra did not ask.

"Where is the goat?" Nia asked. "I gave her to you."

"That is what I asked," Gurryon said.

Nia laughed. "That's not quite what you said."

"Close enough," Gurryon grumbled. "Do you see the stupid goat?"

"If the goat is that stupid, how did she escape from you?" Lyell asked.

Gurryon held up the rope. The collar end had somehow loosened. "Are you sure she's a regular goat and not one of the Caprids?"

"Quite positive," Lyell said. "Everybody, spread out and search for the goat."

Zefra walked in a straight line from the river, while the others split up around her. Carrying the baby made it too difficult to search behind bushes, and she did not have hands free even if she found the goat. The most practical thing to do was keep on the path and wait for the others to return.

It was Nia who came back triumphant. "Look, I found little Gurry!"

"What?" Gurryon exploded. "That is not her name."

Nia grinned at Lyell, but he did not smile back. Nia sighed and looked back at Gurryon. "Sure, it is. I don't see why not." She frowned and retied the goat's leash.

"Are your weapons still ready?" Ludik asked.

"If you ask me one more time, I will hit you with this goat," Gurryon threatened.

"Hush, Ludik." Nemerra hooked an arm around Ludik's elbow. "Here I am, darling."

The puppy whimpered. Zefra increased the heat as much as she dared, but Tala kept crying. She jiggled the basket, and Tala cried harder.

Zefra smoothed the puppy's fur. Tala stuck her nose in the air and squeaked a baby howl.

"What are you doing to her?" Lyell asked.

"Nothing!" Zefra snapped. "I mean, I'm doing everything I know how to do."

"Is she warm enough?" Ludik asked.

"If she were any warmer, I would cook her."

"Zefra!" Nemerra gasped. "Don't say that."

"What? I'm not cooking her, I only said—"

Nia put her hand over Zefra's mouth. Zefra yanked her head away.

Lyell turned his head away for a minute before peeking into the basket.

Tala yowled again.

"Is she tired?" Nia asked.

"She just woke up, I think." Zefra jiggled the basket again. "Hush."

Tala whimpered and staggered to her unsteady feet.

"Is she hungry?" Nemerra asked.

"She just ate. How could she be hungry? Please be quiet!" Zefra tapped the puppy on her nose, but the pup wailed harder.

"Babies eat frequently sometimes, and she didn't eat regularly yesterday," Ludik said. "Try giving her the rest of the bottle."

Zefra grabbed the bottle from under the edge of the blanket and shoved it at the puppy. "Here, is this what you want?"

Tala latched on and drained the last few swallows in seconds, then howled again.

"I guess she's hungry. We need more." Zefra gave the bottle to Lyell.

The Wolf turned around for the goat and did not find her. "Gurryon, where is the goat?"

Gurryon turned around and swore again. He held the rope and showed its chewed end. "Lyell, why in the world did you buy an escaping goat?"

"My neighbor did say she was the smartest as well as the fastest one."

Nia laughed, but Lyell just shrugged.

Everyone divided to find the goat again. By the time they got back, Zefra was so desperate to get the puppy to stop whining, she had even tried letting Tala suck on her fingers. Sharp little wolf teeth made Zefra feel sorry for wolf mothers.

While Nemerra milked the goat, Gurryon wrapped a thorny vine around the goat's end of the leash.

"Why, Gurryon," Nia said, "I do believe Gurry is getting your goat." She winked at Lyell.

Lyell grunted and picked up the bucket without smiling. Nia sighed again.

Lyell refilled the bottle and gave it to Zefra, who frantically shoved it into the puppy's mouth.

"Hush, now," Zefra said.

"You know, Zefra," Nemerra said, "babies cry a lot. This will happen again."

"You'll have to get used to it," Nia said.

"What if I do not want to get used to it?" Zefra felt like wailing herself. Why was the baby so unreasonable? She was doing her best.

"I'll trade you the goat for the baby," Gurryon offered. The goat butted him. He hit at the goat, but she danced away.

"No, thank you," Zefra said. "At least the puppy is soft and cute."

Nemerra frowned. "Is that why you like her?"

"Yes?"

Nemerra did not say anything else, and her frown turned sad.

Zefra still had not deduced why Nemerra was disappointed in her when the puppy whined again an hour later. And an hour after that. Every hour, without fail. She tried to make her hush, but sometimes she would not, no matter how much Zefra fed her or how warm she made her. To make things worse, Nia frowned at Zefra, too.

Enough. "The two of you should tell me why you are upset," she complained. "I do not understand what is wrong."

"It's not what you did," Nemerra said. "It's just..."

"You need to love Tala," Nia said. "She's a baby. She isn't old enough to control herself and doesn't cry to upset you. When she gets hungry, or tired, or cold, or cranky, or she misses her mom, she cries. You can't fix every problem, so you need to just love her. If you can't do that, then you need to give her back to her dad now, and we'll figure out another way to keep her warm."

Lyell scooped his daughter away from Zefra and held her to his chest, murmuring. Tala squeaked and closed her eyes, then snuggled in and went to sleep.

Zefra threw her hands in the air. "Why did that work? I tried holding her."

Nia rolled her eyes at Nemerra.

"Try this," Nemerra said. "I'm sure your parents love you. Try thinking about how they took care of you. We can give this another try."

Lyell held Tala for another minute and then slowly handed her back to Zefra. "I will get her back sometime."

Zefra put the puppy back in the basket. Until then, she would try to calculate how to love a squalling bundle of fuzz.

She was still thinking about it when the group stepped out from the forest. They had reached Kairri without ever finding the scent trail again.

Where had their quarry gone?

26. KAIRRI

(KAIRRI, CANID TERRITORY)

I could not return to the battle with only half my hand. I was hauling water for the healers when the Elephants arrived in a glorious thunder of rescue.

Torao, after The Battle of Sad Laughter

Ludik took a deep breath. The scent should have told him they were getting close to Kairri. The village was almost directly on the beach, with the first house on the border of sand and earth and the others sprawled behind to the forest edge. A couple of seals swam from the mouth of the river into the ocean and disappeared under the waves. Fishing boats were either pulled up to a small wharf or beached for repairs.

The scent of saltwater and rotten seaweed overwhelmed his nose, even stronger than the evergreen fragrance behind them. It was so strong, he couldn't smell anything else, couldn't tell if the murderer's scent was here. Memories flooded him from summer, and the water rose into a tidal wave and buried the beach.

Please, Darravani, let this be the right place. Ludik blinked, and the water flooding the shore of his imagination returned to the gentle tide actually in front of him.

Nia sniffed the air with a huge grin and watched the waves run up and down the coast. "Do you think they'd let me go for a swim?"

Ahjin put a hand on Nia's shoulder. "I don't see why not, but you should ask permission."

Lyell pointed toward the village. "Those are the biggest Dogs I have ever seen. Mastiffs, maybe. I would suggest Bear, but they might bite off my arm."

Ludik turned away from the mesmerizing ocean and silently agreed, keeping his own eyes on the intimidating villagers in case they weren't friendly. The Canids in Kairri were huge, with thick necks and limbs. Most of them were taller than Lyell and a lot wider. Some were taller than Ludik and Gurryon and nearly as massive as Ursids.

"Their children are adorable, though," Nia said.

The Kairri children ran across the beach in a wild game involving plenty of delighted squeals and giggles. Their pounding bare feet turned old crescent marks in the sand into a hodge-podge of little footprints. Their plump mamas gathered in small groups and chattered in their own language while they watched the children.

One of the little ones raced from the group and skidded into the trees, laughing. He tripped and fell at Nemerra's feet.

She picked him up with a smile. He stared open-mouthed at the armor most of them wore and ran back to the beach.

"They have beautiful dark brown eyes," Nemerra said. "Your eyes are light enough to stand out here, Lyell. Mine, too. Yours fit right in, though, Zefra."

Zefra shrugged. "My skin is too light."

"Imagine how unusual our eyes must seem," Ludik said. He and Gurryon widened their silver eyes in unison.

Nia giggled and showed her own bright green ones.

"Grow up," Ahin said almost absently, straightening his shoulders.

The mamas on the beach soothed the little boy, and at his frantic gestures, edged between the children and the strangers.

"I think we scared them," Nemerra said.

"Oh, yes, because we're so terrifying," Gurryon said. The goat butted him again, and Gurryon swore. "This goat is the only horrifying one among us." He yanked on the rope and hauled the goat closer to him.

"I love their dresses," Nia said. "Do you think they'd let us see the designs more closely?"

"That would be wonderful," Nemerra said. "I haven't seen anything quite like their patterns before. They look a bit like a cross between Canid and Nokai. Do they trade with Nokailana? What do you think, Lyell?"

"I know nothing about fashion," Lyell said. "Ruka makes my clothes for me." He swallowed. "Made my clothes. Can you tell who might be the village elders?"

"We could ask him." Nia pointed to their left, where the forest ended and the beach began.

One of the Canids was digging a large hole in the sand. A stack of seal pelts leaned perilously toward his knee. The layers of brown, black, and gray had a single stripe of russet near the top. The Dog looked at the visitors and grunted. He called a few words toward the villagers, then turned to save the pile from toppling. When he returned to digging, the russet stripe was gone.

"He seems busy. What about him?" Nemerra pointed at a Dog who had exited one of the houses and now stood looking around. At his side, he held a spear with a long, arrow-headed tip.

"Wait a minute," Lyell said. "Ludik, could that spear make the killing wound we have seen?"

Ludik squinted. "I don't know. I need a closer look."

"A closer look?" Nia said. "Then we might as well accomplish two things at once."

She marched to the warrior before Ludik could stop her.

"Excuse us, please, will you direct us to one of your elders?" She had spoken in trade tongue, and the Dog stared at her blankly.

Ludik and Lyell rushed after her. Ludik pulled her behind him, while Lyell repeated her question in Canid.

"You're smarter than this, Nia," Ludik hissed under his breath. "What were you thinking?"

The guard narrowed his eyes and lifted his weapon.

"I have my armor, and I thought you could inspect that spear." Nia pointed at the spearhead now hovering in front of their faces.

Ludik examined the spear while he kept her out of the way. It was wide enough, but too flat to have made the wounds from their murderer.

They needed to find something a lot rounder and a little longer. He shook his head at Lyell.

Lyell's shoulders drooped. He turned back to the guard, but before he could repeat his question, a huge man ducked from the doorway of the house behind the guard and waved away the spear.

"My name is Varin," he said in heavily accented trade tongue. "How can I help you?"

Huge was too mild a word. He was immense. Ludik had to bend his neck back to see that Varin's eyes were as dark brown as the pups on the beach. His hair was nearly as dark as his eyes, and a bone-handled knife was stuck in his belt. Despite his bulk, he moved sleekly and did not have a paunch.

Maybe a bit of diplomacy was in order. Ludik didn't want to lose his nose to an irritated punch or worse. "We have been tracking someone," he explained tactfully. "We lost the trail a while ago, but earlier, it led in this direction. Perhaps one of you saw something?"

"Come and tell me about it," Varin offered. "We have not seen such a mixed group before. You must have quite a story." He held open the door.

Ludik motioned everyone inside and waited to go last.

Gurryon made a face at the goat before tying her to a tree and following Varin.

The rest of the group cautiously walked into the house. Lyell put one hand behind Zefra's back and the other near one of his knives. Ludik tried to be more subtle as he did the same with Nemerra. Their group nearly filled the empty space at the front of the house.

The villagers huddled around the table stopped their discussion. Most of them turned over their notes as if to hide what they wrote.

Paranoid Dogs. As if Ludik cared about their records. Once they settled their questions, they would be gone faster than a Dog's bark could reach the ocean. The suspicious Dogs could keep their affairs to themselves.

He looked around the small house, which was crowded with people and things. Old documents and musty books covered the table three and four layers deep. A sharpened walrus-tusk spear leaned against the wall next to a yellowed map with corrections and questions scribbled in charcoal. Paintings of the ocean sat on windowsills and tables and other odd surfaces, as if nobody had gotten around to hanging them.

"Now, who you tracking?" Varin had a heavier accent than Lyell.

"Someone, maybe a Bear," Ludik said diplomatically, "crossed the border into Felid territory and murdered a Cat and a Dog, killing another Dog on the way. On his way back, he and his accomplices burned a village. Several people died in the fire. We are here to find who did this and bring them to justice."

"Justice," Lyell growled.

Zefra pulled Tala out of the baby carrier and shoved the pup into Lyell's arms. "Calm down," she ordered. She stood in front of Lyell and glared at him until he rocked Tala.

"You think this killer was a Bear?" Varin said. "We see no Bears here. We have no visitors at all before you come."

Nia wandered across the room to look at a painting. Zefra left Lyell and drifted toward the map.

Someone at the table jumped to his feet and headed for the women, but Varin raised his hand and barked a short command. The man grunted and sat as suddenly as he had stood.

It was polite to speak a language everyone could understand, instead of using Canid. Zefra should count herself lucky Nia worked so hard to translate for her.

Ludik looked up at the massive elder. "The scent was vaguely Ursid, but the murderer might have been a Dog. We lost the trail right before your village." He forced a smile, as if they both knew the possibility was ridiculous.

Varin barked a short laugh. "I promise, there is no murdering Dog in this village."

"Have you seen anyone suspicious, then?" Ludik asked. "Anyone acting strangely? Maybe someone wearing pointed boots? It is important we find him to prevent war."

"No." Varin folded his muscled arms across his broad chest. "I tell you, no one come before you. All our people are counted. These are our boots." He held out one foot with strangely stitched but non-pointed boots. "You are only people strange to me. Leave this to us. We find this person and protect our village. There will be no war with Cats. You go home."

"That is kind of you, but this task was entrusted to us."

"You may not stay." Varin unfolded his arms and leaned toward Ludik. "You leave this to us. We take care of all needed. There is no war with Cats if you leave quickly."

Ludik exchanged looks with Lyell and Ahjin. A quick retreat seemed wise. They could discuss their options later.

"Another question, then," Ahjin said. "Darravani asked me to discover if anything is wrong in this village. She hasn't heard any prayers from here in several days."

"Darravani?" Varin asked.

Ahjin smiled. "Your goddess loves you and wants to make sure you're well. She worries about her children."

"Ah," Varin said. "Our goddess loves us. I see. All is well here. We are busy lately, but I will tell others what you said."

"I'm sure she'll stop worrying as soon as she hears from you," Ahjin said. "Shall I pass on your regards and let her know you'll be in touch soon?"

"Say whatever you think proper," Varin said.

"Thank you for your help," Ahjin said. "If you do see or hear anything, please send word to Durriel, the next village east."

"I know where it is," Varin said. "I will escort you out."

"Wait," Ahjin said. "I also wanted to ask if anyone here was looking for a job and might like to serve the gods. It's far away, but they pay well. I could tell you more about it."

"Not necessary," Varin said. "No one wants to leave. You leave. Now." He hovered over Ahjin, pressing him toward the door.

Ludik pulled Nemerra out the door.

Zefra left the map with several backward glances and collected Tala from Lyell. She walked out with Lyell following.

Nia said something to the men at the table, waving at the art she had been admiring. Some of them glared and others ignored her.

"Thank you," Varin said. "I will tell artist." He took Nia by the elbow and guided her to the door.

"May I go for a swim?" Nia asked, wandering toward the sand. "You have a lovely beach."

"No swim. Have nice trip home. Travel fast." He shut the door firmly.

Agitated voices exploded inside the house, but Ludik couldn't understand the Canid. He didn't know why the Dogs were so upset. He had been polite, and Ahjin was very diplomatic. Even Nia's request to swim shouldn't have been offensive. Maybe the other Dogs hadn't agreed with Varin's offer to track the murderer.

The pelts were gone from the beach. So was the man who had been burying them, and the children and mamas on the sand. Ludik stared at the seemingly deserted village. The screech of gulls broke the silence. Where had everyone gone?

The goat was gone, too. She had chewed through her rope next to the knot and left a trail of shortened plants behind her.

Gurryon followed the trail of devastation behind the house and dragged the goat back with her now-shorter rope and a much longer string of curses. The goat bleated angrily.

While they waited for Gurryon and the goat to stop cursing each other, Nia stared at the mounded sand where the pelts had been piled. "Is burying hides a step in the curing process?"

"I suppose they could be salting it in the hole," Gurryon said, "although that is not how we do it. Who knows what dumb Dogs do."

Lyell smacked the back of his head.

"Ow." Gurryon rubbed his head and glared at Lyell. "I am sure you did not have to do that."

That was Lyell's cue to list all the things he could do to Gurryon instead, but none of them met with approval.

Ludik didn't disagree with Gurryon's opinion about the Dogs, but it wasn't nice to say so in front of the Wolf.

Nia dragged Gurryon from the village. Zefra did the same with Lyell, and the others followed. Once they were out of sight, they stopped.

"I have to admit, I'm eager to go home," Ludik said, "but I'm not sure Varin is as motivated to catch the killer as we are."

Lyell frowned at Tala. "I agree."

Nemerra smiled at Ludik and laced her fingers through his. "He said he'd send word to Durriel if they found the murderer, so Lyell will hear. Varin seemed positive they would take care of it, and he promised there wouldn't be war."

Ludik kissed her fingers. "He did, *if* we can trust him."

"We could circle the village and check for the trail," Zefra suggested.

"That is a great idea," Lyell said.

Ludik took a few steps back to see the village. "Which way should we go first?"

Large, armed warriors poured out of the house and surrounded the village.

Ludik flinched and shoved Nemerra behind him. "Get back," he whispered frantically, waving his arms at the others.

"Why are they so unfriendly?" Nia asked. "We're nice people."

"Maybe they are crazy Dogs," Ludik muttered, too quiet for Lyell to hear.

Nemerra pursed her lips and shook her head at him.

"We did tell them there's a murderer running around," Ahjin said. "Perhaps they're looking for the killer already."

Lyell looked at Tala and back at the armed warriors. "I do not think we are in a position to argue with this village, and they certainly have enough searchers. When I get back to Durriel, I will have my patrol changed to this area. If they find our quarry, I will know. Or if they do not, I will continue the hunt myself."

"We will report to the temple priests, too," Ahjin said. "With Durriel and Kairri and the Elephants watching for trouble, war won't have a chance to break out later."

"And we will still watch for tracks on the way back," Zefra added.

Gurryon tapped his staff on the ground. "I don't know if that's enough. What if the Dogs decide they don't care?"

Nia tugged a ribbon tighter. "How can we leave while the murderer is still free?"

"With everyone looking for him," Nemerra said, "he won't escape. Someone will find him. Lyell will make sure they do. Ludik, it's time you trust the Canids. They are also Darravani's children."

Ludik grimaced. She was always telling him to be nicer and trust more. Even though her family hadn't been slaughtered by the Hyenas, she should understand it wasn't that easy. The Dogs of Orrik had meant to kill them, with the flimsiest of excuses. And the murderer they chased had killed two of his own kindred and burned down Durriel, killing even more of them.

But not everyone from Durriel was evil. Most of the villagers were like those in Maon. If they stood upwind and didn't shift to their other form, Ludik couldn't tell them apart from Cats. And Lyell was a good ally, despite his origins. The Wolf had stood by them, Felids and outkin-dred alike, even against his own people in Orrik. He sought to bring one of his own kind to justice because it was the right thing to do. If Ludik admitted the truth, he might even call the Wolf a friend.

A lifetime of suspicion struggled against his unexpected friendship until Ludik forced suspicion to submit.

"You're right, Nemerra." Ludik squeezed her fingers. "Let's go home. Whenever the killer turns up, those huge Dogs will handle him."

And Lyell had an even better reason to search for the murderer. He would never stop watching until the killer was found. Their quest was in good hands.

Ludik turned for home with a lighter conscience. It wasn't easy to trust the Dogs, but maybe that was the seed of peace. It wasn't enough to change their minds. He had to change his own.

27.RETURN
(KAIRRI, CANID TERRITORY)

The Elephants now return east. The few of us left in the village must rebuild before winter. With the harvest destroyed by the Hyenas, I fear we will starve.

Torao, after The Battle of Sad Laughter

Ludik walked a little faster as they left the village. Since the Dogs of Kairri had agreed to track the killer for them, and Lyell would make sure they did, there was nothing else to do. The threat of war was gone. It was time to go home to Maon. It had taken them a week to make it here, but he was certain they could walk fast enough on the way back to cut off a day. Maybe two.

He grabbed Nemerra's hand in sheer joy. She smiled and blinked three times at him. He blinked back. I. Love. You.

Ludik would finally marry his lovely sweetheart. He felt like singing, or skipping through the crunchy leaves, or screaming happily as he ran through the forest.

Oh, no, he couldn't act like Nia. Never mind, he didn't care. He was going home, and if he wanted to be silly, it was a good time for it. Ludik inhaled the crisp autumn scents of pine, ripe apples, falling leaves, and cool air. This was what happiness smelled like. They should have apple cake at the wedding, to commemorate.

Only a few more days. He had waited a year for their first wedding date, and nearly two months more for the second, and then more endless, tortured days that weren't over yet. But he was almost there. Nothing would go wrong the third time. It would be perfect.

How long would it take to prepare the wedding after they arrived?

Ludik would have to choose a new bouquet for Nemerra, since the old one was dead by now. That was fine; he loved picking flowers for her. The travel home would give him time to plan what he wanted the flowers to say. His previous bouquet seemed a little short-sighted. He had so much more to say now.

Gurryon dragged the goat forward. "It's your turn for rear guard, Ludik. You take the stupid goat."

Ludik laughed. "I don't want to deprive you."

Nemerra kissed him on the cheek and pulled her hand free. "I'll stay and talk to Nia, dear."

Ludik sighed and worked his way to the back of the group, without the goat.

What else did they need for their wedding?

He was bringing the priest and bride and special guests back with him. His family was either in the village or with him. The bride price was already paid. The decorations needed to be set out again, but Kalliona would boss everyone around as soon as they returned. Haider still had the flower bulb. Hiranya was in charge of Nemerra's ring for the ceremony, but Mama and Papa would watch it until then. Nemerra's clothes and his ring were with her parents. His clothes and the paint were still in his house.

He needed to dust the house again, but he could do it while everyone else decorated.

Yes, if everyone hurried, they could be ready for the wedding an hour or two after they arrived. Maybe it was better to plan for two. He should probably take a bath first, and Nemerra would want to mess with her hair.

Ludik stared at her russet hair waving down her back. She looked beautiful no matter what her hair looked like, but he would wait an extra hour if it made her happy. She turned her head toward Nia, and he caught a glimpse of her lovely face. He was so lucky.

A few days to get home and then a couple of hours after that. He hoped they arrived in daylight so they didn't have to wait until the next day. Yes, the day of their arrival would be so much better. He grinned so hard his cheeks hurt.

Ludik had never been happier. He *would* be happier, though, three hours after he reached Maon, when he stood in front of Ahjin to marry Nemerra.

Nemerra turned to her other side. "Why are you frowning, Zefra?"

His sweetheart was kind. Ludik wasn't thinking of anything but their wedding, and here she worried about their friends. It was hard to listen to what the others said when his daydreams were so pleasant.

"'Tis that map on the wall in the Canid's house," Zefra said. "I have not studied the local maps well enough, because I did not recognize all the borders."

"It was an old map," Nia said, "and we've had a lot of changes lately. I mean, bits of the coast fell right into the ocean."

Ludik looked at Lyell, who swallowed and looked away. Ludik stared at Nemerra as the ash-streaked floor flashed through his mind.

Nia kept talking. "That's why Ruka wanted to re-map it, remember? She had a map with the new dotted lines all over it, to confirm the border changes."

"And if the boundaries were *that* different, maybe it's old enough to have the old territory borders on it," Nemerra said. "It's too bad we couldn't copy it for Zefra's new collection."

"Yes," Zefra said, "but something is still bothering me. I'm not sure what it is." She frowned again and swung her staff at a bush. "It might have helped if I could read the language. Lyell, could you read it from all the way across the room? Some of the markings were fairly large."

"I could not read it, anyway," Lyell said. "It was not in modern Canid. You must be right about its age."

"Well, it didn't say much," Nia said. "Dog, Cat, Bear, Sheep, and so forth, plus markings for fishing spots and seal. The other countries weren't on it at all."

"Until recent events," Ludik said, "Darrendra never cared about the other countries."

"Hmm." Zefra tucked a loose strand of hair into her braided crown. "It still reminds me of something I saw somewhere."

"Did you study ancient Canid, Nia?" Lyell asked. "How could you read the map?"

Nia shrugged. "The same way I understand every language. It was a birth gift from Makanavailea. Ahjin can do the same, but his ability is more recent." She snickered. "I got mine an easier way."

Ahjin flicked her arm with his wing. "Have I mentioned how unfair that is?"

Nia patted his shoulder. "Several times."

"The Dogs did not speak regular Canid, either," Lyell said. "I assumed it was a dialect I do not know. Is that right?"

"Oh, weren't they?" Nia blushed. "I couldn't tell. When it's a new language that hasn't been introduced to me, I don't know what it's called, just how to use it. Languages don't come with labels hanging off them, you know."

"Do you speak non-Caprid goat?" Gurryon yanked on the bleating goat's rope. "Can you understand what this monster is screaming at me?" He cursed.

Ludik winced. Ahjin must be wearing off on him, because his brother's language was less amusing than he used to think.

"Yes," Nia said. "But I won't translate it. Let's say you're two of a kind." She rolled her eyes at Zefra.

Ahjin's mouth twitched. "Somehow, I'm not sorry Darravani only gave me the people languages."

"Stop abusing my daughter's food supply," Lyell said.

The corners of Nia's mouth turned up. She winked at Lyell, but he remained somber.

Ludik almost reached out to pat Lyell's shoulder. Though he expected the Wolf to mourn his wife forever, he hoped Lyell's heart would heal enough to regain his sense of humor.

Zefra ignored their jokes, obviously concentrating on something else.

The goat jumped in the air and came down running. Gurryon was dragged along for several steps before he dug in his heels.

"Who is abusing whom?" Gurryon ranted. "Stupid goat. I should eat her."

"No." Lyell flicked the back of Gurryon's head.

"Oh, I know," Zefra said. "That map looked like Ruka's map. Let me show you."

She handed Tala's carry basket to Lyell so she could rummage through her pack. She flipped gently through the old maps, pulling one to the top of the pile.

Everyone stopped to peer over her shoulder. Ludik used the chance to take Nemerra's hand again.

"See," Zefra said, "this is the old map without names on it, but the territories are marked with heavy borders. Here are the eleven kindreds, and below, where Gurryon says the Murron Isles are now, there is another border, as if it were another territory."

"That is just a fishing ground," Lyell said. "See Ruka's note right here, where she put that as her guess? She is usually right about that things like that. She is very good at what she does." He blinked away tears and put a hand over Tala. "Was good."

"I'm sure your wife was talented, but she admitted it was a guess," Ahjin said. "Look, she added 'needs corroborating evidence' at the bottom of her note."

"That's what it said on the Dog's map, too," Nia said. "Not the evidence part. It said, 'fish and seals.' I read it on my way to that lovely picture with the ocean waves, and the sunset, and the seals on the beach, and the dolphins jumping, and the sailboats. I wanted to talk to the artist, but Varin wouldn't let me." She gave an offended sniff. "As if I'd insult the guy. I wanted to compliment him."

"I'm so confused," Gurryon said. "Why would a fishing ground be labeled as a separate territory?"

"I am sure there is an easy explanation." Lyell rocked his daughter's basket. "It probably belongs to the Bears, but because there is water between, they marked it separately."

"The Canids are just as close," Zefra said.

"Yes, but it does not belong to the Dogs," Lyell said with exaggerated patience. "I am very familiar with Canid territory. I have walked most of the southern border myself, and Ruka showed me the maps many times. The Dogs do not own any islands. The Ursids are close enough for the isles to belong to them. You worry about nothing. Besides, if it matches this map, then it is over a thousand years old and not relevant anymore."

"I suppose you're right." Zefra returned the map to her bag. "Thank you again for the maps, Lyell."

"You are doing me a favor. I hate to think of Ruka's work being wasted."

"You do not mind me sharing the maps with my clan, do you?" Zefra asked, resettling her pack.

"No, please, share Ruka's work as much as you like." He reluctantly handed over his daughter. "Tala is looking stronger and less traumatized. One of these days, she might revert to her two-legger form."

"I'm sure she'll be darling," Nemerra said. "Her black hair is so soft, and her blue eyes are beautiful."

"That is just her baby eye color. She will probably grow to have stunning seal-brown eyes like her mama." Lyell reached for his absent silver chain again, but his hands closed on thin air. He flexed his fingers, tucked them into his pockets, and plodded forward.

"Seal brown." Nemerra stopped walking again, and her hand pulled free of Ludik's. "Fish and seals. Twelve kindreds. The map was right."

"Right about what?" Zefra said. "Do you want to see the map again?" She tried to grab the satchel but couldn't with Tala's basket in the way. "Just a minute. Lyell?"

Ludik reached for Nemerra's hand again, but she didn't take it.

"The goat is gone again," she said.

Gurryon swore.

"Stay here," Nemerra said. "I'll look for her. I want to see something, anyway, and if you kill the goat, Tala will get hungry. I'll be right back." She whirled and ran down the path toward Kairri, moving quickly out of sight.

"What is she doing?" Ludik asked. "I thought we were going home."

He waited for a moment, but Nemerra didn't come back. Had the goat gotten so far? She said she wanted to see something. What had she noticed that escaped the rest of them?

"Let's follow her. Did anyone understand what she was talking about?" Ludik turned around and walked toward Kairri. "Why did she say twelve kindreds? There are only eleven."

Zefra followed him slowly, waiting for the others to turn and join them. "I do not know. She seemed fascinated with the fish and seal hunting grounds."

"What does that have to do with anything?" Ludik asked.

"I do not know." Zefra repeated. "She did not say."

"Was it something about the seal pelts that Dog was burying?" Lyell asked. "By the way, we should have looked for someone wearing a seal-skin coat or boots, too. Those pelts smelled an awful lot like Bear."

"Did they? The village stunk so much, I didn't notice," Ludik said.

"Dogs smell better than Cats." Lyell fell into step next to Ludik, sounding a little smug.

Gurryon stepped out of arm's reach of Lyell before he replied. "That depends how you use the verb. Ow." He glared at Nia.

"Oops," she said. "Was that your smelly foot I stepped on?" She looked down to avoid his retaliation stomp and squinted at the ground. "Stop, Gurryon. I mean it. Don't splash that puddle." She leaned down. "Now, after all this time, now I'm seeing something? Why didn't I see when it would have been useful?"

"What do you see?" Ahjin peered over her shoulder as everyone stopped.

"I can't tell. Something about red hair? Did we miss questioning someone with red hair?"

"Nobody had red fur or hair. All the Dogs had brown or black hair." Ludik stretched his legs into a trot. Something was wrong here, and he needed to catch Nemerra. He glanced over his shoulder to hear Nia's answer.

"Oh, coral wreck." Nia pressed her fingers to her lips and hurried after Ludik. "The russet fur in the stack of seal pelts. Do seals come in red? It was the fox's tail. That's why that man hid it from us. And there were crescent marks in the sand before the children trampled them in their game."

"The sealskins smelled like Bear," Lyell repeated in a stricken voice. He caught up to Ludik and reached for a knife. "I am sorry, I have never smelled seal before."

"So that big stack of seal skins means the Kairri Dogs hunt seals for leather?" Ludik said. "It makes sense, being right by the ocean. But if that is the source of the Bear-like scent, and the red stripe was the fox's tail, and the marks in the sand are the murderer's footprints — that means the murderer is in Kairri."

He couldn't make sense of it. "Why wouldn't Varin have discovered him by now? Why didn't he recognize the evidence when we told him about it?"

Ahjin's voice came right behind Lyell. "What does any of this have to do with twelve kindreds? What is Nemerra thinking?"

"Varin said they didn't know the killer," Nia protested, panting behind Ahjin. "And he said they'd take care of him if they found him."

"Actually, he said they had no visitors before us." Zefra's boots crunched the dead leaves at the back of the group. "He said nothing about their own people." She pointed it out as if it were a mere logic problem.

Ludik's heart stuttered, and he hurried faster. Where was Nemerra?

Gurryon ran one step behind his brother. "If the killer is one of their own, how do you think they plan to take care of him?"

"Did we not decide the killer took the fox's tail and the dog's paw as trophies?" Zefra half-shouted to be heard. "Or evidence the deed was successful? To whom would he take them?"

"That is why Varin promised there would be no war," Lyell growled. "He knew who was responsible. They are hiding him, protecting him. They have no intention of turning him over."

"And Nemerra went back there alone." Ludik drew his ax and broke into a dead run.

28.SEAL
(KAIRRI, CANID TERRITORY)

The Pinnipeds include the Seals, Walruses, and Sea Lions.
A Brief Sketch of Mysterious Darrendra

Ludik and the others raced back to Kairri. At the edge of the village, they found the goat hiding in the bushes, but no Nemerra. Where was she?

Ludik searched desperately and finally found her backing away from the beach with her hands in the air. Varin scowled as he held a heavy walrus-tusk spear against her chest.

Ludik's blood froze in his veins. He charged toward the shore, howling.

Beyond Varin, seal pups crawled for the ocean as fast as their mamas could herd them. The sand was scuffed with the dragging trails of their bodies and crescent tracks from their flippers. Hulking men guarded their escape with long spears.

"This is a Dog village," Lyell panted as the others joined Ludik. "Where did all the seals come from?"

Nia's eyes widened. "Narrasiman thought Agu said 'see'... or something before he died. Maybe he meant 'seal.' Could the killer be a seal?"

"How could he be?" Ludik asked. "Seals are just animals."

Nia gasped. "No, they're the twelfth kindred! That's what Nemerra figured out."

Zefra groped at the map case, then wrapped both arms around Tala's basket-sling.

Varin spat out a string of foreign words as Ludik and the others skidded to a stop.

The goat bleated wildly, yanked the rope from Gurryon's hands, and fled into the woods. Gurryon blew on his hands and swore.

"Oh, that's not nice," Nia said to Varin, ignoring the goat incident. "Didn't your mom teach you manners?"

Ludik grabbed her arm, but she shrugged him off, glaring up at the huge man as if she could squish him with her sandals. Ludik tightened his grip on his ax.

"*You* have no manners," Varin retorted in trade tongue, his accent heavier and now obviously foreign. "Was it not enough to invade our village once? I let you go to spare the infant and outkindred. Why you come back?"

"*Your* village?" Lyell growled. "Are you one of these Seals? Kairri belongs to the Canids. Where are they all?"

"Most of them already pay for their crimes," Varin said. "We catch rest after we rid ourselves of you. We already send word to Walruses, our kin and allies." He briefly lifted the sharp tusk-spear.

The spear! It matched all those deep, round wounds in the dead bodies. Ludik could have protected Nemerra if he had realized the connection when he saw that spear leaning against the wall inside Varin's house.

But it wasn't Varin's house. Ludik's stomach churned. It belonged to some poor slaughtered Dog family. If all these people were Seals, there were a lot of missing Dog families.

Behind Ludik, Ahjin strung his bow.

"Let her go," Ludik pleaded. "She's done nothing to you." He looked at Nemerra, fear cramping his heart. "What were you doing, Nemerra?"

"Just looking," she whispered. "I remembered the maps, and how brown everyone's eyes are, and the seals in the ocean. I was excited to think Ruka might be right about another kindred. I thought maybe, since we left, they would shift and I could prove her theory."

"Oh, Nemerra." Ludik shook his head. "You should have waited for me."

Nia glared at Varin. "She's right, isn't she? You and the Walruses are Darrendrakar."

"Our myths say we were," Varin said, "long ago, before land broke into islands. I believe it is only story, and we were always our own people. We live on islands until recent earthshakes. Then our islands crumble in tiny pieces. We cannot always live in ocean, must have land sometimes. We could not go north to Walrus kin. It is too cold, and our little ones cannot swim that far."

Ludik shuddered. Last summer, the shaking had been bad enough on solid ground and worse when the ship threatened to sink under waves taller than the mast. For the Seals, trapped between dissolving land and tidal waves, it must have been terrifying.

"We swim here, scouts and families, to barter for land," Varin continued. "A small piece, enough for home. But while we sleep on beach, the Dogs" — he spat — "take us for common seals and slaughter us. One of us try to talk to Dogs, but they kill him, too. The rest of us hide in ocean."

Ludik pressed his elbow against his knife and wished his bow were strung. Though he regretted the Seals' misfortune, it was no reason to threaten Nemerra.

Varin's voice broke. "We watch Dogs skin our kindred and butcher them for meat. Then we swear revenge. Next night, we take village as blood price for murders. When mongrels send for help, we chase their messengers. Finally, our avenger returns with proof of deaths."

The giant Seal-man glared at them. "Now all that is left is few who escape and *you*." Varin pressed his spear against Nemerra's chest until blood welled through her dress.

Nemerra cried out and backed up a step, pressing her hands to her wound.

Ludik's vision turned red, and he lunged forward.

Varin raised the spear. "All stop, or she dies now. This land is ours now."

Ludik screeched to a halt, shaking in rage. "It is not yours," he protested. "Of course you were taken for common seals. You were gone so long you were not even a legend anymore. How were the Dogs to know?"

"Your islands were not really that far away," Zefra said. "You must have tried hard to be forgotten. Why did you do it?"

"We know your pathetic worship of nonexistent gods, and we want no part of it." Varin sneered. "Darravani loves us, you say. I say there is no Darravani."

Ludik gasped at the disrespect, as did the other Darrendrakar, but Ahjin laughed.

"Nonexistent gods? No Darravani?" Ahjin said. "That might be nice, but they do exist. And they don't approve of your murders."

"We kill only those who slaughter us. Is fair," Varin insisted.

"What about Durriel?" Lyell asked. "We did nothing to you."

"We need more land for when rest of our people come," Varin said. "We burn, what you call it, Durriel, to chase away Dogs without killing. See how merciful? We allow them to leave. But *you* will not leave. Why do you not accept mercy? Now I can not let you go. I was generous first time, but I think outkindred too dangerous to anger. Now we have no choice. We get rid of you and then anyone who knows you."

The Seal pups and mamas had made their escape. They hovered in the waves at the edge of the beach while the guards rushed across the sand toward Varin.

In a moment, Ludik and his friends would be badly outnumbered. He stretched his arm uselessly toward Nemerra.

Nia dumped her pack and rummaged in a pocket. She pulled out her perfume bottle and replaced the stopper with a ribbon from her braids.

"Zefra! Light it." Nia threw the bottle.

Zefra caught it, then snapped her fingers and lit the ribbon with her flame.

Ludik and Gurryon took a step forward. Varin took a step backward and raised the spear to stab Nemerra.

Zefra tossed the bottle at Varin's feet and turned to shield Tala.

The delicate glass shattered. Flames burst across the spilled perfume. Varin threw his arm across his face and backed away to the Seal guards. The hem of Nemerra's dress caught fire, and she screamed.

"Nemerra, move," Zefra yelled.

Nemerra took two quick steps, and then Ludik threw her to the ground. They rolled away from the Seal warriors, smothering the flames that ate her dress and nibbled her skin.

Gurryon and Lyell stepped in front, weapons raised in a pitiful defense.

The Seal warriors flanked Varin, feet braced and spears forming a bristling hedge.

Ludik pressed on Nemerra's chest to stop the bleeding while Nia rummaged through the pack on his back.

Ahjin jumped between the opposing forces and spread his wings. "Everyone, stop," he yelled. "I command you, as the Mouth of the Gods, to put down your weapons and stop!"

"There are no gods," Varin shouted. "That is belief of weak-minded people." He raised his spear again.

Ludik peeked under his hands at Nemerra's wound. The spear hadn't penetrated her ribs. He pressed down again and closed his eyes in relief.

"Oh, really?" Ahjin's bellow made Ludik glance at the conflict.

"Irajahan, tell Darravani I need her now!" Ahjin stepped behind Gurryon and Lyell and drew his bow.

Zefra tucked herself behind a tree, curling over Tala, drawn sword in hand. Ludik put his ax next to him, keeping one hand pressed on Nemerra's wound.

Varin thrust his spear toward Lyell, but Gurryon blocked it with his staff. Ahjin shot an arrow into another Seal's weapon-hand. Varin shouted, and the Seals spread out to surround the three defenders.

Then Nia shoved Ludik's salve at him. He listened to the sounds of battle as he bandaged Nemerra's chest. He would rather cut off Varin's head, but Nemerra needed him, and the others could handle the Seals for a few minutes. They could, couldn't they?

Ludik brushed aside his doubt and turned to Nemerra's burns. At least her boots had protected most of her legs. Only the strip between her boots and knees had been burned.

"I'm sorry, Nemerra," Nia babbled. "I'm so sorry."

"Don't be," Nemerra gasped, squeezing Nia's hand as Ludik worked. "The burns aren't that bad. It would be a lot harder to heal a gash through my heart. You did a great job."

Ludik jerked and dropped a bandage in the dirt, feeling like he had a hole in his own chest. He couldn't lose her. Taking flowers to her funeral would kill him. They might as well bury him with her. He left the dirty bandage on the ground and fumbled for a clean one.

Ahjin had to stop this before war spread across Darrendra. Ludik spared a quick glance at the fight behind him. Lyell and Gurryon stood back-to-back, surrounded. Ahjin flew circles above them, firing arrows at shoulders and legs. While several Seals moaned on the ground, no injuries seemed fatal.

Ludik would have to finish healing Nemerra later. He handed the bandage to Nia and reached for his ax.

Two figures popped into existence just outside the fight. Both had such sharp visual edges, it hurt to look at them. Ludik recognized them both.

Kassian had tan skin, brown hair cut to his ears, and black eyes. The short, slight man's plain green shirt and blue trousers made him look like a common workman instead of the eldest god.

The graceful woman in his arms was Ludik's own goddess. Darravani had darker brown skin than Ludik's, and the ash-blonde hair waving halfway down her slender back was streaked with tawny brown. Her hands were subtly clawed, and her long tunic idly shifted colors and patterns.

Vines sprouted from the ground and engulfed the Seals. Their muscles shook as they strained to move.

So much for Varin's claim the gods did not exist. And now Ludik could take the time to heal Nemerra. He wrapped bandages around her legs and checked for other injuries.

"Are two gods enough, or do you need all five?" Ahjin shouted. He landed and relaxed his bow but didn't lower it.

Varin bared his teeth behind the vines.

Kassian let go of Darravani. "These are your people," he said, "so I'll leave you to it."

Darravani pulled herself to her full height, nearly as tall as Ludik. "Oh, my children." She spoke in trade tongue, but her voice echoed in another language. "You ignored me for a long time, but this is enough. I love you whether or not you want me, but when you left all those millennia ago, you promised to leave my other children alone. If you can't keep that promise, your choices will have consequences."

She examined the crowd of warriors before she stared into Varin's eyes. "Now, are you finished here, or should I fight you myself?"

The Seal guards quavered and dropped their weapons. Ludik would have done the same in their pawprints. Only Ahjin had the nerve to defy the gods.

The vines gradually retreated into the ground. The Seals on the beach, suddenly transformed by Darravani back to their clothed, two-legger state, crept closer to the goddess. The warriors stayed where they were and watched Darravani with wide eyes and ashen faces.

Kassian knelt by Nemerra and helped her drink from a glass bottle chosen from his belt of potions. "You'll be fine," he said. "Watch my sister impress these louts. I have other things to do and only brought Darravani for speed." He vanished as quietly as he had appeared.

Ludik gathered Nemerra into his arms to watch the goddess deal with the Seals.

"Explain yourselves," Darravani commanded. "Why did you start this war?"

"Our islands crumble," Varin choked. "We need more land. When we come here, Dogs kill us. We only defend ourselves."

"Did you tell them who you were when you arrived?"

"No." His voice got softer. "We plan to watch first and be sure they are safe."

Nemerra leaned into Ludik's shoulder and cried as he smoothed her hair. He would feel a lot sorrier for the Seals if they hadn't killed so many people.

"After the first death," Darravani asked, "did you tell them you're Darrendrakar and not dumb animals?"

"We are not Darrendrakar," Varin mumbled. "We are Pinniped."

"You are." Darravani nodded. "And the Pinnipeds are Darrendrakar. I know my children. I left you alone these long years to honor your wishes. You may have forgotten me, but I have not forgotten you. Now, did you tell the Canids you are not dumb animals?"

"They not understand our language," Varin protested, "and they kill the Seal who try to speak to them while they slaughter our kin."

Ludik winced. Maybe he felt a little sorry for them, watching as their friends died.

Darravani continued firmly, "Did you shapechange as proof, or send for one of your people who speaks trade tongue, like you?"

"No." Varin looked at the ground. "After so many die, we want revenge."

"Did you stop killing them when the actual murderers had died?"

Varin shook his head silently and clasped his shaking hands together.

"Why not?"

He swallowed hard. "We take their land as pay for murders? Is fair price." He glanced at Darravani, and the color drained from his cheeks.

Darravani frowned. "And you chased the fugitives to keep all this secret?"

Varin nodded slowly, and Ludik stopped feeling sorry. It was Varin's fault the others had died. He could have prevented the rest of this tragedy. Even Agu was not Ludik's fault.

"Would you kill everyone who came to trade or visit?" Darravani asked. "What of the bordering territories? You already killed an innocent Cat and burned a village to scare away its people."

Varin squeezed his eyes shut, wavering on his feet. "Please let our women and children go. Let our warrior deaths be enough to cleanse the stain on our honor."

"No, I don't think that will do," Darravani said slowly, her voice still echoing the Seal language.

His face crumpled, and a single tear escaped. "Please," he begged. He fell to his knees and pressed his face against the earth. "Mercy. Our families are innocent."

Behind him, his warriors copied him. The women and children screamed and ran to join their men. Families huddled together and wept.

"Their families don't deserve to die," Nemerra whispered into Ludik's neck.

"*You* killed innocents, didn't you?" Darravani's voice was firm as she addressed the Seals. "You planned to kill more innocents." She waved her arm at Tala and the rest of Ludik's group.

Ludik tightened his embrace. If he had lost Nemerra...

The Seals wilted into sobbing misery.

"We are sorry." Varin clasped Darravani's feet. "Please, spare our children. Please, Lady, we beg you."

Darravani beckoned Ahjin. He handed his bow to Gurryon and

picked his way through the kneeling crowd to join the goddess. She bent to whisper in his ears, waving her hand toward the Seals.

Ahjin frowned at Varin, running a hand through his wild curls.

When Darravani stopped talking, she raised her head and waited.

Ahjin's wings twitched while he thought, spreading and furling over and over. After a minute, he folded his wings neatly and stood on tiptoe to whisper to Darravani.

She listened with a thoughtful expression, then nodded.

"All of you will pay." Darravani raised her echoing voice. "Listen to the price the Seals will pay."

Nemerra leaned forward to hear. Ludik held his breath, not sure what he hoped would happen. It was fair for the murdering Seals to pay, but what about their families who hid their bloody secrets and benefitted from their misdeeds? How far did justice run?

Varin let go of the goddess' feet. He wrapped his arms around himself, head bowed.

Darravani looked at Ahjin and dipped her head a fraction. "They will bury everyone they killed with full honors and give their families the proper blood price. If the entire family was killed, they will pay twice the price to the kindred. They will rebuild every building they damaged."

The Seals stopped wailing and inhaled.

Ahjin smiled. Ludik saw his lips form the word, "mercy."

Darravani continued. "They will properly negotiate for a small territory along the coast of Canid and Ursid lands with the help of the temple shamans and His Holiness the Mouth of the Gods, and they will look for other places they might live."

In the background, Zefra whispered an offer of help to explore. Lyell shifted from foot to foot.

Darravani kept talking. "They will contribute one tenth of their entire people for five generations, at all times, to work on projects benefitting other kindreds or peoples, including sending workers to His Holiness."

Ahjin rubbed his hands together. "Gardeners," he whispered. "And guards."

Ludik frowned. This plan was merciful, but was it just?

Darravani raised her arms. "And for the rest of their lives, everyone here, down to the smallest babe in arms, will never fight against another

Darrendrakar, even in self-defense. If they do, they will suffer banishment or death, at the choice of their opponent."

Some Seal's protest was quickly smothered. Lyell growled almost
inaudibly.

"Gardeners are good enough," Ahjin murmured.

"The rest of the Seals may still defend these few," Darravani said.
"But if their kindred refuse this offer, which is their right, they will be
banished forever. All their kindred, not just those here." She sighed heavily. "I wish you hadn't pushed me to this."

"You cannot make us do this," Varin said.

"I can," Darravani said. "If you don't choose either obedience or
banishment, then every plant or animal you eat for the rest of your life
will be poisonous. How long do you think the rest of your life will last
when every bite is fatal? Is this what you choose for your children?"

The Seals stared at her in horror. Ahjin flinched, and his mouth
dropped open. Lyell bared all his teeth in a savage grin.

Ludik nodded. And there was the justice behind Darravani's mercy.
Did the murdering Seals deserve anything gentler? They had not spared
the Dogs, though the Canids had not even realized their crime.

Varin lowered his forehead to the ground again. "Thank you, merciful
goddess. We accept your grace. You also require our worship?"

Lyell scowled ferociously.

"I'm glad my children have returned to me," Darravani said, "but
mandatory worship is meaningless. You must make your own choices.
You can disobey my commands, if you accept the consequences."

Varin shook his lowered head. He remained on the ground, head
bowed, hands clasping his knees. Even from where Ludik sat, he could
see the Seal tremble.

Darravani walked among the kneeling crowd, touching their heads
and talking to the children in their own language.

Lyell shadowed her at a distance, watching with narrowed eyes.

After Darravani had talked to everyone, she sank into the ground and
vanished.

Ludik helped Nemerra to her feet. "That was a good call, Ahjin."

Ahjin grimaced. "Thank you."

"You convinced the goddess to give them justice," Ludik said. "If they
disobey, they will die."

Ahjin winced. "That wasn't what I intended. I wanted a true peace."

Ludik snorted. "You won't get that between the kindreds. This is the best you could do."

Lyell clenched his fists. "This is not any kind of peace," he shouted. "She cannot let them go free! They killed my family!" He threw himself into wolf shape and lunged at Varin.

"No!" Nemerra cried. She flung herself between the Seal and the charging wolf.

Lyell's jaws snapped shut on her.

29. WOLF
(KAIRRI, CANID TERRITORY)

A jaguar can bite through a skull or a turtle shell. A wolf's jaw, while not as strong, can still break bones and has a faster snap.
A Brief Sketch of Mysterious Darrendra

Ludik's heart stopped as Nemerra screamed and collapsed in a shower of blood.

In an attempt to kill Varin, Lyell had clamped his powerful jaws in a death grip on Nemerra's shoulder, close to her neck.

"Stop," Ludik shouted. He fell to his knees by Nemerra, heart pounding, while Gurryon and Nia grabbed Lyell.

Most of the Seals ran screaming to the beach or the houses. Ahjin stood between Nemerra and the few remaining Seals.

Ludik slid one arm under Nemerra's neck to support her and tried to press on her wound with the other hand. He couldn't see how bad the damage was until Lyell let go. His vision grayed, and he blinked to clear his sight. If he had to cut off the Wolf's head to free Nemerra, he would.

Gurryon pried his fingers behind the wolf's teeth and tried to unlock his jaws. "Let go, monster, or I will rip your head apart."

Nia twisted the wolf's ear and glared in his eye. "Broken coral, Lyell, let go now! What are you doing?"

Lyell growled and shook Nemerra like a rat, pulling her from Ludik's arms.

Nemerra screamed again.

Ludik's blood felt cold in his veins. He looked for a stick to smack into Lyell's head. If the mad Wolf didn't let go, Nemerra would die from blood loss or be ripped to shreds. Wolves were exceptional at tearing prey.

Nia smacked the wolf. "That's Nemerra, you idiot, not Varin. Have you gone blind? Ruka would be so disappointed in you."

Lyell stopped mid-growl. He dropped Nemerra and backed away, whimpering.

Ludik gasped; there was so much blood. He grabbed Lyell's half-split tunic, ripping it through the hem and yanking it off the Wolf. With trembling hands, he pressed the torn fabric against Nemerra's neck and shoulder.

"Plague fleas," he croaked. "Nemerra, stay with me."

Her blood soaked through the shirt and painted his hands red.

"I'll try, darling."

He barely heard her whisper, but he knew what she meant when she blinked three times.

I love you, too, Ludik blinked back, squeezing his eyes the last time to blot his tears.

Gurryon let go of Lyell, but Nia kept a hand on the Wolf's ear.

"I — I am so sorry. I did not realize." Lyell lowered his head and stared away. "I was aiming for Varin. Everything went red, and I did not see her move between us." He tucked his tail between his legs and flattened his ears.

Nia let go of his ear and smacked him again.

"Why did she get in the way?" Lyell lowered his body to the ground and crawled to Ludik's side. "I am sorry." The wolf rolled over and exposed his belly, head flattened to the side.

Ludik ignored the continued apologies and tried to stop the bleeding. He peeked under the edge of the tunic, and chills ran up his spine. Nemerra looked almost as bad as Ahjin had when the scorpion nearly pinched him in half. Blood poured from the wound, making it hard to see details. Her skin was shredded, and he thought her muscles were torn to the bone in a few places. He slapped the tunic back down and pressed harder.

"Why did you do it, Nemerra?" he groaned.

"Varin couldn't defend himself," she whispered. "It wasn't fair. And to end a war, both sides must stop fighting." She sighed, closed her eyes, and went limp.

"Move it," Nia ordered Lyell. She pushed on him with her foot until he rolled away. "How can we help, Ludik?"

"Press here," Ludik said. "I need supplies from my pack." He lifted one hand and pressed both of Nia's over the wound before moving his other. He shrugged out of his pack and reached to open it, but Gurryon shoved his hands away.

"Go wash your hands," Gurryon said. "I'll have your stuff ready by the time you get back."

Zefra, who had stepped back to protect the baby earlier, stood ready. With Tala's carrier slung across her chest, she used both hands to juggle soap and the rags and a jug of water a cringing Seal-woman passed out a window.

Zefra dropped a glob of soft soap into Ludik's hands. He lathered frantically, keeping an eye on Nemerra. The cloth Nia pressed against her neck didn't seem to be getting redder, but he scrubbed his fingers quickly, cursing the ground-in dirt that kept him from helping Nemerra.

Zefra rinsed his hands with a stream of water, then poured the rest of the water into a pot next to Nemerra.

Ludik slid back into place by his sweetheart, hands held carefully above the dirt and blood. Gurryon handed him clean rags to exchange for Lyell's tunic. He had bandages, needle and thread, and Ludik's ointment laid on another clean rag.

Ludik took deep breaths to calm himself. "Has the bleeding slowed?" he asked Nia.

"This part has." She twitched her little finger to indicate the shoulder end of the wounds.

Ludik nodded. He folded the rags and held them above Nemerra's neck, then nodded again to Nia. At the same time she pulled away the saturated tunic, he slapped the new cloths on Nemerra's neck, leaving an inch of the shoulder end free.

Nia slid her hands back into place, and Gurryon handed a wet cloth to Ludik. After Ludik cleaned a section of the wound, Gurryon gave him a threaded needle.

"You can do it," Gurryon said. "One step at a time."

Ludik took a deep breath and slid the needle under Nemerra's skin, glad she was unconscious.

Nia gradually slid her hands up Nemerra's neck, keeping pressure on the wound while Ludik sutured below her grasp. In the eternity it took Ludik to stitch Nemerra back together, he had plenty of time to curse the Seals for starting this war, curse Lyell for continuing it, and curse himself for not pulling her out of the way or being good enough at healing.

His heart ached. His eyes burned, but he couldn't afford to let tears blur his vision. The only thing that kept his hands from shaking was the need to make steady, precise stitches and the knowledge that no one here could do it as well as he could.

As he sank his healing magic into every stitch, Ludik tried to remember everything Shri Okechuku had taught him. If only he'd had time with the Iskrin healer to learn more than a bit.

If Nemerra survived, he would ask her how she felt about him going to Iskra for that apprenticeship. Hunting was more fun, but healing was more important.

If Nemerra didn't live, well, it wouldn't matter. Nothing would matter then.

Gurryon was the perfect assistant, always handing Ludik what he needed before he had to ask, murmuring encouraging words and reminders of the next step. Ludik had snuck into many of Gurryon's healing lessons, but not all, and now he was grateful his brother had attended more of them.

Ahjin ferried water while he stood guard. The Seals did not approach. Most of them stayed out of sight, but Varin and a few of his guards cowered not far away.

In the background, Lyell howled, and Zefra nagged him to change form and put on some clothes. She said she would call the Seal guards. She offered to have Ahjin call back the gods. It was only when she threatened him with the permanent loss of his daughter if he couldn't pull himself together that he finally stopped wailing.

With Nemerra's blood staining his fingers, Ludik couldn't make himself feel sorry for the Wolf.

Zefra left Lyell changing in the woods and helped Ahjin guard Nemerra until the puppy whined again.

"Make Tala be quiet," Ludik said. "She's distracting."

"She's hungry," Zefra said, "but the goat disappeared."

"That I can fix." Ahjin turned and bellowed, "Varin."

The enormous Seal-man dragged his feet to Ahjin's side. "Yes, Your Holiness?"

"Our goat ran off in the chaos," Ahjin said. "I need her back, please."

"Yes, Your Holiness." Varin bowed and went back to the houses. A few minutes later, a horde of subdued Pinnipeds crept into the forest in search of the ornery goat.

"Yes, Your Holiness," Ahjin mimicked sourly. "Do they have to do that?"

"They will find the goat, though." Zefra stopped petting Lyell's daughter long enough to pat Ahjin on the shoulder.

Ludik had reached the last part of his stitching, and he turned all his attention back to Nemerra. When he finished sewing, he trickled healing magic across the entire wound, then let Gurryon bandage her while he washed. The stitches ran for half a foot, tracks of disaster marching across Nemerra's shoulder and neck.

When her blood was off his hands, Ludik leaned his head on her uninjured arm and wept.

Tala howled behind him.

He had done the best he could. He'd learned a lot from his experiences with Ahjin and had used it all on Nemerra. But he didn't know if it would be enough.

He had to save her. They were so close to being married — again — that he could see it, taste it, smell it. Every time they got delayed, it broke his heart more. He couldn't do this again. It wasn't fair. And if she died, it would be worse than unfair.

Tala's howls choked into whimpers, and Ludik remembered Ruka and her other babies. Life wasn't fair. He knew that, but somehow it always came as a surprise when it happened to him.

When he ran out of tears, he sat up.

Zefra bounced the puppy in her basket, murmuring soft words, though her eyes were wide and panicked.

Most of the Seals were gone. Only Varin hovered on the beach.

Despite his bandages, Lyell was milking the goat slowly, his face pressed against Gurry's side. The bit of cheek Ludik could see had a distinct tinge of gray under the brown.

Ludik turned his face away from the heinous Wolf. He had been wrong to trust someone from another kindred.

Gurryon guarded Nemerra's other side with a drawn knife. Nia screwed the cap back on Ludik's salve jar and wiped her hands on her clothes, then awkwardly wound a bandage around Gurryon's free hand.

Ludik took the bandage from her. "What happened? Why didn't you tell me?" He peered at Gurryon's hand. Nia had done a good job of washing and salving the abrasions.

Gurryon unclenched his jaw enough to talk. "It was the stupid goat. A little rope burn can wait for a better time."

"We'd better get it done now," Ludik suggested, bandaging him quickly, "before it stops being a better time."

Gurryon helped him move Nemerra to a litter brought by a shame-faced, cringing Pinniped, and then they and Nia joined the ongoing religious discussion.

Lyell stood and poured the goat milk into the baby bottle. "Why did Darravani not intervene again? Why did she not stop me from hurting Nemerra?"

As soon as he took Tala from Zefra and put the bottle in her mouth, the puppy stopped squalling. Zefra and Lyell sighed almost identically.

"Why didn't she stop the Seals and Dogs from hurting each other in the first place?" Ahjin said. "Why didn't she keep the Seal out of Felid territory? Why didn't she keep Orrik from arresting us? The gods rarely interfere in mortals' affairs. They must allow us free will, even when we hurt each other."

"But—" Lyell gestured helplessly toward Kairri with the bottle and Durriel with the arm burdened with his daughter. Zefra grabbed the wolf pup before he dropped her.

Ludik glared silently. Why *didn't* the gods protect their children? How could Darravani let Lyell attack Nemerra, who never hurt anyone in her life?

"Sending the rain to Durriel didn't take away the Seals' free will," Ahjin explained. "It just doused the fire. And Darravani didn't make the Seals stop fighting, either. She just gave them an impeccable incentive to stop. Remember, she left them alone for thousands of years when they wanted. She didn't keep them from coming back to the mainland, either. It was only when they proved their hearts were set on murder and declared their intent to sweep through the continent that she insisted they stop.

"If the Seals weren't atheists, a simple priest could have told them to stop and enforced it with the help of the other Darrendrakar. Since the Seals don't believe in the gods, it took a personal demonstration to convince them anyone had that kind of authority over them." Ahjin looked at Ludik and changed the subject. "How's Nemerra?"

Ludik felt his eyes burn again. He swallowed twice before he could answer. "She's breathing fine, and the bleeding has nearly stopped. She lost a lot of blood, though, and I don't know how well her muscles will knit."

"Will she live?" Nia asked.

"We must wait and see." Ludik's voice croaked through his dry throat. "If she survives the blood loss, infection could kill her, or a blood clot from the injury might destroy her brain." So many things could go wrong. His mind trotted out an unwelcome list from Akamu's lessons. So many ways she could die. So few chances for her to be his wife.

Ahjin watched the Seals peeking over their windowsills. "Can she be moved?"

Ludik shrugged. "I don't know, but we can't stay here."

"Oh!" Nia ran a few steps and came back with Kassian's abandoned bottle. She shook it vigorously. "There's a few drops left. Maybe it can help?"

"We can try." Ludik blinked hard and sprinkled the potion under Nemerra's bandage.

Lyell clenched his fists. "I— I am sorry. If you want, you can apply Darravani's verdict to me as well. I offer my life in exchange if Nemerra dies. If it would compensate for my offense, you may kill me now." He turned to Zefra. "Will you take care of Tala for me?"

Zefra nodded with tears in her brown eyes. "I will love her like my own child."

Lyell was offering his life for hurting Nemerra. Ludik's heart pounded in his ears. "That sounds fair."

Gurryon nodded fiercely.

"Don't be ridiculous," Ahjin said. "There's nothing fair here, but you can't feed the hate. I promised Torao I'd keep you from war. That also means keeping war from you."

He took a step forward, but Gurryon grabbed his arm, covered his mouth, and nodded at Ludik. "Stay back, all of you. This is our affair."

Zefra turned away with Tala. Nia bent across Nemerra, shoulders shaking.

Lyell bent one knee and bowed his head.

Ludik bared his teeth and reached for his ax at his side, but his fingers came back empty. He had dropped the weapon to care for Nemerra. He spun to look for it. There it was on the ground. And there was Nemerra on the litter, so still, almost lifeless.

Ludik's vision clouded, and heat rushed through his body. Yes, Lyell deserved to die.

He ground his teeth and grabbed his ax. "This is for Nemerra, her revenge."

His revenge.

Ludik raised the ax above Lyell, still kneeling for his execution. And after Lyell, he would kill Varin, too, for starting this entire situation. Then he would find the Seal murderer and finish *him*.

The burning, freezing, aching weight of anger and loss drained a chasm in his heart and killed his soul. Justice would fill the gaping breach in his heart with fire and numb the pain.

The ax shook in Ludik's hand.

This was what Lyell must feel for his dead wife and children.

This fire was what the Dogs in Durriel had felt when they argued for retribution, what the other victims' families would feel when their papas didn't come home.

This was what started the Seals' rampage of vengeance against the Dogs that killed their scouts.

This was the feeling of war.

The ax sagged in Ludik's hand. He was sent to prevent war.

But it was his right to claim justice for Nemerra, and sorrow fueled the heat in his veins.

Ludik lifted the ax higher. Gurryon understood. They couldn't let the Dogs dishonor their kindred.

Ahjin struggled in Gurryon's grip. When he failed to free either his arm or his mouth, he squirmed his free hand behind his back and pulled Grandpapa's journal from the side pocket of his pack, waving it at Ludik.

Ludik scoffed. "Your promise to Grandpapa does not apply anymore. Lyell's death is justice for Nemerra."

Ahjin waved the book again, then let his arm sag at his side. His purple eyes watched Ludik above Gurryon's brown hand.

Ludik tightened his grip on the ax. Justice.

He froze. Not justice — vengeance and hate.

This hate was what ruined Grandpapa's life, filling it with suspicion and misery. This was why the Darrendrakar couldn't even cross their neighbors' borders. This was why the village of Orrik wanted to strike first.

This hate was why Lyell hurt Nemerra in his attempt for revenge on Varin.

Ahjin was right. Hatred was poisoning Ludik's soul and Gurryon's integrity as a shaman. Only hours ago, Ludik had counted the Wolf as a friend, and now he was ready to execute him — and in revenge for an accident. He was as bad as the Seals.

Ludik looked at Nemerra on her stretcher. Her injury wasn't Lyell's fault. She had jumped in his way to save Varin.

She had sacrificed herself for peace.

She wouldn't want this. If he killed Lyell, what would she think of him? If he surrendered to hate, he would betray her sacrifice and everything she believed.

Nemerra was good and kind and brave enough to forgive. He had always known he didn't deserve her, but if he couldn't remember friendship and trust in the face of tragedy, he never would.

For an eternal moment, his overwhelming anger fought with his love for Nemerra.

The anger finally drained and left a softer sorrow in its place. If Nemerra died, his life would still be over, but he wouldn't take anyone else down with him.

He would make her proud of him. He would honor the peace she desired and build a place for forgiveness in the ruins of his heart.

He turned back to Lyell, exhaustion sweeping through him. His ax sagged toward the ground.

"No," Ludik said. "This ends here. If Nemerra lives, you can take up reparations with her." He turned and picked up his pack. "Gurryon, let go of Ahjin. Let's go home and find out if I'm having a wedding or a funeral."

30. RITE

(MAON, FELID TERRITORY)

Red carnation: my heart aches for you. Orange blossom: eternal love. Helenium: tears. Iris: wisdom and valor. Kitten willow: bravery and compassion. False hellebore: sorrowful remembrance. Purple hyacinth: please forgive me. Primrose: I can't live without you.

Flowers and Their Meanings: A Guide for All Darrendrakar

L udik looked out his window. Home again, after weeks away, but it would never be the same. He put on his green tunic and his old, scarred boots and wiped his tears.

The funeral song Lyell had sung for his wife floated through his mind. *You will take my breath...*

He propped a small mirror on the table and opened the jars of ceremonial paint. He clenched his fists to stop them from shaking, then dipped a finger in the paint. Intersecting yellow lines went on his left cheek for Papa's lion whiskers. An orange zigzag on his right cheek indicated Mama's tiger heritage. A black circle with a center dot marked his own jaguar shape on his forehead.

And now it was time. He screwed the lids back on the jars and picked up the flowers he had spent hours choosing. *Share my heart's bouquet...* He was as ready as he could be for the circumstances.

He opened the door and stepped out into the middle of his family. His parents led the way, Gurryon and Haider guarded his sides, and his other siblings brought up the flank. When he staggered, his littermates grabbed his elbows.

"You can make it through this," Gurryon said. "Your life isn't over yet."

"Joy follows sorrow," Haider said.

And I cannot mend...

Autumn leaves had been raked to border the path with red, orange, and yellow. A few hardy fall flowers augmented the display.

Everyone from his village was there. He had expected that. They always came for important life and death events. They stood soberly now, waiting for him.

Nia and Zefra stood near the front. He had expected them, too. Zefra wore her embroidered sash over her carefully cleaned robe, and her red hair flamed in a braided crown around her head. Nia wore a purple skirt and a blouse with so much rainbow embroidery that the white fabric barely showed. Her newly trimmed hair was braided only halfway down her back before falling past her knees in a lavender torrent.

Ludik had invited Lyell without expectation of him coming, yet here he was with his infant daughter. She was finally out of her fur and wearing a tiny dress with an alarming number of ribbons decorating it. Nia had been busy.

Ludik had not expected the Canids and Ursids hovering around the edges of the clearing, some in their fur and some out. Even the yapping little guard from Orrik was here.

He also hadn't expected the Seal's headman, Varin, clearly nervous between Maon's headman and their priest. More Seals stood at the back of the crowd, packed bags behind them and hands clasped carefully behind their backs. Grandpapa watched all the strangers with narrowed eyes.

Haider jiggled Ludik's elbow to redirect his attention toward the distant end of the path where His Holiness stood in front of a large hole, waiting to perform the ceremony.

At the end of day, I will sit with you...

Despite his bursting heart, it was hard for Ludik to keep a straight face when he looked at Ahjin all dolled up in his new, priestly outfit.

Ahjin normally wore shockingly plain shirts and trousers. Now he shifted his weight and fussed with his regalia before clasping his hands and freezing still, only to repeat it a moment later. Even for Darrendran preferences, Ahjin's clothing was outrageous. His orange brocade robe clashed with a scarlet headband with three flames stamped in black. Neither coordinated with the lavender sash embroidered with purple waves and multi-colored dolphins, or the bright green boots. The only discreet bit of insignia was the silver star medallion around his neck.

Then Ahjin stepped aside and Ludik saw Nemerra. Everything else fled from his mind, and his heart stopped for a moment. Living without her would kill him.

You are still my light and my everything...

He had thought waiting the customary year to marry his sweetheart was bad enough. Missing the wedding had been torment he'd endured for good reasons. The long two months and more he'd waited for his friends to come had been horrid. Then he'd had to leave on the very day of the second time he'd planned to marry her, and it had nearly killed him.

Their journey had been no easier. Worrying about her while they chased a murderer was agony. Waiting in jail for their execution was misery, and the near-miss of a guard's sword was torture.

But nothing was as bad as when Nemerra collapsed in the jaws of a wolf.

His heart stuttered again with the memory. Without her, his life had no meaning.

Looking at her now, his heart restarted with a roar.

Nemerra stood in front of him with a smile, as beautiful as she was brave and kind. She wore a plain green dress with leaf embroidery around the collar. Rings of brown spots marked her right cheek and her forehead, for both herself and her mama. A black circle and dot designated her papa's jaguar lineage on her left cheek. Her arm hung in a matching green sling. She had never looked more beautiful.

Ludik stumbled forward to give her the bouquet. His original choices for her two weeks before had spoken of her beauty and charm. While those blossoms were still present, today he had added flowers that spoke of her deeper qualities and his own resolves.

The crowd cheered.

Ludik and Nemerra held hands and walked toward the priest.

We will walk along with your hand in mine, the song continued haunting him.

When they stopped in front of Ahjin, he leaned forward and whispered. "You both still want the new ecumenical words rather than the traditional Darrendrakar blessing?"

At their nods, he straightened and spread his wings halfway. He looked surprisingly impressive, despite his clashing colors. Ludik had rarely seen him so imposing.

The horde quieted as Nemerra and Ludik turned to face each other, hands clasped.

Ahjin turned to Nemerra's parents. "Has the bride price been paid?"

"It has been paid and accepted."

Ahjin turned to Ludik's parents. "Is there a sacrifice from the wedding hunt?"

Ludik stopped breathing. He had forgotten they needed to redo that. Now what would they do?

"There is," Papa said. "They hunted war and found peace."

Mama stretched out her arms and presented the broken pieces of a walrus-tusk spear and a brief note. Ludik twisted his head to read it. "Orrik has abandoned the invasion."

Ahjin took the spear, and after a nervous glance at Varin, dropped it into the deep fire pit and dedicated it to Darravani. After the fire died, the pit would be filled in as a symbol that Ludik's and Nemerra's single lives had ended and a new life had begun.

"Are you prepared to start a new life together?"

"Yes," Ludik and Nemerra chorused.

Ahjin lifted a clay pot. Ludik poked a hole in the dirt that was suspiciously warm for this time of year. He glanced thankfully at Zefra as Nemerra gently settled a small bulb in the hole. They covered it together, then handed the pot to Nemerra's parents.

Ahjin turned to Ludik. "Ludik, do you give yourself in marriage and take Nemerra as your wife?"

Ludik looked into Nemerra's eyes. "Yes." It was not enough of an answer, but nothing would be. It was the most important word. At Ahjin's encouraging nod, he remembered he could say more. "Nemerra, I will love you forever. Your needs will come first. I will protect you and care for you always. You encourage me to improve myself."

Ahjin turned to Nemerra. "Nemerra, do you give yourself in marriage and take Ludik as your husband?"

Ludik held his breath. This was her last chance to change her mind and decide he wasn't worth the trouble.

Nemerra smiled at Ludik. "Yes. Ludik, I have loved you for a long time. I've watched you learn and grow into a wonderful man. I will love you forever."

"We witness your pledge," the village elders said, led by Ludik's grandmama.

Ahjin placed his hands over their clasped hands. "We beg the gods to protect the ones we love," he said. "We honor all you created as Ludik and Nemerra pledge their hearts and lives together. May earth support their marriage as it grows stronger through the seasons. May fire warm the love in their hearts. May wind carry them through life safely. May water clean and soothe their relationship, that it may never thirst for love. May the universe give them harmony as they enlarge their souls together. Amen." He removed his hands and smiled.

It was time for the marriage rings. Both mamas stepped forward. Ludik's mama pulled a needle from her collar and handed it to Minali, who waved it through the fire to purify it and then handed it to Ahjin.

Ahjin swallowed visibly. "Ludik, please kneel."

Ludik let go of Nemerra and knelt in front of Ahjin. He turned his head, took a deep breath, and closed his eyes. When nothing happened, he opened his eyes again. The needle shook in Ahjin's hand.

"Just do it quickly," Ludik whispered. He turned his head again, but watched from the corner of his eye until Ahjin gulped and reached for his left ear. The sharp pain was over in a moment.

Nemerra slipped a small hoop into Ludik's ear, then took his place at Ahjin's feet. The priest's hand shook even more when he approached Nemerra's right ear. She smiled at Ahjin and waited.

"You can do it," Ludik muttered. He held his breath until Ahjin winced and poked the needle through Nemerra's ear. Ludik carefully slid the other hoop into Nemerra's ear before pulling her to her feet.

Ahjin sighed and handed the needle back to Minali.

"The gods have given me the authority to now declare you man and wife," Ahjin said.

You are mine lifelong; I am always thine! Now the plaintive song in Ludik's head changed to a triumphant refrain.

Nemerra picked an orange blossom from her bouquet and tucked it into Ludik's collar. She untied the ribbon and threw the rest of the flowers to the crowd. Anyone lucky enough to catch one cheered.

As they walked toward their house, everyone threw flower petals over him and Nemerra. By the time they reached home, their green clothes were a mere background for the petals.

"We put your gifts inside your house," Mama told them.

The corners of Nia's mouth twitched as she presented a floppy bundle. "You should open my gift before we leave."

Nemerra reached for the package, but Ludik glared at Nia.

"What are you up to?" he said.

Nia's eyes opened wider. "You are always so suspicious of me," she complained. "Do I deserve that?"

Nemerra unfolded the wrappings to reveal a thick quilt. "It's so warm and colorful, thank you."

"What kind of picture is that?" Ludik asked. The way it was folded, he couldn't tell, but Nia's twinkling eyes made him wary.

Nemerra handed him two corners and backed up with a third. The unfolded quilt revealed a large, lavender fish with a small, black-on-black-spotted jaguar kitten dangling from its mouth. The picture was amazingly detailed.

Ludik's mouth dropped open.

Nia laughed. Ahjin snorted and slapped a hand over his mouth. Zefra grinned. Ludik's brothers howled with laughter and slapped their knees. All four parents gasped.

Nemerra squeaked and tears leaked from her eyes.

Ludik snarled, shoved the quilt at Nemerra, and headed for Nia.

"Stop, stop," Nemerra gasped. She thrust the quilt back into Ludik's arms and held on to him.

He wrapped one arm around her shaking body and glared at Nia. "I'll get you," he started. His threat died off when Nemerra's laugh finally broke free.

"I love it," she wheezed between giggles, looking between Ludik and the quilted kitten, and between Nia and the lavender fish.

"It's time for your friends to leave," Papa said.

"Thank you, Ahjin." Ludik reached for Ahjin's arm, then pulled him into a hug instead.

Nemerra hugged Ahjin with one arm. "Thank you for everything. Keep well."

"Fly high," Ahjin said, then stepped aside to make room for Nia.

"You're invited to my coming-of-age party in five months." Nia stretched on tiptoe and still couldn't reach Ludik's cheek. He gave in and bent for her kiss.

"I'm sorry, I'll be busy," Ludik said. "I'm going to Iskra. It's past time I took that apprenticeship."

"If we go to Iskra, we'll be close enough to slip over," Nemerra said. "We'll come."

Nia squealed and clapped her hands as she moved on. "Pleasant journey, then."

Zefra bowed as she stepped in front of Ludik. "Warmth to you. You will let me guide you in Iskra?"

"Who else?" Ludik hugged Zefra before turning her over to Nemerra.

Lyell was next, holding his pretty, dark-haired baby protectively. Tala had stuffed one of her ribbons in her mouth.

"Keep well, Lyell," Ludik said.

"Keep well." Lyell turned to Nemerra and reached softly toward her bandaged arm. "I'm very sorry."

Nemerra smiled. "You've said that every day." She pulled the ribbon from Tala's mouth and tickled her with it.

"I've meant it every day." Lyell said. "I'm so sorry."

"Try to stay out of trouble from now on," Nemerra suggested. "Make a new life for yourself."

"I'll apply for a job with His Holiness," Lyell said. "Will that make you happy? The Darrendran isolationist policy isn't working. If I go help Ahjin, maybe we can change things."

Nemerra clasped Lyell's still-outstretched arm. "I think it's wonderful."

Ahjin stepped closer to smooth Tala's fuzzy hair. "I had Chief of Staff in mind."

"I'm afraid that won't do," Lyell said.

"It won't?" Ahjin's smile died. "Why not? I thought you'd be perfect for the job."

"I absolutely refuse to carry a big stick." Lyell walked off laughing as Nia cheered.

Ludik burst out laughing. First contractions and now a joke. Despite the mourning stripes on his tunic, Lyell was beginning to heal.

Ahjin grinned and threw his arms around Nia's and Zefra's shoulders, turning them toward the guest houses.

Ludik held Nemerra's hand and watched his friends leave with Asad. They would sleep in the village tonight and be escorted to the ocean tomorrow, along with the Seals and other Darrendrakar going to serve His Holiness.

Ludik's and Nemerra's families gathered around the newlyweds. With so many helping hands, it didn't take long to plant a token garden of perennial herbs, bulbs, and berries. If they had married in the summer as planned, they would have had a real garden.

It wouldn't have taken long to stuff their new mattress, either, if fewer jokes had been made. Instead, it took forever, until Ludik declared it fat enough and drove everyone from the house.

He slammed the door and leaned against it. When the sounds of his teasing relatives faded into silence, he heaved a sigh and looked at Nemerra.

"Are they gone? Are we alone now?" She smiled, glowing with happiness.

She *was* beautiful, but her sling and the bandage peeking above her collar marked her with courage and honor and compassion.

"Yes," he said, "and I'm the luckiest man in Darrendra." He took her hand and drew her to him for a perfect kiss.

YAY! NOW OUR HEROES WILL LIVE HAPPILY EVER AFTER, AND NIA'S PARTY WILL GO PERFECTLY!

Will it, dear reader?

DEAR AUTHOR, YOU ARE MAKING ME NERVOUS.
EVERYTHING WILL BE PERFECT, RIGHT? RIGHT??

Well… Maybe not. More surprises await our poor heroes. Turn the page for info about **Wave of Dreams**, wherein Nia discovers her mom has been hiding a secret for seventeen years. And it will change her life… forever.

WAVE OF DREAMS

A treasure map could change her life or lead to her death.

For a sixteen-year-old mermaid, the best part of becoming an adult is the party. Even though Nia must host it on land for the sake of her gill-less friends, she can flirt with all the cute boys.

But her mom's gift is unexpected — an old map and the news her long-lost dad disappeared in the Dragon Isles.

With her friends and a charming suitor, Nia follows her missing dad's trail on an adventure to the supposedly cursed islands. Will she find love and discover her dad's fate?

Maybe. Unless the curse is real.

Romance and danger swirl with the tide, and undercurrents could sweep her away.

*Wave of Dreams is an immersive fantasy with adventure, pirates, and sweet romance, where victory is found through friendship and teamwork. It is the third book in the **Unexpected Heroes** series of clean YA secondary world fantasy and is best read in order for the most enjoyment.*

Check my website MCLeeBooks for links to buy the next story or get the entire series at once.

Still want more? Get free stories by joining my newsletter. Every two weeks, I chat about my current writing or my life and offer book news and deals. And did I mention free stories?

Sign up at MCLeeBooks.com

Free Story: The Cat's Fortune

So long ago that truth has faded into legend, a cat and a boy seek their fortune together.

Orphaned and homeless, young Aktar travels to the city of Rapata for a better life. But it seems the rumors of gold-paved streets are false. Can he find a home and a job before he starves? Maybe with the help of a foundling kitten.

A retelling of Puss in Boots and Dick Whitting-ton, with timeless themes of belonging, courage, and self-discovery, set on the fantasy world of Kaiatan, home of the **Unexpected Heroes***.*

If you liked this book, please leave an honest review on any retailer or reader site. Seriously, it would really help me. :)

If you found a typo, you're welcome to report it at mcleebooks.com/re-port-a-typo/

CHARACTER LIST AND PRONUNCIATION GUIDE

IF YOU ARE INTERESTED IN THE
MEANINGS OF THE NAMES,
PLEASE SEE MCLEEBOOKS.COM

Name (Pronunciation) Identity

<u>People</u>

Agu (AH-goo) Darrendrakar, Maon hunter

Ahjin Machol (AH-jzhin MACK-ole) Iojif, 16 years old, skydancer

Akamu (Ah-KAH-moo) Darrendrakar, Maon shaman

Asad (Ah-SAHD) Darrendrakar, Maon headman

Askari (Uh-SCAR-ee) Iskrin, guard

Darravani the Omnifarious (DAR-uh-VAHN-ee) Darrendrakar
Goddess of Earth

Gurryon Moriko (GURR-yon) Darrendrakar, Ludik's brother

Haider Moriko (HIE-der) Darrendrakar, Ludik's brother

Hiranya Moriko (Her-AHN-yuh) Darrendrakar, Ludik's younger
sister

Ilani (Ill-AHN-ee) Darrendrakar, Gurryon's fiancé

Irajahan the Omnipotent (Ear-AH-jzuh-han) Iojif God of Air

Izo Ashvakosha (EE-zoe) Iskrin, Zefra's older brother

Kassian the Omnipresent (KASS-ee-an) Fifth god, oldest brother

Kalliona Moriko (Kal-ee-OH-nuh) Darrendrakar, Ludik's older sister

Ludik Moriko (LUD-ick) Darrendrakar, 18 years old, healer

Lyell Ulriksin (LIE-el UL-rick-sin) Darrendrakar wolf, border guard
in Durriel

Makanavailea the Omniscient (Mah-KAHN-uh-vie-LEE-uh) Nokai Goddess of Water

Minali (Min-AH-lee) Nemerra's mama

Mingan (MEENG-an) Darrendrakar, Durriel's headman

Narrasiman Moriko (Nah-RRAHS-ih-man) Darrendrakar, Ludik's older brother

Nemerra (Neh-MERR-uh) Darrendrakar, Ludik's betrothed

Niamolenulanami (NEE-ah-moe-LEN-noo-la-NAHM-ee) Nokai, 15.5 years old, singer

Resef the Omnificent (RES-eff) Iskrin God of Fire

Ruka Sassabadin (ROO-kuh Sah-SAH-bah-din) Wife of Lyell

Shri Okechuku (SHREE OH-keh-CHOO-koo) Iskrin, healer

Tala Lyelldin (TALL-uh LIE-ul-din) Darrendrakar, Lyell's second-born child

Tema (TEEM-a) Darrendrakar, Durriel's shaman

Torao (Tor-AY-oh) Darrendrakar, Ludik's grandpapa

Varin (VAHR-un) Darrendrakar in Kairri

Ya'eel (YAH-eel, with click between syllables and a squeal-whistle) Nokai dolphin, Nia's friend

Zefra Ashvakosha Kezhekori (ZEF-rah ASH-vah-KOASH-uh KEZ-eh-KORE-ee) Iskrin, 15 years old, Hotaru guide

Groups, Locations, Languages

Arupa (Uh-RUPE-uh) Island of the Mouth of the Gods

Darrendra (Duh-RREND-druh) Northern country

Darrendrakar (Duh-RREND-druh-car) People of Darrendra, shapeshifters

Darrendran (Duh-RREND-drun) Darrendrakar language

Durriel (DUHRR-ee-ell) Canid village

Hotaru (Hoe-TARE-oo) Iskrin tribe, specialty: maps

Ioj (EYE-ojze) Eastern country

Iojif (Eye-OH-jziff) People of Ioj, avians

Iojo (Eye-OH-jzo) Iojif language

Iskra (ISK-ruh) Southern country

Iskrin (ISK-ree) People of Iskra, desert-dwellers

Iskrit (ISK-rit) Iskrin language

Kairri (CARE-ree) Village in Canid kindred

Kanshi (KAHN-shee) Darrendra capital, in east
Maon (MAY-on) Felid village
Murron Islands (MURR-on) Islands south of Darrendra
Nokai (NO-kie) People of Nokailana, aquastrians
Nokailana (NO-kie-LAHN-uh) Western islands
Noki (NO-kee) Nokai language
Orrik (OR-rick) Village in Canid kindred
Vasi (VAHS-ee) Capital of Ioj

ACKNOWLEDGMENTS

Thanks to my Day Group, Carol Malone, Cheree Myatt, Donna Gonzales, and Gail Porter, for their excellent advice, and to my extraordinary alpha and beta readers, Ammon Rasmussen, Jessica Bullough, Maria Farb, Matt Peel, Patricia Parker, Robin Cranney, Virginia Cummings, and Wendy Allott.

Special thanks to Laura Dotson for her musical help,
to Kyle Adams for his expert plotting,
to Chris Cornetto and Michelle Henrie,
who brainstormed and read endless iterations,
and to my editor, Anna King.

ABOUT THE AUTHOR

Marty C. Lee told stories for most of her life, but never took them seriously until her daughter asked her to write this one. Between writing and spending time with her family, she reads, embroiders, paints-by-number, and gardens.

She has lived in five states, seven cities, and ten houses so far. She currently lives in the West, but not in a tropical paradise. She doesn't like flying, even in an airplane. She wishes she could produce her own fire to warm her hands. She's glad she didn't have to wait a year to marry her sweetheart, who also wishes she could warm her hands.

You can find her at
    MCLeeBooks.com and on Facebook and book sites